A Study in Crimson

A Study in Crimson

A PREQUEL TO THE DAKOTA STEVENS MYSTERY SERIES

CHRIS ORCUTT

A Study in Crimson

A Prequel to the Dakota Stevens Mystery Series

by Chris Orcutt

First Print Edition: 2018

First Ebook Edition: 2018

This is a work of fiction. Names, characters, places and incidents either are the product of the author's imagination or are used fictitiously. Any resemblance to actual persons (living or dead) is entirely coincidental and is not intended by the author.

ISBN-13 (Print book): 978-0996278393 (Have Pen, Will Travel)

The publisher of this work and cover artist is Have Pen, Will Travel Publishing. Book cover image, "Inscription lipstick hugs and kisses," (stock photo ID # 676186567) by Golubovystock, used under license from Shutterstock, Inc.

Also by Chris Orcutt:

Nick Chase's Great Escape (A Comic Novel)
I Hope You Boys Know What You're Doing! (Short Stories & Poems)
A Real Piece of Work (Dakota Stevens Mystery #1)
The Rich Are Different (Dakota Stevens Mystery #2)
A Truth Stranger Than Fiction (Dakota Stevens Mystery #3)
The Perfect Triple Threat (Dakota Stevens Mystery #4)
The Man, The Myth, The Legend (Short Stories)
One Hundred Miles from Manhattan (A Novel)
The Ronald and Other Plays (Plays)
Perpetuating Trouble (A Memoir)

www.orcutt.net

For Sir Arthur Conan Doyle & Ian Fleming, the two peerless masters whose creations inspired me to become a fiction writer.

"Dr. Watson, Mr. Sherlock Holmes," said Stamford, introducing us.

— From *A Study in Scarlet*
by Sir Arthur Conan Doyle

1

One-Way Ticket

I no longer worked for the Bureau, but the Director had summoned me to headquarters, so I was going, and that was that.

My lack of resistance surprised me. Maybe it's something they subliminally program into you during your training at Quantico: If the FBI Director summons you to Washington, you go, no questions asked.

At 4:30 a.m. on a Monday, there was a knock at my door. The Director had sent two agents from the Manhattan field office to pick me up. After waiting in the hallway while I dressed and wrote Ashley a note, they drove me downtown in silence, handed me a ticket for the 6:00 a.m. Amtrak, and dumped me in front of Penn Station. They didn't even wish me luck. Boarding the train, I noticed the ticket they'd given me was one-way. This was mildly disconcerting. Either the Bureau was being cheap, or they knew I wouldn't be returning to Manhattan.

The train slogged into Union Station half an hour late. In the great hall upstairs, another pair of reticent agents whisked me out to a car. We sped down Pennsylvania

Avenue to that behemoth, sandy brown building whose overhanging top floor looks as if it will shear away at any moment and topple to the sidewalk: FBI Headquarters.

Descending into the garage beneath, we drove around for a while and finally stopped at a guarded elevator. I'd heard about this elevator when I worked here, but I'd never seen it. Unarmed but dressed in my best Hickey Freeman navy pinstripe suit, I boarded the elevator with the agents. One of them inserted a key and punched a button. The doors closed and we rose quickly to the top floor.

When the doors opened, the agents led me into a waiting room and pointed to a chair. I took my time sitting down; I didn't want them thinking I was taking orders. They strode away, leaving me in the hands of MRS. GREER, a homely older woman whose frigate-sized desk formed an imposing barrier between the waiting area and the heavy double doors of Director Reeves's office. MRS. GREER typed fast enough to provide electricity to Appalachia, and she wore headphones attached to a Dictaphone. I didn't think people still used those things, but apparently Director Reeves did.

"Excuse me, Mrs. Greer," I said. "Do you have any idea what the Director wants with me?"

"No, Mr. Stevens," she said, continuing to type. "But he should be with you shortly."

I settled back into the chair to wait. This outer office was a sensory deprivation chamber. There were no clocks, and because I'd been in a rush this morning, I'd forgotten to put on my watch—a vintage Omega that had belonged to my grandfather. There were no windows.

There were no magazines, no reading matter of any kind. The only sound was the relentless, mercurial clicking of Mrs. Greer's computer keys, like a thousand tap dancers running the New York City Marathon.

It all seemed calculated to wear down the resolve of the visitor, to impress upon him—in this case, me—the power of the man with whom you were about to meet. Even the air itself seemed party to the conspiracy, perfectly odorless as it was, and seemingly composed of the minimum amount of oxygen necessary to sustain human consciousness. For all I knew, this wasn't even the real waiting room; this could be a special one for people the Director wanted to torture before granting them an audience. A single mirror behind Mrs. Greer's desk forced me to stare at myself. I suspected that the Director had a camera behind the mirror so he could observe my every expression. Or was the mirror there only to make me paranoid?

Nobody came out. Nobody went in. Nobody called. Nothing happened but the incessant clicking of those keys. Mrs. Greer could have been typing gibberish, and I had no way of telling otherwise. Time crawled across a desert. I began to seethe. What was this about? Why had I been rudely roused at four thirty this morning and summoned to Washington? I hadn't done anything illegal—at least not that I knew of. Maybe I hadn't completed my exit paperwork properly when I'd resigned last year. Or maybe they wanted me back and the Director was going to make a personal plea. Yeah, right.

Across the room a water cooler gurgled, but there were no cups for it. Another subtle torture device. After a while I found myself staring at the beige carpet, trying to find a stimulating pattern in it. Eventually I closed my eyes. Heat was building under my suit, and I became aware of a prickly sensation on my neck. By now I'd been waiting for at least an hour, and I was plenty irritated. To calm myself, I breathed slowly and deeply, and meditated on something pleasant: beautiful redheads.

I remembered the cinnamon redhead bank robber who had whispered promises of sexual favors in exchange for letting her go; luckily my partner was with me, so I didn't take her up on her very enticing offer. I thought of the more strawberry than blonde, and married, waitress at the diner on Broadway, and how often I found myself there flirting with her. I thought of curly redhead Bernadette Peters, whom I'd seen in *Annie Get Your Gun* from a second row seat—close enough to observe the perspiration beading on her upper lip. And lastly I thought of the petite Texas redhead whose name I never learned but with whom I made out in the most remote nook of Strand Bookstore near Union Square. A heady bouquet of lilacs stuck out of her shoulder bag. I had literally pinched myself at the time, because I couldn't believe my luck: a redhead with soft lips, and the piquant aroma of my favorite flower wafting around us.

"Mr. Stevens?"

When I came to, the little Texas firebrand was gone, sadly supplanted by Mrs. Greer.

"The Director will see you now," she said.

"*Already?*" I said, getting to my feet.

"There's no need to be sarcastic, young man," she said.

"To hell there isn't," I said, "but I'm not going to argue with you. So, where's Oz? Through there?"

She smirked. "He can hear everything you say, you know."

"Good," I said, "he can hear this then—I'm leaving." I headed for the elevator.

"The elevator is locked, Mr. Stevens. You might as well see the Director."

I checked it, and sure enough, you needed a key to call it. I turned around and marched straight past Mrs. Greer, into the Director's office. As a minor act of rebellion, I left the doors open, making her have to get up to close them.

I'd only seen Director Reeves in person a few times. Once, when I was nominated for a Service to America Medal (which I didn't win), he dropped by my cubicle to commend me on solving the Hagerstown Kidnapping case. A couple other times, I'd seen him and his entourage striding down the hall in the Lab.

Even in his late sixties, Director Reeves was an imposing man. Six-and-a-half feet tall, with iron-gray, closely cropped hair, he had survived two tours in Vietnam, graduated *magna cum laude* from Yale, and worked his way up from a lowly Special Agent in Boston to become head of the Bureau. He remained seated. In the window behind him, towering over the buildings across Pennsylvania Avenue, was the Washington Monument. I cleared my throat. Director Reeves glanced up from some papers. He was not amused.

"*Oz*, Stevens?" He pointed across his desk. "Sit down, please."

Easing into the chair, I noticed another man in the chair next to mine. Ruddy-faced and white-haired, he had that broad-shouldered but puffy look of aging former football players, as though if you could strip away the layers of fat and time, you'd find a star of the gridiron underneath. The Director put down his papers.

"Mr. Stevens," he said, "this is Harold Standish, a friend of mine from college. He has a situation with his daughter, and I told him you'd be glad to help."

"Excuse me, sir," I said. "I don't work for the Bureau anymore."

"Yes, I know that," he said. "But I also know you're starting a private investigations firm, and that you're leveraging your experience with the Bureau to do it."

He held up a sheaf of papers. Among them I recognized my applications for a New York State PI license, and a New York City handgun concealed carry permit. On all of my applications I had listed the FBI as my former employer. He put the papers down.

"Never mind that you've been doing investigations without a license for several months," he said. "It's amazing how quickly these things can go to the top or the bottom of the pile with one phone call."

"Point taken, sir," I said.

The Director nodded at Mr. Standish, who breathed heavily and began. He had a strident voice that didn't match his ursine frame.

"Well, Mr. Stevens," he said, "my daughter is a sophomore at Harvard. Actually I should call her my *youngest* daughter, as she is the issue from my second wife and myself."

He actually said "issue." I stifled a laugh.

"Sally has always been academically gifted," he continued. "Valedictorian of her class at Miss Porter's, straight A's her freshman year at Harvard. However, in this first semester of sophomore year, she's barely passing. She's never in her dorm when I call, and her mother receives only the occasional short email from her. She didn't come home for our Labor Day house party either, without a word of explanation as to why, and—"

"Pardon me, Mr. Standish," I said. "It sounds like you need a family counselor, not a detective."

"Let him finish, Stevens," the Director said. "Go on, Harold."

"I have reason to believe that Sally is"—Mr. Standish gulped—"*involved* with an older man." He scowled at me. "A professor—about your age, I think. Doctor Malone. He's a '*sexuality researcher*' or some such nonsense, and Sally has been working as his assistant since early August."

"Well, if she's over eighteen," I said, "it's not illegal. Unethical, maybe. Did you talk to the university?"

Standish's face flushed. "I…yes, I spoke to multiple people in the administration. Apparently, Dr. Malone is not employed by Harvard. He has some 'independent research grant,' so he isn't bound by the university bylaws governing faculty, which means there's nothing they can do. So, I hired a Boston private detective, who reported that Sally comes and goes from Malone's apartment at all hours."

"Due respect, sir," I said, "if you have a detective, what do you need me for?"

"Because Stevens," Director Reeves said, "the PI is dead. Shot in his car a week ago, while staking out Dr. Malone's North End apartment."

"Could be a coincidence," I said. "Besides—and I'm sorry if this comes off callous—isn't his death a state matter?"

"It is." The Director nodded at Mr. Standish. "Which is what I told Harold when he contacted me. I explained I can't put Bureau resources on a case that isn't under federal jurisdiction. Of course if you discover evidence that indicates a *federal* crime, then the Bureau can get involved. Until then, however"—the Director smirked at me—"*you'll* have to suffice."

Standish set his jaw. "Mr. Stevens," he said, "Director Reeves tells me you're well-trained, persistent and that you don't scare easily."

"Yes, except sharks and rats," I said. "Oh, and also—"

"I want you to make contact with this *Doctor* Malone," Mr. Standish said. "That's Dr. *Geoff* Malone, spelled with a 'G.' I want you to discourage him from seeing my daughter anymore."

"Spelled with a 'G,' huh?" I said. "I don't like him already."

"I'm quite serious, Mr. Stevens," Standish said.

"So am I. The 'G' spelling is pretentious."

"I want this man to stay away from my daughter!" He pounded a fist on the Director's desk. "I want my little girl back!"

He doubled over in his chair and wept into his hands. Director Reeves glared at me with his jaw clenched, looking like he ached to kick me, which he probably would have, had his desk not been in the way. We waited for Standish to blow his nose into a handkerchief, and when Standish re-pocketed it, I decided to take a mulligan with him.

"Sir," I said, "please forgive me for being flip. I'm a little punchy. I've been up since four thirty, I've been on a train for three hours, and"—I glanced at the Director—"I've been waiting in the outer office for an hour. Mr. Standish…are you asking me to *beat up* your daughter's boyfriend?"

"Of course not," Standish said, scowling. "But I think a few firm words might scare him off."

"So you're asking me to *threaten* him?"

Standish shrugged.

"Do you really think that's a good idea?" I said. "In front of the Director of the FBI?"

"Harold and I are old friends, Stevens," the Director said, "going all the way back to our days at New Haven. Harold believes, and I concur, that Dr. Malone may be engaged in something nefarious. We would like Sally extricated from the situation—quietly."

"I have a few questions, sir," I said.

"Naturally."

"Well…for starters, why me?"

"A combination of things," Reeves said. "You're the right age. You went to college"—he flipped a page in my personnel file—"right down the road, so you know the area. You were an excellent Special Agent, if only for eleven years. And, apparently…you're quite good-looking, something we might be able to use in luring Sally away from Dr. Malone."

"Why, thank you, sir." I crossed my legs and waggled my foot. "I'm flattered."

He made a huff that was half growl and leaned across the desk.

"That's what some of the *women* in the building have said about you, Stevens. Personally, I don't get *what* they see in you."

"Well, would you let me know, sir?"

"Let you know what?"

"What they see in me," I said. "Whatever it is, I'd like to hone it."

The Director shook his head, glanced at his wrist-watch. "Do you have another question, Stevens?"

"Yes. If I'm doing this privately, how can I traipse around Harvard without—"

Reeves held up a hand, silencing me. "I will direct an agent in the Boston office to assist you—*unofficially*. I'll also arrange for you to be at the university as a postdoctoral Fellow. Harvard Fellows basically have the run of the place, and your specialty will be in criminal psychology and profiling—an area in which you have some expertise."

"That I do, sir."

"There you have it then," he said. "I'm expediting the paperwork so you'll be fully licensed in Massachusetts as a private investigator. You'll have everything except a handgun. As you know, Mass is extremely restrictive."

"Sir," I said, "given that my predecessor was murdered, I won't be taking this case *without* a gun."

Staring at me, the Director drummed his fingers on the desk blotter.

"Fine," he finally said. "But it might take a day or two. The Boston agent will bring everything to your hotel. Mr. Standish will be putting you up at the Charles in Cambridge." The Director raised an eyebrow. "No objections, I trust."

"I'll make do."

"Anything else, Stevens?" the Director asked. "I meet with the A-G in fifteen minutes."

"Mr. Standish," I said, turning to him, "I'll need a recent photo of Sally, a copy of her schedule and—"

"You will be provided with everything you need," the Director said.

"Then the only item left is my fee, which—"

"—you will graciously waive for my old friend," the Director said with a grin. "However, Harold *will* cover any reasonable expenses, of which you are to keep a strict record."

"Fair enough," I said.

The Director stood. "Do a good job on this, Stevens. It's smart business to be on the Bureau's good side. By the way, I want you in Cambridge A-sap. That means tonight."

"Understood, sir," I said. "There's just one last little thing."

"What?"

"The train," I said. "The New York agents gave me a one-way ticket."

"Because I told them to," he said. "Buy your own and expense it." Reeves looked at Standish. "Anything you'd like to add, Harold?"

"Just get Sally out of whatever she's into and bring her back safe, Mr. Stevens," he said. "Please."

"I'll do my best, Mr. Standish."

A door opened on the side of the room, and two agents came in. Craning my head to see out the door, I glimpsed an oasis—a posh waiting room with a covey of leggy secretaries that looked like they moonlighted as Vegas showgirls. The agents closed the door behind them and crossed the room. The agent in the lead took a briefcase from the Director. Reeves stood and shook hands with Standish.

"Ah, before I forget," the Director said, staring at me.

"Yes, sir?" I said.

"I expect daily reports on your progress, Stevens."

"Can't, sir," I said with a sheepish grin. "No laptop."

"Then get one," he said. "Anything else?"

"Hmm…Red Sox tickets?" I said. "They *are* in the playoffs, sir."

"We're done, Stevens."

While he walked into Mrs. Greer's outer office, I drifted toward the door with the beauties behind it.

"This way, Stevens," the Director said.

Following the agents and Mr. Standish out, I paused in the doorway for one last look at the Director's office. I imagined what the place must have looked like when J. Edgar Hoover occupied it—mahogany paneling, heavy velvet drapes, and a minimum of light—and vowed this was the last time I'd ever be here.

2

NEW YORK, NEW YORK

Generally it's not my nature to brood, to dwell on the negative things in my life. Like an action movie hero, I pride myself on taking defeats in stride and always looking forward. That afternoon, however—alone in my window seat on the New York return train, gazing out at the late September countryside—I have to admit, I brooded a little.

Part of me wondered if I'd made a mistake leaving the Bureau. I'd been in private practice for close to a year and had a few cases, but I spent most of my time navigating the bureaucracy of licensing, and hustling for new clients. The cases I'd been forced out of financial necessity to take were nearly all divorce work, which, after having helped to solve high-profile murders, kidnappings, bank robberies and the like, made me feel slimy at the end of each day.

Ironically, returning to FBI headquarters today reminded me that I missed the very thing that had caused me to resign from the Bureau in the first place—the routine. I missed my partners, our morning coffees in the bullpen, and the swapping of stories about funny interviews and arrests. I missed the modest but regular paychecks, and the comprehensive health insurance.

Out the window, we passed a roadside farm stand where a smiling elderly woman handed a bag to a young mother. A breeze rustled the ash tree above the farm stand, and all of its gold leaves sparkled in the bright sunshine. It was a gorgeous day, but I wished it were raining. At least then I could justify feeling sorry for myself.

What I needed more than anything, and what I'd been trying for months to get, was a competent assistant. My strengths were questioning suspects, detecting, forensic science, legwork, and, when necessary, throwing the occasional devastating punch. What I needed was somebody who could handle the business stuff: running an office, getting clients, getting *paid*.

We passed through a railroad crossing: lights flashing, bells clanging, drivers sulking. I took out a pen and pocket notebook, and started a list. My ideal assistant would be more than just an assistant. I needed somebody who could help me to solve cases, somebody who possessed skills and qualities I didn't have. My dream list went like this:

> Extremely organized, yet adaptable
> Enjoys research
> Computer skills
> Knowledge of accounting
> Good with money
> Can deal with red tape

Heck, while I was shooting for the moon…

Speaks Spanish
Patient, can perform surveillance
Willing to travel
Contacts—brings me business
Doesn't mind making coffee
Doesn't need a big salary or health insurance
Elegant dresser with great legs

I tore the sheet off the pad and jammed it in my pocket. Who was I kidding? I'd never find somebody like that. I had put postage stamp-sized classifieds in the Sunday *Times*, but so far only three people had been qualified enough to merit an interview. Adding insult to injury, since I didn't have an office yet, I'd had to interview the applicants at a Starbucks on Broadway, a few blocks from my apartment. I would buy a black coffee, sit at a table by the window and wait for each applicant to arrive.

My first applicant had been a young man, barely 25, who'd already failed the Bar exam twice. He was working as a paralegal until he could take the exam again. He'd been "dealing in theory far too long," he said, and was "eager to participate in real-world applications of the law." He spent so much time asking me about my experiences at the Bureau that I barely got to ask him any questions. After costing me an hour and two cappuccinos, I was glad to see his peach-fuzz face disappear back onto Broadway.

The second applicant, a woman who, now that I thought about it, bore a resemblance to homely Mrs. Greer, had ten years' experience as the executive assistant to the head of corporate security for Citibank. In many respects, she was perfect. She understood investigations and was organized and skilled in accounting and administration. She even had some useful contacts in the NYPD and the Securities and Exchange Commission. Sharp and well spoken, she would have been ideal for handling my back office work, but…she kept interrupting me. During our half-hour interview she probably interrupted me twenty times.

With the third and last applicant, I never learned whether she'd be a good fit, because the moment she strutted into Starbucks in a tight blouse and scanned the café with a pair of shimmering sapphire eyes, I knew I had to leave. On paper, she was great—a recent NYU Accounting graduate who'd interned in the New York Attorney General's office—but she had a quality common to all devastatingly sexy women: even standing still, she drew attention to herself. She simply couldn't help it. If I hired this young woman, her mere presence would constantly blow my cover. Spotting me at my table, she flashed a beaming smile that radiated total confidence and began her approach.

"Mr. Stevens," she said with a voice that sounded like warm apple pie, "it's an honor to—"

Sighing through my teeth (*Dear God, what a beauty; if only I were unscrupulous*), I snatched my messenger bag off the floor and shook her hand. "I'm sorry, miss. The position has just been filled."

Although it pained me to be rude to her, for my own good I nodded goodbye and dashed across Broadway.

This was probably how Goldilocks felt. I doubted I'd ever find the right person.

When the train reached Penn Station, I walked deject-edly upstairs to Seventh Avenue, where I hailed a cab back to 201 West 77th Street. As I entered the apartment, the woody sounds of drawers being wrenched open and slammed shut echoed down the hallway. A black Rollaboard leaned next to the credenza. I walked into the bedroom. Ashley was there, jamming clothes into a Zabar's bag. Unfortunately, this scene was all-too-famil-iar to me. I decided to play it cool.

"Hey, beautiful," I said. "Making a trip to Goodwill?"

Ashley and I had been together only four months, but I could tell when she was angry with me. Her ears and hairline would turn red, like now, and her nostrils would flare. Under other conditions these would also indicate she was having an orgasm, but I was pretty confident that wasn't happening at this moment.

"I am *so* over this." She slammed another drawer shut, brushed past me with the bag, and stormed into the bathroom. She grabbed her personal items and makeup and jammed everything in the bag. "I woke up this morning and you were gone. Gone!" She batted the shower curtain aside, glowered at the bottles standing around the tub. "No clue when you were coming back. Who do you think you are—Batman?"

A few tiles around the tub needed to be re-caulked. I leaned against the sink.

"Didn't you see my note?" I asked.

"Yeah, I saw it," Ashley said. "And what a love note it was"—she mimicked my voice—" 'Hey, Ash…had to go to D.C. on business. Back this afternoon. Sorry. Dakota.' Ugh. We were supposed to spend the day together."

"Well, considering how little warning I had," I said, "I think it was pretty decent of me to leave the note."

"Yes, you're a saint," she said.

"Let me explain, Ashley."

I told her the Director of the FBI had summoned me, and if I wanted any kind of career in law enforcement, private or otherwise, I had to stay on his good side. Ashley considered what I'd said, and, after cleaning out the medicine cabinet, shook her head.

"You could have invited me to come with you," she said. "We could have spent the day in D.C. together. You know how hard it is for me to get a day off during the week."

With a final look around the bathroom, she went out to the living room.

"I can't do this anymore, Dakota," she said. "This is the third time you've disappeared or broke off our plans. In case you haven't figured it out yet, I'm the *last* woman who needs to put up with this crap." She gave me a contemptuous look. "You could have at least *called* me. Oh, but I forgot…you're the stubborn square who refuses to get a cell phone."

She started down the hallway. Her long bronze hair—thick, heavy hair I would miss burying my face in—gleamed in the overhead light. Soon, every cell phone tower in the Tri-State Area would be white-hot as word of her renewed availability circulated through the singles scene. In the Wall Street pub where I'd first met her, men had been fluttering around her like moths around a bug zapper, and I knew that, despite a few months off the market, her allure would be as strong as ever.

I'd been questioning a stockbroker regarding a divorce case when I noticed Ashley staring at me. When I finished with the stockbroker, I bought her a drink and told her a joke, which made her laugh but irked a Queens Cro-Magnon who'd already set his sights on her. The Cro-Magnon made the mistake of grabbing my arm, so I torqued his thumb and wrist, and he ended up on the floor begging me not to break his thumb. Excited by seeing me display my dominance (right then, I should have realized this girl was trouble), Ashley sprang off her barstool and followed me out of the bar. She started kissing me in the cab with the lights of Eighth Avenue flickering over our faces. Her tongue was in my mouth during the elevator ride to the 12th floor, and it stayed in my mouth while I unlocked my apartment door and we groped into the living room together. There, she stopped kissing me long enough to hastily shed her clothes and reveal, with an impish grin, a pink and black lingerie ensemble so torridly sexy, it sent a chill down my spine.

Now as Ashley put on her coat, I reached over her collar, pulled out her silken hair, and let it sluice over my hands one last time. Then I gently turned her around and kissed her on the cheek.

"You bastard," she said. "Don't you care about me? Won't you miss me?"

"I do, and I will," I said, "but you've clearly made up your mind."

"And you're not willing to change?"

I shrugged. "This is my life, Ash. Being a detective is who I am."

"Your *job* isn't keeping you from letting someone into your life," she said. "You don't let *anyone* in. It's like you were abandoned by your parents or something."

"I was…in a way," I said. "But that's not relevant."

"*That* is exactly what I'm talking about." Clenching her jaw, she slapped her apartment key on the hallway credenza and towed the Rollaboard and Zabar's bag to the door. "Goodbye, Dakota."

She slammed the door behind her. I watched her through the peephole while she waited for the elevator, and was grateful she didn't start crying. If she had, I probably would have thrown the door open and apologized. But when the elevator arrived, she stepped inside and left without further incident.

At the sight of her leaving, I felt a terrible emptiness. Like all uniquely beautiful women, Ashley haunted a space long after she'd left it. I wandered back into the apartment and stared at the living room. The place looked like the break room in the FBI forensics lab. The desktop in the built-in bookcase, the dining table, the club chair and hassock, the bar counter and all four TV tray tables—everything was covered with books, file folders, paperwork, a microscope, and several containers of half-eaten Chinese takeout.

I spent an hour straightening up and vacuuming, packed a suitcase for Boston, then changed into running clothes. I stretched in the lobby, then jogged slowly down

77th Street, past the Museum of Natural History, and turned onto Central Park West heading downtown.

This was my usual route—Central Park West to the Dakota building at 72nd Street (where John Lennon had lived), then across the street into Central Park and through the memorial for him: Strawberry Fields. Even though it was a workday, and a hot day at that, dozens of Lennon pilgrims surrounded the "IMAGINE" mosaic, placing flowers and lighting candles. I skirted around a man strumming on a guitar, and, turning onto the path that headed uptown through the Park, I thumped down the hill. The guitar sounds faded into the stirring trees behind me.

Yes, Ashley was a loss, but I'd get over her. She thought my work was a mere *job*; the woman never would have understood me. Being a detective was my *passion*, my life's purpose, and people without a life's purpose can never understand those of us who have one. To them, our choices seem rash and unbalanced. Ashley could never fathom the idea that following a trail of clues was more interesting to me than, say, meeting her parents. I wanted to become a master private investigator, one sought after by the wealthy and powerful, and becoming a master at anything required total commitment and focus.

As I ran, I couldn't help replaying the conversation with Ashley. One thing she'd said—"You don't let *anyone* in"—really grated on me. She was wrong about that. It wasn't a case of my not letting people in; I was ready to let people in, but I wanted them to be the *right* people, people who understood my desire to master a discipline few others cared about—whether those people turned out to be romantic partners or business partners.

From Strawberry Fields, I took a circuitous route northeast across the park, jogging around the lake, past the Great Lawn, behind the Met, and on the running track alongside the reservoir, to the very top of the park at 110th Street, where I ran a few blocks north to the parking garage on 113th.

This remote garage is where I kept my car: my grandfather's 1970 Mercedes 280SE. It was a venerable dark maroon sedan with stylish rounded fenders and headlights, walnut grain dashboard, and leather upholstery. If it ran better, I would have referred to it as "vintage." When my grandfather was alive, he'd kept it in the garage across the street from the apartment, but when I inherited the car, the only garage I could afford was this one in Harlem. I drove back, and the second I turned onto 77th Street, I lucked out: another car vacated a spot directly in front of my building.

Upstairs, I showered and dressed. Slipping on my grandfather's Omega wristwatch, I gazed at Ashley's photo on my bureau one last time before placing it in the bottom drawer with those of other past girlfriends. I went into the living room and behind the bar, and poured myself a highball of Macallan 18-year on the rocks. Strolling over to the '60s Zenith hi-fi console that looked like a sideboard, I put on a favorite Sinatra LP and stared down at Amsterdam Avenue while sipping my scotch.

As Sinatra belted out "New York, New York," I caught myself singing along. And then I realized something: Despite what had happened with Ashley, despite being coerced into taking a non-case by the FBI Director, I, Dakota Stevens, had the world by the balls. I was an American male in the prime of his life, setting out on a new adventure. As the song played on, my confidence soared and I became filled with an inner knowing that, someday, somehow, my struggling PI business would take off, and that my leaving the Bureau would prove the best decision I'd ever made.

When the song ended, I finished my drink, shut off the hi-fi, grabbed my packed suitcase and left. I hadn't visited my estate in Millbrook for several weeks, and as I waited at the stoplight to cross Columbus Avenue, I considered swinging by there first, on my way up to Boston. But Director Reeves had been adamant: I was to get out to Cambridge ASAP.

When the light turned green, I took a deep breath—a breath that felt a lot less free than ones I had taken just yesterday—and grudgingly made my way to I-95 north.

3

PSYCHOPATHS AND PSYCHOPATHY

The next morning, I rose early in my room at the Charles Hotel and went running in the cool, late September air. As I crossed the Harvard Bridge, the river below was as still as a millpond. A crew team in a racing scull whisked under the bridge.

I ran around the football stadium and the Harvard Business School, noting with a smile the hidden tennis courts where I had once made out with a beautiful redhead on the hot court surface in a cold rain—and ran back to the hotel. After a short workout in the hotel fitness center and a fast twenty laps in the pool, I returned to my room and had breakfast sent up.

Since I wasn't getting a fee for this "case," I planned on splurging a bit on my expenses, and that meant starting my day with a legendary breakfast: three scrambled eggs, bacon, sausage, home fries, blueberry pancakes with Vermont maple syrup, Jamaican Blue Mountain coffee, and freshly squeezed orange juice. Watching the news as I ate, I noticed the WBZ morning anchor was the same buttercream blonde who'd anchored when I was in college. The woman was sexy then, and she *still* was—a fact that, in this constantly changing world, I found oddly comforting.

Today I'd meet my quarry—Miss Sally Standish. Since my task was to tempt her away from Dr. Malone, I had to look good enough to make a college girl's heart throb. The trouble was, I had no idea what college girls found attractive nowadays.

Thinking back to the coeds I'd known in my undergraduate days, remembering the grad students or professors they'd pined for, I opted to wear jeans and a chocolate tweed blazer. For a shirt—because it was supposed to be warm today, and because my arms were one of my best features and it was a sin to keep them covered all the time—I wore a snug polo shirt. My blazer didn't have elbow patches, but I was confident my academic peers would forgive this egregious breach of sartorial decorum.

Director Reeves had said an agent from the Boston office would "unofficially" assist me and bring the identification I needed (e.g., Harvard ID, handgun and PI licenses). But by the time I was ready to leave, nothing had been delivered. It seemed that, for this first day at least, Dr. Dakota Stevens would have to survive by his wits. I went downstairs to the lobby.

As I stood among the sumptuous leather sofas, and the walls of brick and dark paneling, it occurred to me that a hotel of this caliber must have a business center. *Maybe the Boston agent emailed you,* I thought. The front desk clerk, a lovely cobalt-eyed blonde named Augusta, directed me to the business center, where I logged into my email account. My inbox contained one email, from Director Reeves's personal email address.

He wrote that Dr. Norman Cantor—world-renowned expert in criminal psychology, and one of Sally's professors—would corroborate my cover story that I was a Ph.D. on sabbatical from the FBI. The Director was still lining up an agent with the Boston office who would bring me the other materials I needed. He ended his email with a gibe: *"Finally, Stevens, a word of advice: If you wish to convey a professional image for your new investigations firm, I strongly suggest you acquire a better email address than 'dakotapi@YAHOO.com.' Son…get your own domain name, for Pete's sake. I look forward to reading your first report this evening. —Director Reeves."*

I frowned. Most annoying about his comment—once again, he was right.

Attached to the email were Sally's class schedule and activities list, and a picture of her. At first blush, Sally Standish was rather plain looking. Although her complexion was smooth and makeup-free, she had a prominent—almost bulbous—forehead, and she wore nerdy black cat-eye glasses. Her hair, the dull brown of a beaver pelt, was parted in the middle.

When I went to print the photo and schedule, I couldn't figure out how to print attachments, so I had to ask Augusta to do it for me. As she stooped over the keyboard, some of her lustrous hair fell over one shoulder. The shimmer of those locks—the color of wet straw drying in the sun—evoked part of a Yeats poem: "Only God, my dear/Could love you for yourself alone/And not your yellow hair." Augusta's pleasant efficiency reminded me how sorely I needed an assistant. Maybe I should hire Augusta.

While she was printing things, I also had her print out a map of the Harvard campus for me. After all, it had been over a decade since I'd lived in Cambridge. Finally, after I thanked Augusta and forced a sawbuck into her hand, I did a web search and found some information about Dr. Malone, including a photo of him. He was a Caucasian in his late 30s with blonde hair. A fairly handsome guy, but he looked soft. He was no heartthrob by any means. What a 19½-year-old Harvard girl saw in him, I had no idea.

Finished, I scanned Sally's class schedule. Her first class of the day, beginning in half an hour, was "Psychopaths and Psychopathy," taught by Dr. Cantor. Once I located the lecture hall on the map, I stowed everything in my messenger bag, shouldered it and left.

Outside, the sun was well up now, hinting at the hot Indian summer day to come. The sidewalks were still wet from the previous night's rain, and I had to hop puddles. When I got to Harvard Square, it occurred to me that my bag was empty and that a Harvard Fellow would at least have something to write on. Inside the university bookstore, the Coop, I bought a legal pad, a clipboard, and a couple of pens. I also bought a copy of Raymond Chandler's *The Little Sister* (for detecting inspiration), a bag of cashews and an apple juice, and stowed it all in the bag. Now I felt like I belonged in Harvard Yard. It was time to see if I passed muster with the real academics.

Crossing the brick plaza in front of the Au Bon Pain café, where the chess hustlers were setting up under the trees, I attached myself to a covey of chirping coeds and followed them across Mass Ave into Harvard Yard—the brick buildings that date back to the earliest days of the college. The 200-year-old maples and oaks in the Yard gleamed with vibrant reds, oranges and yellows. I checked my watch. Only ten minutes until class. I started to jog.

Out of habit I glanced over my shoulder and noticed a tall Japanese woman—her hair in a bun—following me. When I ran faster, she picked up her pace to match mine. I had no idea who this woman was, but I wasn't taking any chances.

Once past the steps of Widener Library, I scooted down a narrow, hedge-lined walkway on the side of the building. The Japanese woman followed. At the rear of the building where the path turned, I backed into some bushes near the top of a staircase and waited.

I could hear the hedge rustling as she drew nearer. A couple of prep school boys tossed me a jaded glance as they tramped up the stairs beside me; apparently, encountering men in tweed coats skulking in bushes was a routine occurrence for them. Turning the corner, they continued up the path, toward the front of the library. I heard the woman's footsteps approaching. She muttered, "pardon me" as she edged past the boys. Meanwhile, I stood absolutely still with the hedge branches making my face itch.

As the woman jogged around the corner, I thrust out a leg and tripped her. She careened toward the bushes, but on her way to the ground she somehow morphed her fall into a front somersault, grabbing my messenger bag strap and pulling me down with her. While I landed hard on my back, tangled in the hedge, she tumbled smoothly onto her feet and brushed herself off. I tried to stand up, but I was caught in the branches.

Damn, Dakota...talk about hoisted by your own petard.

I was thrashing around, struggling to get out of my blazer, when she reached into a large handbag. So this was it: I was going to be gunned down by a Japanese woman assassin, without even knowing who'd sent her or why. I tried kicking her, but she had wisely placed herself out of reach. Then she showed me a badge.

"Special Agent Jennifer Suzuki, Mr. Stevens." With a simper on her face, she tossed me a large padded envelope. "Compliments of Director Reeves."

Finally on my feet, I rummaged through the envelope. There was a Harvard Fellow ID, a Massachusetts PI license and pistol permit, and a Smith & Wesson .40 semiautomatic in a shoulder holster.

"So, Miss Suzuki," I said, "may I ask...are you of the violin school or motorcycle Suzukis?"

My comment elicited no reaction from her; not even a raised eyebrow. It was a little annoying because I considered it a pretty good impromptu line.

"Mr. Stevens," she said, "I'm doing a favor for Director Reeves. He asked me to give you a message. This case involving Miss Standish is, and must remain, *off the FBI's books*. He does not want any attention drawn to the Bureau. Finally, regarding the gun, he said you are to refrain from using it at all costs, unless—"

"I know the drill," I said. "Thank you, Agent Suzuki."

She wore a snug-fitting navy pantsuit and a white blouse with turn-back cuffs. While admiring her splendid curves in the outfit, I extricated my blazer from the hedge and started to put it back on. Miss Suzuki approached me.

"Hold still, one moment." She reached behind me and pulled a leafy twig off my back.

"Thanks," I said. "Nice take-down, by the way."

"I know." She smiled. "Too bad I can't say the same of you."

"I'm rusty," I said with a shrug. "But maybe we could get together and practice our grappling."

"Hmm…and throws and arm-locks?" she said.

"Sure, if you're up for it."

She smoothed out her suit jacket. "That can be very sweaty work, Mr. Stevens."

"No problem. My hotel has a pool."

"And what if I can't swim?" she asked.

"I'll teach you. Or we could just frolic in the shallow end."

"*Frolic*? That sounds like fun."

"Oh, it is," I said. "I'm staying at—"

"The Charles. Yes, I know."

"So…see you after work then?"

"I highly doubt it," she said. "I have friends in the District, Mr. Stevens. I'm afraid your reputation precedes you."

"Really? What *reputation* is that?"

She was about to say something else when a light-skinned African American man, maybe 25, ran up the walkway. One look told me everything I needed to know about him; it was practically stamped across his forehead: "NEW FBI SPECIAL AGENT." He eyed me warily.

"Suzuki," he said, "you okay?"

"Yes, Winters," she said. "Let's go."

"Agent Suzuki," I said. "Please *do* get in touch. I think we could both benefit from practicing together. You know where to find me."

She walked away with a smirk forming on her lips. Winters followed her.

"Practicing *what* together, Suzuki?" he asked her.

Their voices faded. I brushed myself off, stuffed the padded envelope with the gun into my messenger bag, and located Sally's lecture hall on the map.

Already late, I set off at a brisk jog.

———◆———

The lecture hall doors were shut when I got there, and although I was able to *open* one quietly, when I stepped inside and let the door close, it emitted a loud groan behind me. Pacing back and forth down in the amphitheater pit, Professor Cantor stopped short and frowned up at me.

"Sorry, professor," I said.

Having worked up a sweat getting here, I removed my tweed jacket and took an empty aisle seat in the back row. The room was packed; apparently a lot of young people were interested in psychopaths. I scanned the students, looking for Sally Standish, but the hall was dim and the students were all facing away from me.

A beam from an LCD projector shone onto a screen behind Professor Cantor. It was a PowerPoint presentation on the research of Dr. Robert Hare, a criminal psychologist renowned for developing the Psychopathy

Checklist. I'd met Dr. Hare during a stint with the FBI's Child Abduction and Serial Murder Investigative Resources Center, so I was conversant with his work.

Professor Cantor clicked a remote in his hand. A new slide came up on the screen. On the left was a picture of serial killer Ted Bundy; on the right, Hare's psychopathy checklist.

"*Doctor* Stevens," he said, gesturing grandly to the top rows of the amphitheater. "I'm pleased you could join us this morning—albeit extremely tardy."

"Pleased to be here, Dr. Cantor," I said.

"Class, Dr. Stevens is a criminology expert and profiler with the F-B-I."

The entire class turned in their seats to face me. I waved broadly.

"He's also a Harvard Fellow," Cantor said, "doing a sabbatical with us as he continues his research. Dr. Stevens?"

"Yes, professor?"

"Of the traits listed in the Interpersonal Quadrant of the PCL-R, which one do you think best applied to Ted Bundy?"

Unwittingly, Professor Cantor had pitched me a softball. Every Special Agent candidate at Quantico studied the Bundy case in detail.

"I think it's a tie, professor," I said, "between glibness-slash-superficial charm and conning-slash-manipulative. Unfortunately, Mr. Bundy was apparently very attractive to the ladies, and they often fell for his charm. In fact, it was only when one young woman escaped from him that Bundy was eventually caught."

"Exactly, Dr. Stevens," Cantor said. "Did everyone hear that?"

Pleased with my answer, I leaned back in my chair and laced my fingers behind my head. Glancing at the students now facing me, I spotted Sally Standish: smooth complexion, prominent forehead, brown hair and cat-eye glasses. She was in the opposite aisle seat, three rows down. Seeing her in person from a few feet away, I observed several details that hadn't come across in the photo. Her hair was tucked behind a pair of slightly forward-facing ears, and gathered in a ponytail. Her teeth were straight and white, but almost horsey in shape and size. Her lower lip was considerably fuller than her upper one, and it seemed to hang, glistening, in a perpetual pout. I couldn't imagine what a grown man, Dr. Geoff Malone, saw in this almost nebbishy-looking girl. And then I understood her appeal: seen in a photo, Sally's individual features made her seem plain, almost an ugly ducking; but in the flesh, she was much more than the sum of her parts; in the flesh, the girl was striking.

While the other students turned back to Dr. Cantor, Sally continued to stare at me. With my fingers still laced cockily behind my head, I flexed my arms in the snug polo shirt. The swelled muscles strained the sleeve cuffs. Sally's eyes widened. After she'd been staring at me for a few seconds, I winked at her, jolting her out of her trance. She spun around and whispered to her girlfriend. During the rest of the lecture, Sally and her friend kept stealing glances at me.

When class finished, I stayed in my seat and made sustained eye contact with Sally, smiling at her as she filed out with the other students. My first encounter with Miss Standish was an unmitigated success. I'd piqued her curiosity—step one in getting her away from Dr. Malone.

Eventually Dr. Cantor and I were alone in the amphitheater. He waved me down to the pit. Putting on my jacket and grabbing my messenger bag, I walked down and shook his hand.

"Interesting comment today, Mr. Stevens," he said.

"Thank you, professor. Great lecture. I haven't thought about Bundy since my training days."

He stowed some papers in a briefcase and hoisted it off the lectern.

"I haven't much time—appointment over at Grossman," he said. "Perhaps you could walk with me?"

"Certainly."

I followed him out a side door and down a hallway, and then we were outside, walking across campus.

"When Director Reeves called and asked for my help in this charade," he said, "I must admit I was initially skeptical. But...I don't care for Dr. Malone, so I'll be happy to vouch for you."

"I appreciate it, professor," I said. "If you don't mind my asking, sir, why don't you care for Dr. Malone?"

"Because he's a charlatan who gives those of us doing *real* psychology research a bad name," he said. " 'Sexual Attractiveness *Study*,' my eye. Honestly, I don't understand why the administration allowed him here."

"Maybe because he's controversial and a minor celebrity," I said. "Due respect, professor, this university *does* seem to enjoy controversy."

"Yes, I suppose you're right. Anything to keep that endowment growing." He turned to me with a wry smile. "There's a joke in academia, maybe you've heard it—that we're actually a multi-billion-dollar hedge fund running a university on the side."

I chuckled. "No, I've never heard that, but it sounds apt."

When we reached Grossman Library, Professor Cantor said goodbye to me, walked up a couple steps, then stopped suddenly and considered me over his shoulder.

"Mr. Stevens?"

"Professor?"

"I know Miss Standish is the reason you're here." He looked around to make sure no one was within earshot, and spoke softly. "But somebody needs to look into Malone's background. I mean *really* look into it—not the pro forma box-checking our illustrious HR department does. You could start by contacting the *long* list of prestigious institutions that have hosted his ridiculous sideshow. My gut tells me there's something *off* about the man. Frankly, I've never met anyone who reminded me more of Ted Bundy than Dr. Malone." He swallowed and gave me a trepidatious look. "Fair warning, Mr. Stevens...I think you're dealing with a psychopath."

"Thank you for your counsel, professor. I'll be careful."

Nodding perfunctorily, the professor spun on his heels and went up the steps and into the building. Even with the warm sun on my back, thinking about the professor's warning, I shivered.

4

THE DOPPELGÄNGER OF A
PREDATOR-EYED SUPERMODEL

After saying goodbye to Dr. Cantor, I was passing Widener Library again when I noticed a tall, lanky man standing on the library steps with his nose in a thick book. As I got closer, I noticed the book was *Moby Dick* and the man was my college freshman roommate, Stanley Ford, whom I hadn't seen in over a decade.

I climbed the steps toward him. His glasses were several prescriptions thicker. Looking up from the book, he paused as his eyes refocused, and then, recognizing me, his face lit up. He clapped the book shut and hugged me.

"Dakota Stevens! So wonderful to see you!"

"You, too, Stanley." When he let go of me, I tapped his book. "*Moby Dick*, huh?"

"Ah, yes," he said, sneering at the cover, "haven't read it since Professor Green's class. Remember him and his Phi Beta Kappa key on the watch chain? Quite a pip. As for *Moby*"—he thumped the book—"it doesn't hold up to a second read unfortunately. An interesting study about the whaling industry in the nineteenth century; however, as far as a novel goes, it's dreadfully slow. But never mind that. Where were you last summer? Our ten-year reunion. Did you not receive an invitation?"

"No, I did," I said, "but I was working that weekend."

"And what *is* your line of work, Dakota?" Stanley gestured with the thick novel. "I've heard all sorts of rumors over the years—FBI, CIA, NSA. There's even one that you moved to Alaska and became a bounty hunter. So which is it?"

"Until recently, FBI," I said. "Now I'm in private practice."

"Ah, a regular gumshoe then. Like Sam Spade."

"Mm, more like Phillip Marlowe," I said, "but yes, a private detective."

"And what brings you to Harvard?" he asked. "Study?"

"No, a case," I said. "But it's confidential. What about you, Stanley? Are you working here now?"

"Yes, I'm the special events liaison for the university. Half-babysitter, half-goodwill ambassador for important guests."

Stanley explained that his job was to act as a buffer between the administration and the often high-maintenance visiting celebrities, athletes, politicians and artists. His latest charge was a champion chess player.

"Have I heard of him?" I asked.

"Her," Stanley said. "Depends on how well you know chess."

"A woman?" I said.

"Yes, an international grandmaster, and you should see her," he said. "Gorgeous and brilliant. The woman speaks three languages. Been wiping the floor with the men in her exhibition tournaments all week long. Hm…I seem to recall your playing a bit in college."

"Yeah, but I sucked then, and I suck even more now," I said.

Stanley checked his watch. "She was supposed to meet me here. She's late, but I have an idea where she is. Care to join me? She's something to see—a wonder of the world, I assure you."

I had planned to infiltrate Sally's dorm and search her room. But, never one to pass up a chance to meet a gorgeous woman, I opted to tag along.

"Sure," I said.

"Splendid." Stanley led us down the steps and along a path that headed to Harvard Square. He checked his watch as we strolled past a horde of undergrads. They looked shell-shocked, like they'd all just failed an exam.

"By the way, Stanley," I said, "what's this woman's name?"

"Svetlana Krush."

"Wait," I said, "you're telling me this woman is a chess player and her last name is 'Crush,' as in she *crushes* her opponents?"

"Sorry," Stanley said, "mispronounced it. First off, her surname is spelled with a 'K,' not a 'C.' Also, she uses an umlaut over the 'U'—you know, those two little dots—so it sounds like 'crewsh.' "

"Svetlana Krüsh," I said. "Got it."

Outside the brick wall that surrounded the Yard, Stanley nodded at the plaza in front of the Au Bon Pain café across the street.

"That's where we're headed," he said. "See the hub-bub? You can bet she's the cause of it."

A throng around the café tables said something was going on. At a lull in the traffic, we crossed the road.

The crowd was an odd assortment of businessmen, students and homeless men. There were no women among the onlookers that I could see. Spunky sparrows pecked at crumbs around the crowd. Through gaps in the crowd I glimpsed a tall woman who was the doppelgänger of a predator-eyed supermodel I'd seen in a Victoria's Secret catalog. As we wended through the onlookers, I heard the snap of chess clocks interspersed with the clip-clop of boots on the brick courtyard.

"Make way, please!" Stanley said. "Pardon us. We're with Miss Krüsh."

There was some grumbling, but gradually the men moved aside and we were in the inner circle of the crowd, gazing down a long row of café tables. Hunched over chessboards on one side of the tables were ten men of various ages and socioeconomic backgrounds. On the other side, a woman moved a piece, pressed a button on a chess clock, and slinked to the next table.

It didn't seem possible that a woman chess player could be blessed with such talent *and* beauty; I'd always imagined them to be sickly pale, hirsute brutes. That did not describe Svetlana Krüsh. Her hair was glossy and shoulder-length, flipped up at the ends so it flounced on her jacket collar. The jacket, a black old-fashioned frock coat that draped nearly to her knees, made her look like a woman gunslinger.

When she reached the next table, she paused to contemplate her move, putting a finger to her pillowy lips. Deep in thought, she pushed the jacket off her hip, exposing a long and denimy thigh. They were runway legs, trim and confident. Light makeup accentuated her delicate bone structure. Her eyelashes were Norwegian ski jumps. Beneath the frock coat she wore a cream silk blouse, and the fact that it was undone a couple of buttons seemed to be premeditated; whenever she dipped forward to make a move, her opponent's eyes strayed from the board.

And there we stood, Stanley and I, for half an hour while, one by one, her opponents tipped over their kings. A couple of curmudgeonly holdouts played down to pawns. Kibitzers chatted and gesticulated about the various games, but Miss Krüsh silenced them with her gaze. The woman had a pair of almond-shaped, widely spaced eyes that seemed to be continually sizing up everything in their purview as prey.

When her one remaining opponent finally resigned, Miss Krüsh stood fully erect, snapped her frock coat taut and glared around, daring someone else to challenge her. Her eyes landed on me. I could tell she was accustomed to people withering in the heat of her stare, but I had a pretty good stare myself. After a short staring contest, she averted her eyes and walked gracefully down the row of tables toward Stanley and me. The sparrows and awed spectators moved aside to make room for her. Indeed, the very air seemed whipped up by her approach: a sudden gust rustled the albizzia trees overhead. When she reached us, a college boy thrust a vinyl roll-up board and

CHRIS ORCUTT

a black Sharpie at her. Hastily autographing the board, she shoved it back at him. He darted away to show his buddies.

"Svetlana Krüsh—this is my college roommate, Dakota Stevens," said Stanley, introducing us.

She held out her hand with the wrist firm but bent, so I wasn't sure if she expected me to shake her hand or kiss it. In the end I opted to shake it. Something about her—her excellent posture, her unflinching eyes, or the deadly serious brain behind them—something told me this was not a woman to be trifled with. Normally relaxed around women—a bit too accustomed to gorgeous creatures materializing in my life like manna from heaven—I found myself nervous in this one's presence. Our handshake probably only lasted a few seconds, but it seemed like it went on for hours, both of us with faint smiles on our lips. It was as though we sensed that meeting each other was a destiny moment for both of us, and neither of us wanted it to end.

"I require a double latte, Stanley," she finally said, letting go of my hand. "And...*un pain au chocolat, s'il vous plaît.*"

"Certainly," Stanley said. "That will give you two a chance to talk. Dakota, want anything?"

"Just a black coffee, Stanley. Thanks."

While Stanley went inside, I led Miss Krüsh to an empty table beneath a tree. I was about to sit down when Miss Krüsh hesitated at her chair. Caught in the awkwardness of the moment, I walked over and held the chair for her while she sat and crossed her legs. Then I pushed it in for her.

47

"Can I do anything else for you, madam?" I said. "Run a lint brush over your jacket, perhaps?"

She gave me a piqued sidelong glance. I sat down.

"So, Mr. Stevens," she said, "what is your profession?"

"I'm a private detective."

She shook her head minutely and shrugged.

"A private investigator," I said. "People hire me to solve crimes and problems for them. Haven't you ever seen a PI movie or TV show?"

"Ah, yes. *Magnum, P.I.* is one, correct?"

"Yes," I said. "But I'm not as whiny when Higgins won't loan me the Ferrari."

She didn't even smile, which annoyed me; anyone familiar with the show would have found my line hilarious.

"Does this work attract undesirables?" she asked.

"Often."

She nodded again, without expression.

"But, hey"—I nudged her boot under the table—"what's life without a few undesirables around?"

The corners of her mouth flickered in a short-lived smile.

"So," I said, "when you're not jet-setting around playing chess, where do you live?"

"Manhattan." She said this curtly, as if with disdain for every other city in the world. I decided to have some fun with her.

"Manhattan, Kansas?" I said. "Really?"

"Of course not, New York Ci—"

"Relax, I'm joshing you. I'm on the Upper West Side myself. Seventy-seventh and Amsterdam. Where's your place?"

CHRIS ORCUTT

"Eighty-two and a half East Tenth Street," she said.

"And a *half?*"

"That is correct."

"The East Village," I said. "Nice."

"Where is your office located, Mr. Stevens?"

"I'm without an office space at present. You could say I'm in the market."

"Our meeting might prove fortuitous, Mr. Stevens," she said. "The basement level of the building I own is available. It is zoned for commercial use and has a sidewalk entrance. Perhaps you would like to see it when we are both in the city."

"Sure, that'd be great."

Stanley arrived with a tray of food. He placed coffee and a *pain au chocolat* (looked to me like a simple chocolate croissant) in front of Miss Krüsh, and a black coffee in front of me.

"Dakota," Stanley said, "perhaps you'd like to come to Svetlana's tournament tomorrow night—a twenty-board exhibition. Afterward, the three of us could go to dinner on the university. What do you say?"

"I'm game."

"Svetlana?" Stanley said.

"A nice meal and some adult conversation would be a welcome distraction," she said.

"Shoot," I said, looking at Stanley. "Does that mean I can't bring my book of knock-knock jokes?"

Stanley laughed, but Miss Krüsh cracked a smile, which I considered the greater accomplishment.

"Then it's settled," Stanley said. "Where are you staying, Dakota? I'll send a ticket over."

"The Charles," I said.

"Fine," Stanley said. "Tomorrow night, seven o'clock."

"It's a date."

I glanced at Svetlana, then checked my watch. Sally was at class for another hour, which made this an ideal time to search her dorm room. I picked up my coffee and stood.

"You'll have to excuse me, but I'm on a case and I need to get back to work."

"Oh, of course, Dakota," Stanley said.

"Mr. Stevens?" Miss Krüsh said.

"Yes?"

"I hope you do not encounter any undesirables today."

"So do I, Miss Krüsh."

"Until tomorrow then."

I shook hands with both of them and wended through the café throng with a buoyant feeling in my chest. Somehow I sensed that my life was about to get better, and that Svetlana Krüsh would be a part of that.

5

BDSM

From Harvard Square I wandered down J.F.K. Street toward the river, looking for Sally Standish's dormitory on Memorial Drive. She lived at Banister House. According to her class schedule, she was busy until the mid-afternoon. This would give me time to snoop in her room.

I had no idea whether Sally had a roommate, or if she'd be there. Regardless, I was confident I could pull it off. Having watched the TV show *The Rockford Files* since I was a boy, I'd picked up more than a few of PI Jim Rockford's tricks.

I couldn't get Svetlana Krüsh out of my head. Her posture projected total self-confidence, and her charisma was palpable. There was an air of superiority, too, but I supposed if one were an internationally famous chess genius, it might be difficult to be humble.

It started to sprinkle when I walked into the Banister House courtyard. A pack of male students in designer prep wear brushed past me on the walkway, boisterously singing a song I didn't recognize. There was a security desk inside the main entrance, but I wasn't going in that way. Cutting across the lawn, I circled the building to the loading dock. A couple of women in chef's outfits were standing under the overhang, smoking.

When I was with the Bureau, all I had to do in situations like this was flash my badge. Private practice, however, required stealth and subterfuge. Recalling how Jim Rockford routinely handled these situations, I pulled out my clipboard with the legal pad and a pen, clipped my ID to my jacket, and went up the stairs and under the loading dock overhang. Just then, the light sprinkling rain turned into a downpour. The women looked at me. I jutted my head at the rain.

"Boy, that was close." I pointed at my ID. "Harvard Fellow. Efficiency audit." I gestured at the door with my clipboard. "This the way in?"

They nodded wearily.

"Thank you, ladies."

I continued inside and through the kitchen, looking around with my pen and clipboard poised, nodding superciliously. I emerged into a large parlor.

A piano trio—pianist, cellist, violinist—played something by Beethoven. At least it sounded like Beethoven. A small audience of students and adults frowned at me as I crossed in front of the trio, heading toward the lobby. I put away the clipboard and pen. Beside the door was a table with tea, coffee and a platter of sandwiches. Turkey club. Not my favorite, but one makes do. With the audience facing the other way, I grabbed a sandwich and gnashed into it. The cellist, a slender spinster type, scowled at me as she played. I winked at her in reply, causing her to flub a few notes. I took another bite of the sandwich and left the room.

Having dated a Renaissance literature major who'd lived here, I remembered the Banister House layout well. It helped that they hadn't changed it. I walked through a TV common room, the dining room, a computer lab and the library before reaching the main hall.

Dominating the room was a grand staircase that led to the residence rooms. The security desk and main entrance were through a doorway on the side of the main hall. As soon as the security guard was facing outside, I ran upstairs.

At the top I paused to eat my sandwich and to read a sign announcing the Annual Connect Four Championship. It was tonight, in the Banister House Grille. A championship for an obscure '80s board game? Until now, I'd forgotten something: While most Harvard students are undeniably smart, many of them are about as socially adept as Venus flytraps. Sally's room was on the third floor. Wolfing down the sandwich and dusting my hands, I continued upstairs.

The third-floor hallway was surprisingly dim. Considering the astronomical cost of this university, you'd think the facilities people would spring for more light bulbs. A cacophony of rock music wafted out of open bedroom doors. Walking along, noting the room numbers as I went, I heard someone playing a car racing video game, smelled marijuana, and spied two girls scurrying across the hall in their underwear. Their panties, I observed, had cartoon cats on the front that read, "HELLO KITTY." As far as I recalled, when I was in college, girls' panties didn't have messages or cartoons on them. A wave of existential angst crashed over me. Although youthful and in excellent shape for my age, I was a decade older than any of the students in this building, and I would never be that young again. *Sigh*. I let this thought sink in before continuing down the hallway.

Finally I found Sally's door. Inside, a television played. Feeling frisky, I knocked "shave-and-a-haircut, two bits." A second later, the door flung open and I was staring at a female hardbody in an electric blue sports halter and gray Spandex athletic shorts. She had short blonde hair. I was forced to improvise.

"Excuse me," I said. "Is Sally in?" I said.

"No." Her back was bowed, such that the crown of her head and the marble curve of her butt touched the doorjamb. "Who are you?"

This girl had a stomach you could literally wash clothes on. In my younger and more vulnerable years, I could imagine myself persuading her to try such a thing.

"Dr. Dakota Stevens, Harvard Fellow." I showed her my ID. "Pardon me for barging in like this, but Dr. Cantor—that's Sally's 'Psychopaths and Psychopathy' professor—he said she needed some extra help."

"Extra *help*, huh?" She sniffed. "Sorry, Harvard Fellow Guy, but she's at class. *If* she comes back, it won't be for another hour."

"May I use your phone?" I said.

She fanned the door open and waved at a phone on a desk. "Sure."

"It's a local call," I said.

"Call Bangladesh for all care," she said. "It's Sally's phone."

I stepped inside. It was a typical dorm room—two beds, two bureaus, two bookcases, two desks, two closets—with each girl's things on one side of the room. Above the headboard of the right-hand bed was a framed photo of a women's racing scull crossing a finish line, the rowers' arms raised in victory. A brass plaque on the bottom of the frame read, "MEGAN ARCHAMBAULT — HEAD OF THE CHARLES, FIRST PLACE."

"So...Megan," I said, "you're on the Crew team."

"How observant of you," she said. "Yeah, I row. Look...hurry up and make your call. "

The window was open, and the maples outside swayed in the wind. The breeze coming in caught an open book on the desk and flipped the pages like a ghost was speed-reading them.

"Better grab that book," I said.

She tossed it on the bed and shut the window.

"Hey, Megan," I said. "What did you mean before, when you said '*if* she comes back'?"

"I meant she's hardly ever here. Stays at her boyfriend's place most nights. That's him." She pointed at picture frames on the desk: Sally and Dr. Geoff Malone at Boston sites—Bunker Hill, the Boston Tea Party ship, Fenway Park. "Meanwhile, some *boy*friend—the guy's a visiting *professor*. Dr. Malone. Maybe you've heard of him?"

"Peripherally."

"Guy's a total lech," she said. "First time he came over here, he was totally scamming on me. Every time

Sally turned her back, he'd be checking me out. He even grabbed my ass once. He's one of those accidentally cop-a-feel guys, you know?"

"Not really," I said. "That's not my style."

"I don't care if he's a Ph.D.," she said. "Far as I'm concerned, the guy's nothing but a slimy troglodyte."

"Damn," I said. "Impressive vocab word, young lady."

"Perfect SAT verbal." She shrugged it off with a smile. "Anyway, I told Sally all about the lech, but she wouldn't listen." Megan grabbed some keys and a wallet, stabbed her feet into flip-flops, and walked toward the door. "Listen, Dr. Stevens…I'm going down to the Grille. I assume I can trust you alone in here for five minutes."

"Of course," I said. "I'll be on the phone."

"Yeah, well…I'm leaving the door open, so don't get cute with anything in here."

"Yes, ma'am." I gave her a little salute, sat at the desk and picked up the phone.

Squinting at me, she backed out of the room and sauntered down the hall, her flip-flops slapping her heels with every step. I counted to ten, then quietly closed the door.

Sally's desk had three small drawers on the right and one wide one above the space where the chair was stowed. The top two small drawers contained only office supplies. But in the very back of the bottom drawer, along with a few rolls of quarters, I found a box of condoms and a bottle of K-Y lubricant.

Then I checked the wide drawer. At first it was jammed, but I yanked it open and a fluorescent green flyer fluttered out. There was a stack of them in the drawer. I picked up the one that had fallen on the floor. On either side of the flyer were cartoon figures: on the left, a curvaceous coed in lingerie, covering her mouth in mock surprise; on the right, a muscular young man in nothing but a pair of briefs. Down the center was the following text:

INTERESTED IN
SEX?
THEN JOIN VISITING RESEARCHER
DR. GEOFF MALONE,
IN THE MOST IMPORTANT
AND CONTROVERSIAL
SEX RESEARCH PROJECT
SINCE MASTERS & JOHNSON.

THE MALONE SEXUAL ATTRACTION STUDY
WILL FOREVER CHANGE
HUMAN SEXUALITY.
CURIOUS?
ARE YOU BETWEEN 18 AND 25?
IF SO, BECOME A SUBJECT!
APPLY AT VOLVAP HALL,
MON–FRI, 10AM–4PM.
APPLICATIONS STRICTLY CONFIDENTIAL.

I folded up a copy and slipped it in my messenger bag. The rainstorm raked so savagely against the window, I couldn't hear if anyone was coming from down the hall. However, it was doubtful I'd get another crack at this. I simply had to forge ahead and risk getting caught.

Moving on to Sally's bureau, I found questionable items in the top and bottom drawers. The top one was filled with panties with the word "JUICY" emblazoned

A STUDY IN CRIMSON

across the seat; the bottom drawer, I discovered with a wince, contained myriad sex toys and a nest of racy lingerie. Maybe searching her room wasn't such a good idea after all. No matter what, I wouldn't be mentioning these items in my report to Director Reeves.

I was about to check Sally's closet when I heard grumbling from behind the hallway door. Darting back to Sally's desk, I picked up the phone and pretended to be talking to my hotel.

Megan squinted at me as she came inside. She tossed her wallet and keys on her desk and stabbed a fork into a salad.

"So he didn't leave a message?" I said to the dial tone. "All right...thanks."

I hung up.

"Hey, I told you to leave the door open," Megan said.

"Sorry, I needed some privacy."

"Mm, well, it's been nice meeting you, Dr. Stevens, but I have to study. If you want to wait for Sally, please do it down in the library."

"You two don't get along, do you?" I asked.

Megan shrugged and ate some salad.

"It's sad when friends drift apart," I said.

She gave me an eye-roll that would have made a fifth grader proud.

"Whatever," she said. "If Sally shows up, I'll tell her you're in the library."

"Thanks, Megan," I said.

I made my way downstairs. Like a lot of rooms at Harvard, the dorm library had the feel of an English club: dark paneled walls, built-in bookcases, and chandeliers. A few students hunched over study tables, while others lolled on leather sofas. The windows were shut, and I could hear the rainstorm slashing against the windowpanes.

I took out my copy of *The Little Sister* and plopped into a club chair and put my feet up on a hassock. Four pages into the novel, when I read the line, "She was a small, neat, rather prissy-looking girl with primly smooth brown hair...," there was a tap on my shoulder. As I was emerging from the fictional dream, I thought the woman in the novel had come to life. Sally Standish was standing in front of me.

"Mr. Stevens," she said softly, "Megan said you came over to help me with today's lecture. Funny, but I don't recall asking for private tutoring. I don't recall introducing myself or even telling you my name."

"No, you didn't."

I stood up and motioned toward an alcove in the corner of the room. She followed me inside.

"After class," I said, "I peeked at Professor Cantor's seating chart and I looked you up in the college directory. Then I came over here and asked around until somebody told me your room number."

"But why go to all that trouble?"

"I was thinking we could go out sometime."

"I have a boyfriend," she said.

"Yeah, Dr. Malone. I heard."

"I'm sorry, but we're exclusive," she said. "What made you think I was interested in you anyway?"

"During the lecture," I said. "I saw how you were looking at me."

"I just wanted to"—she fidgeted—"see who was speaking, that's all."

I chuckled.

"What's funny?" she said.

"You. You're adorable," I said. "Look, how about tonight? We could go over to Boston and have dinner— Atlantic Fish on Boylston Street. I was a waiter there in college."

"I can't. I have an appointment."

"All right, then—tomorrow night."

"Geoff is in a chess tournament tomorrow night," she said. "Against some woman professional or something. But even if he weren't, I couldn't—I mean...I *wouldn't* be interested."

She averted her eyes when she said this. At the very least, she was intrigued. I wasn't thrilled with what I was about to do—trifle with a young woman's emotions—but I reminded myself that Sally's father was worried about her, that he'd essentially sanctioned my wooing her, and that the successful completion of this job would establish me in private practice.

I took a deep breath and thought of England.

Moving closer to Sally, I backed her up until she was against a floor-to-ceiling bookcase. She was almost a foot shorter than me and had to tilt her head back to look me in the face. Her eyes were a soft brown, almost amber, and the chandelier lights shone in them. Easing closer still to her, moving with hypnotic slowness, I caressed her cheek with my hand and glided it over her jawbone. Her cheeks flushed, her breathing faltered.

I was planning to caress her teasingly down her neck but ran into a thick turtleneck sweater. I probed a couple inches underneath, and my fingers touched something hard, like a piece of steel. Gently I pulled the fabric down, revealing a quarter-inch-thick pewter loop that fit snugly around her neck. Dangling off the loop was a small metal ring, and at the bottom, where the two ends of the necklace came together, was a heart-shaped lock.

"This is the strangest necklace I've ever seen," I said. "What is it, some kind of choker?"

"No." She pushed my hand away. "It's my BDSM collar."

"Excuse me?" I said. " 'BDSM'?"

"It stands for 'Bondage, Dominance, Sadism, Masochism,' " she said. "I'm the submissive, or slave, to my boyfriend, who is my master."

I shook my head fiercely, like a cartoon character that had just smashed into a brick wall.

"What?" I said. "A 'slave'? Some guy is your *master*? Sally, you're an Ivy League student, and a young woman from—" Thankfully, I stopped myself before adding "a wealthy family," which would have blown my cover. "Why would you—"

"Being submissive is how I get in touch with my femininity," she said.

"Who told you that? Your *master*?"

"Never mind, you wouldn't understand." She smoothed out her sweater. "Like I said before, I have a boyfriend."

"Well, when you change your mind," I said with a smile, "I'm staying at the Charles."

"You don't lack for confidence, do you, Dr. Stevens?"

Harvard student or not, Sally was still a 19½-year-old girl. Pick-up lines that might repulse women my own age would indubitably arouse young Sally's interest.

"It's confidence born of experience, my dear," I said. "Long, *hard* experience."

Her mouth went slack, and she coughed out a nervous giggle. Leaning close to her, I breathed in the clean scent of her neck. I'd forgotten how nice college girls smelled. Unsullied by time, and with the natural scent of their fertility obviating the need for perfume, they were like new cars, and their aroma was addictive.

I put my mouth close to her ear as though to whisper something scandalous, and breathed hotly there. She shivered and wilted her body against mine, taking hold of my arms. That lower lip of hers—that glistening, pouting, full lower lip—was begging to be kissed, but I kissed her on the cheek instead, next to her ear. While she was still plastered against the bookcase with glassy eyes, I hitched up my messenger bag and slipped away. Scurrying after me, she caught up to me in the main hall.

"Wait, it's Dakota, right?" she said. "Stay, let's talk!"

"Uh-uh." I wagged a forefinger. "You have a *boy-friend*, remember?"

"Yeah, but—"

"Take care, Sally."

I went out the front door and stepped into the rainstorm.

Acting the scoundrel with women is not without its pitfalls. In order for my leaving not to be anticlimactic, I had to depart when the autumn storm was at its worst.

And because finding a cab in Cambridge in the rain is as impossible as getting one in Upper Harlem at three o'clock in the morning, I had to walk back to my hotel. Arriving sopping wet and chilled, I made myself a cup of coffee, filled the tub, stripped, and settled into a hot bath.

This afternoon's discoveries at Sally's dorm had daunted me. Especially that "BDSM" collar of hers. I'd taken this case believing it was just a matter of my enticing Sally away from another older man. But that collar, her referring to herself as the "submissive" or "slave" in the relationship, and Malone as her "master"—these behaviors were similar to those of people under the influence of cults.

This "non-case" might prove a lot tougher than I originally thought.

For starters, I now had fairly definitive proof that Mr. Standish's little girl was sexually active. I'd also found a drawerful of flyers advertising Dr. Malone's sexual attraction study, which suggested that Sally was posting them for him, perhaps even acting as a "talent" scout. I knew that Sally's dorm mate, Megan, loathed Dr. Malone; she called him a "slimy troglodyte," said he'd groped her. I'd learned that Malone was one of Miss Krüsh's opponents in tomorrow night's tournament. Finally, a world-renowned psychologist, Dr. Cantor, had remarked that Malone reminded him of serial killer Ted Bundy and that I should be looking closely into Malone's background.

All of this made me wonder, *What the hell are you going to say in your report, Dakota? Should you mention the lingerie and sex toys? The BDSM collar?* And then I remembered something: I didn't have a laptop to type my report on. I supposed I could use the computer in the hotel business center downstairs, or trek over to Widener Library to do it.

I sighed. Reports were one of the reasons I'd left the Bureau.

Screw it—I'd write it tomorrow.

I soaked in the tub until the water turned tepid, then lounged for a long time on the king-sized bed while watching the Weather Channel. By tonight, they said, the storm would blow out to sea. I fell asleep listening to the smooth jazz they played in the background.

6

THE PERSISTENCE OF A BLOODHOUND

By seven thirty the next morning, I had been staked out in front of Sally's dorm for an hour. Thanks to my early-rising New England genes, I'd woken at five, worked out, showered, dressed, eaten breakfast, walked along the river to Banister House, and parked myself on a bench in a remote corner of the courtyard. Now I was sipping coffee and reading *The Little Sister* in the autumn morning sunshine, and scrutinizing the students that emerged from her building to see if she was among them. She wasn't.

You'd think with eleven years' experience with the FBI, and another year doing private work, this part of the job would have become easier, but it hadn't. If I ever wrote a book about detecting someday, I had a good opening line for it:

> More than flashy Sherlock Holmes skills of observation and deductive reasoning, the good detective must possess two ordinary qualities in abundance: the patience of a Zen monk to endure long periods of tedium or inactivity, and the persistence of a bloodhound to tirelessly follow clues wherever they might lead.

Waiting for Sally was testing my limits with the first of these qualities—patience. Given that her first class started at eight o'clock, by quarter-to I realized she wasn't coming out. She had probably stayed in Boston with Malone last night and would be going directly to class from his apartment. Tossing the book in my messenger bag, I threw out my now-cold coffee and hotfooted it over to campus.

The class, "Great Psychological Literature," was held in a classroom in Widener Library. I peeked in the window on the door. A woman professor spoke animatedly to nine yawning students leafing through paperbacks of *The Brothers Karamazov*. Sally wasn't one of the students. For half an hour, I waited in a study carrel at the end of the corridor—but she never showed.

After a quick restroom break, I went to Sally's next class: "Abnormal Psychology." Again I waited, but she didn't show up to this one either.

Stumped, I examined her class schedule and activities list. She hadn't gone to either of her morning classes, and she had only one other class today, in the afternoon. She was in two activities: intramural tennis, which met again tomorrow afternoon, and the school newspaper, the *Harvard Crimson*. There were no scheduled times associated with the *Crimson*, but having written a few forensic science articles for *my* college newspaper, *The Tech*, I remembered that students often worked on the paper between classes, or catch-as-catch-can. The Renaissance literature major I'd dated here at Harvard had been managing editor for the *Crimson*, and the two of us spent many late nights alone there together. Thus I was very familiar—*intimately* familiar, you might say—with the building's layout. I decided to drop by the *Crimson* and see if Sally was there.

Stepping outside into the bright sunshine, I paused on the steps to slip on my American Optical square-framed aviator sunglasses. As weather goes, today's—clear blue skies, low chance of precipitation, and the perfect balance between the warmth of late summer and the coolness of autumn—was ideal for tailing someone on foot. Taking a deep, satisfying breath, I hustled over to 14 Plympton Street.

The venerable brick building looked exactly as it had the last time I was here, twelve years ago: the two flagpoles and small balcony, "The Harvard Crimson" engraved in the frieze over the entrance, and the crimson red door. However, when I swiped my ID to get in, it didn't work. Frowning, I waited until two girls came out carrying stacks of newspapers. I grabbed the door before it closed.

"Hold it," said one of the girls, a tall brunette. "Are you a student here?"

Leaning against the door, I slowly removed my sunglasses and smiled. "Dr. Dakota Stevens." I flashed my ID like it was my old FBI badge. "That's right, ladies—I'm a Harvard Fellow. Drink…it…in."

They sniggered. The other girl, a freckle-faced redhead, hitched up her newspapers and used them to push her bangs out of her eyes.

"Hey," she said, "is it true you guys have, like, *carte blanche* all over campus?"

"Are you kidding?" I said. "I could burn Kirkland House to the ground and nobody would say 'boo.' "

They laughed.

"Please not Kirkland," the brunette said. "That's *our* house."

"All right. I was going to, but since you two gorgeous creatures live there…"

They giggled. I nodded at the open door.

"Editorial still upstairs?" I asked.

"Yeah," said the brunette.

"What do you have there?" I asked. "Latest edition?"

"Uh-huh," the redhead said. "We have to deliver—"

"Here, let me give you a hand." I slowly slid the top copy off the redhead's pile, which provoked another laugh from them. "Have a great day, ladies," I said over my shoulder, and stepped inside.

"Bye," the brunette said. "Hey, what's your name ag—"

The door slammed shut behind me, guillotining her question. The lobby was empty, save one man: a workman painting the foyer walls Harvard crimson red. He dipped the roller in the paint tray, and every time he rolled it on the wall, it emitted a piercing squeak. He grinned awkwardly at me over his shoulder.

"Roller, she-a-squeak," he said.

I wasn't sure how to respond to this, so I just nodded. The same bench I used to sit on while waiting for my girlfriend was still here. I sat and opened the newspaper to a full-page version of the "Malone Sexual Attraction Survey" flyer I'd found in Sally's dorm room. Then I turned to the newspaper masthead. Although I didn't see

Sally's name listed, near the bottom an entry caught my eye: "Sex & Relationships Advice Columnist: Mustang Sally." Somehow I sensed that little Sally Standish was "Mustang Sally." I turned the page to her column, "Ask Sally Anything":

> *Dear Sally,*
>
> *There's a girl in my house I'm really into, and sometimes we flirt and stuff, but I can't tell if she's just flirting or she's waiting for me to make a move. What should I do? Help!*
>
> *Sincerely,*
> *Desperate in Dunster*

> Dear Desperate,
>
> Sounds like somebody needs to man-up and make a move!
>
> Seriously, it depends on how intensely she's flirting. Watch her body language the next time you two are together. Is she brushing her hair away from her face or touching her neck to draw attention to her breasts? If so, the girl's raring for action! Does she step into your personal space or moisten her lips a lot? Those are also sure signs she's into you.
>
> Try this—find out what her favorite snack is and show up at her door with it some night. If she invites you inside and makes any of the above-mentioned gestures…feed her some food and make your move!
>
> Good Luck,
> Mustang Sally

The second question and answer in her column discussed the merits of various battery-operated phallic devices. Too modest to read it, I shoved the newspaper in my bag and went upstairs. I was at the doorway to the editorial offices and about to go in when I spotted Sally sitting next to a desk inside the room. She was talking to a young man who was clearly her editor: he leaned back in his chair with his feet up on his desk, and had a pencil jammed behind his ear. I couldn't hear what they were saying, but I noticed Sally was making notes in a Franklin planner.

That was it—her personal planner. If I knew where and when Sally's appointments were, I wouldn't need to follow her; I could simply go wherever she was headed, arriving before her. But in order to do that, I needed a copy of her planner. How? I'd just have to keep following her and wait for an opportunity.

She spoke to her editor for another five minutes. When she got up to leave, she stuffed the planner back in her knapsack. It was a pink plaid knapsack, which would make her easy to tail from a distance. I hustled downstairs and outside, where I crouched in a narrow alley on the side the building. When she emerged, I waited until she reached the corner of Plympton Street, and then, slipping my sunglasses back on, I followed her from the opposite sidewalk.

From the *Crimson* offices, Sally wended down so many streets that I lost count. Thirty minutes into tailing her, I realized with a shudder how disturbingly Bundy-esque my behavior was. Bundy would often stalk his chosen victim for days or weeks before making a move.

However, I reminded myself, while Bundy had been a rapist and serial killer, I was a detective; I was one of the good guys.

Eventually she arrived at Volvap Hall. I recognized the building name from the flyer and the newspaper ad. Located a good mile from the main Harvard campus on a quiet, tree-lined street, it was a plain two-story brick building that looked more like a college infirmary than a research center.

While Sally entered the building, I sat inside a bus stop shelter on the opposite corner with a view of the entrance. I checked my watch, noticed it was noon, and realized I was starved. Remembering I had some cashews in my messenger bag, I fished them out and wolfed them down in less than a minute. Rather than satisfying me, all they seemed to do was remind my stomach of how empty it was.

When would I ever learn? If you're following somebody on foot, you have to pack sustenance. I'd passed a delicatessen at the end of this street, about a quarter mile away. If I hurried, I could run there, get a couple sandwiches and drinks, and be back in twenty minutes or so.

But what if Sally left before that? I wouldn't know where she went. What I really needed was somebody to watch the building for me, but the street, although crammed with parked cars, was devoid of people. I didn't even see a squirrel. I looked up and down the street, hoping somebody would show up to wait for the bus, and that person could watch for me, but nothing happened. Eternally optimistic, I fished in my bag again for something else to eat, and my hand touched my digital camera.

Ah, old trusty—that's how I'd do it.

Walking to a big Norway maple across the street from the building entrance, I placed the camera on an exposed root in the ample shade, trained the lens on the walkway of Volvap, and set the video function to record. Then I spread a page from the *Crimson* over the camera, such that the lens peered out the end of the tented newspaper, and put small stones on the newspaper corners to hold it in place.

Stepping back to observe my handiwork, I noticed how much the newspaper stood out. If anybody with a soupçon of civic pride happened by while I was gone, they'd go to throw away the paper and discover the camera. But detectives with empty stomachs can't be picky. The camera had a half-hour recording time. Grateful I'd worn my running shoes today, I glanced at my watch and set out at a fast jog for the delicatessen.

I made it there and back in twenty-two minutes. The camera was still recording when I retrieved it from under the newspaper. Resuming my seat inside the bus stop shelter, I ate my first sandwich (an exquisite Italian sub on freshly baked bread, as good as any I'd had in Manhattan) while watching my "movie" of the building entrance at 16x speed.

I had placed the camera far enough back so that both the front entrance and the street along the side of the building were in the frame. This was good, in case she slipped out the back of the building. She didn't. In fact, during the entire 22 minutes I was gone, no one came out of the building; only two girls who looked like graduate students went inside. I shut off the camera and ate my sandwich, glancing catty-cornered at the building entrance from time to time.

A taxi whisked by. A few minutes later, a mailman slogged past, his bulging mailbag bouncing against his hip. A yellowjacket, probably attracted by the smell of my sandwich, buzzed into the shelter and landed on a tomato slice peeking out from under the sub roll. I didn't have the heart to kill him, so I shooed him away and laid the tomato slice on the cement outside. He returned to it. We seemed to have reached an accord: I ate my sandwich while he nibbled on the tomato.

I thought about meeting Svetlana Krüsh yesterday. That woman was one of the most distractingly beautiful creatures I'd ever seen. She was also visibly brilliant. Looking into her eyes, I could see some impressive machinery churning away in there. It surprised me how much I was looking forward to seeing her in tonight's chess tournament. We seemed to have shared a moment, and I *had* managed to make her smile once or twice. I wondered if she'd thought about me at all. Doubtful. She'd probably written me off as a foolish merry andrew.

Oh, well. They can't all think you're amazing, Dakota.

A group of young men and women exited Volvap Hall and headed back toward the Harvard campus. A woman pushing an exercise stroller jogged past. Then the yellowjacket made another run at my sandwich. This time I backhanded him outside, where he flew off in a panic. Take that, tough guy.

An hour passed like this. I finished my first sandwich, a bag of Humpty Dumpty potato chips, and a bottle of seltzer, and was debating whether to start my second sub when a bus screeched to a halt in front of the shelter. The door opened. The driver stared down at me.

"Well?" he said. "You gettin' on or what?"

"Changed my mind," I said.

He scowled, shut the door and roared away, leaving me—intentionally, I'm sure—in a miasma of diesel fumes. I had to stagger out of the shelter to get some air. Fortunately I happened to glance down the street and saw Sally hotfooting it back toward campus. Tossing my trash in a wastebasket, I resumed tailing her from the opposite side of the street.

From Volvap Hall, she walked to Widener Library, dumped her knapsack on a corner table in the main reading room, and walked away. When she left the room, I knew this was the best chance I was going to get. Students occupied the tables in the center of the reading room, but they were all hunched over books and weren't paying attention to their surroundings.

I went to Sally's knapsack. Glancing around the room, I unzipped the main pouch, removed her planner and hustled to a photocopier out in the hallway.

Attached with velcro to the inside flap was a key-chain wallet that contained several keys, including one labeled "Dorm" and another labeled "Geoff's—2468." The keys could be useful, but they'd have to wait. For now, I photocopied the planner pages—today's through next week—stuffed the copies in my messenger bag, and walked the planner double-time back to her knapsack.

The whole process had taken two, maybe three, minutes, but it was still in the nick of time. The second I returned the planner to the knapsack and zipped it closed, Sally emerged in the far corner of the reading room. Triumphant, I swaggered out the opposite end, paused outside to slip on my sunglasses, and jogged down the library steps.

Jim Rockford couldn't have done better.

Back at the Charles, I savored my second sandwich while perusing the copied pages from Sally's planner. Each entry was detailed, the handwriting tiny and meticulous. I focused my attention on tomorrow's entries. Her class times were noted, but I ignored them; I'd learned the hard way that Sally wasn't attending her classes regularly. Besides, I was more interested in her extracurricular activities. They could be ideal opportunities to make contact with her:

> 6:30 A.M.: Swim, Blodgett
> 10:30 A.M.: Hand out flyers, Harvard Square
> 11:45 A.M.: Lunch, Berg D-Hall, meet w/ sorority ldrshp.
> 12:45 P.M.: Crimson, meet with Kyle
> 1:30 P.M.: Volvap, interviews
> 3:00 P.M.: Tennis, Beren

Exhausted from being on my feet all day, when I finished my second sandwich I undressed and lay down for a nap. I was awakened by the telephone. The front desk clerk said someone named Stanley Ford had just dropped off an envelope. Ah, my ticket for the chess tournament. I asked for it to be delivered to my room.

It was six o'clock when the ticket arrived, which meant there was only an hour until the tournament. I showered and shaved. Emerging from the bathroom in a cloud of steam, I turned on the TV and flipped through the channels.

The Lifetime channel was showing one of their light romantic comedies, and I'd happened upon it precisely when the guy and the girl first meet. The two of them were in an office records room, in adjoining aisles with a shelving unit between them. When they reached for the same banker's box of files on the top shelf, the box broke open, showering them with papers.

What was this part of romantic comedies called? Yes…the meet-cute. Well, Sally Standish had no idea, but tomorrow I was going to orchestrate half a dozen "meet-cutes" with her, starting with swimming at Blodgett—which would also give me an opportunity to introduce her to another one of my best features: my shirtless torso. I chuckled to myself and shut off the TV.

It was time to get ready. I mulled what I should wear. All I had were casual clothes or my Hickey Freeman suit. I chose the suit, with a white dress shirt worn with the collar open, and a black pair of square-toed Kenneth Cole oxfords. I strapped on my gun in its shoulder holster, slipped into the suit jacket, and eyed myself in the mirror. Liking what I saw, I fired a finger-gun at myself and hurried out.

I couldn't wait to see Svetlana Krüsh again.

7

ZWISCHENZUG

When I got there, I was glad I'd chosen the suit, but wished I'd worn a tie. The law school auditorium, where the tournament was being held, was packed with students and faculty in Harvard ties, prep school ties, bow ties, even a couple of nutty-crunchy types in bolo ties.

Everyone was staring at the lit stage, where a large "U" of tables held 20 chessboards, sets of pieces, and clocks. There were chairs on the outer side of the tables, but none on the inside; apparently Miss Krüsh didn't get to sit down.

The hall buzzed with anticipation until the MC (one of the deans) walked onstage. She started by introducing the opponents. Malone was number eighteen. When all of the players were seated, she explained that the tournament was a charity exhibition to benefit Boston Children's Hospital. She then introduced Miss Krüsh:

"Born in the Ukraine under the scrutiny of the Soviet Union, Miss Krüsh was trained to become a chess champion for the State. In 1984, during a tournament in Washington, D.C., her family defected to the United

States, and she has been the darling of the U.S. chess world ever since. An International Grandmaster at nineteen, Miss Krüsh is ranked number one in the U.S. and two in the world. Ladies and gentlemen, I give you… Svetlana Krüsh…"

I was looking around for Stanley, wondering what was keeping him, when the lights dimmed. It became almost completely dark in the auditorium. Then, out of the darkness, over a PA system, rose up John Williams's "Imperial March" from *The Empire Strikes Back*.

When the horns began to blare, a spotlight illuminated the corner of the stage. Miss Krüsh strutted onstage in a glittering black sequin evening dress, trailing a black cape like Darth Vader's. Ridiculously long, it flowed from her shoulders across the length of the stage. The audience laughed and applauded. As the music faded, she unclipped the cape and handed it to an assistant who ran offstage with it.

Slowly the lights came up, revealing a roving cameraman onstage. Her opponents filed out and took their seats. Upstage hung a giant HDTV with a 2D representation of a chessboard and its pieces. A digital clock appeared on the TV, counted down from 10 seconds, and the match began.

Miss Krüsh demonstrated the same ruthless efficiency she had shown at the tables in front of Au Bon Pain, pausing stone still over each board, her predatory eyes devouring the pieces and ignoring the player. With sharp, decisive flicks of her hand, she moved a rook, a pawn, a bishop, snatching up each opponent's captured soldiers with a twist of her wrist.

When she reached Dr. Malone, I got my first good look at him on the giant TV. He wore a charcoal suit and a white band-collared shirt. His face had that "bad boy" beard stubble made popular in the '80s by the TV show *Miami Vice*. His hair was unnaturally blonde and close-cropped, a step above a military cut. When Miss Krüsh leaned forward slightly to appraise the board, the camera caught Dr. Malone leering into her décolletage.

Over the next hour, one by one her challengers resigned or were checkmated. Each shook Miss Krüsh's hand and strode offstage to sympathetic applause. Eventually there were only two left: Dr. Malone and an Asian woman, Sally's age, from the Harvard Chess Club. It was while playing this young woman that Miss Krüsh showed her only sign of hesitation during the entire match. While reaching for her bishop, she stopped and withdrew her hand. Then, with a wry smile on her lips, she whispered something to the girl. They agreed to a draw, and the girl bounced offstage to cheers.

And then only Dr. Malone remained. Somehow he had managed to last into the endgame. Despite having less than five minutes left on her clock, Miss Krüsh studied the board for a full minute. On Malone's side of the board were three pawns, his king and two knights; on Miss Krüsh's side were three pawns, her king, a knight and two bishops. The camera zoomed in on Miss Krüsh's face; she squinted down at the pieces. Malone sat with hands folded, staring up at her with a simpering grin on his face.

"He's got her, and he knows it," said a man behind me. "His pawns are closer. He'll promote sooner."

"No, he won't," his buddy said.

These two sounded like they knew what they were talking about. I cocked an ear in their direction and kept my eyes on the TV.

"She's going to do a minor piece mate on him," the second one said. "Those pawns are a millstone around his neck. They're going to deprive his king of critical flight squares. Watch."

On her next move, Miss Krüsh put Malone's king in check with her bishop. Her eyes narrowed. Never before had I seen a person with such predatory eyes.

What followed was Miss Krüsh inexorably strangling Malone: checking his king with one of her bishops, advancing her king up the board, and checking him again with her knight or a pawn. Malone attempted to retaliate with his knights, but Miss Krüsh's planning was brilliant. The one time Malone was able to put her king in check, Miss Krüsh moved her king out of the way, exposing her bishop behind it, and checking Malone's king in reply.

"Exposed check! Brilliant!" said one of the men behind me. "This woman is a chess *machine*. I saw her at the European Championships five years ago. Seventy-eight moves to beat the reigning champion. They don't call her the Queen of the Endgame for nothing."

Miss Krüsh gradually worked Malone into the corner, promoted a pawn to Queen with a red fingernail, and checkmated Malone. He rose, grudgingly shook her hand, and sauntered offstage. While the audience gave her a standing ovation, an assistant brought her a bottle of water. Miss Krüsh bowed to the audience, sat in a director's chair under a spotlight, and crossed her legs. The black sequin dress had a long slit up the side, revealing the runway legs I'd admired earlier today. I admired them some more, until the MC came onstage and handed Miss Krüsh a microphone. Two assistants climbed up the auditorium aisles with additional mikes.

"Miss Krüsh will now answer your questions," the MC said.

A young woman a few rows ahead of me stood up.

"How'd you become so good at chess?"

"I was raised in Soviet Ukraine," Miss Krüsh said. "The State trained me to beat corrupt Western capitalists. If I lost, my family did not eat."

The girl gave a start. "Oh my God, that's terrible!"

"I joke," Miss Krüsh said. "Ha, ha."

The crowd laughed.

"Practice, young lady," she said. "That is how one becomes good at anything."

From the very top of the auditorium, a preppy young man shouted down at her: "I love you! Can I have your phone number?"

"That depends," she said. "What is your net worth?"

The crowd tittered. The young man pouted.

"I don't get my trust fund until I'm twenty-one," he said glumly.

"Too bad," she said. "When you get it, and *if* it is over ten million dollars, you may look me up."

Another laugh. Across the aisle from me, a studious-looking kid with a beard jumped to his feet.

"In the game against *Professor Quincy*—"

"Board nine," she said.

"Yes," he said. "Could you explain the series of exchanges beginning with"—he consulted a notebook—"uh…"

"Move seventeen?" She sipped some water.

"Right. You captured his rook. What was your tactical thinking there?"

"An excellent question," she said. "I sensed that Professor Quincy was attempting to gain a pawn on my queen side, so I devised a *zwischenzug*, which is German for an 'in-between' move. American players know this as an intermezzo or a 'swishy.' I allowed the first two pawn exchanges to happen, but before he could make the third capture, I placed him in check. That was the *zwischenzug*. Since his rook was skewered on the same diagonal, when Dr. Quincy moved his king out of check, I captured his rook." She smiled and morphed her voice into a comical German accent. "Vun could say I use zvishen*sook* to capture *rook*."

The audience clapped and chuckled. A middle-aged woman across the auditorium asked the next question: "How do you remember all of your moves?"

"How does a litigator memorize her arguments?" Miss Krüsh said. "How does a painter make art or a doctor heal the sick? They just *do*, because that is who they are. Chess is who I am."

She answered questions for another half hour, and when the exhibition ended, fans flocked down to the stage to get her autograph. The seat next to mine, Stanley Ford's, was still empty. Stanley was supposed to be my buffer with the chess goddess during dinner. I supposed I'd just have to go it alone.

I went out to the lobby and bought a copy of her chess primer, *Krush Your Opponents*, and hustled back into the auditorium. Squeezing through the throng, I held the book out for her to sign. She signed it with a Sharpie and glanced over my shoulder.

"Mr. Stevens…where is Stanley?"

"I thought *you* would know," I said. "He never showed tonight. Great tournament, by the way. You're amazing."

"One should be excellent in one's profession," she said. "Are you excellent in yours, Mr. Stevens?"

"I do my best."

A student thrust a book at her; Miss Krüsh scribbled her signature on the flyleaf.

"So, Mr. Stevens," Miss Krüsh said, "I assume you will be taking me out to dinner."

"Without a chaperone?" I feigned a look of shock.

She smiled and signed the sleeve of a girl's T-shirt, which read, "CHESS GIRLS KNOW ALL THE BEST POSITIONS."

"I'd be delighted," I said.

Across the room, Sally Standish gave me a finger wave; I replied with a roguish smile and a slit-eyed stare that caused her to blush and fidget her feet. Finally Miss Krüsh finished with the last of her fans. As she took her overcoat and handbag from a student assistant, Dr. Malone accosted her and performed a *zwischenzug* of his own: he kissed her hand.

"*Enchanté*," he said.

I seethed—mostly because I knew I should have kissed her hand when *I* met her, but I'd been chicken.

I was also annoyed because Malone did it with such panache, even saying something charming in a foreign language—French, probably. His eyes were a faint gray with a wraith of blue in them, and as much as I hated to admit it, their unusual paleness made them mesmerizing. He grinned at Svetlana wolfishly.

"I should have asked for a draw."

"Yes," Miss Krüsh said, "but I would not have given you one."

"Nonetheless, it was a pleasure being dominated by you." He handed her a card. "Perhaps while you're in town you'd like to visit my lab and partake in my study."

"What do you study?" she said.

"Sexual attraction."

"No, thank you."

"A shame," Malone said. "You would have been an *ideal* subject." He turned to me. "Excuse me...aren't you Stevens, the FBI profiler?"

"I am. *Dakota* Stevens—not 'Stevens.' "

"What are you doing here at Harvard?"

"I'm on sabbatical," I said. "Harvard Fellow. Doing research on psychopaths."

"Interesting," Malone said. "But this hardly seems like the ideal environment for that kind of research."

"You'd be surprised," I said. "In my experience, academia affords psychopaths ideal hiding places and hunting grounds. I've only been at Harvard a few days, and my research has already proven quite fruitful."

"Well, good luck with it." He shook my hand half-heartedly and turned to Miss Krüsh again. "I'll have an invitation sent to you in case you change your mind."

Before she could object, he started for the exit. He met Sally by the door at the top of the amphitheater. Sally smiled over her shoulder at me, and the two of them wandered out into the lobby. I tapped Miss Krüsh on the arm.

"Listen, are you up for an adventure?" I said.

"Pardon?" she said. "I thought you were taking me to dinner."

"I will, but I'm working, and I need to follow Dr. Malone."

"I barely know you, Mr. Stevens." She looked around the empty auditorium. "Explain what you mean by 'an adventure.' "

"While we walk," I said. "Are you in or out, Miss Krüsh?"

I leveled my eyes on hers.

"Very well," she said.

I helped her into her overcoat and led us outside. I was afraid I'd lost Malone and Sally, but Malone—a smoker apparently—had stopped in the courtyard to light a cigarette. Miss Krüsh, mincing behind, caught up to me at the lobby doors, where I stared out the windows at Malone and Sally.

"Okay, Mr. Stevens," she said, "*why* are you following Dr. Malone?"

"Shh," I said. "I'll tell you, but you've got to keep it down."

As we followed Malone and Sally across campus, I explained how Mr. Standish had hired me to extricate his daughter from a relationship with Malone. When I mentioned that Mr. Standish was a friend of the FBI

Director, and that I used to work for the Bureau, Miss Krüsh thrust her hands in her coat pockets.

"*Ah*, the FBI," she said. "After my family defected and we settled in Manhattan, they watched us for over a year. They thought we were Soviet spies."

"Different time," I said.

"I must say, Mr. Stevens…this case of yours seems foolish. Why did you not simply refuse to take it?"

"Because I can't say no to the Director of the FBI, that's why."

Ahead, Malone and Sally crossed Mass Ave to the T entrance and rode the escalator down. Miss Krüsh and I followed, staying a good fifty feet behind them.

"I certainly hope there will be dinner sometime this evening," she said.

"Well, little lady," I said with a bad Texan accent, "if'n you're good, I might just buy y'all a steak dinner."

She gave me a withering look. "I suppose other women find that line to be amusing."

"Hilarious, actually," I said.

"You will find, Mr. Stevens, that unlike the women you are probably accustomed to, I am *not* easily impressed."

"Noted, Miss Krüsh. Walk faster, please."

When we reached the turnstile, I gave Miss Krüsh a T token, and we followed Malone and Sally down to the Red Line platform to Boston.

8

ENOUGH SAID

With a deafening screech, a train rolled into the Harvard T stop, and we boarded one car down from Malone and Sally's. I guided Miss Krüsh to an open seat near the door and kept an eye on our quarry through the window at the end of the car.

Malone and Sally rode to the Park Street stop and took the escalator up to the street at the corner of Boston Common. There, they strolled hand-in-hand to the state-house, where they turned down Park Street Place.

"Where are they going?" Miss Krüsh asked, mincing along beside me.

"If I knew that," I said, "I wouldn't need to follow them, would I?"

When we came to a cobblestone alleyway, Miss Krüsh wobbled in her high heels. I held out my arm, and she took it.

"I have played in several tournaments here," she said, "but I rarely leave my hotel. I have seen very little of Boston."

"Well, stick with me, kid," I said. "These are my old stomping grounds."

" 'Stomping grounds'?"

"I went to college here."

"Ah," she said.

Ahead, the lights of the Parker House Hotel, home to many a Boston debutante's ball, splashed across the sidewalk. The entry overhang gleamed gold. As Malone and Sally approached the entrance, the doorman tipped his cap and held the door open for them. I tapped Miss Krüsh on the shoulder.

"We might be in luck," I said.

"Good. I am not dressed for following people."

When we reached the chandeliered lobby, Malone and Sally were already being ushered into the dining room. Miss Krüsh started to follow them.

"Hold it." I grabbed her arm. "They'll see us."

"Perhaps not," she said.

She edged past a gaggle of women to the maître d'. She spoke to him, and the maître d' smiled and grabbed two menus. Miss Krüsh waved me over.

"They do not have a table available until ten o'clock," she said, "but I told him you would give him a hundred dollars if he could seat us now."

"I don't have that kind of cash on me," I said.

"Then get it," she said. "The maître d' said he would seat us in the corner farthest from them. There is an ATM in the lobby."

"You've got this all figured out, don't you?" I said.

She lowered her eyes and shrugged minutely. "Please, Mr. Stevens...I am famished."

I knew it was futile to argue with her. Clearly, Miss Krüsh was a woman who, by her virtue of her beauty and talent, was used to getting what she wanted, when she wanted it.

Without another word, I went down to the ATM and withdrew $500 of the remaining grand in my checking account. I folded up five twenties, palmed them to the maître d', and he seated us in a corner, beneath a portrait of famous Bostonian Henry Cabot Lodge. From here, I had a view of the entire dining room—its carved mahogany moldings, its gold sash drapes on the windows, its ornate table settings, and Malone and Sally at the far end.

When the waiter came, Miss Krüsh ordered filet mignon, "exceedingly rare," with béarnaise sauce; I ordered the Boston scrod. When a server brought us a basket of the hotel's legendary Parker House rolls, Miss Krüsh took one, buttered it, and ate it with gusto. Across the room, Dr. Malone and Sally talked quietly, sipping drinks. Several patrician Beacon Hill couples eyed the odd pair; it was impossible not to notice the near 20-year gap in their ages.

"I don't get it." I shook my head at them. "What could she possibly see in that guy?"

Miss Krüsh turned in her chair and cast an appraising glance across the dining room at them. "I imagine she is like many other young women—seeking approval from a father figure."

"Don't tell me you're a psychologist, too."

"No, but my father controlled my chess career for a long time," she said. "There was a time when older men strongly appealed to me."

Whatever Sally and Malone's conversation was, it wasn't very animated; they acted like a couple that had been married forty years.

"I wish I knew what they were saying," I said.

"You *can* know," she said. "For another twenty."

The waiter brought our food. As he was about to leave, Miss Krüsh put a hand on his arm.

"I need you to do something for me," she said.

The story she gave him was this: her boyfriend, Malone, was here with another woman. If the waiter would find out what he and the girl were saying, her friend (me) would pay him an extra $20 when we left. He agreed, and off he went.

"Creative," I said. "And duplicitous. You could have a future in my business."

She sliced her filet mignon into thin, equal-sized strips. They lay on her plate like fallen red dominoes.

"It is merely looking at a position," she said, "seeing what material you have, and devising tactics that leverage your positional advantages."

"Oh, is that all?" I said.

"In this case, the waiters are our material, and we can get them working for us."

"Sure…using *my* money," I said.

She shrugged indifferently. I ate some scrod and kept an eye on Sally and Malone. Miss Krüsh and I were nearly finished eating when Malone snapped his fingers at his waiter for the check. Our waiter drifted back over to our table. While I pulled out my billfold to pay him, Miss Krüsh played the scorned woman perfectly.

"Go ahead, young man," she said, "I am quite used to his indiscretions by now."

"He was talking about how he had to go to Montreal soon," the waiter said. "Then he said, 'After this, how about Acorn Street?' And she said, 'All right,' and that's it."

Acorn Street was an old cobblestone alleyway on Beacon Hill. What reason could they possibly have for going there? A romantic walk?

"Thanks." I handed him $40 and my AMEX card to cover the bill. "We're in a hurry."

The waiter jogged away.

"What is this 'Acorn Street'?" Miss Krüsh asked.

"Hard to describe," I said. "Look, I have a feeling we're going to be on foot again from here. Are you sure you're up for this? Or would you prefer to go back to Cambridge?"

"I have nothing better to do," she said. "Stanley has clearly abandoned me, and I have only my room at Cabot House to look forward to."

I noticed Malone signing his check. Once the waiter returned with my card and check, I signed it and waited until Malone and Sally left the dining room. As soon as they walked out, I helped Miss Krüsh out of her chair.

"Okay, let's go," I said.

We followed Malone and Sally out to the street. Waving off a cab, they hiked back up the hill toward the statehouse, stopping at the corner of Park Street. The gold dome of the statehouse was brightly illuminated, as if taunting crooks to steal it. Malone and Sally kissed, and then they split up. While Malone headed down

Beacon Street along the dark Common, Sally went up Bowdoin Street, along the side of the statehouse. I wasn't sure which one to follow. Miss Krüsh and I stood in the shadows on the corner, watching them get farther apart.

"Well, detective?" she said.

If I was going to be spotted by one of them, I preferred it was Sally. I could always say I'd followed her after the tournament because I was interested in her. I'd have a harder time explaining such a coincidence to Malone.

"Let's follow her," I said. "Come on."

Sally turned left onto Derne Street, which ran behind the statehouse. She was heading into the heart of Beacon Hill, with its old-fashioned streetlamps, brick sidewalks, and black-shuttered brick townhouses that had long been the homes of Boston's elite. Miss Krüsh and I stayed a block behind Sally, walking on the opposite side of the street. Quietly, I told Miss Krüsh some of the history of Beacon Hill, including how, back in Colonial times, the hill had been much higher; that is, until much of its dirt was excavated to fill in the swampy Back Bay.

"Fascinating," Miss Krüsh said, stifling a yawn.

Sally wove through the streets of Beacon Hill, around shadowy corners, along wrought-iron fences with the autumn leaves tumbling along the sidewalk in the night breeze. Then she took a sharp turn down a narrow alleyway: Acorn Street. A street in name only, it was one of the original cobblestone byways in Boston. While Sally continued down Acorn Street, I pulled Miss Krüsh close to me, ducking us behind the corner at the alley entrance.

"I thought we were following her," Miss Krüsh said.

The chess diva seemed to be adapting to detective work.

"It's too exposed," I said. "We'll wait here."

Far down Acorn, light from tourist-heavy Charles Street spilled into the alley. Staring at the distant end of the alley, I noticed the backlit figure of a man hiking up-hill as Sally wobbled downhill in high heels. The breeze stirred the oak trees around us and blew Miss Krüsh's hair across my cheek. She smelled good.

Sally had only gotten about fifty feet down Acorn when the man coming up the street rapidly closed the gap. They were side by side now. The man looked like Malone, but with the backlighting from the other end of the alley, it was hard to tell. Then the man grabbed Sally, I saw a flash of pale blonde hair, and I knew it was Malone. Beside me, Miss Krüsh stiffened. I sensed she was about to shout, so I clamped a hand over her mouth.

"Don't," I said. "It's Malone. I think this is a game between them."

We crouched and watched them. We watched them, that is, until their antics got out of hand, at which point we stared uncomfortably at the cobblestones and gri-maced at the sounds they made.

It was rough sex. Enough said.

When they finished, a light went on in a second floor window, and a voice shouted: "What the hell is going on?! Who's out there?!"

Malone hurried down Acorn toward Charles Street. Shortly afterward, Sally stood, calmly brushed herself off, and followed him. When they were both gone, Miss Krüsh and I got to our feet.

"Well, that was repulsive," she said.

"Yup."

"I cannot believe I let that man kiss my hand."

"One of the dangers of being sophisticated, Miss Krüsh," I said.

"We have just been through an ordeal together, Mr. Stevens," she said. "Please…call me Svetlana."

"Dakota."

She took a deep breath and pensively considered the cobblestones.

"Dakota, I would appreciate it if you escorted me back to Harvard now."

"Sure." I started back toward Park Street. "I hope this didn't ruin your evening."

"Why should it?" she said. "What woman does not enjoy watching simulated rape?"

"Yeah, I hear you."

We retraced our steps to Park Street station and caught a cab back to Harvard Square. From there, I walked Svetlana over to Radcliffe Quad, where we stood on the sidewalk at the mouth of the broad courtyard between the brick buildings. Lights in the windows made the lawn gleam luxuriantly. A breeze came up, stirring the leaves in the oaks above us.

"Sorry to ruin your evening." I held up her chess book. "Thanks for the autograph."

A band of drunken, reveling students staggered by on the sidewalk. Svetlana waited until they were gone, then said, "I would thank you for a lovely evening, but given what we witnessed…"

"How about a do-over then?" I asked. "Care to join me for lunch tomorrow?"

"Perhaps," she said. "What time? I have individual meetings with the team in the morning."

"How about quarter to twelve? The Berg D-Hall?"

"Pardon?"

"Sorry," I said. "Harvard-speak. Annenberg House dining hall. You could invite some of the kids, and we could eat among the troops so to speak."

Since Sally was scheduled to be there at that time as well, I knew there was a good chance she'd see me with Svetlana, which might make her jealous.

"Yes, that could work for me," she said. "I suppose I *should* spend more time with them in a social setting."

"Then I'll see you there?"

"You shall."

Taking hold of her hand, I was about to kiss it when she yanked it away and started down the walkway toward the building.

"Good night, Dakota."

"You too, Svetlana."

Walking back to my hotel, I put my hands in my trouser pockets and felt a slip of paper. I stopped under a streetlamp, unfolded it and read. It was the list I'd made on the train from D.C.—the qualities my "dream assistant" would have. Considering the person I'd just dropped off, I laughed out loud when I read the last item on the list: "Elegant dresser with great legs."

I carefully refolded the paper, slipped it in my jacket breast pocket, and started back to the hotel. I had a busy day tomorrow to prepare for.

9

TASTY

As luck would have it, Blodgett Pool, the scene of Meet Cute #1, was located near the football stadium, directly across the river from my hotel. At six o'clock, I rolled out of bed, put on my swim trunks and a warm-up suit, packed a change of clothes in my messenger bag, and hoofed it over there.

I was in the first person in the pool. By the time Sally arrived and got into the lane next to mine, I had already swum six laps. I much preferred this regulation-sized pool to the rinky-dink one back at the hotel.

Once Sally had swum a lap, I decided to have some fun with her. When she started her second lap, I dove under the lane rope into her lane and swam underwater facing up so she couldn't avoid seeing me when she neared the end of the pool.

She had a red kickboard under her torso and was doing such an awkward breaststroke, it was indistinguishable from a dog paddle. Swimming backwards, I waited until she noticed me, then waved to her. It was difficult to make out her face because she swam with her head out of the water. At the end of the pool, she stopped and held onto the side. I surfaced beside her. She was wearing a swim cap and goggles, but the BDSM collar around her neck made her unmistakable.

"Excuse me," she said, raising her goggles. "This is *my* lane."

"Hi, Sally." I raised my goggles. "I didn't know you swam."

"Dr. Stevens?"

"In the flesh." I winked at her.

Up on the pool deck, the lifeguard blew his whistle.

"Sir! No swimming under other swimmers!"

"Relax, young man," I said to him. "I'm a Harvard Fellow."

Sally giggled.

"What?" the lifeguard said.

"Never mind," I said. "Carry on, son."

I treaded water in front of Sally. She was holding onto the side ladder with both hands. Her kickboard, which had a big white capital "H" on it, floated between us. I snatched it up.

"What the heck...?"

"It's a kickboard," she said.

"I know what it is," I said. "Why do you use it?"

"Because...I'll sink without it."

"Nonsense." I winged it out of the pool. It landed on the pool deck beneath the lifeguard chair. "Don't worry," I said to Sally, "I'll rescue you if you drown. I'm very good at mouth-to-mouth."

She smiled and shook her head faintly. Her shoulders and chest were above the water. She was wearing a sleek one-piece maraschino cherry swimsuit, the plunging, divided neckline of which revealed her to be much more shapely than I'd first surmised.

Approaching her, I took a few seconds to appreciate how flattering the suit was, not to mention the delicious contrast between the satiny red of her suit fabric and the creaminess of her skin. Holding onto the pool deck beside her with one hand, I lifted the BDSM collar off her collarbone.

"How can you swim with this thing on?" I asked. "Doesn't it act like an anchor?"

"It's pretty light actually," she said.

I gently snapped one of her shoulder straps. "I like your suit. You look very nice in it."

"Thanks."

"But…you're not a very experienced swimmer, are you?"

"Um…well," she said, looking down at the water, "I only learned a few months ago."

"Then it's a good thing I'm here," I said. "Meet me down at the shallow end, and I'll teach you how to do the crawl."

"I really shouldn't, Dr. Stevens."

"No, you really should." I lowered her goggles and stroked her cheekbone with my thumb. "And my name's 'Dakota,' not 'Doctor Stevens.' Come on, beautiful—let me teach you something."

She nibbled her lower lip. "Mm…all *right*."

Lowering my goggles, I pushed hard off the wall, dove under the lane rope, and swam to the other end like a crocodile was chasing me. There, I drank from my water bottle and waited for her. When she finally reached me, she was out of breath. I let her have a sip of my water.

"Okay, here's what you're going to do." I put the bottle aside. "I want you to lie face-down on the water while I hold you. I'm going to put my arms under your hips and ribs, and I want you to kick your legs with your knees straight, like this."

I demonstrated by wagging my forefinger and middle finger.

"What do I do with my arms?" she asked.

"Easy. You just cup your hands a little bit and alternate them in front of you. You want to kind of 'pierce' the water with the tip of your hand, then push down and back. Every second stroke, turn your head to the side and take a breath. Ready?"

"Wait," she said. "*When* do I breathe?"

"I'll tap your side when it's time." I laid my hands on her waist underwater. "All right, ready?"

"I think so," she said.

"Okay. Lie face-down in the water."

She made a pout. "Dakota...I don't *like* putting my face in the water. I'm worried I'm going to breathe in water and drown."

"You're not going to drown," I said. "I'm here, and sonny boy is in the lifeguard stand."

With a snort, she lay face-down in the water. I slid my forearms under her ribs and hips, remarking to myself how petite she was. Out of the water, the girl might have weighed 100 pounds; in the water, she weighed next to nothing.

I grinned thinking of the opening credits of *Magnum, P.I.*, when Magnum mugs at the camera because he's holding a bikini-clad woman on top of the water, teaching her how to snorkel. Here in the pool, as Sally kicked and stroked with her arms, every second stroke I tapped her ribs with my fingers. She turned her head out of the water, exhaled and took a breath. Her kicks were ungainly and produced a lot of splashing. Her arm motions looked more like random flailing than coordinated swimming strokes.

I let her continue like this for thirty seconds or so, and then I suddenly curled her out of the water. Flipping her over so she was on her back, I cradled her in my arms.

"Did I do something wrong?" she said.

"Nope...conference time." I carried her to the edge of the pool and nodded at the water bottle. "Have a drink."

While she drank, I gave her notes on what to do differently on the next attempt. The second and third times I held her and gave her notes, she relaxed in my arms, and, with goggles raised, gazed into my eyes.

"How am I doing, Dakota?"

"Not bad." I curled her body up once, like she was a barbell. "Hey, would you mind if I did a few reps with you? I didn't have time to hit the gym this morning."

"What are you—"

"You're the perfect weight. Now straighten your body out, like a board. Good."

With her sniggering the whole time, I curled her out of the water and up to my chest ten times. When I finally plopped her back in the water, she was laughing loudly.

"You're so weird!" she said.

"All right, the crawl," I said. "Ready to do it for real?"

"Uh…"

"Know what I think? You're ready."

She was standing in the water beside me. I kissed her cheek and lowered her goggles.

"Swim to the other end. I'll meet you there."

"Okay, I'll try," she said.

"No," I said, "don't *try*. Do it. Now go!"

With a determined nod and a deep breath, she thrust off the side of the pool and began swimming a crawl toward the other end. At first her strokes were choppy, but soon she settled into a rhythm—albeit a slow one—and made steady progress down the pool. I let her get halfway before I dove under the lane rope into the adjoining lane, sprinted to the far end, and waited for her. When she grabbed the pool edge beside me, her face was one giant smile.

"I did it," she said. "I can't believe it! Thank you, Dakota!"

"You're welcome, beautiful." I kissed her on the cheek again.

"Dakota…you shouldn't do that."

"Shouldn't do *what*?" I said. "Give you a congratulatory peck on the cheek?"

She shrugged. "I told you—Geoff is my boyfriend."

"Look, I want to finish my workout now, but what are you doing after this?"

She let go of the wall and treaded water. "You mean after swimming?"

"Yes."

"I have class, and then—"

A Study in Crimson

"I have a proposition," I said. "You wouldn't let me take you to dinner the other night, but how about breakfast? We can have a friendly breakfast together, and then I'll walk you to class."

"Jeez, I don't know."

"Come on, Sally," I said. "Who just gave you a free swimming lesson?"

"*You* did."

"I bet *Geoff's* never given you a swimming lesson."

She gazed over my shoulder, then looked me in the eyes and nodded. "All right…breakfast."

"Good. We'll meet outside in half an hour."

"Okay."

"Keep practicing," I said, and swam away.

I swam fifteen more laps, and when I went to get out of the pool, I noticed that the surly non-shaver had been replaced in the lifeguard stand by a dazzling tawny-haired coed with a heart-piercing smile. She watched me climb up the ladder with the water sluicing off me, and continued to watch me as I cranked out twenty reps on the pull-up bar against the wall. Strolling by her stand afterwards, I noticed that her eyes were a shimmering blue-green like the swimming pool, and positively epic. I smiled and wished her a nice day.

I showered, changed into jeans, an FBI T-shirt and my chocolate blazer, and waited outside for Sally. Luckily I had the Chandler novel to read, because, like all men have done for women from time immemorial, I ended up waiting for her.

She emerged from the building twenty minutes late, but the sight of her was worth the wait. She wore a cute

CHRIS ORCUTT

powder blue cardigan with a matching scarf around her neck, a white blouse, powder blue capris, and white Keds tennis shoes. Her pink plaid knapsack, clearly jam-packed with books, drooped down to her butt. I chuckled.

"What's funny?" she said.

"Your knapsack. It's drooping."

"It's heavy!"

"I can see that," I said.

"I've got a lot of books in it!"

"Stop whining and come here." I grabbed her by a shoulder strap, tugged her close to me and cinched both straps tighter. "There, how's that?"

"Better. Thanks." She gazed at the bridge, then turned to me. "Where are we going for breakfast?"

"Hmm," I said. "If this were ten, twelve years ago, I might take you to The Tasty, but they're not around anymore. How about the restaurant in my hotel? The Charles."

"All right."

We started walking across the bridge.

"Dakota?" she asked.

"Yes, Sally?"

"What was 'The Tasty'?"

"Ah. Take my arm and I'll tell you a story."

She held onto my arm with both of hers and even rested her head on my shoulder.

"Once upon a time," I began, "there was a very greedy restaurant…"

The Tasty, I explained, was a Harvard Square greasy spoon when I was in college. While the food had been pretty good, it was exorbitantly priced: a thimble-sized glass of orange juice cost four dollars. The last time I went there, after ordering breakfast I drank from a carton of OJ I'd smuggled in with me. The proprietor, unyielding on his "no outside drinks" rule, forced me to leave. I never went back.

Inside the Charles hotel restaurant, a hostess grabbed two menus and escorted us to a table by the window with a view of the river.

"So," Sally said, "whatever happened to the Tasty?"

"Oh, yeah," I said. "The bank that owned their building raised the rent so high, they couldn't afford it and had to close."

"Oh, that's terrible!" she said.

"No, my dear," I said, "that's *karma*."

Over breakfast I asked her questions about her coursework and interests, complimented her on her outfit, and described my "work" as an FBI profiler. When we finished, I charged the meal to my room, and we discussed movies as I walked her to class. She paused at the lecture hall doors.

"Do you want to come in?" Sally asked. "We could sit together."

"I'd love to, but I have research to do," I said.

"Thank you for breakfast. And the swimming lesson."

"My pleasure."

A couple of stragglers brushed past us and went inside.

"I should get in there," she said.

"You should. Have a great day, Sally."

As I started to walk away, she lunged and grabbed my arm. "Dakota, wait! When will I see you again?"

I suppressed a grin. "Oh…soon enough, I'm sure."

"How? I mean, don't you at *least* want my cell number?"

"No, let's leave it up to fate," I said. "If we bump into each other again, we'll know it's meant to be. Okay?"

She nodded hesitantly.

"You be good today, beautiful," I said.

Her glasses were a bit wonky; I straightened them. And that's when my eyes zoomed in on that pouty, glistening lower lip of hers. Glancing up and down the empty hallway, I leaned in toward her mouth. She sunk into the doorjamb and closed her eyes.

When my mouth was half an inch from hers, I stopped and breathed her in for a second. The warmth from her face smelled of lavender shampoo. Her lips were irresistible. Well…*almost.*

"Bye, Sally."

Her eyes sprang open. "Aren't you going to kiss me?"

"It's too soon," I said. "Besides, if it's meant to be, it will be. Have a great day." I squeezed her shoulder and walked away.

"Dakota?"

"Yes?"

"I'll be thinking about you today!"

I smiled and waved over my shoulder as I walked out of the building.

From the lecture hall I strolled through the Old Yard, attaching myself briefly to a tour group. Then I walked over to Au Bon Pain, had a cup of coffee and watched the chess hustlers set up for the day.

Twelve years ago I would come here a few times a week to meet my girlfriend, and while waiting for her I would fantasize about my future—as a forensic scientist with the FBI Lab. At the time I thought I'd spend my entire career working in a lab. I never imagined I'd become a successful field agent, and then a private investigator.

When I finished my coffee I still had another hour before Meet-Cute #2, so I took a long walk along the river, returning to Harvard Square at ten thirty. Sally was scheduled to be here now.

Starting at a couple of bookstores, I window-shopped along Mass Ave and J.F.K. Street. I was looking in the window of a miraculously still-extant typewriter shop, admiring a gleaming red typewriter, when a reflection appeared in the glass. Sally was behind me. I pretended not to notice her.

"Dakota?" she said. "What are you doing here?"

I spun around. "Oh, hi, Sally. Just window-shopping. What are *you* doing here?"

She held up a stack of fluorescent pink flyers. "Distributing flyers for Geoff's study."

"May I see?"

She handed me one. Even though it was the same flyer I'd found in her desk drawer the other day, I pretended to read it closely.

"So," she said, "what do you think?"

I shrugged. "I don't know. I guess it has to be brazen. But don't you think these illustrations are a bit over the top?"

"Yeah," she said with a sigh. "I mentioned them to Geoff, but he said that's the flyer he's used at every college. According to him it works, so he's not changing it."

I nodded at the stack in her hands. "There don't seem to be many takers."

She stared at the sidewalk and shook her head grimly.

"I have a little time," I said. "Let me give you a hand."

"Really?"

"Sure." I took half of the stack from her. "But if you're trying to hand them out to random people on the street, you'll be out here all day."

"What do you suggest then?"

"Watch and learn, young one," I said.

For the next hour, I went into a dozen businesses along J.F.K. Street with her and convinced eight of them to post a flyer and to keep a small stack next to their registers. When we emerged successful from a jewelry shop, Sally gazed up at me.

"So, Dakota?"

"Yeah?"

"Do you think this is a sign?" She looked up at me with a raised eyebrow.

"Do I think *what* is a sign?" I asked.

"Us bumping into each other again—and so soon!" Pedestrians on the sidewalk streamed around us like we were stones in a rushing river. "You know—what you were saying earlier…that if we see each other again, we'll know it was meant to be."

"Maybe," I said. "But I think once is coincidence." I glanced at my watch. "Gosh, look at the time. Sorry, doll—lunch date. Gotta go. Maybe we'll see each other later, okay?"

"Okay."

I pecked her on the cheek and crossed the street with the other pedestrians.

10

IMPROMPTU STUDY IN CRIMSON

Walking to Annenberg Hall, I felt guilty for toying with Sally like this, but I'd been hired to do a job: extricate Sally from her relationship with Dr. Malone. Therefore, my Casanova act was a necessary evil. The good news was, it seemed to be working.

However, now that I'd piqued Sally's interest, it was time to pull back a bit. Pull back and, if the opportunity presented itself, make her jealous.

I hadn't been in the Annenberg dining hall since I was a freshman at MIT and the Harvard girl I was dating was living here. I'd forgotten how majestic the place was. The moment I entered and saw the Gothic vaulted ceiling, the rich wood beams and arches, the giant gold chandeliers on long chains, and the stained glass windows, a flood of memories came back to me. Taking a breath, I scanned the dining room for Svetlana.

In the far corner a crowd was gathered around one of the tables. Above the din of hundreds of freshmen eating and talking, I heard two rapid, staccato sounds: the plunks of chess pieces against a board, followed by the snaps of a chess clock. I wormed my way through the crowd. Sure enough, there she was, Svetlana Krüsh, playing speed chess against an Indian young man. The young man sat hunched over, elbows on his knees, staring across the board from the level of the pieces. Svetlana, meanwhile, stood leaning forward and glaring at the entire board, her fingertips deftly pressing the tabletop. Her entire body was tensely coiled, as if she were about to pounce across the table and devour her opponent.

All the spectators' eyes were riveted to the board, surely admiring Svetlana's strategy in the endgame. But not mine. Mine were riveted to the curves of Svetlana's backside, admiring how snugly encased it was in a deep crimson red pencil skirt. Dear Lord—a red pencil skirt, dark stockings, and black kitten heels. Each time she moved a piece, she shifted her legs, causing the skirt fabric to catch the light and stretch delectably taut across the sweep of her backside.

While enjoying this impromptu study in crimson, I had to remind myself not to pant. After a few seconds of this, I forced myself to walk away, take a few deep breaths and think about something else. Other guys typically murmur the starting lineups of their favorite baseball teams; I prefer the periodic table, column by column. During my turn around the dining room, Sally slogged in and dumped her knapsack on a table near the cafeteria entrance.

When I returned to Svetlana's table, the game was over and the crowd was breaking up. Svetlana sat next to her opponent, going over moves from the game. A couple minutes later, with a weary and resigned nod the young man packed up the chess set and trudged away. Svetlana and I were alone.

"Where are your students?" I asked. "I thought you were going to eat among the troops today."

"No troops." Looking up at me, she flipped her hair over her shoulders. It was then that I noticed her lipstick—crimson red, deep and shimmering, that matched her skirt. "I have been working with them individually all morning. I need some time with adults."

"One adult, at your service."

"I suppose you will suffice."

"Come on," I said, jutting my chin at the cafeteria, "I'll buy you lunch."

"No, I will buy *you* lunch. You paid for dinner last night."

"Thanks. I'm what you might call *financially challenged* at present."

I proffered a hand. She took it to help herself up, then let go and walked on her own.

"That's a lovely skirt you're wearing, Svetlana," I said.

"Yes, I noticed you admiring it earlier."

"What? I wasn't—"

She peered over her shoulder at me with hooded eyes. "I have excellent peripheral vision, Dakota."

"All right, you caught me." I sidled up to her. "Sorry, Svetlana. My eyes have a mind of their own sometimes. I didn't mean to objectify you."

She scoffed. "Please—you could not *objectify* me even if you wanted to. I know I am much more than a sex object. I chose to wear this skirt today because I know it looks great on me, and I like the confidence that comes with wearing nice, well-fitting clothes. You do not need to apologize for your perfectly understandable behavior."

"What behavior?"

"Ogling me."

"I wasn't *ogling*. I was admiring."

"You were ogling," she said.

"Let's agree to disagree." Entering the cafeteria, I grabbed a tray and put two sets of silverware on it. "Seriously, I apologize. I'll try not to do it again. Just do me a favor, though?"

"What is that?"

"Don't wear that skirt around me anymore."

She shook her head. "I cannot promise that. It is one of my favorite skirts."

At the serving line, I put a cheeseburger, salad and bottled water on the tray. Walking alongside me, Svetlana added a steak sandwich and a slice of Key lime pie. She paid the cashier.

"How is your case progressing?" she asked. "Any new developments?"

"Yes," I said. "In fact, I could use your help."

As we approached Sally's table, I told Svetlana about my plan for today, adding that if she could behave affectionately toward me when Sally was around, it would help to make Sally jealous.

"*Avec plaisir,* Dakota. *C'est fait accompli.*"

With one corner of her mouth turned up in a smile, Svetlana held my arm, and we stalked toward Sally's table.

At the head of the table with her back to us, Sally didn't see Svetlana and me walk up behind her. However, she did see the dozen poised young women at the table turn to look at us. The young women all wore pastel skirts and sweaters, and they sat with their legs uniformly crossed and their smiling faces slightly canted. The blonde ones had deep tans, and their faces seemed to sparkle. As we got closer, I whispered in Svetlana's ear.

"Is that *glitter*?"

"Yes," she sighed.

"Do I detect a hint of disapproval?" I asked.

"Yes."

Sally turned around to see what the other girls were staring at. Her face fell.

"Hi, Sally," I said. "Hi, ladies. Sally…aren't you going to introduce me to your friends?"

"Yeah…sure. Everyone, this is Dr. Dakota Stevens, a friend of mine. Dakota, this is the Harvard sorority leadership. I was telling them about Dr. Malone's study and—"

"Dakota," Svetlana said, "I go back to table now. Do not make me wait too long."

Softly, seductively, she muttered something in a foreign language—Russian, I think—and, with Sally and the sorority sisters looking on, kissed me on the cheek. She pulled her lips away so slowly, I could feel them stretch and peel away from my cheek, leaving the warm, wet imprint of her lipstick.

"Oh, goodness…that will not do." Svetlana grabbed a napkin off Sally's tray and wiped the lipstick off my cheek. "I see you soon, Dakota." She took our tray and sashayed away.

"Wow, who was *that*?" said one of the blondes.

"Some chess grandmaster," said another blonde.

"Yeah," another girl blurted out, "I heard she played like fifty people last night and beat all of them!"

"So, Dr. Stevens," said the alpha, a tall brunette in a crested blazer. "We know who your lady friend is, but not who *you* are."

"Well, I have something in common with you girls." I touched my chest. "I'm a Lambda, Lambda, Lambda," I lied, citing the infamous fraternity in the '80s comedy *Revenge of the Nerds*. "MIT chapter."

"MIT?" the alpha said. Her eyebrows clenched. "*You* went to MIT? The guys I know at MIT are all major nerds. They—"

"—don't have arms like mine? You know what... you're right." I removed my blazer, revealing my snug FBI T-shirt underneath. Tossing Sally my blazer, I flexed for the girls. "Then again," I added, "I've always been something of an outlier."

All of the girls chuckled—except one.

The one next to Sally, a bookish, waifish redhead who defied the sorority girl stereotype, gazed rapaciously at my arms. She faintly squirmed in her chair with excitement, like a child eyeing chocolate chip cookies hot out of the oven. The alpha rapped on the table, instantly silencing the other girls.

" 'F-B-I,' huh?" the alpha said. "Let me guess...'Female Body Inspector'? How original." She rolled her eyes at the others. They tittered.

"Actually," I said, "this one stands for 'Federal Bureau of Investigation.' My 'Female Body Inspector' T-shirt is in the wash. It gets a *lot* of wear."

This triggered a laugh from the entire table, after which I went into my now-familiar spiel: that I was a Harvard Fellow on sabbatical from the FBI.

"So you, like, solve crimes?" said one of the blondes. "Like on that TV show?"

"I do."

The waifish redhead was still staring at my arms. I pulled up a chair and sat beside her.

"Hey, lovely…what's your name?" I asked.

She swallowed. "Alice."

"Really? I love that name."

She blushed.

"Alice," I said, "have you ever held a muscular man's arm?"

"Ch'yeah, right," the alpha said. "Alice hasn't held a muscular man's *anything*."

The other sorority girls laughed.

"Madison, *please!*" Alice hissed.

"Alice, today's your lucky day." I flexed my bicep and held it in front of her. "Go on…feel that baby."

Tentatively she touched the curved peak of the muscle with her fingertips like it was a red-hot stove. Then, with a gulp, she squeezed the muscle with one hand. An eye blink later both hands were fondling my entire upper arm. Her eyes, a limpid blue, widened. Despite having all of her sorority sisters watching, she seemed to forget herself.

"Alice, honey?" I said softly.

"Mm?"

"We need to stop now." Gently, I pulled my arm away. "You're getting me excited."

The girls—even Alice—laughed hysterically, slapping each other and the table, but Sally wasn't laughing. Her face was flushed. I couldn't tell if she was on the verge of crying or shouting at me. Once again I felt guilty about my behavior. I got up and smiled at her.

"It's been a pleasure meeting you, ladies," I said, "but as you can see"—I pointed across the dining room at Svetlana—"my friend awaits."

"Your friend, huh?" the alpha girl said. "I think Alice would be your *friend*."

"Madison!" Alice said.

"Bye, ladies."

Slipping on my blazer again, I gave Sally's shoulder a reassuring squeeze and returned to Svetlana's table.

Svetlana was gnashing into her steak sandwich and staring up at the corner of the ceiling. She was obviously thinking about something. Across the table from her was the tray with my food. Not wanting to interrupt her train of thought, I sat and ate my burger in silence. She was still thinking when I finished it.

"What are you thinking about?" I asked.

Appearing to recall something that pleased her, she nodded to herself and put down her sandwich. "I was replaying my game with Gaurav, seeing if I had missed any earlier mating opportunities. I did not."

"Wait a second," I said. "You can remember *all* the moves? Yours and his?"

"Of course."

"Amazing." I shook my head at her. "I've never met anybody like you."

She flashed me a smile—all lips, no teeth. "How goes your *case* with young Sally?"

While eating my salad, I told her about my interactions with Sally so far today, and how I was feeling guilty for toying with her emotions.

"I've never played games with women," I said, "so I don't like it. That being said…"

"Yes?"

"It seems to be working," I said.

Svetlana gracefully cleaved off a forkful of Key lime pie, savored it, and waved the empty fork at me.

"You will be doing more of this foolishness tomorrow, I suppose," she said.

"What *foolishness?*"

"This *case* of yours."

"Yeah," I said.

"And what will you be doing exactly?"

"Hard to say," I said. "When you're poking into other people's business, every day is different, and you have to be able to deviate from your plan. Tomorrow morning, I was planning on driving over to South Boston."

"Why? What is there?"

"Another PI's office," I said. "My predecessor on the Sally case."

She didn't ask why I'd taken over for somebody, and I was glad for that. The truth—that the man was killed while staking out Malone's apartment—might have scared her away.

"Does this involve Dr. Malone?" she asked.

"I'm not sure. I won't know until I investigate."

She cleaved off another piece of pie and gestured with her fork. "Perhaps if it would not be—"

"Svetlana, are you asking me if you could come along?"

"I have seen so little of Boston," she said, "and...I should get to know my future tenant better."

"I don't know," I said. "You might not like what you see."

She scoffed and flapped a hand. "Nonsense. I am an excellent judge of character."

"I plan on starting early," I said. "Tell you what...can you be at the Charles Hotel by eight o'clock?"

"So early? Must I?"

"The early bird gets the clue, my dear."

"Very well," she said. "Eight o'clock. I will ring you from the lobby."

"Good. It's a date."

"No...it is a business appointment."

"Of course," I said. "That's what I meant."

Across the dining room, the sorority girls picked up their things and filed out. I could tell from Sally's slumping in her chair that her meeting hadn't gone well. I had planned to "bump into" her again at the *Crimson* offices, but between the rejection from the sorority girls and Svetlana's kissing me, Sally was probably reeling right now. This was a critical moment: If I didn't show her some affection, pronto, she might run to Dr. Malone.

"Svetlana, I have to go," I said, getting up. "Thanks for lunch. See you tomorrow morning."

By the time I brought my tray to the bussing station, Sally was already marching out of the dining room. I caught up to her outside, on Quincy Street. Her knapsack straps had loosened again, so the pack was drooping on her back. She walked hunched over like a depressed Charlie Brown.

"Hey there, beautiful," I said.

"Hey yourself," she said.

"Why so glum?"

She shrugged and continued walking. "They don't want to do Geoff's study."

"So what? That's Geoff's problem, not yours. Stop for a second."

"I can't. I have to get to the *Crimson.*"

"Stop. Please?"

She halted suddenly and heaved out a sigh. I tightened her shoulder straps again.

"There," I said. "Mind if I walk with you?"

"Whatever," she said.

She marched down the sidewalk, continuing on Quincy Street along the eastern fence of Harvard Yard. Her jaw was set, and she marched leading with her head, fiercely determined, like a petite, female Theodore Roosevelt. Teddy, a Harvard student himself back in the late 1870s, was once called a "steam engine in trousers." I chuckled. From now on, I would think of Sally as "a steam engine in capris."

"Are you laughing at me?" she said.

"No, admiring you. You're adorable."

"Dakota," she whined, "what's the deal with *Svetlana?*" She glanced at me. "Is she your girlfriend?"

"Hardly. We just met the other day. We're friends. Less than friends, actually—acquaintances."

"*Acquaintances*? You're sure? She seemed *really* friendly. She kissed you!"

"Just on the cheek," I said. "Look…she's European—from Russia, I think. They're all like that."

"Whatever, I don't care." Eyes down, she kicked a stone into the street. "What about Alice? Do you like her?"

"Do you mean, why did I let her feel my arm? I'll tell you. Because she seemed like a sweet girl who's never touched a man before. Come on, would you really begrudge poor, waifish little Alice the chance to squeeze a man's muscle?"

Sally shrugged again. I waited for a group of students to pass us, and then I grabbed her knapsack, stopping her short.

"Hey!" she said.

"Sally…are you *jealous*?"

"No."

"I think you are, but there's no reason to be. I just met Svetlana Krüsh, I don't have a girlfriend, and I'm not interested in Alice. I promise. I'm interested in *you*, Sally. What about you? Are you interested in me?"

She took off marching again, this time swinging her arms.

"Well?" I said.

The words blurted out of Sally's mouth so fast, and with such force, they were like exploding steam.

"Why would you possibly be interested in me? I'm an ugly, dumb undergrad, and you…you're a handsome Ph.D."

I tugged her into me and kissed her. For a split second she tried to pull away, but then she closed her eyes and relaxed in my arms. Her lips were every bit as soft and succulent as they looked. When I ended the kiss, her eyes had tears in them. I fished a napkin out of my pocket and handed it to her. I took her knapsack and slung it over my shoulder and talked to her while she removed her glasses, dried her eyes and blew her nose.

"First of all, Sally," I said, "you're far from ugly. You're a striking young lady."

"Uh-uh. An ugly duckling maybe, but—"

"Hush. I'm talking. You're uniquely attractive. Period. Some of the best models aren't classically attractive, but their combination of interesting features makes them beautiful. That's you, Sally. And as for dumb, you're kidding, right? You're an honors student at one of the best universities in the world. You're *light years* from dumb. You don't know what dumb is, Sally. Trust me…I've dated more than my share of dumb girls, so I know what I'm talking about. True story—one girl I dated was so dumb…" I nudged Sally.

She rolled her eyes and sighed. "How dumb was she?"

"While vacationing on Nantucket together, we went to the same beach every day," I said. "Then, on our final day there, we went at low tide and she looked at some rocks in the water and said, 'Dakota…those rocks have grown since yesterday.' I tried to explain tides to her, but she wouldn't hear it. In her world, rocks *grew*."

Sally sniggered like a cartoon cat and put her glasses back on.

"See?" I said. "You're beautiful, and you're far from dumb."

"Thanks."

"So?" I said. "Are you interested in me or not?"

"Yes. Very much."

I grinned. "I think you're special, kid—one in a million." I put an arm around her and led her to the end of the block. "Come on, I'll walk you to the *Crimson* offices."

"How do you know where it is?" she asked.

"I used to date one of the editors. Years ago."

We crossed the street. At the corner of Plympton Street, in front of Harvard Book Store, I helped her put on her knapsack again and walked her the short distance to the *Crimson* office.

"There's one thing I want to know, Sally," I said. "And I want the truth."

"*Truth*? About what?"

I looked at her askance. "Have you been following me today?"

"Excuse me?"

"Everywhere I've gone today, you've shown up right after me—the pool, Harvard Square, the Berg. You're not *stalking* me are you, Sally?"

"Don't be ridiculous," she said. "It's fate. It *has* to be. What you said this morning, when you walked me to Cantor's class, remember? About how 'if it's meant to be, it will be'? You know what I think? I think it's a sign we're meant to be together."

"Maybe," I said. "But if we bump into each other again today, then we'll *know* it's a sign."

The brunette and the redhead I'd met here yesterday waved to me on their way into the building.

"I'm nervous, Dakota," she said.

"What are you nervous about?"

"That I won't see you again. Can't we at least exchange phone numbers?"

"If you really want to talk, I'm staying at the Charles," I said. "Call me anytime."

"Anytime? Really?"

"Well, don't call in the middle of the night unless it's an emergency, but otherwise, sure—anytime."

"I like you, Dakota. A lot."

"I like you, too, Sally."

She waved at the building. "I'm late. Call you later?"

"Sounds great."

She hugged me a final time and skipped to the door. "Bye, Dakota!"

"Bye."

When the door of the *Crimson* closed behind her, I was overcome by a deluge of exhaustion. Before my next meet-cute, at the tennis court, I needed to rest. I headed back to my hotel.

11

TOTALLY 'THE DIRTY DOZEN'

Technically speaking all I'd done today was follow and spend some time with a 19½-year-old girl. So why did I feel like I was back in the Bureau, with my brain fried from interrogating a suspect for three hours?

Exhausted when I reached the hotel, I sat in the sauna for half an hour, showered, and took a nap. By the time I woke up, it was quarter to three. Sally's tennis intramurals started in fifteen minutes. I quickly changed into tennis clothes, drove across the river to the Beren tennis center, and grabbed my racquet and a can of balls out of the trunk.

When I was at MIT, I'd only played here once. Since Harvard was a Division I school and MIT was Division III, it was an exhibition tournament. Naturally we lost to Harvard that day, but we got our revenge weeks later.

We broke in one night and meticulously repainted the lines on one of the courts so the playing area was three inches shallower and narrower. Our prank wasn't discovered until the following season, when a visiting player, who kept hitting his ball out, insisted the court be measured.

Overall, this was the best tennis facility I'd ever played in. With the courts' blue playing surfaces, white lines and green sidelines, and their seating for hundreds of fans, the complex was like a miniature version of the U.S. Open Tennis Center in Queens, New York.

Entering the first section of courts, I expected to see Sally and a bunch of girls, but there was only one other person there—a dark-haired man, early 30s, wearing a Harvard baseball cap.

He stood at the baseline with a basket of balls. I watched him serve. His windup, toss, body extension and racquet contact with the ball—I sensed that I'd seen this serve before. The man serving was a bit heavier and softer around the middle, but I was pretty sure I recognized him as my old arch tennis rival from Brandeis—Joshua Cohen.

"Josh?" I said. "Is that you?"

With a cursory glance at me, he served another ball. It whizzed dead-on into an empty ball container in the opposite service box. Smiling wryly in my direction, he bounced a tennis ball with his racquet.

"Well, I'll be damned," he said. "If it isn't Dakota Stevens."

I walked over and shook his hand. He eyed me up and down, eagerly nodding. Honestly, it was a bit uncomfortable.

"And still in killer shape, I see," he said. "Damn. So, what brings you to the big H?"

"Harvard Fellow." I flashed my ID.

He whistled. "So, it's *Doctor* Stevens now?"

"Yeah. I'm a criminal profiler for the FBI, doing a sabbatical at Harvard for a while."

"Sounds like a sweet gig."

"It's all right," I said. "What about you?"

"Wanna hit it around a bit? I've got a dozen girls coming in a few minutes."

"Sure."

Tossing my racquet cover on a bench, I ran over to the other side of the court, tossed the ball container against the back fence, and waited at the baseline for Josh to deliver a flaming serve.

Instead—probably to test my skill level—he lofted a ball across. I drilled a forehand return down the line, deep into the corner.

"Nice shot," he said. "Yeah, so I'm assistant A-D for the college, and I run the girls' intramural tennis program. I'd like to coach the Men's team someday. Anyway, I'm married now—wife's a big-time Boston litigator—and I've got two kids, boy and a girl. We live in Newton. How about you? Married? Kids?" He fed me another ball.

"No and no." I hit a backhand crosscourt.

I thought my shot was hard-hit until Josh replied with a down-the-line forehand that, had it been any faster, would have caused a sonic boom.

As I ran for the ball, Josh rushed the net. Miraculously, I got my racquet under the ball and lobbed it over him.

Sprinting back to the baseline, he let the ball bounce and chipped it back deftly with a backhand drop shot.

Now I rushed the net. When the ball bounced on my side of the court, it lurched toward the net and dropped before I could reach it.

"Nice shot yourself," I said.

"Good to see you're still playing," he said.

"When I can find the time."

A cell phone rang. Josh pulled a phone out of his shorts pocket.

"Sorry, it's my wife," he said. "I've got to take this."

"No problem."

I mimed practicing my serve while he paced around the court. Then he hung up abruptly and ran to the net. His face was drawn.

"My little girl's been in an accident at school," he said.

"Oh, Josh—that's awful." I met him at the net. "Is she okay?"

"I think so. Something happened in gym class. Listen, normally I wouldn't ask, but could do me a solid?"

"Anything. What?"

"Run the intramurals for me today?" he asked. "Drills and maybe a round-robin? It's a piece of cake."

He glanced over his shoulder at the entrance. A group of girls in a mishmash of polo shirts and tank tops, shorts and tennis dresses, shambled in. He lowered his voice.

"Most of them aren't very good," he whispered. "Basically, I just need you to babysit them for two hours. Could you do that for me?"

"Of course, Josh. Go."

"I'll make it up to you, I promise." He hurriedly collected his things. "Where can I reach you?"

"The Charles," I said.

The girls, including Sally, had gathered on the other side of the court. They were all slouching and looking at Josh with anxious faces. Slipping on my sunglasses, I strolled over bouncing a ball in the air off my racquet strings.

"Mr. Cohen, what's wrong?" one of them asked.

"Family emergency, girls," he said. "But you're in good hands. My friend here, Dr. Dakota Stevens, was almost as good as me in college. He's generously offered to fill in for me today, so be easy on him. Bye."

The girls watched Josh run out, and when he disappeared out the gate, they turned their heads in unison to face me.

Sally wore a canary yellow tennis dress, the clingy fabric of which was enticingly smooth and sheeny. The look was marred, however, by the garish glint of her BDSM collar. Smiling and waving her tennis racquet, she mouthed, "It's a sign, Dakota."

The rest of the young ladies stared back at me with their eyes half closed and their mouths pinched up in jaded sneers. Chomping on gum, swinging their racquets metronomically like grandfather clock pendulums, scuffing absently at the court with their sneakers, these girls were the Bad News Bears of Ivy League intramural tennis.

None of them said anything, so the loudest sound was the "tung-tung-tung-tung-tung" of the ball bouncing on my racquet strings. I paused in front of them for effect before introducing myself.

"Good afternoon, ladies," I said. "As Mr. Cohen mentioned, my name is Dakota Stevens. I'm a Harvard Fellow, and I'm going to be your substitute coach today."

A tall blonde on the end stepped forward. She cocked her head and stood with her arms akimbo.

"What happened to Mr. Cohen?"

"His daughter got hurt," I said. "That's all I know."

All at once, the group of them winced and said, "Oh, no! Not little Hannah!"

"I don't think it's anything serious," I said.

"You just said you didn't know," the tall blonde said.

"I'm sure Hannah's going to be fine." I kept bouncing the ball on my racquet: *tung-tung-tung-tung-tung*.

"Well…what happened to her?"

This question came from an Asian girl in a Harvard tank top and a pair of gray Spandex shorts. Her hair was pulled back tightly in a high ponytail, accentuating her inscrutable, exotic features.

"Something involving gym class," I said. "That's all I know."

Again the girls winced collectively.

Then they began positing theories about what had happened:

"Bet she was climbing the rope. Yeah, fer sure, she prob'ly fell."

"Hannah's seven years old, Peyton. They don't make *seven*-year-olds climb the rope in gym!"

"Maybe she got sick. Little kids puke all the time. I've done a *lot* of babysitting."

"Kids are the worst. I'm never going to have kids."

"She probably got hit with the ball during dodgeball and got a bloody nose. That happened to me once, and it hurt like—"

"Ladies!" I batted the tennis ball somewhere behind me. "You're here to play tennis, not gossip. Now let's begin. Line up for inspection."

"Inspection?" the Asian girl said. "What is this, the *Army*?"

Putting my racquet under my arm like General Patton used to do with his riding crop, I swaggered up to her and stared at her through my aviator sunglasses.

"What's your name, soldier?" I said.

She sighed. "Jade Lee."

"Line up according to height, Miss Lee," I said. "Toes on the baseline, please, and stand up straight. No slouching, ladies."

It took a few seconds, with them dawdling and grumbling while they did it, but eventually they got lined up and were standing at attention. I stepped back and took in the row of them.

"Very nice, ladies. Very nice."

"Why are we doing this, Dr. Stevens?" the tall blonde asked.

"Because," I said, "few things are more beautiful than twelve young women in shorts and skirts standing up straight. Ever heard of *The Dirty Dozen*? Well, you ladies are 'The Divine Dozen.' "

"That's what *you* think, Dr. Stevens," said the tall blonde, glancing down the row of girls. "We're *totally* 'The Dirty Dozen.' "

"You know it, girl!"

Peyton bumped fists with the blonde, then, turning and squatting slightly, started humming a song and gyrating her behind—much to the delight of the other girls, who laughed and hooted.

"Careful, Doctor Stevens," the Asian girl said. "Lexie's father's a lawyer. What you said sounded pretty sexual harass-y to me."

I waited for Peyton to finish her dance and get back in line, then said, "All of you…tell me how you feel right now."

A pixyish blonde turned to Sally. "What's he mean?"

"I *mean*," I said, "when you stand up straight, how do you feel inside?"

"I don't know…strong?" the tall blonde said.

"Good," I said. "Now I want all of you to hold your arms over your head and arch your back slightly. Imagine you're crossing the finish line of a marathon. Then, with your eyes closed, tell me how you feel."

"Confident."

"Powerful," said Jade.

"Right," I said. "That's because this is a power position. Remember the feeling you have right now. If you ever feel depressed, make this position for a minute and visualize yourself accomplishing your goals."

"Wow…it works!" Peyton said.

"Thank you, Tony Robbins!" Jade shouted.

The girls laughed.

"All right." I grabbed a basket of balls. "Let's do some drills. One at a time, on the baseline. Hit a forehand approach shot, rush the net, then a backhand volley. Okay? Let's go, chop-chop!"

In retrospect, I probably spent too much time individually with Sally. After the second time she asked me to correct her form, the other girls parodied her, saying, "No...correct *my* form, Dakota." Even Jade warmed to me, wagging her behind and asking me, "How's *my* form, Dakota?"

After drills, I made them pair off and play a set of doubles. As I walked court to court correcting their serve or volleying technique, I spotted a man sitting at the very top of the grandstand, peering down at us with a pair of binoculars.

I hadn't seen him enter the tennis complex. Aside from him, the stands were utterly empty. In fact, the man in the grandstand was the only non-player I'd seen in the entire facility since I came in. When Jade walked to the sidelines for a drink, I approached her.

"Why aren't you on the tennis team, Jade? You're an excellent player."

"My parents won't let me." Working the spigot, she filled a cup from a giant cooler of Gatorade. "They think it'll distract me from my studies."

"That's too bad."

"Yeah, it bites all right." She sipped some Gatorade.

"Let me ask you something," I said. "Does Mr. Cohen ever have scouts here watching you girls play?"

Snorting at my question, she spit up some of her drink.

"*Scouts*? Really, Dr. Stevens—do you *see* them playing over there?"

We both looked at the courts. Sally served a ball and drilled her doubles partner in the back. The tall blonde tried to return a serve while rolling back on her heels, and the ball sailed over the fence behind her. Peyton played air guitar on her tennis racquet and spanked her partner's butt with it, then spun around and gyrated her behind for the girls.

"*Oh, Peyton.*" Jade shook her head with a faint smile on her lips. "See what I mean, Dr. Stevens?"

"Jade," I said, "I need you to do something, but you have to be discreet about it."

"Okay."

"Look up in the grandstand."

She did.

"Have you ever seen that man before?" I asked.

"Mm…I don't think so," she said. "Binoculars, dude? Really?"

"Thanks. Take over with the girls for a few minutes, would you?"

"Me?"

"Absolutely."

"What are you going to do?" she asked.

"Go talk to the guy."

"Careful, Dr. Stevens. He looks creepy."

"Relax, doll." I curled my bicep into a muscle while she was drinking, and she spit up Gatorade again.

"Holy crap!" she said.

Over thirty, Dakota, and you've still got it.

"*Yeah,*" I said. "I'll be fine."

I went out the door in the fence, crossed the walkway behind the courts, and started jogging up the aisle into the stands. The man was at the very top, peering down with a small pair of binoculars.

As I got closer, I saw he had short blonde hair. He was smoking a cigarette and writing in a pocket notebook. Noticing me, he lowered the binoculars and put away the notebook.

"Dr. Malone?" I said.

"Oh, hello, Dr. Stevens." He exhaled a cloud of smoke and ground out his cigarette under his shoe. "Marvelous day for tennis, isn't it?"

"Excuse me, Doctor," I said, "but you can't be here."

"Don't be ridiculous," he said. "I come all the time to watch Sally play. No one's said anything before."

"Why the binoculars, Doctor? And why were you taking notes?"

"This is outrageous, Dr. Stevens. Because I study Sally's play and give her notes afterward. I don't know if you're aware or not, but Sally and I *are* a couple."

"That might be the case," I said, "but your presence is making the girls nervous."

Frowning, he sprang to his feet and stomped down the stairs.

"What about you, Dr. Stevens?"

"What *about* me?"

"Why are you here?" he said. "Where is Coach Cohen?"

"I'm filling in for him today."

At the bottom of the grandstand, he slowed to a stroll, heading toward the exit.

"I saw you instructing my Sally earlier."

"*Your* Sally, Dr. Malone?" I said. "You say that like she's your property."

"The two of you seemed quite friendly."

I shrugged. "What can I say? I have a natural rapport with girls her age."

"I suppose that explains it." He stared through the fence at Sally, who was having her butt spanked with a tennis racquet by Peyton. "Please tell Sally I'll be in my car when practice is over. Good day, Dr. Stevens."

"Dr. Malone."

When I returned to the courts, the girls were packing up. I checked my watch: it was five o'clock. Jade carried two full baskets of balls to the gate. Stowing her racquet in her tennis bag, she leaned into my shoulder.

"Who was that guy?" she asked.

"Nobody to worry about," I said. "A women's tennis enthusiast, that's all."

"Mm, I bet. More like a women's tennis *perv*. Thanks for bouncing him." She shook my hand. "Nice meeting you, Dr. Stevens."

"You too, Jade."

"Will you be back?" she asked.

"Not sure," I said. "Maybe."

I shook hands goodbye with each of the girls except Sally, who waited until the others left before approaching me.

"Jade said you had to tell a man to leave," she said. "Who was it?"

"Sally," I said, "I need to ask you something."

"Yeah, what?"

"Does Geoff ever come to your practices and give you notes later about your play?"

"No," she said. "Well, *once* he did. Why, was that him?"

"Yes. He's waiting in his car for you."

Her face blanched. "What did he say? Was he angry?"

"He saw me correcting your form, and didn't like it."

She gazed across the courts as though in a trance.

"Crap…I'm in trouble."

I put my hands on her shoulders. "Sally, you don't *have* to leave with him. And if you don't feel safe, I don't *want* you leaving with him. I can drive you back to your dorm, or you can stay at my hotel."

This snapped her out of her trance. "What? Like *sleep* with you?"

"Of course not. You'd have your own room."

Her eyes darted around, and then they fixed on me.

"What should I *do*, Dakota?"

"I think you—"

Her cell phone rang. She glanced at the screen.

"It's him," she said.

"Don't answer it," I said. "Or, better yet, let *me* talk to him."

"No, I can handle this."

She answered the phone. I couldn't hear what Malone said, but I saw its effects on her. It was as if he spoke a subliminal code word, because Sally's face suddenly went blank and all she said was, "Yes. Yes, Geoff. Yes, Master."

After a fifteen-second one-sided conversation, she hung up, tucked her racquet under her arm and moved robotically toward the door. I blocked her way.

"Dakota," she said, "I have to go!"

"All right," I said. "But at least call me later so I know you're okay. The Charles, room three-one-six. Will you do that for me?"

"Yes."

"Try to call when you're alone. And if you don't feel safe, even if it's the middle of the night, call me and I'll come get you."

"Okay, fine. Let me go."

She squirmed around me, darted through the gate, and marched toward the exit. She didn't turn around.

The little steam engine kept marching.

12

THE FACE THAT LAUNCH'D
A THOUSAND SHIPS

Without a punching bag handy on which to take out my frustrations, when Sally stormed out of the tennis center I practiced my serve with a basket of balls, serving each ball as hard as I could. I managed to make ten balls wedge in the chain link fence on the other side of the court. A couple went clear through.

After cleaning up and changing at the hotel, I walked to the Border Café, an upscale Tex-Mex restaurant and watering hole near Harvard Square. It was mobbed with the after-work crowd. The hostess said the earliest a table would be available was nine o'clock, so I took an empty stool at the bar. I ordered a Macallan double and shrimp and steak fajitas. When my drink arrived, I relished the warmth of the scotch in my throat, and how each sip made me temporarily forget today's setback with Sally.

The day with her had been going so well—until Malone showed up. As soon as Sally talked to him, it was as if a switch in her got tripped. I wished I knew the hold Malone had over her. Between following her yesterday, and all of the "meet-cutes" today, I'd put a lot of time and energy into luring her away from Malone. I'd compromised my integrity by telling her what she wanted to hear. I'd kissed her. And enjoyed it. Now, after all that, what if I failed in my assignment? Even worse, what if Mr. Standish had hired another PI to keep tabs on me, and that PI reported my activities to him? Or, what if Director Reeves had Miss Suzuki watching me?

Relax, Dakota, you're being paranoid. Relax and enjoy your scotch. Relax and maybe chat up a woman in here.

A woman with long bronze hair paused in the bar doorway and looked around for somebody. At first blush, she resembled Ashley. The sight of this beautiful stranger made me think about Ashley for the first time in days. No question, I would miss the sexual chemistry between us. But, with a bracing pang of sadness that I curbed with another slug of scotch, I realized there was virtually nothing else I'd miss about our relationship. Like every other woman I'd been involved with, Ashley had been attracted to my looks and my physicality, and occasionally my humor, but never to my intelligence or ambition.

When I drained my glass, I gestured to the bartender for another scotch, and scanned the bar. Mostly couples, late twenties to early thirties. There were a lot of professionals in suits, and a few who were clearly third-year law students, which I deduced from the dark circles under their eyes and the legal pads jammed in their briefcases.

Sitting at a cocktail table near the bar entrance were four young women with the overtly vamping behavior of single girls out husband-hunting. They wore little black dresses and took turns glancing in my direction. While they pretended to straighten their hair or adjust themselves in their chairs, they weren't very subtle about it.

One of them, a dusky Latina, was more creative than her friends. She checked me out over her shoulder using a compact mirror, and when my chiding eye met hers in the mirror, she blushed and the four of them burst into nervous laughter. I raised my drink to them. They were attractive, but I'd had my fill of young women recently. Their transparency and, frankly, vapidity, bored me.

I kept scanning the bar. When my fajitas came and I started to eat, I noticed a studious-looking woman at a corner high table on the other side of the bar. She sipped a glass of red wine while reading Homer's *The Odyssey*. She was a good deal older than me—in her mid-forties, I surmised—wearing a green tweed skirt suit and sitting with her legs crossed, wagging one foot. They were very nice legs, long and well-proportioned. Her shoes were narrow Oxfords with a high heel, and with the tweed suit they were, antithetically, very sexy.

The Odyssey was dog-eared, the pages sprouting dozens of colored plastic tabs. She had neither a wedding ring nor an indentation on her ring finger to suggest she used to have one. Every now and then she smiled contentedly, put down her wine, and jotted something in the book margins, or she mused into space across the bar. It looked like she was envisioning a scene in Odysseus' world.

The woman had grey-green eyes, huge and pensive, and her hair, a rich chestnut, was rumpled on one side from her absentmindedly running her fingers through it. She had the smooth, pinkish face of a schoolgirl, hinting at the stunner she must have been twenty years earlier.

Overall she looked like a woman who, for most of her adult life, had subordinated her sexual passions to her academic ones. For all of these reasons—the eyes, the legs, the shoes, the classic text, the smoldering sublimated sexuality, and the contented smile—when I finished my fajitas, I ordered myself another scotch, her another wine, and ventured over to introduce myself.

The bartender had just finished delivering our drinks to her table when she looked up from her book. At first her eyes were out of focus, as though she were still in Odysseus' world, and it took her a couple seconds to return to present day. Then she saw the new glass of wine in front of her. With a start, she looked at me incredulously.

"What is this?" she asked.

Several pick-up lines occurred to me—lines I'd used successfully on young women over the years—but this woman was a Classics scholar. If I wanted to hit it off with her, I'd have to raise my game considerably.

"Pardon me, professor." Picking up my drink, I slid onto the stool across from her and recited a quote about Helen of Troy, considered the most beautiful woman of the ancient world. I gestured at her cheek. " 'Is this the face that launch'd a thousand ships, / And burnt the topless towers of Ilium?' "

She chuckled and raked her fingers through her hair.

"Ah, the great Christopher Marlowe...*Doctor Faustus*," she said. "Wonderful. Would you believe, kind sir, that my name actually *is* Helen?"

"You're *kidding*," I said.

Smiling, she narrowed her eyes at me. "Did you ask the bartender my name?"

"I didn't, I swear."

"I believe you," she said. "Helen Hale. And you are…?"

"Dakota Stevens."

We shook hands. Her hand felt fragile, so I was exceptionally gentle.

"Oh my, what a marvelous name," she said. "A hero's name."

"I'm happy with it," I said.

"Dakota, how did you know I'm a professor?" she asked.

"Elementary, Doctor Hale. Your copy of *The Odyssey* is marked with color-coded plastic tabs, and over the past half-hour I've seen you make a dozen notations in the margins. I believe you're a professor of Classics and that you can both read and write ancient Greek and Latin."

She put down her book and clapped. "Spot on, Dakota Stevens. Spot on."

"But with a first name of 'Helen,' I guess you were somewhat predestined for your work."

"I suppose so." She finished the glass of wine in her hand, put it down and picked up the one I'd bought for her. "Now what about you, Dakota? Are you a professor as well?"

At first I was going to give her my Harvard Fellow cover story, but she smiled so sweetly at me. Besides, I didn't feel like lying anymore today. I wanted to share the truth about my situation with someone, so I wouldn't feel so damn lonely.

"I'll tell you, Helen," I said. "But you have to swear not to tell a soul. Okay?"

"Certainly, Dakota. I swear."

Moving my drink and stool to her side of the table, I sat close to her and told her my story. I explained how, until a year ago, I'd worked for the FBI; how I'd been a very good agent; and how, if I'd stayed, I likely would have become the SAC (Special Agent-in-Charge) of a field office. But now I was on my own, struggling to start a private investigations firm, taking non-cases to pay the bills, and being forced by the Director of the FBI to woo a Harvard student out of an inappropriate relationship. Helen listened intently the entire time, cradling her head in her hand with her elbow on the table, gazing at me with those fathomless grey-green eyes of hers.

"Mmm," she said when I finished, "although I know nothing about investigations— I've only ever been an academic—your plight is actually reminiscent of the ideas of Joseph Campbell, particularly his text *The Hero with a Thousand Faces*. Have you heard of it?"

"Peripherally," I said. "Isn't he the guy who deconstructed the journeys of great heroes in literature and film and showed the commonalities? And didn't George Lucas consult with him when he was creating the *Star Wars* movies?"

She chuckled. "Yes, I believe he did. But the reason I bring him up—the idea that I thought apropos to your life's journey—is his contention that every hero, once he accepts what Campbell terms 'The Call to Adventure,' faces a dark period in the wilderness, when he is cut off from everyone and everything. He undergoes a series of tests which Campbell refers to as 'The Road of Trials,' and the hero must get himself through them." She sipped some wine and, canting her head, stared thoughtfully at me.

"In forming your own agency, Dakota, you accepted the Call to Adventure," she said. "Now I think you're on the Road of Trials. This will be a dark time for you, a time of struggling in the wilderness, alone without the support of a big government agency. But...I believe if you fight your way through this period and overcome the challenges you're faced with, on the other side will be success and satisfaction beyond anything you've ever known."

"Wow," I said. "I thought all I did was quit my job with the FBI. But when you say it like that"—I tapped her book with a forefinger—"you make me sound like Odysseus."

"You are like Odysseus," she said with a smile. "A modern-day one."

With that, I decided I really liked this woman. I wanted to take her to bed if she was agreeable to the idea. I downed the rest of my drink and gestured to the bartender to bring us two more. Locking my eyes on her, I asked her to tell me about herself.

"Hmm, well, where should I start?" she said with a rake of the hair. She was distantly related to the Revolutionary War patriot Nathan Hale; she went to the University of Pennsylvania for undergrad; she received her Ph.D. from Oxford University; and she had been an associate professor of Classics at Harvard for seventeen years. Currently she was working on a new translation of *The Odyssey* from ancient Greek and wanted to be the first woman to translate the text. I listened to her story as intently as she listened to mine, admittedly feeling humbled by her academic accomplishments, yet also feeling myself more and more attracted to her as she talked. We were both sipping our third drink and studying each other's faces when the Border Café mariachi band sauntered not so subtly into the bar.

"Helen"—I jutted my chin at the sombrero-wearing quartet loudly approaching our table—"I don't know about you, but I have an aversion to mariachi bands like other people have to telemarketers."

Squinting her eyes and smiling, she nodded vigorously. "I concur, Dakota. Entirely."

I looked her straight in the eyes with complete stillness. "Let's get out of here."

"Oh…okay…let's." She stared back at me in wonderment. Clearly, being picked up was not a regular occurrence for her. "But…your place or—"

"Yours," I said. "I'm interested to see your decorating style. Especially in your bedroom."

She laughed and gave me a knowing wink. After I settled with the bartender, Helen put her book in her purse and I escorted her outside.

During the two hours I'd been in the restaurant, a cool autumn dusk had enveloped Cambridge, cloaking the brick walls and buildings of Harvard Yard in shadow. Strolling silently, the two of us on autopilot, we crossed Mass Ave and walked along the wall of the Yard. Helen was swaying a bit, and the third time she bumped into me, I held her around her waist to steady her.

"Where are we going?" I asked.

"You tell *me*, Odysseus." She leaned her head on my shoulder. "This is *your* Odyssey."

Helen snorted, which turned into a full-blown cackling laugh. A group of passing students seemed to recognize her. They looked shocked. One of them started to say, "Hi, Professor," when another girl stopped her. We crossed Mass Ave again and started down Garden Street, toward Radcliffe Quad.

"Helen?" I said.

"Yes?"

"How many wines did you drink tonight?"

"Um…before or *after* you came over?" she said.

"Total."

"Five or six, I suppose."

I winced. "Okay. Where do you live?"

She flapped a hand in the direction of a row of warmly lit streetlights that faded into the darkness.

"Up there, near Radcliffe Quad," she said. "Faculty apartment. Hector and I."

"Hector?" I said.

"My cat." She nuzzled my cheek; her breath was piquant with wine. "Made you nervous, didn't I?"

The farther we walked, the more Helen's energy flagged and the more I effectively had to drag her. As we were passing Radcliffe Quad, she wrenched out of my arms, scampered into the bushes, and, holding her hair, quietly retched. Not wanting any students to see her like this, I stood guard on the sidewalk and was relieved when she finished. Wiping her mouth with a tissue, she led us across the street and plopped down on the stoop of a brownstone, panting.

"This is your building, Helen?" I said. "You're sure?"

"Quite sure." She rummaged through her purse and produced a ring of keys for me. "Three-B, Dakota. I… just need…to catch….my breath."

Her eyes fluttering closed, she slumped against the steps, which jolted her awake again. I bit my lip in exasperation and shook my head. The visions I had nurtured just half an hour ago—of making love with this woman on a rug in front of a fireplace while she vehemently declared me her hunky Odysseus and shouted cries of ecstasy in ancient Greek—had now sadly evaporated.

Taking her keys, I heaved her to her feet and up the stoop. I opened the door and dragged her inside, the toes of her shoes scraping the threshold, to the foyer. By the way she was wobbling, I could tell that everything was spinning for her. There was no way this woman would be able to climb three flights of stairs, so I told her to close her eyes and keep them closed. I then slung her over my shoulder and began climbing the stairs.

Upon reaching the first floor landing, I nodded at a dignified silver-haired couple on their way downstairs. To break the tension of the situation, I smiled and said hello (just another man carrying a drunk woman up some stairs). In reply, the husband raised a snooty eyebrow, but the wife flashed me a whisper of a smile. Being in great cardiovascular shape has its advantages, one being that I didn't begin to perspire until halfway up the second flight of stairs. By the third flight, however, I regretted ever meeting Helen and wished I'd instead hooked up with one or two of the vapid 20-somethings.

Now breathing heavily and sweating, I climbed the final steps to the top landing and staggered to Helen's door, keys at the ready. With the sound of the turning deadbolt, Helen unexpectedly came to on my shoulder, muttering my name into my back.

"Dakota...Dakota, where are we?"

Considering the state she was in, I was impressed she remembered my name.

"Home, Helen." I opened her door, felt around and switched on a light. "I'll have you tucked into bed in no time."

"Don't leave, Dakota. Please." Her hands dangling down my back started rubbing my butt. "I'll rally, I promise."

I laughed to myself.

Rally. Sure you will.

Once inside with her, I kicked the door shut and tossed the keys on a table. I was in a typical Boston brownstone apartment. In front of me was a living room with a fireplace. A stack of wood on the hearth and a thin bed of ashes behind the screen told me it was a working fireplace, too, damn it.

There were stools lined up against a kitchen peninsula, and although the kitchen itself was tidy, it was outdated with pink Formica countertops, linoleum floors, and an antediluvian refrigerator. Something nudged me in the calf. It was Hector the cat, bunting my legs.

Gently shoving him aside with my foot, I carried Helen into the apartment. Towering bookcases, overflowing with books, formed a scholarly gauntlet down a long hallway. Once I located the bathroom, I switched on the light and finally put her down.

"Helen, can you stand on your own?" I asked.

"Yes, I think so," she said.

"Good. Brush your teeth and use the bathroom, and I'll tuck you in, okay?"

She lurched against me and kissed my cheek. "Don't leave...please...I'll rally."

While she attended to her ablutions, I went in the kitchen and poured her a glass of water. I got her some aspirins from the bathroom medicine cabinet, and met her in her bedroom.

She was sitting on a crisply made double bed. A framed print of Vermeer's *Girl with a Pearl Earring* hung over the headboard. I made Helen drink some water and swallow the aspirins, and then, with her swaying in tiny circles, I undressed her to her underwear. I draped her suit carefully over a chair back and tucked Helen under the covers. I was about to turn and leave when her eyes sprang open. She was wide awake and perfectly lucid.

"Don't leave yet, Dakota. Hold me for a while? Until I fall asleep? Please?"

"Of course," I said.

I got on the bed and spooned her. She turned on her side and kissed me for a long time.

"You're so handsome," she said. "Great Zeus, I wish I weren't so drunk! I bet you're something under those clothes—*mmm, built*—like strong, swift-footed Achilles!"

"Hush, beautiful Helen," I said. "Go to sleep."

13

KISSING AROUND

Once Helen was asleep on her side (in case she got sick again), I went out to her living room, fed the cat, downed a couple scotches, shut off the lights, locked her apartment door, and left.

Back at my hotel, Augusta—the arresting cobalt-eyed blonde who'd helped me with printing during my first morning here—waved excitedly from the front desk.

"Dr. Stevens!" she said.

"Augusta?"

"There's a message for you." She plucked an envelope out of a pigeonhole. Handing it to me, she leaned over the counter and lowered her voice. "From a girl about *my* age—one of your students, maybe? Hm?" She gave me a smile, a furtive and beguiling smile that was not learned at the Cornell School of Hotel Administration. "She came by a couple hours ago. When I told her you were out, she wrote this and asked me to—"

"Thanks, Augusta, you're a doll," I said. "I can handle it from here."

The envelope was closed, but not sealed. I opened it and headed for the elevator. The note was written on

Charles Hotel letterhead. Sally's tiny, precise handwriting took up less than half of the page:

> Dakota—
>
> Seems I missed you. Guess you're at dinner.
>
> Sorry I freaked at the tennis courts earlier. Turns out Geoff wasn't angry at all. He did ask about you, though, and whether I was cheating on him. He won't say it, but I can tell he's <u>super</u> jealous.
>
> After tennis, I had him drop me at my dorm, which is why I was able to walk over here. I wanted to see you tonight—<u>so</u> much. I feel really close to you, Dakota. I know it's only been a few hours, but I miss you already.
>
> God, I loved it when you kissed me today. You're such a good kisser! I have to see you tomorrow! Maybe I'll drop by and surprise you!
>
> I want to please you, Dakota. I'll be thinking of you.
>
> ♥ Sally xoxo ♥

When she'd stormed away after tennis, I'd worried she might run back to Dr. Malone, returning me to square one with her. But this was worse. Apparently I'd gotten in her head. Had I been *that* manipulative with the poor girl? As much as I hated to admit it, I probably had. Tomorrow I was going over to South Boston to do some actual investigating for a change, and on Saturday I'd pick up where I left off with Sally. Hopefully, her passions would cool a bit in the interim.

Folding up the letter and putting it in my jacket, I stepped wearily into the elevator and jabbed the button for my floor. It had been a long day, and I was ready to collapse into that luscious king-sized mattress upstairs. As the elevator doors closed, so did my eyes, but I was jolted awake by the doors clanking and reopening.

A long, slender hand with ruby fingernails had slipped between the doors. A tall brunette stood in the doorway. It was Special Agent Suzuki. I glanced at my watch: eleven fifteen.

"Working late, Agent Suzuki?" I said.

"Yes, forced overtime you might say."

Her hair was down. Coal-black and obscenely long, it cried out to my fingers to glide through it.

"Can we talk?" she asked.

"I was just going up to bed."

"Please? It's important."

"All right."

I followed her off the elevator. She had a messenger bag over her shoulder, and her hands were in the pockets of an open trench coat.

"I got a delightful call at home from the Director," she said. "He's pissed. Apparently you haven't submitted a report all week."

I couldn't help noticing what Suzuki was wearing: heels, tight jeans, and, underneath the trench coat, a ruby camisole that suspiciously matched her nails.

"Left your place in a hurry, I see."

"Well, have you written a report?" she asked.

"Nope," I said. "No computer."

She sighed and unzipped the messenger bag, revealing a laptop computer.

"I've been instructed to assist you in filing one—*to-night*. There's a business center in the lobby. Why don't we—"

"I've got a better idea." I gently laid my hand on the small of her back. "Let's have a nightcap. I need to talk out the case with somebody, and *then* we'll file the report—together. What do you say?"

She unconsciously sucked her cheek for a second, then turned to me with a resolute expression on her face.

"*One* drink. I mean it, Dakota."

She gulped when she said this, so I knew there was wiggle room with her one-drink limit. I raised the middle three fingers of my right hand.

"Scout's honor," I said. "And that's coming from an Eagle scout, doll."

In the hotel bar, we both had scotches to start. Immediately Jen began to unwind, and we leaned against each other in our stools at the bar. We got laughing swapping stories about cases we'd worked, and then we switched to tequila. Finally we switched to Sam Adams beer and shared a piece of Boston cream pie, which we took turns feeding each other. It was a little past one o'clock when Agent Suzuki grabbed my wristwatch to look at the time.

"Ohmigod, we've *got* to do your report, Dakota," she said. "The Director was adamant!"

"Adamant," I said. "Screw him. He's always *adamant*."

She grabbed her purse and stood. "Come on. We'll use the business center."

Out in the lobby, we discovered the business center was closed—lights off, doors locked.

"Relax, Jen." I walked us to the elevator and punched the button. "We can work in my room."

"But we're *just* doing the report, right?"

"Yes," I said. "Scout's honor."

Upstairs in the room, I hung up my jacket. Agent Suzuki put her coat and purse on the bureau, sat at the desk, and opened her laptop.

With her elegant ruby fingernails poised over the keys, she glanced at me over her shoulder. "All right, Dakota—report."

"Okay, here we go," I said. "Director Reeves—colon—Sir, the first few days of the case were eventful. On Tuesday morning, after a great run along the Charles and—"

"Get to the point, Dakota," she said, typing away.

"—an excellent full breakfast, I went over to Harvard, where I made contact with Special Agent Suzuki, a sexy, smart, hard-working asset, whom you should—"

She stopped typing and frowned at me over her shoulder. "I can't say that."

"Sure you can," I said. " 'Whom' is the objective case."

She chuckled. "Go on, Dakota."

As I dictated what had happened since I got to Cambridge, Agent Suzuki typed with her back to me, never noticing me behind her, removing my shoes and shirt, and quietly hanging up my pants. I omitted the private details about Sally's sex life from the report, and the fact that I'd kissed her.

"Is that it?" Suzuki asked.

"Yeah, read it back to me."

While she read, Agent Suzuki fashioned her long hair into a braid and draped it over one shoulder. To read the text on the screen, I had to lean forward and get very close to her neck. She wore a sweet perfume, mixed with some kind of jasmine body powder, and these smells, not to mention her shadowy cleavage in the silk camisole, knocked the wind out of me. It occurred to me that Jen might have used the Director's demand for my report as an excuse to get hastily dressed and visit me at my hotel. When she finished reading, I started massaging her shoulders. She made a long exhale, slumped into the chair, and then, catching herself, sat up straight again.

"So...what do you think?" she asked.

"Well, I think you're carrying a lot of stress in your shoulders." I kept massaging, working my thumbs down along both sides of her spine. "Your rhomboids, too, actually."

"No, Dakota...the report."

"Oh, that," I said. "It's fine. Send it."

There was a "whoosh" sound on the computer. She closed the laptop, stood and turned around to face me. By now I was wearing nothing but my undershorts and a smile. Her eyes devoured my torso. A tiny gasp escaped her lips.

"Where are your clothes?" she said.

"I took them off. It's bedtime, Agent Suzuki."

She swallowed and reached for her coat and purse.

"Don't you want to practice grappling and take downs?" I pressed on the corner of the mattress, bouncing it a few times.

"Dakota..."

"Suppose I came up to you like *this*."

Swiveling her around, I spooned her from behind and placed my hands on her ribs, against the smooth silk of her camisole. From her ribs, I slid my hands slowly up over her breasts, which stiffened and tented some of the silk between my fingers. I kissed her neck from her ear down to her collarbone, all the while gently guiding her toward the bed, until our legs touched the edge of the mattress. And then I held us there, precariously close to tipping onto the bed.

"So, Special Agent Suzuki," I said. "What would you do in this situation?"

In one smooth motion she knocked my hands off her with an upward thrust, grabbed my wrist, pivoted, and slung me over her hip with such force that I bounced across the bed and into the headboard. Pretending I'd hit my head, I groaned loudly.

"Oh, gosh! I'm so sorry, Dakota!" She crawled onto the bed in a panic. "Are you okay?"

When she got closer, I batted her arms out from under her and flipped her on her back.

"Nice one," she said.

We kissed and undressed each other in a frenzy. Once she was lying nude on her back, consuming me with her bewitching feline eyes, I clambered up the bed and kissed up her long legs from her toes. When I reached her thighs, I rose slowly to my knees, as if I were having second thoughts.

"Mm, I don't know if this is such a good idea."

"What?" she said. "Why not?"

"You're a Suzuki."

"Excuse me?"

"I've only ever ridden a Honda," I said.

A look of delight and disgust flashed across her face. Lunging at me, she clobbered me in the head with a pillow, whereupon I pretended to "die" happy, falling over and landing face-first between her breasts. She laughed so loudly, I was afraid other hotel guests would call the manager.

When she caught her breath, she lifted my head up by the chin.

"Dakota?"

"Yes, Jen?"

"Stop kidding around and start *kissing around.* Understood?"

"Perfectly." I reached for the bedside lamp to shut it off.

"No," she said, stopping me. "Leave it on."

14

NEVER AGAIN

Before I even opened my eyes, as I hovered in that normally delicious state between sleep and consciousness, there was only pain—a throbbing pain in my head, and, bonus, a steady humming pain throughout my entire body. It was as if all of my cells were screaming. Which in a sense they were—for water.

Ugh, Dakota—alcohol. Drinking. You were up all night drinking, followed by vigorous sportive exploits... with...ah, yes...the ravishing Jen Suzuki. Is she still here? Reach over. Yup, there she is. The two of you, drunk and spent, must have fallen asleep only a couple of hours ago.

And there had been drinking earlier in the evening, too. Some woman at the Border Café. Had an old-fashioned name. Penelope? No...Helen. Helen of Troy. That's right—a Classics scholar. Visions of carrying her up five flights of stairs. Is that why your legs ache? Tucked her in, fed her cat. Did you actually do all of that or did you dream it?

On the periphery of the pain, reaching my senses muffled as though through a dense fog, was a ringing sound. But not a ringing like a bell. No. This ringing sounded more like electronic bleeping. Steeling myself for an intense stabbing pain, I slit my eyes open. Light streamed in from a crack in the blackout curtains, providing just enough illumination to display the carnage in the room.

Beer bottles littered the bureau and desk. Where the beer came from, I had no idea. An open pizza box, one slice hanging precariously over the lip. Jen's ruby red camisole. A light flashed on my nightstand—the telephone. Something hard—Jen's elbow—poked me in the back.

"Ugh, *Dakota*," she moaned, "make it stop! Answer it already!"

"All right!"

I groped for the handset, knocking a beer bottle onto the rug, and finally answered the phone.

"Director Reeves," I said, "if that's you, sir, I sent my report last night, so would you please, for the love of—"

"Dakota? This is Svetlana Krüsh. I am in the lobby."

"What?" I sprang up in bed. "What time is it?"

I noticed the clock radio on the nightstand just as Svetlana said, "It is ten minutes past eight, Dakota. I thought we were meeting in the lobby at eight o'clock."

It took a moment for this to compute.

"We were—I mean *are*—yes." I swung my legs out of bed. "Sorry—overslept."

"Perhaps I should leave. I seem to have caught you at a bad time."

"No, don't leave. Give me—tell you what, have breakfast in the hotel restaurant and charge it to my room—three-one-six. I'll be down in twenty minutes or so."

Someone was knocking on my door.

"Dakota." Jen elbowed me. "The door."

"Take your time," Svetlana said over the phone. "Make it half an hour."

"Thanks," I said. "See you then."

As I hung up the phone, the knocking on the door continued. Jen grumbled. I found my pants, put them on and staggered to the door, stubbing my toe on the suitcase stand. Swearing to myself, I looked out the peephole. It was Sally. She knocked again.

"Dakota?"

"One second, Sally," I said. "I'm not dressed. Hold on." I limp-jogged back to the bed and roused Jen. "Sally's here. I need you to hide. She can't find you in here with me."

"Hide?" she said. "Where?"

"Behind the blackout curtain," I said.

"Jesus," she whispered, "I'm not dressed, Dakota."

"Please, Jen. Just for two minutes. I'll get rid of her fast, I promise."

"What time is it?" she asked.

"Like quarter after eight," I said.

"All right, but be quick about it."

As she sprang out of the bed, I guided her behind the blackout curtain, admiring her nude body in the light.

"I'm really starting to regret coming over last night," she said, tightly squinting her eyes shut.

"Shh. Quiet. Two minutes, I promise. Try not to squint, by the way. We don't want you to get crow's feet."

"*Crow's feet*...you assh—"

I kissed her and snapped the curtain closed. I looked around for a shirt, couldn't find one, and had to hurry to the door and open it shirtless.

"Jeez, took you long enough," Sally said.

She started to come inside, but I pushed her back. Seeing my naked torso, she smiled—a smile that rapidly disintegrated into a scowl.

"Ohmigod, do you have a *woman* in there?" she said.

"Don't be ridiculous," I said. "I just drank too much last night. I haven't showered or anything, and the room's a mess. Let me meet you downstairs in half an hour."

"I can't," she said. "I have to get to class. At least let me use your bathroom. Please?" She shrugged off her knapsack. "Hold this for me?"

"Fine."

Unsure if there was something in the bathroom that might give Jen and me away, I tentatively flipped on the bathroom light. I was relieved to see only my personal articles. As soon as Sally went inside and shut the door, I remembered the keychain wallet in her planner. She had a key labeled "Geoff's" in there. Since I was going over to Boston today, I could search Malone's apartment.

Quickly I turned on the foyer light, unzipped the knapsack, removed and opened her planner, slid the "Geoff's—2468" key out of the keychain wallet, pocketed the key, put everything away, and switched off the light again—in less than a minute. When the toilet flushed and Sally re-emerged, I opened the door to the hallway.

"Okay, have a nice day, Sally."

"Uh-uh, not yet." She slithered her arms around me. "I want a kiss first. I didn't sleep at all last night. I kept thinking about our kiss yesterday. Kiss me, Dakota. And tell me again what you said yesterday…you know, how I'm beautiful and smart."

"I haven't brushed my teeth yet, Sally," I said.

"I don't care."

With half of her face glowing from the hallway light, and the other half in shadow, I whispered into her ear those things she wanted to hear, and kissed her firmly and long on the lips.

"Okay, time to go." I put the knapsack on her. "Get to class, young lady."

"Can I see you later?"

"Sorry. I'm working today."

She pouted. "And I have to work tomorrow. Hmm… but"—her face brightened—"maybe you could come over to the lab? Saturday's a big day for the study. It'll be packed. Will you come?"

"Maybe," I said.

"Can I call you later?"

"Sure, I'd like that."

Bouncing on her tiptoes, she pecked me on the lips.

"Hey, one last thing," she said.

"What?"

"I saw that woman Svetlana downstairs when I came in. Is she here to see you?"

"Yes. She's helping me with my research."

"Just research?" she said. "You promise?"

"Just research, Sally."

She hugged me again. I kissed her on the forehead and nudged her into the hall. Closing the door, I glanced out the peephole. Sally stepped onto the elevator, the doors closed, and she was gone. Back to Jen.

For one instant of clarity, during which I thankfully didn't feel hungover at all, it occurred to me that I hadn't had to juggle women like this since my sophomore year in college, when I had a different girlfriend on each floor of my dorm. Smiling to myself, then feeling the hangover return with a vengeance, I rescued Jen from behind the blackout curtain.

Groaning, she held her head by the temples and sat unsteadily on the edge of the bed. I rustled up some aspirins for her and a bottle of water from the mini-fridge, then got the "Hers" hotel robe out of the armoire and slipped it on her.

"Ugh, Dakota, I feel awful," she said.

"Yeah, me too. Sorry." I rubbed her back. "Guess we blew off some steam last night, huh?"

"I guess so." She snorted a laugh, then grimaced and held her head. "How much did we drink?"

"A lot. In the bar we each had like five shots and a couple of beers. And up here"—I waved a hand at the hotel room—"more beer."

"Beer? Where'd we get it?"

"I don't know. Room service maybe?"

"Ugh," she said. "And is that…a *pizza*?"

"Yes."

"Did I imagine it," she said, "or were you *kissing* Sally a minute ago?"

"A friendly kiss goodbye," I said. "I'm trying to lure her away from Dr. Malone, Jen. I have to show the girl a *little* affection."

"Okay, okay, stop shouting." She stared at the rug and shook her head. "Oh, God…that report we wrote for you last night. Did we send it to the Director?"

"Yeah, we did."

She groaned again. "All of that stuff about you calling me sexy…I can't remember if I left it in the report. Well, at least we sent it from—oh, crap! We used *my* computer, didn't we? And *my* email address?"

"Yeah? So what?"

She turned to me with an angry, nauseated look on her face.

"So what?" she said. "I'll tell you *so what*—I sent that email from here at like one thirty in the morning. If the Director looks at the email header, he'll—"

"Relax," I said. "Director Reeves is *not* going to look at the header on your email."

She put her face in her hands. "Damn it…what was I thinking? I knew you were nothing but trouble. But the Director made me come over, and—"

"Hey, Jen," I said, "I didn't force you to stay."

"You think I don't know that? I'm just as much to blame for this as you are." She guzzled some water. "Dakota, do you really want to know what those women in D.C. said about you? They called you 'The Hot Mess'— that you're smart and funny and crazy good-looking, but you have this cloud of chaos and poor choices around you, and every woman who gets involved with you makes *bad* decisions and loses her self-respect."

I rubbed her back quietly for a few seconds.

"But," I finally said with a shrug, "we had fun, didn't we?"

She raised her head and smiled. For a millisecond her hangover seemed to go away like mine had earlier.

"A lot of fun, Dakota."

"Me too."

We kissed, until Jen suddenly pulled away and swayed. "Whoa, head rush," she said. "I feel like I'm still...*drunk*. Is that even possible?"

"Unfortunately, yes. Listen, I have to meet someone downstairs in a few minutes. Why don't you call into the office and go in later? Stay here for a bit and sleep it off."

"I'm working a major Charlestown bank case right now, so I really shouldn't. But I'd better." She sighed and crawled back into bed. "I'm in no shape to *drive*, much less work."

I put the covers over her and stroked her hair until she fell asleep. Then I took four aspirin, chugged a bottle of water and a can of Orangina, showered, and dressed. Jotting a funny note to Jen, I propped it by her pillow, got my keys and wallet, put the "DO NOT DISTURB" sign on the door, slipped on my sunglasses, and left.

Downstairs, the lobby was empty, but I heard commotion in the restaurant. I went inside. A group of salesmen were having a breakfast meeting. I deduced they were salesmen because they all wore suits and, like a group of stand-up comics, they were all trying to talk over each other. Several of the men were staring at someone across the dining room. One of the men called out, "Hey miss! You look lonely over there all by yourself. Wanna join us?"

"No, thank you," the woman said.

The woman was Svetlana Krüsh, in jeans, boots and a slinky crimson sweater under a brown suede jacket. The sweater had a big white "H" across the chest. On the floor beside her chair was one of those designer handbags—Coach, Gucci, I couldn't tell which—and she wore a pair of oversized sunglasses, so I couldn't see her eyes.

"C'mon, sweetheart," the man persisted, "there's plenty of room over here. We'll make a space for you."

"Yeah," said another man. "On my lap!"

The entire table laughed. My instinct was to walk up to the guy who made the "lap" comment and pound his face into his Belgian waffle, but I stopped myself. My hangover had caused my usually cool, composed demeanor to call in sick today, leaving me short-tempered. I looked at Svetlana. If the man's comment had bothered her, she didn't show it; she was calmly eating her steak and eggs. I walked up to the table of salesmen, stood at the end and stared silently at them until they shut up. Then I joined Svetlana, asking a passing waitress to bring me a tall Bloody Mary and a bottle of Tabasco sauce.

"But, sir," she protested, "we're not allowed to make drinks this early."

I glanced at her name tag and handed her a twenty-dollar bill. "Please, Gabrielle? It's an emergency."

"I'll see what I can do," she whispered.

As I sat down across from Svetlana, she gestured at the table. "I took the liberty of ordering breakfast for you. Since you are clearly an athletic type, I assumed you would prefer the 'heart healthy' option."

On the placemat in front of me was an egg white omelette with toast and potatoes.

"This is perfect," I said. "Thanks."

The omelette, which contained tomato, spinach, onion and mushroom, was excellent. As I was eating, the hangover nausea surged through me again. I groaned. Svetlana sat up in her chair with her hands folded on her lap.

"Late night?" she said.

"Something like that."

Gabrielle the waitress arrived with the Bloody Mary and the Tabasco sauce. She whispered into my shoulder as she placed them in front of me.

"One Bloody Mary, sir," she said. "With *extra* vodka."

"Gabrielle...you're an angel." I shook Tabasco into the glass.

"Hope you feel better," she said.

"So do I. Thanks."

She glided her fingers down my arm as she walked away. I shook more Tabasco into the glass.

"That is quite a lot of hot sauce," Svetlana said, glancing up from her plate.

"It helps me sweat out the impurities."

I stirred the drink and took long sips of it.

"Impurities?" Smiling faintly, she speared a piece of rare steak and twirled it on her fork. "Please forgive my curiosity, Dakota, but is this your status quo?"

"What? No, not at all," I said. Then I thought about what Jen had said—how other women referred to me as "The Hot Mess"—and revised my answer. "Well...not very often."

She ate the piece of steak, then reached out with her leg and tapped my calf with her boot.

"May I make another observation?" she said.

"Sure, go ahead—I can take it." I sipped the Bloody Mary with one hand and ate the omelette with the other.

"Do you think it wise to be drinking during a case involving the daughter of a close friend of the FBI Director?"

"No," I said. "It's very *un*wise. Stupid, actually."

"And the woman I heard in the background when I called you?" she said. "That was not young Sally, I hope."

"God, of course not," I said. "That was an FBI agent from the Boston office. She's helping me with the case."

"Helping you…at eight-ten in the morning?" Svetlana said.

"We were up all night writing a report together."

I drank the rest of the Bloody Mary and put the glass down. The ice cubes rattled. I sighed, nodded crisply.

"Well, Svetlana, you're hearing it first. Never again."

"What never again?" she said.

"Drinking while on a case—never again," I said. "That's my new policy. *After* a case, to celebrate or drown my sorrows? Sure. But *during* a case? No way."

Svetlana sliced off another piece of steak. "A very sound decision."

We finished our breakfast in silence. When I signed the check, the loudmouth from the big table—the one who had made the "sit on my lap" comment—piped up again, this time cupping his hands around his mouth.

"Hey, miss…what's the 'H' stand for? 'Hottie, Hussy, or Hooker'?"

The entire table of men laughed. I threw my napkin down.

"That's it."

I started to get up when Svetlana grabbed my wrist. Still wearing the oversized sunglasses, she turned to the man who had made the comment and beckoned him over with a finger. The man, grinning to his buddies, shoved out his chair and swaggered over. A tall, heavyset guy, he wore a disheveled off-the-rack suit. He was over 250 pounds, but I could tell from the heavy jowls under his chin that it was mostly flab. I was aching to punch him in the face and see those jowls jiggle like Jell-O.

"Yeah, little lady?" he said. "What can I do you for?"

"What is your name?" Svetlana asked softly.

"Greg," he said. "Why?"

"And your last name?"

"Dwyer," he said.

"Greg Dwyer…very good. And where do you live?"

"Framingham, Mass," he said. "Why…you wanna go out or something sometime?"

"Actually, no," she said. "You see, Greg Dwyer, my father is Oleksander Krush. Perhaps you have heard of him? The head of the Ukrainian Mob in New York City? When I tell him that Greg Dwyer from Framingham, Massachusetts publicly disrespected me, he will almost certainly send some very big men to have a chat with you. Goodbye."

Instantly all of the color drained out of Greg's face. Sweat beaded up on his brow. I'd questioned a lot of suspects and witnesses in my time, and not one of them ever exhibited these physiological responses so quickly. Greg loosened his tie.

"Listen...lady...I was only joking around, I swear. I didn't mean to—"

Svetlana hissed something at him in a language I didn't recognize—it might have been Russian or Ukrainian—causing the man to stagger backwards and bump into the table behind him, as if a witch had just cast a spell on him. Even though I didn't understand what she said, the viciousness of her tone made the hairs on my neck stand up.

"I'm sorry!" Greg said, backing away. "Really, I am! Please, I have kids!"

At his table, the man whispered something to the others. Within seconds they all got up and left.

"*Voilà*," Svetlana said, waving at the now empty dining room. "See...no need for violence."

"No, just the threat of it." I smiled and shook my head. "Impressive. But...what you said about Oleksander Krush being your father—is that true? Your father is *the* Oleksander Krush?"

She nodded. "He is a card I never play...unless I am faced with a lout who refuses to leave me alone. Only then do I exercise the nuclear option. As you can see, it is quite effective."

"Yes it is," I said. "So, are you ready to do some investigating?"

"I am and have been looking forward to it. Are you feeling better?"

"Some. The food helped." I stood and dropped my napkin on the table. "Let's get to work."

15

Tommy O'Toole, P.I.

Outside beneath the hotel *porte cochère*, I handed a valet the ticket for my car. When my Mercedes pulled up to the curb with its embarrassingly flatulent exhaust, the valet looked like he wanted to comment on it. At first I considered silencing him with a deftly palmed ten-dollar bill, but since I was running out of cash, I gave him a mean look instead. A mean look was cheaper, and with my sunglasses and hangover, I wasn't running out of them anytime soon.

Once Svetlana got in, I set out for South Boston. I needed to search the office of the dead PI. Every time I accelerated, the muffler blared and Svetlana slid down a little more in her seat.

"My, what a lovely automobile," she said.

"Hey, be nice," I said. "This was my grandfather's. It's vintage."

Svetlana held her purse on her lap. A biography peeked out of the top. The spine read, "*Tragic Genius: The Brilliance and Madness of American Chess Wunderkind Paul Morphy*." I nodded at the book. "I thought you Soviets scoffed at American players."

"I used to," she said, "but I am American now. So, tell me again—what is it we do today?"

"We're gaining illegal entry to an office," I said. "The office of the PI who preceded me."

"I see," she said. "And by 'gaining illegal entry,' you mean…"

"Breaking and entering," I said.

"Ah. Then it is a good thing I wore my *incognito* outfit."

"You mean the sunglasses?"

"Yes, and this." She fished a long silk scarf out of her handbag, draped it over her head and tied it in a bow under her chin. "Tell me about the PI who preceded you. Why are you on the case now? Was he fired?"

"No, murdered," I said.

"Murdered?"

"Afraid so. Why, would you like me to take you back?"

"No," she said, "but if the PI is dead, why are you searching his office?"

"I need to see if there's a connection between his murder and Dr. Malone."

"Yes, which reminds me." She reached into her purse and pulled out a note. "*Doctor* Malone invited me to his lab tomorrow, to observe his 'study.' I was going to throw this away, but perhaps you would like to accompany me? If Sally is there, you could drive a wedge between her and Malone."

"That's a great idea," I said. "She's working at the lab tomorrow. I take it you're not busy."

"That is correct. I have no engagements until the evening, when the chess team will be playing a charity exhibition match against Yale."

"Okay, let's do it. But this morning, South Boston."

On our way past the MIT campus, I told her about my studying chemistry and criminalistics there, then going to work for the FBI. As we continued down Mass Ave into Boston, I described a few of the major cases I worked on while with the Bureau, including the infamous Hagerstown Kidnapping case. With both of us wearing sunglasses, I couldn't tell if Svetlana was listening to me until I stopped talking and she said, "I envy you, Dakota. You have been free to have a far more adventurous career than I."

Svetlana proceeded to tell me how she was raised from the age of three to become a chess champion, and how, until recently, her father Oleksander had controlled her career with an iron fist. I glanced at her. This woman was manifestly beautiful and brilliant, not to mention internationally famous, but she envied *me*. Something about her demeanor told me that, deep-down, she was very sad and craving a change in her life.

When we reached South Boston, I was amazed at how gentrified the neighborhood had become. Places where I remembered burned-out storefronts and junk-ridden vacant lots were now galleries and cafés, bistros and real estate offices. And the sidewalks, formerly garbage-strewn, were pristine.

I found the office of "TOMMY O'TOOLE, P.I." in a brick building on the corner of E Street and West Broadway. I parked across the street and looked the place over. The faded lettering on the entrance awning said this business had been here a long time—perhaps as far back as the 1970s—and the encroaching trendy eateries said that if Mr. O'Toole hadn't been murdered, he soon would have been priced out of this location. I patted my pocket to be sure I had my lock picking set, and nudged Svetlana.

"Ready?" I said.

"That is the establishment?" she said.

"Yes."

"You seem to be feeling better."

"I am. The hangover's still there, but it's kind of in the background, and the Tabasco is making me sweat."

"Delightful," she said. "Now what exactly am *I* doing?"

"You're keeping lookout while I pick the lock."

"Oh, goody."

We got out and crossed the street. The entrance door was in a shady alcove, so I couldn't see the doorway clearly until we were beneath the awning. The doorway was composed of two side-by-side glass doors, the metal handles of which had been chained together and locked with four heavy padlocks. Ordinarily I'd welcome the challenge of picking four locks, but today I felt like a hit-and-run victim. I stopped in my tracks and breathed out the first part of a naughty word. I sounded like a tire leaking air.

"What?" Svetlana raised her sunglasses, saw the snarl of chains and locks. "Oh. This is problem, yes?"

"Yeah, it's a problem, but"—I deepened my voice to sound like Arnold Schwarzenegger—"I'll be *back*."

Svetlana stared blankly at me.

"*The Terminator*?" I said. "Don't tell me you've never seen that movie."

"I have not."

I shook my head. "Your loss."

We drove around for an hour before I found a hardware store, where I bought the biggest pair of bolt cutters they had. When we returned to O'Toole's office, however, the inside lights were on, the front door was open, and the chains and locks were gone.

"Shoot."

I glanced at the bolt cutter handles jutting between the front seats. Svetlana tapped the handles and made a pouty frown.

"And you were *so* looking forward to using them," she said.

"As a matter of fact, I was." I thumped the steering wheel and opened my door. "Come on, let's go talk to whoever's in there. Maybe it's O'Toole's partner."

We crossed the street and walked inside the office. All the way in the back, a white-haired woman was pulling files from a filing cabinet and tossing them on a desk. Each time she did it, the files made a loud slap.

"Hello?" I said. "Ma'am?"

The woman didn't hear me. She just kept pulling files and dropping them on the desk.

"Excuse me, ma'am?" I continued toward the back. "Could we speak with you? Ma'am?"

Svetlana leaned into my shoulder. "She seems hard of hearing, Dakota."

"Seems?"

We walked slowly down the middle of the room. Halfway toward the back, I bumped into a chair. It screeched against the floor. When I looked up next, the old woman was leveling a sawed-off double-barrel shotgun at us. Instinctively I stepped in front of Svetlana with my hands raised.

"Who the hell are you?" the woman shrieked. "State your business!"

"Ma'am," I shouted, "this woman and I are private detectives! We need to ask you a few questions about a case Mr. O'Toole was working on! Lower the gun, please!"

"Detectives, eh?" She partially lowered the shotgun. "Let's see some ID. Right quick—on the desk there."

"Yes, ma'am." I slowly reached into my jacket, pulled out the Mass PI license and tossed it on the desk. She doddered toward us and peered down at the license. With a nod, she laid the shotgun on the desk and sat in the chair.

"All right, Dakota Stevens," she said. "What do you want?"

"Well, first, ma'am…may I ask who you are?"

"I'm Mrs. O'Toole," she said.

"We're very sorry for your loss," I said.

I pulled up chairs for Svetlana and myself. When we sat down, I explained to Mrs. O'Toole that after her husband's murder, Mr. Standish had hired me to take over the Malone investigation. For a second I wasn't sure she'd heard me because she just sat there.

I was about to repeat myself, louder this time, when she slumped over in her chair and began to sob. While I went over and patted her shoulder, Svetlana disappeared into a back room and returned with tissues and a glass of water. She handed them to Mrs. O'Toole and sat down again.

"Oh, you're a dear," she said to Svetlana. "Sorry, young man, but I'm still grieving."

"I understand, ma'am. Let me ask you, do you think Malone is behind your husband's death?"

"Oh, yes, definitely." She blew her nose and sipped some water. "But I can't prove it, of course."

"Did your husband obtain any evidence the police don't know about?" I asked.

"Yes indeedy, he did." With surprising spryness, she sprang out of the chair and tottered to the back of the office. She rifled through a desk drawer, pulled out a photo and returned to Svetlana and me.

"The night before he was killed, he entered Malone's apartment and took this picture. I think it's a page from one of those Franklin planners, you know the kind I mean?"

"I do," I said. "May I see the picture, please?"

She handed it to me. It was a close-up of a day planner page from early September, with a handwritten list of items in the "NOTES" section:

1. perky brunette, very short hair, nose and tongue piercings

2. Asian girl with long hair (very black hair), athletic

3. young Jane Fonda lookalike

4. debutante, society-type girl; tall, long legs, nice posture

5. mousy brunette, glasses, petite; saddle shoes

~~& short skirt~~

~~6. buxom girl, early 20s, blonde, like a German barmaid~~

7. pale-skinned redhead with pale blue eyes, foreign accent

~~8. female athlete, hardbody type; blonde or Latina~~

"Strange." I handed it to Svetlana. "Mrs. O'Toole... what did your husband think of it?"

She shrugged. "Tommy never mentioned it. But Malone's been doing that Sexual Attractiveness Study around the country, right? Maybe the girls on this list were ones he observed during one of the sessions."

"Maybe," I said. "The thing is, this page was dated early September. It's doubtful Malone's study was up and running that soon."

Svetlana handed the photo back to me. "Yes," she said, "it would take him time to acquire subjects."

"Good point," Mrs. O'Toole said. "What do you think it is then?"

"I'm not sure," I said. "But the fact that this was in a day planner might be significant."

"What do you mean?" she asked.

"Well, if these were observations taken during one of his sessions, they'd probably be in a lab notebook. They'd include other details, too, like the girls' behavior. Also, I'm not sure why half the entries are crossed out."

Mrs. O'Toole drank some more water. When she put the glass down again, she smiled grimly and nodded.

"You seem like you know what you're doing, Mr. Stevens. Are you a good detective?"

"I was good when I was with the Bureau," I said, "but I'm fairly new to private work."

She looked at Svetlana. "And what about you, dear?"

"I am a professional chess player," Svetlana said.

Mrs. O'Toole tapped the stock of the shotgun. "Sorry I pulled this on you when you came in."

"It's understandable," I said. "But you really shouldn't be here alone."

"My nephew's coming this afternoon with a truck to help me clean the place out."

"That's good." I held up the photo of the list. "May I keep this, ma'am?"

"Yes, on one condition," she said. "If you find out Malone killed my husband, you have to promise me you'll take him down."

"I'll do my best, Mrs. O'Toole."

"Okay, take it then. And be careful, you two."

"We will, ma'am," I said. "Thank you."

Svetlana said goodbye to Mrs. O'Toole and we returned to the car. For the first part of our ride back to Cambridge, the two of us were quiet, but when we passed the Christian Science Church on Mass Ave, I glanced at the photo of the list again and had an epiphany. I tossed the photo on Svetlana's lap.

"What do you make of it?" I asked.

"It does not read like a list of girls Malone observed," she said.

"No, it doesn't."

"It reads like—"

"—a wish list," I said.

"No, Dakota." Svetlana slowly turned to me and removed her sunglasses. A look of horror shone in her eyes. "A *shopping* list."

A fresh wave of the hangover nausea, combined with a sensation of dread, came over me.

"Damn, I think you're right," I said. "When people go shopping and find something on their list, what do they do?"

"Cross the item out," she said.

"Right," I said. "One of the girls on the list sounds a lot like Sally Standish. Read number five aloud, would you?"

Svetlana picked up the photo. " 'Mousy brunette, glasses, petite; saddle shoes and short skirt.' "

Even though my head was sweating from the Tabasco, a tingling chill cascaded down my neck and back. Somehow I knew, without a scintilla of doubt, that the "mousy brunette" described was Sally Standish, and that she was in danger. I had no idea what *kind* of danger she was in though. I needed evidence. Good thing I had Malone's key in my pocket.

At Boylston Street, I veered sharply toward downtown.

"Where are we going?" Svetlana asked.

"The North End," I said. "It's time to take a closer look at Dr. Malone."

16

A Time-Honored Secret of the Detecting Trade

Few city neighborhoods are more problematic for a detective than Boston's North End. It's a maze of narrow streets with no parking, and many of the buildings, including Malone's, have been converted to lofts with solid steel doors at the entrances.

After spotting Malone's building, we had to drive all the way to the Old North Church before we found a parking spot. Then, as we walked back along the main drag of Hanover Street, all of the old Italian men at the sidewalk cafés rubbernecked watching Svetlana pass.

This was another problem with Boston's North End: it's an insular community where outsiders—especially exotically beautiful outsiders like Svetlana—are conspicuous. Suddenly I questioned the wisdom of bringing her along.

I bought a box of latex gloves at a pharmacy, and when we finally reached Malone's building, I discovered that the key from Sally's planner didn't fit the outside door.

"What now, detective?" Svetlana said.

"Watch and learn, Miss Krüsh. You're about to witness a time-honored secret of the detecting trade. Ready?"

"Yes."

I paused for effect, then swiped my hand down all the intercom buttons. Svetlana stifled a laugh. The speaker blared with six different voices asking, "Who is it?" I replied with gibberish, and the door buzzed open.

"*Voilà.*" Waving Svetlana inside, I glanced at the intercom directory. "He's in unit four-A."

The staircase was wide and metal, and the building seemed to have once been a factory or warehouse. When we reached the fourth floor landing, we were faced with two giant sliding steel doors, about twenty feet apart. Neither one was labeled, so I couldn't tell which one was unit A and which was B. I tried the key in the lock of the first one, but it didn't fit. I pointed at the other door.

"*That* must be unit A," I said.

"Amazing deduction, Holmes," Svetlana said.

I sneered at her. I knocked on the door a few times, waited, and inserted the key in the lock. Pocketing my sunglasses, I opened the box of latex gloves and slipped on a pair.

"Here," I said, handing her the box, "put on a pair and stow the box in your purse."

I unlocked the door, removed the key, and, with a deep breath, heaved the door open. We walked inside, and I quickly slid the door shut behind us. The entryway was dim, but right next to my shoulder was a flashing light. It was the control panel for an alarm system. The LCD read, "ARMED—ENTER CODE TO DISARM."

Adding to the good news, the display was counting down from 30.

"Uh-oh," I said.

"Uh-oh?"

"I didn't think his apartment would be alarmed. Who puts an alarm in their *apartment*?"

The counter reached 20.

"Someone who has valuables or secrets he does not want others to find," Svetlana said. "Do you not know the code?"

"No, well"—I thought for a moment and remembered the notation in the keychain wallet—"I might, actually."

The counter was down to 9. On the panel, I pressed "2-4-6-8" and "DISARM." There was a beep, and the LCD now read, "DISARMED—ENTER CODE TO ARM."

"That was close," I said.

"What are we looking for exactly?" Svetlana asked.

I shrugged. "A diary. A computer. Phone records. Anything unusual or that relates somehow to the list Mrs. O'Toole gave us, or to his sexual attraction study. It's hard to say. We'll search each area together. As much as possible, try not to disturb objects. If you do pick something up, put it back exactly where you found it— make sure the dust lines match up, okay?"

"Understood."

As I took a step into the loft, Svetlana put a hand on my arm.

"Dakota? Thank you for bringing me along today," she said.

"A bit more exciting than the Nimzo-Indian Defense, right?" I said.

She nodded. "Quite. My legs are trembling."

"That's the adrenaline, kid," I said. "Take slow, deep breaths and you'll be fine. All right, let's do this." I led the way inside.

The apartment wasn't what I'd expected. Instead of a vast open space like a typical loft, this one was much smaller, maybe 25′ by 25′. Instead of giving the place a hip, trendy feel, its exposed brick walls and wood beams, and its steel support columns and unfinished floors made it seem like a dungeon; the only things missing were a medieval rack and shackles chained to the walls.

There were two windows—one on the left, which looked out on the street, and another one at the far end of the space, which looked out on another building. Running diagonally between the far corner of the room and the entrance was a ceiling track.

One thing that stood out was the dearth of furniture. In the living area were one leather couch and an HDTV. The bedroom area had a king-sized bed, two foot lockers for nightstands, a small bureau, and a rolling clothes rack that held a few men's suits and some petite dresses. The kitchenette contained a small refrigerator, stove, microwave, and a breakfast table. The bathroom—the only walled-off space in the apartment—had a toilet, sink and corner shower.

On the far end of the loft was an office area, with a bare desk and chair, a bean-bag, a stack of newspapers, and a steel storage cabinet. The storage cabinet was locked. Taking out my lock-picking set, I was about to pick the lock when Svetlana pulled some kind of cord out of the far corner of the room and walked toward me holding it. As she pulled it, the ceiling track made a scraping sound.

"What is this for?" she asked.

It was an 8- or 10-foot steel cable with one end attached to the ceiling track and a padlock dangling from the other end. At first I had no idea what purpose the cable served, but then I remembered the metal ring on Sally's BDSM collar, and the picture became painfully clear: Malone would lock the cable to the ring on Sally's collar, leaving her chained up like a dog. The sadistic bastard probably left her like that for hours, days even.

Anger, along with a fresh dose of my hangover, swelled up in me. Suddenly lightheaded, I had to steady myself on the storage cabinet.

"Are you okay?" Svetlana asked.

"Yeah, I'll be fine," I said. "I don't think I told you this, but…Sally has one of those 'BDSM' collars. I think that cable connects to it."

Scoffing in disgust, Svetlana pinched the cable gingerly in her fingers and flung it back into the corner.

"This place disturbs me, Dakota," she said. "I want to leave now."

"We can't," I said. "We haven't found anything yet. Tell you what…start searching the desk while I check this cabinet."

"Very well."

I started picking the cabinet door lock. These locks are much easier to pick than door locks, and I had it open in thirty seconds. Office supplies filled the top shelves.

On the middle shelf were a small, insulated cooler and an international express shipping label. Lastly, on the bottom shelf, were a couple banker's boxes containing older versions of Malone's Sexual Attraction Survey flyer from previous colleges. Jammed in the boxes were also dozens of folders containing questionnaires and study applications. Attached to the folders were headshots of the applicants. All of them happened to be young women.

I took out my digital camera. There wasn't enough time to document all of the applications, so I photographed only the first ten. As I was putting the boxes away, I brushed against a black cloth and discovered it was covering a mini-fridge inside the cabinet. There was a padlock on the fridge. Why would someone lock a refrigerator? My curiosity aroused, I started picking the lock.

"Svetlana," I said over my shoulder, "how are you making out over there?"

"Excellent. I found a flash drive hidden in one of the drawers. The files are encrypted, so I am decrypting them now."

"What?!"

I spun around to see Svetlana standing over a notebook-sized computer on the bare desk. The screen was filled with a bunch of settings and flashing letters and numbers that made no sense to me.

"Where'd you get the computer?" I asked.

"Where do you think?" she said. "My handbag."

Finished picking the padlock, I opened the mini-fridge. Inside was only one item: a tray containing twenty test tubes sealed with rubber stoppers. Fourteen of the test tubes were filled with a purple liquid. During my tenure with the FBI Lab, I'd done enough serological work to recognize blood when I saw it. I snapped a photo of the entire tray, then quickly photographed each test tube. Each of the fourteen test tubes had a single label with two initials on it.

"Done," Svetlana said behind me. "What have you found? Anything?"

"Blood."

"Blood?"

"Yeah, I'm pretty sure, but never mind that right now." I put the tray away, shut the fridge and stepped over to Svetlana. "Show me what you found."

"There are fourteen folders on the flash drive," she said, "each one labeled with two initials."

"Same thing with the test tubes I found. Go on."

"As you can see"—she double-clicked on the computer touchpad—"each folder contains several photographs, and each photograph is labeled with the same initials as the folder, plus a number. For example, in this case we have 'T.G. One,' 'T.G. Two' and so on."

"Interesting," I said. "One of the test tubes of blood over there is labeled 'T.G.' Bring up the photos."

She selected all of the photos in the "T.G." folder and opened them. The photos were all of a curvaceous, dark-haired young woman. The first few were photos taken covertly from a distance, like surveillance shots. In the other photos—which looked like stills from a closed-circuit camera—the young woman was nude, looking at someone or something else off-screen. Svetlana put a hand on mine. Hers was shaking.

"I very much want to leave, Dakota."

"First of all, Svetlana, relax." I pinched open my coat, revealing my gun. "I'm a trained FBI Special Agent, my dear. Nothing's going to harm you. Not while I'm around." I gave her a consoling wink. "Second, *this* is precisely when we need to slow down and be ultra-methodical. Let me ask you—did you copy these folders over to your laptop?"

She nodded.

"Good," I said. "Then put the flash drive back *exactly* where you found it, and then I need you to go to the pharmacy for me."

"The pharmacy? Why?"

"There's no time to explain." I pulled out my pocket notebook and pen. "Here, I'll make you a list."

While she put the flash drive away, I wrote out a list, tore off the sheet and handed it to her.

"Leave your laptop," I said. "And hurry."

Shouldering her purse, she walked briskly out of the apartment. I opened the other folders on the computer and glanced at the photos inside. Like the first one, each folder contained surveillance photos and nude stills. Closing the computer, I rummaged through the rest of the desk, but didn't find anything. I gave the rest of the apartment a cursory search, checking first for obvious traps like slips of paper wedged in drawers or strands of hair across cabinet doors, but I didn't find anything.

Finally it was time get things ready for Svetlana's return. I removed a newspaper from the bottom of the stack and spread it out on the desk. I'd just moved Svetlana's laptop aside when she returned, closing the apartment door behind her.

"Good, you're back," I said. "Bring everything to the desk, please."

She put the bag down and let out a deep breath.

"Fourteen eyedroppers," she said, "medical tape, Ziploc bags, blood typing kit, two instant ice packs, lunch cooler, and one fine-tipped Sharpie pen."

"Good show, Svetlana." As I emptied the bag, I pulled out an item with "Revlon" printed on the cardboard backing. "What's this?"

"*This* is a new mascara," she said, snatching it away. "It spoke to me."

"You took time to shop for *makeup*?"

"I did not *shop*." She batted her eyes. "It simply jumped into my basket."

"Fine," I said. "Not that you need it. You have the lushest eyelashes I've ever seen."

She smiled. "Now, what are you doing with all of this, and how can I help?"

I took the tray of test tubes out of the mini-fridge and set it on the desk.

"First, using the eyedroppers, I'm going to take a tiny sample from each of these test tubes," I said. "You can help by tearing off pieces of medical tape. Each time I take a sample from a new test tube, I'll say the initials out loud. Please write those initials on a piece of tape, put the tape on a Ziploc bag, and I'll place the eyedropper in that bag. You then seal the bag and put it in the cooler. When we're finished, crack the instant ice packs and place them on top of the Ziploc bags. But don't open the blood typing kit yet—that's for later. Okay?"

Nodding, she opened the medical tape, Ziploc bags and Sharpie pen, and laid everything in front of her.

"You may begin, doctor," she said.

"All right," I said. " 'T.G.' "

Uncorking the test tube, I laid the rubber stopper carefully on the newspaper, tilted the test tube to the side, and sucked up enough blood in the eyedropper to reach the 1 ml mark. I returned the test tube to its slot in the tray and re-corked it. Finally, I sealed the nozzle end of the eyedropper with a piece of medical tape, and put it in the Ziploc bag that Svetlana held open for me.

"One down," I said. "Thirteen to go."

The first four took a good minute each, but after that Svetlana and I were a well-oiled evidence-stealing machine, completing the process on the remaining test tubes in about five minutes. While I returned the test tubes to the mini-fridge and locked it and the cabinet again, Svetlana cracked the ice packs, closed the cooler and stowed her computer and the packing refuse in her purse. I refolded the newspaper and returned it to the bottom of the stack, glanced around to make sure I hadn't forgotten anything, and entered the alarm code on the panel. The alarm was now set.

Out in the hallway, I locked the door. We hurried downstairs, paused to remove our latex gloves and put our sunglasses on, and exited the building.

We stuffed our gloves and the packing refuse in a wastebasket on the corner, and instead of walking back to our car along Hanover Street, I turned us down North Bennett—little more than an alley that zigzagged through the North End. The second we were safely in the car, we looked at each other, smiled and heaved a sigh of relief.

"Exciting?" I said.

" 'Exciting' is one word for it," she said.

I patted her arm. "Good job, Svetlana. You're a natural."

"Once I got over the jitters from the adrenaline, it was rather enjoyable," she said. "My first 'B and E.' "

"Well, you performed like a pro." I started the car and pulled away. "Hey, that stuff with the computer back there. Where'd you learn that?"

"I have a degree in computer science from NYU," she said. "I knew a day might come when I did not wish to play chess professionally anymore, so I decided to expand my skillset. I was always talented in computers. I have also studied mathematics and languages."

And here I thought I my dual bachelor's degrees in chemistry and English were impressive.

"Really?" I said. "Where?"

"Several universities. Moscow State. The University of London. The American University of Paris." She held up the cooler. "So where do we take this? The police?"

"No, my alma mater," I said. "We're going to perform some tests on the samples ourselves—under the radar."

"I assume your alma mater is okay with your waltzing on campus with a cooler full of stolen blood samples."

"Nope," I said. "But my mentor will be. If he's still there, that is. It's been a while."

17

THE PRODIGAL PROTÉGÉ RETURNS

Returning to Cambridge, we parked on Memorial Drive and walked across the MIT campus from the river. Along the way, I gave Svetlana the nickel tour, pointing out buildings where I'd taken various classes, and noting to myself with a smile the building that housed my freshman English professor's office, where I'd once spent a rainy, quiet, watershed afternoon with her, receiving, shall we say, some special, private tutelage.

Then Svetlana and I entered the courtyard in front of building 18—Dreyfus—which, as a sandy brown rectangle with rows of small square windows, bore an uncomfortable resemblance to FBI headquarters in Washington, D.C. I held open the door for Svetlana, boarded the service elevator with her, and pressed the button for "B3"—the deepest bowels of the building, where my mentor used to have his office and private lab. The elevator doors closed and we slowly descended.

"So, who is this mentor of yours?" Svetlana asked.

Knowing how long the elevator ride and walk to his office would take, I told Svetlana about him. When I was an undergraduate here, I explained, MIT didn't officially have a forensic science program. What MIT *did* have was Dr. Steven Lenz, or simply "Steve" as he insisted we students call him, who would attend his colleagues' chemistry lectures and poach promising students who showed an interest in forensic science and criminalistics.

Steve had begun his academic career in the 1970s doing pure biochemistry research; but shortly after receiving tenure, he experienced a terrible tragedy: his wife and daughter were murdered. From that day on, Steve became obsessed with forensic science—not only to try to find the killer of his wife and daughter, but also to improve forensic science for law enforcement in general. Some of his early research in DNA helped to develop DNA "fingerprinting" for criminal investigations, and he had consulted for the Massachusetts State Crime Lab, the FBI, Scotland Yard and Interpol.

When the elevator doors opened, I led Svetlana down the long, dingy hallway. The air was still filled with the same acrid chemical smell that I'd come to associate with Steve and his "secret" lab.

"He sounds like a fascinating man," Svetlana said.

"He is," I said, "but don't get the wrong picture of him. He's not a typical white-haired 'mad scientist.' The guy's a total maverick. Used to drive a motorcycle. Not sure if he does anymore, but if he's still here at MIT, I'm sure he's just as much of a rule-breaker as he always was."

Our footsteps echoed in the empty hallway. I chuckled to myself remembering another aspect of Steve's personality.

"By the way, Svetlana—fair warning." I glanced in the lab windows as we passed them. "Steve was always a notorious ladies' man. He's in his late fifties now, so I'm sure he's mellowed, but don't be surprised if he flirts with you a little bit. Ah, here we are."

A cracked plastic name plaque beside the door read, "DR. STEVEN LENZ," and a card beneath it listed his office hours. Steve was scheduled to be here later this afternoon. I peered in the window on the door. Both Steve's office and his lab were dark.

"This is unfortunate." Svetlana tapped a fingernail on the office hours card. "Perhaps we should go have coffee and return when—what are you doing?"

"Getting the key," I said.

I jogged down the hall, opened the fire extinguisher locker, felt inside and removed the Hide-a-Key box.

"Should you be doing that?" she said.

"He won't mind. His favorite students always knew about this key."

"I assume you were one of his favorites."

"Yup."

I unlocked the door, stowed the key back in its hiding place, led Svetlana inside the lab, and switched on the lights. Nothing had changed.

A sprawl of lab apparatus still cluttered the stainless steel countertops. There was the same Sherlock Holmes poster on the wall—now yellowed and frayed at the corners—with famous Holmes quotes, and the same giant periodic table of elements suspended from the ceiling in the back. On the side of the lab was his adjoining office, his *sanctum sanctorum*, which we students never entered uninvited, and in the far corner of the lab was Steve's "gym"—a speed bag, heavy bag, weights, weight bench, boom box, and mats. There, Steve worked out with us while teaching us criminalistics by Socratic method.

"Wow," I said. "It's like I went out for Chinese take-out and just came back."

"Did you spend much time here as a student?" Svetlana asked.

I smiled and looked around fondly at the place. "Yeah, a lot."

Svetlana set the cooler on an empty countertop. "Should we get started?"

"Yes, let's."

I hung our jackets on hooks, taking down two lab coats for us. Once we'd slipped on the coats and some latex gloves, I laid fourteen small glass testing trays on the counter and squirted the three antibody liquids into three different cups on each tray. This took a few minutes. When I finished, I placed a notepad and pencil in front of Svetlana.

"Okay, here's what we're going to do," I said. "You're going to hand me a bag containing an eyedropper, writing down the initials of that sample. I'll test it, announce the blood type, and you write down the blood type next to the initials. All right?"

"Yes," she said, "but how does the blood typing work?"

"You really want to know?" I asked.

"Yes."

I took a deep breath and pointed at each cup on the first tray.

"These cups each contain a different antibody," I said. "Left to right, the first one is an antibody to Rh factor, the second is 'A' antibodies, and the third is 'B' antibodies. I'll be putting a drop of blood into each cup. If the blood clots in the first cup, we'll know the sample is Rh-positive. If it doesn't clot, then it's Rh-negative. Then, with the next two cups, it works like this. If the blood drop reacts only to cup number two, then the blood is type A. If it only reacts to cup number three, then it's type B. If it reacts to cups two and three…well, you tell me."

"Type 'A-B'?" she said.

"Correct," I said. "And if the drops don't react with either cups two or three, then the blood is type 'O.' Got it?"

Svetlana yawned and nodded.

"Okay," I said. "First sample."

From out in the hallway, a familiar baritone voice boomed out: "Who the *hell* is in my lab?!"

A second later, Steve walked in wearing a black leather motorcycle jacket and carrying a helmet. His hair was now silvery at the temples, but it was as thick as ever. At his side was a blonde woman, maybe 30, also carrying a helmet. Over her shoulder were a purse and a tote bag brimming with blue exam booklets. When Steve saw Svetlana and me, the stern expression on his face vanished. He beamed at me and nodded.

"The prodigal protégé returns," he said. "Gretchen, I want you to meet a former star student of mine, Dakota Stevens."

"*Former* star, my ass, Steve," I said. "I'm still a star."

Steve glanced at Gretchen, said something in German, and put his helmet on the floor. Then he turned to me, thumped his chest and extended his arms. I walked over and hugged him. He introduced Gretchen, and I introduced Svetlana. The three of them spoke some German, and then Gretchen, nodding and grinning, excused herself to Steve's office and began correcting exam booklets.

"Gretchen's a Ph.D. candidate from Austria," Steve said, turning and winking at her through the open doorway. "I'm teaching her the ropes." Without warning he grabbed me by the shoulders so I couldn't turn around. "Quick! Group zero of the periodic table! Go!"

"The noble gases," I said. "Helium, neon, argon, krypton, xenon and radon."

Squinting, he pursed his lips and gave me a nod of approval. "So what are you up to nowadays? Still at the Bureau?"

"Nope," I said.

I gave him the abridged version of my saga of starting a private detective agency.

"Yeah," he said when I finished, "you're like me, Dakota—to really thrive, you need *entropy*." He patted me on the back, slipped on a lab coat, and clapped his hands together sharply. "So, what've you brought me, young Grasshopper? What insurmountable forensic challenge? What mystery? What—"

"I need to type fourteen different blood samples," I said.

"*Fourteen* samples?" Steve said. "Are you investigating a serial killer?"

Without giving away Sally's identity, I described Dr. Malone and his "Sexual Attraction Study," and how my investigation of him had led to today's discovery of blood and photographic evidence. I finished by telling Steve that, while the evidence was circumstantial at best, it was deeply suspicious, warranting further investigation.

"Based on what you're telling me, Dakota," Steve said, "I agree it's suspicious, but…you're working from a hypothesis based on an assumption."

"What assumption, Steve?"

"That the test tubes you found contain human blood and not some other liquid that resembles human blood," he said. "Did you perform any tests to determine whether the samples are indeed human blood?"

"No, I didn't, Steve," I said. "The pharmacy was fresh out of Luminol and UV lamps, not to mention RSID readers. Besides, why would this guy keep pig's blood locked up in a mini-fridge?"

"Hey, there's no need to be testy," he said. "I'm not questioning your investigative skills, Dakota. I'm just trying to remind you to follow the process and to not make assumptions."

I sighed and leaned against a mass spectrometer. My whole body was weary.

"You're right, Steve," I said. "Sorry. I was up late last night, and I drank too much."

"Been there, done that." He patted me on the back. "C'mon kid, follow me."

Steve went to a refrigerator across the room. He pulled out a bottle of water, a beaker and a foil package of Alka-Seltzer. Pouring the water in the beaker, he dropped in the Alka-Seltzer tablets and handed me the fizzing concoction. I chugged it down.

"Thanks, Steve."

"You're welcome," he said. "Now…let's get to it."

Over at the lab table, I showed him the setup and described my plan.

"Not bad," he said. "One suggestion, though. Before you type the samples, how about I do a quick RSID strip test assay on all of the samples *first*, verifying they're human blood?"

"Good idea, Steve," I said, gesturing at the cooler. "I have been assuming these are human blood."

Steve opened a drawer and pulled out an RSID test reader, reader cassettes and a box of test strips.

"Once I get the sample on each strip, it only takes ten minutes," he said.

"I know. Go ahead."

While Steve went to work with the samples, Svetlana surveyed everything on the counter and said, "I do not understand. What will this 'RSID' test tell us that the blood typing kit will not tell us?"

"The RSID test tests specifically for human Glycophorin A," I said.

"Oh, that makes it much clearer," she said.

"Glycophorin A is a protein of the membrane of human red blood cells," I said. "If the test is positive for Glycophorin A, it means it's a human red blood cell. Steve is going to test for it, and then, any samples that come up as human blood, we'll do the typing test on them."

"Now I understand," she said. "Thank you."

I wandered over to Steve's gym area, removed my lab coat and put on a pair of practice gloves. I tried to work the speed bag, but it had been a long time since I'd used one and I couldn't find a rhythm, so I switched to the heavy bag. Punching it with rapid combinations as hard as I could, hearing and seeing the bag buckle and the chain jolt, I felt myself being purged of some of my frustrations.

I became so deeply focused on working the bag that I completely forgot where I was. It was only when Steve shouted my name that I came back to reality. I had sweat through my T-shirt.

"If you're done beating my bag to a pulp, Dakota," he said, "we're ready for you to do the typing. Your instinct was right—they're all human blood."

"Great."

I washed my face and hands, dried off, and joined Steve and Svetlana at the lab table. Svetlana handed me the first eyedropper, and I put a drop of blood from it in each of the three cups. After waiting a few seconds, there was no clotting in the first cup (the one that tested for the presence of Rh factor), so I knew the blood sample would be Rh-negative. However, there was a reaction in cups two and three, which meant the sample was reacting to both 'A' and 'B' antibodies, making it type AB.

"The first sample is A-B negative," I said.

As I went through the same tedious process for the other thirteen samples, I was reminded of why, after only a year, I'd transitioned out of the FBI Lab into fieldwork. The repetitive, painstaking nature of lab work made my mind wander. Ultimately it left me more exhausted than chasing a suspect on foot—like I'd once done across half of Pittsburgh.

CHRIS ORCUTT

Soon, the results were in: all of the samples were human blood, type AB negative. While Svetlana made sure everything was documented, and I sealed the samples and placed them in a refrigerator, Steve walked Gretchen out to the elevator. She had an appointment across campus. When he came back, he invited Svetlana and me into his office, where he poured coffee for the three of us, and we discussed our findings.

"Tell me about the photos you found," he said.

"We don't need to tell you," I said. "Svetlana, show him."

She removed her laptop from her purse and opened all of the photos in a photo viewing program.

"Now, these initials," he said, flipping through the photos. "You're sure they correspond exactly to the initials that were on the test tubes? In other words, you didn't make a mistake copying any of the test tube initials, did you?"

"No," I said. "And I have photos of the test tubes."

"And do you have *any* idea who these young women are?" he asked.

"No, not yet."

Svetlana blew on her coffee and peered over the mug at Steve.

"For the photos with a clear view of the young woman's face," she said, "I plan on doing a search based on the image. I have contacts at some internet companies that are developing reverse image search algorithms that take a sample image and scour the web for similar images. I am hopeful we will identify at least a *few* of these young women this way."

"Svetlana has a degree in computer science," I said.

"A gorgeous international chess champion *and* a computer expert?" Steve stared at her. "Svetlana, my dear, you probably already know this, but you can do way better than Dakota."

Svetlana gave me a look that was half amusement, half annoyance.

"Svetlana and I aren't an item, Steve." I sipped some coffee. "We just met the other day. But can we get back to the facts here?

"We've got fourteen sets of photos, both surveillance photos and nude video stills, of fourteen different girls. Then, locked up in close proximity to the photos we found fourteen test tubes of blood labeled with initials that correspond to the fourteen sets of photos. All of the blood is type A-B negative.

"Let's assume for now," I continued, "that each test tube of blood is a sample taken from the young woman whose photos bear the same initials. For example, the blood from the 'T.G.' test tube was taken from the young woman whose photos are labeled 'T.G.' Steve, given these parameters, I'd like your thoughts on what we're dealing with."

Steve drank some coffee and put down his mug. Then, crossing his ankles on top of his desk, he laced his fingers behind his head and stared up at the ceiling.

"It seems to me," he said, "that two facts stand out here. First, that each group of photos is labeled with the same set of initials as one of the test tubes. Second, that all of the blood samples are A-B negative—the rarest blood type there is."

"Less than one percent of the population," I added.

"Precisely," Steve said. "Now…the fact that A-B negative is so rare makes it *what*?"

"Valuable," Svetlana said.

"Correct, Miss Krüsh."

"So," I interjected, "let's continue that line of thought. Suppose Malone knows someone who is willing to pay top dollar for A-B negative blood. Once he identifies people who could serve as blood donors, he'd want to keep tabs on them, right? That would explain the surveillance photos."

"But not the nude video stills," Steve said.

"They do not fit within your hypothesis, Dakota," Svetlana said.

"Svetlana's right," Steve said. "Your theory of a person desperate for A-B negative blood doesn't account for the nude photos."

"Maybe it's not *logical*," I said, "but we could be dealing with a weirdo—either Malone or our hypothetical A-B negative blood-seeker. Maybe Malone or the 'client' just likes having nude photos of his blood donors."

"Which begs the question," Steve said, "of how Malone came to possess such photos."

"All of the stills seem to be from a ceiling-mounted camera, and the backgrounds are sterile, like…a hospital or—"

"—a psychology lab," Svetlana said, glancing at me.

"Right," I said.

Steve gazed up at the ceiling for a minute, then put his feet down, sipped some coffee and shook his head.

"There's not enough data," he said. "Listen, we're making two other major assumptions here, okay? One is that the type A-B negative blood in each test tube was *taken* from the individual whose initials are such-and-such. Right?

"But the second assumption is even slipperier—that each test tube contains blood from a different individual. We don't know that. Without a DNA workup, we *can't* know that. All we know right now is that we have fourteen samples of A-B negative blood. They could be fourteen samples of the *same* A-B negative blood."

"Steve—you're right," I said. "This is why *you* are the master." I swore and pounded the armrest on my chair.

"Easy, Grasshopper," he said. "This is easily rectified. There's enough blood left in all of the eyedroppers to run a DNA test on the samples. I can do it tonight."

"Really, Steve? I can't tell you how much—"

"No worries, kid."

"I appreciate it, Steve," I said. "While you're doing that, Svetlana and I will look into the photos and the other evidence we found in his apartment."

"I'll call you in the morning with my results," Steve said, reaching for a notepad and pencil. "What's your cell number?"

"I don't have one," I said. "I'm staying at the Charles, though. You can reach me there."

"Will do."

He sprang out of his chair, walked over and yanked me to my feet.

"Dakota, this moping around with a hangover doesn't suit you. Doctor Lenz prescribes the following: go back to your hotel, get some sleep, have a nice meal and start fresh tomorrow."

"You're right, *sensei*," I said. "I'll do all of that. But first I have to drop something off."

18

JUICY

According to the page I'd copied from her planner, Sally had intramural tennis practice again this afternoon. I needed to return Dr. Malone's apartment key to her keychain wallet before she discovered it missing and got suspicious.

Once I dropped off Svetlana, I started driving over to the tennis center when it occurred to me that I couldn't just go over there, march onto the court, and open Sally's knapsack in plain sight of everyone; I needed a reason to open her knapsack. After giving it some thought, I decided that bringing her a present would be an ideal reason.

Stopping at my hotel, I went into the gift shop, bought a boxed pair of silver and turquoise earrings and a card, and charged them to the room. I jotted a quick, flirty message on the card. Then, in the lobby phone booth I called Svetlana and explained the situation, asking her to call the tennis center in fifteen minutes and request to speak with Sally Standish. She agreed, and I left.

Traffic was backed up on the Harvard Bridge, so I arrived at the tennis center just in time. I was hustling down the walkway outside the courts, the present tucked in my jacket pocket, when, ahead, I heard a gate door clang shut.

Sally was jogging toward me in her pretty yellow tennis dress. She looked worried—that is, until she saw me. Her mouth bloomed into an ecstatic smile.

"Dakota, what are you doing here?" She ran over and bear-hugged me. "I thought you were working all day."

Her unbridled ardor unleashed a fresh surge of guilt inside me.

"I was." I hugged her back. "Still am, actually. But I wanted to drop by and say hello. What are you doing right now?"

"Tennis practice," she said, "but there's a call for me in the office. Don't leave until I get back, okay?"

"I won't. I'll go in the court area and wait for you."

"I'm so glad you're here!" Standing on her tiptoes, she pecked me on the lips, and started jogging toward the main building.

As soon as she disappeared, I walked double-time to the court entrance and went inside. Josh was on the far court, doing drills with some of the girls, so he didn't notice me.

Spotting Sally's pink knapsack leaning against the fence, I grabbed it and unzipped it, and pulled out her planner. I put the key back in the keychain wallet, bookmarked the planner with the card I'd bought for her, and slid the planner inside the knapsack. I was about to put the gift box in there when I was startled by a loud woman's voice.

"Excuse me...*what* are you doing?!"

It was Jade. She strolled over bouncing a ball between her racquet and the court surface.

"Oh, Dr. Stevens," she said. "I didn't recognize you."

Holding a finger to my lips, I pulled the gift box out of my jacket pocket.

"A gift for Sally," I said.

"Sally?" Jade gave me a disapproving look. "Dr. Stevens...don't tell me you're involved with *her*."

"No, she's just a friend." I put the gift box in the knapsack, zipped it up and leaned it against the fence again. "How's life, Jade?"

She shrugged. "I'm studying a subject I hate, but I suppose things could be a lot worse. I *could* be at one of my safety schools."

"Thattagirl—look on the bright side," I said. "Hey, let me ask you...did Binoculars Guy show up again today?"

"No, haven't seen him," she said.

"Good. Take care, Jade."

I was heading for the gate when Peyton and a couple of the other girls ran over.

"*Hiya*, Dr. Stevens," Peyton said.

"Hi, girls. How's 'The Dirty Dozen' doing?"

They giggled.

"Whatcha doin' here?" Peyton said. "Are you gonna coach us again? Please?"

"No, afraid not," I said. "You're in better hands with Mr. Cohen."

I waved to him. Peyton raised an eyebrow and tapped my leg with her tennis racquet.

"Mm," she said, "but...what if we prefer *your* hands, Dakota? Huh?"

I wagged a finger at her. "Peyton…you're lucky I'm *not* your coach. If I were, I'd give you an *epic* spanking, young lady. Your ass would be redder than your Harvard T-shirt."

Peyton's jaw dropped. "Dr. Stevens!"

While the girls all gasped and snickered at my curtain line, I slipped out the gate. I bumped into Sally just as she came out of the main building.

"You're leaving?" Sally said. "You said you'd stick around."

"I can't. Work."

"Can I see you later?" she said.

"I'm working, Sally."

"No, like *later*. You know…like, at your hotel tonight."

"Absolutely not. We don't even know each other yet." I kissed her forehead. "But if I came over to your lab tomorrow, would you give me a tour?"

"Sure, whatever." She kicked a bottle cap into the shrubbery. "It's Volvap Hall. Know where it is?"

"I'll find it," I said.

"We get there at noon on Saturdays," she said.

"Hey, don't pout," I said. "Go look inside your knapsack. I left a surprise for you."

She looked up at me and smiled. "A present?"

"Maybe."

"Oh, Dakota…you're the best!" She hugged me and started to run away, but I yanked her into me and kissed her hard on the lips.

"All right," I said. "See you tomorrow, Sally."

"I can't wait to see what you got me," she said.

"Well…go!"

As she ran away, the skirt of her tennis dress flapped up and down, exposing a pair of canary yellow panties with "JUICY" emblazoned in baby blue across her stellar backside. The girl also had two of the smoothest, trimmest, loveliest legs I'd ever seen on a woman.

I sighed and grit my teeth. In just a few short days, and in more than one way, this case had gotten harder.

Much harder.

19

Nobody Takes a Stinky Guy Seriously

I was in great shape for my age—for someone half my age, actually. From the time I was a teenager, I'd put thousands of hours into developing and maintaining my fitness level and physique. During high school and college, during my tenure with the FBI, and during and between relationships, my daily workouts always came first.

And on the rare occasion when I missed a workout, I made up for it the next day. Having been out of commission with a hangover yesterday, I resolved to make this morning's workout one of those extra-hard ones.

Beginning with some stretching and light calisthenics in the room, I changed into running clothes and took a long run along and across the Charles to the hatch shell (where the Boston Pops played to fireworks on July 4). Back at the hotel, I jogged straight into the fitness center and did my entire regimen, which included pull-ups, push-ups, incline pushups, handstand pushups, crunches with a medicine ball, and two sets on each of the Nautilus strength training machines. As I cooled down with yoga stretches in the corner, a pair of trophy wives made not-so-subtle eyes at me from their stationary bikes. On my way into the locker room afterwards, I nodded at them and gave their bulletproof backsides an admiring, lingering look.

"Ladies," I said, "keep up the great work."

Smiling in reply, they stood up on their bikes and pedaled like they were crossing the Alps in the Tour de France.

In the pool, I swam twenty slow laps, concentrating on lengthening my strokes and stretching out my muscles. Finally, I capped off my workout with half an hour in the sauna. Between the vigorous exercise and the heat, I had succeeded in sweating out the last vestiges of alcohol, so by the time I showered, shaved, dressed, and went downstairs for breakfast, I felt reborn.

On my way into the restaurant, Augusta the desk clerk handed me a large manila envelope, saying that a man in motorcycle garb had delivered it at three o'clock in the morning. I thanked her, and when the hostess seated me, I opened the envelope and pulled out a sheaf of papers.

The cover sheet was on Steve's MIT letterhead. It was a handwritten note in Steve's almost illegible scrawl:

> Dakota,
>
> Great seeing you yesterday. Gretchen and I are jetting off to London for a few days, but I wanted to give you these results before I left.
>
> I tested all 14 samples. There wasn't time to do full workups, but I was able to establish two facts:
>
> 1. All 14 blood samples are from <u>women</u>.

2. The DNA in each sample is unique. In other words, the samples are from 14 <u>different</u> women.

The enclosed printouts give the other details.

If you're still in town next week, give me a call. Maybe the four of us could get together for dinner. For now, I've got a plane to catch.

Later,
Steve

I put the papers away. Over a healthy breakfast of oatmeal, fruit, and an egg white omelette, I mulled what the test results meant and how they might be connected to the fourteen sets of photos Svetlana had found. More to the point, since Svetlana and I were going to his lab soon, there was this question: *Why did Dr. Malone (ostensibly a psychologist who specialized in studying sexual attraction) have the photos and blood samples of fourteen different women?* At least I *thought* the photos and blood samples belonged to the same women. For all I knew, the photos might have nothing to do with the blood samples, in which case I was dealing with twenty-eight different women.

Ordinarily I'd be hopeful about visiting Malone's lab today, but I sensed it was only going to raise other questions and create new problems. However, such is the plight of the detective: You have to follow the leads the detecting gods give you, even if you think they're dead-ends, and even if they mean more work.

After breakfast I strolled around Harvard Square—a nostalgic tour down memory lane—and when I returned to the hotel, at eleven thirty, I drove over to Radcliffe Quad.

It was the quintessential New England autumn morning—tangy crisp air and cloudless skies. Svetlana got into the car sipping from a to-go cup. She was noticeably dressed down, as if for fall-weather outdoor work—picking apples or digging potatoes—wearing a floppy wool newsboy cap, a denim shirt beneath a frumpy down vest, and jeans tucked into olive Hunter wellies.

Pulling away from the curb, I told her about Steve's findings with the blood samples and asked her if she'd been able to establish the identities of any of the women in the photos.

"No, unfortunately," she said. "The reverse image-search technology is still in its infancy, and all the photographs were either blurry or taken from awkward angles."

"Bummer," I said.

"Yes," she said. "Bummer."

As I drove toward Malone's lab, I shared the questions I'd been mulling during breakfast. And then I remembered something Professor Cantor had mentioned: Malone wasn't employed by Harvard University; he had an independent research grant.

"Do me a favor today, will you?" I asked.

"What is that?"

"Professor Cantor said Malone's research is funded by an independent research grant," I said. "See if you can find out who his benefactor is."

"Certainly."

"Hey." I gestured at her clothes. "Why the Tom Joad–*Grapes of Wrath* look?"

"Pardon me?" She sipped her coffee.

"Why do you look like a hobo from the Great Depression?"

"Because I do not want to give Dr. Malone any ideas," she said. "For this reason, I visited a consignment shop yesterday and acquired this unflattering outfit."

I shook my head. "Sorry, but it won't work."

"What do you mean?"

"Svetlana," I said, "you could be wearing *sackcloth* and you'd still turn men's heads. Women's, too."

She looked at me askance and smiled.

When we arrived at Volvap Hall, there were no open parking spots near the building, so we had to park in a garage a few blocks away and hike back. As we started up the walkway, we were halted by a commotion at the entrance.

A stocky, barrel-chested man, maybe 5'7" tall, with greasy, matted black hair and a shaggy beard that could have given Moses' a run for his money, stood defiantly in front of Dr. Malone and Sally. He was blocking them from entering the building. The man wasn't wearing a belt, so every few seconds he had to hitch up his pants. I moseyed toward the entrance, paying close attention to their conversation.

"I wanna know where my daughter is, you son-ovabitch!" the man said.

"I haven't the slightest idea who you're talking about," Dr. Malone said, "nor do I know who *you* are. Now, let me pass, sir. Can't you see you're scaring this young lady?"

He gestured at Sally. Cowering beside him, wearing a short red-and-black plaid skirt, white blouse, and saddle shoes, Sally looked about sixteen years old. The man held out a photo of a young blonde woman.

"She was a student at the University of Chicago," he said. "She participated in your *study* back in January and disappeared in May."

Dr. Malone tried to force his way past the man, but got shoved back.

"You're going to hear this, both of you." He hitched up his pants again and turned to Sally. "So in May, when she disappears, I find out a professor came on to her over the winter. My daughter told him she wasn't interested. Guess who I'm talking about, young lady?" He gestured at Sally, then pointed at Malone. "*This* guy."

"This is preposterous." Dr. Malone pulled out a cell phone. "I'm calling the police."

"Go ahead," the man said. "Fine by me."

The man sat on the steps, took out a cigarette, and lighted it. Suddenly he grabbed Sally's arm.

"Honey, I don't know what your name is or what you're doing with this guy, but I'm telling you—run. Right now. Run! Get away from him, or you'll end up like my little girl! God only knows what's become of her!" He held Sally by the elbow and shook her.

"Let go of me!" Sally said.

I stepped forward. As I came into the man's proximity, I was overcome by his body odor. He smelled like he hadn't showered in weeks, and that he didn't know deodorant had been invented.

"All right," I said, "that's enough. Let go of her."

"Who are you?" The man took a puff off his cigarette and flicked it into the shrubbery along the building. "Hey, buddy, here's a tip—keep your nose out of stuff that's not your business."

Smiling like Mother Theresa, I took hold of his fingers on Sally's arm and pried them off. "And I have *three* tips for you." Torqueing his thumb, I twisted his arm until he yelped and lay flat on his back on the cement. "First, *don't* throw burning cigarettes into shrubbery. That's how fires get started. Second"—I tweaked his thumb; he yelped again—"don't grab women. And third…if what you're saying is true, go to the police. Don't harass—"

"I *am* the police, you jerk! Des Moines P.D."

"I hate to break it to you," I said, "but you're a bit out of your jurisdiction. If I let go, will you be nice?"

"Screw you."

A siren blared in the distance. Malone pocketed his cell phone and walked over to us.

"That's the police now," he said with a smirk.

"All right, I'll leave," the man said. "Let me go."

"I'll walk you out," I said.

When he got to his feet, I stepped behind him, bent his arm up at the elbow, and steered him down the walkway. At the gate, I released him.

"Seriously," I said, "if what you're saying is true, go to the police."

"You haven't seen the last of me, buddy." He hitched up his pants and marched down the sidewalk.

"Tough talk for a guy with no belt," I said. "Here's a final tip—take a shower. And put on some deodorant. Nobody takes a stinky guy seriously."

He gave me the finger over his shoulder, hitched up his pants, and tramped down the sidewalk. I returned to Svetlana, Sally and Dr. Malone, who were waiting at the entrance with the door open.

Sally smiled at me and mouthed, "Thank you, Dakota."

"Dr. Stevens," Malone said, "where did you learn how to"—he made a twisting motion with his hand—"disable him like that?"

"Self-defense class," I said with a shrug. "The Learning Annex in Manhattan. They've got classes in everything."

"Yes, I'm sure," he said. "May I talk to you...in private?"

Hands in his blazer pockets, he walked over to the corner of the building and stood beside a rhododendron.

"I want to apologize," he said.

"For what?"

"Our quarrel. At the tennis courts the other day."

"There was no quarrel," I said. "Your presence was making the girls uncomfortable. I asked you to leave, and you left. There's no need to apologize."

"Well, irregardless—"

"You mean 'regardless,' Dr. Malone," I said. "The 'I-R' prefix is a superfluous hypercorrection that actually negates the meaning of 'regardless.' "

"Yes, yes, I knew that. I meant to say...*regardless*, I appreciate your discretion in the matter." He walked back to the entrance. "I'm glad you and Miss Krüsh could make it today. Sally will escort you inside. I'll join you as soon as I talk to the police."

"Fine," I said.

Inside, Svetlana and I followed Sally down a hallway to a windowless steel door. She swiped a card key, the door lock buzzed, and she opened the door and went in.

"Here we go," I whispered to Svetlana, "down the rabbit hole."

20

Babe in the Woods Routine

The first thing I noticed was a large observation window that looked into a white room in which test subjects sat. The white room was divided in half widthwise by a sheet of plexiglass. There were male and female subjects in the room, with all the female ones sitting on one side of the plexiglass barrier, and all of male subjects on the other side.

Ceiling-mounted cameras peered down at the test subjects, all of whom wore baggy white nightshirts and white socks. Electronic leads were attached to their heads and arms. Finally, at the back of the white room, on either side of the plexiglass barrier, were two doors: one on the female side, one on the male side.

Here in the observation booth, technicians sat at a long workbench, taking notes and watching computer screens and TV monitors. On each computer screen were several program windows displaying a headshot of a test subject and that subject's vitals—including pulse, blood pressure, respiration, and other data. In addition to video images of the test subjects, the TV monitors displayed close-ups of the subjects' pupils.

On the far wall inside the observation booth, a massive HDTV showed a young woman and man (who were not in the white room) facing each other through another sheet of plexiglass. Unlike the solid plexiglass barrier separating the test subjects in the white room, the plexiglass on the monitor had large holes in it above the subjects' waists.

I glanced at Svetlana. She was studying the data on the computer screens. Sally, on the other hand, was transfixed by the scene on the HDTV. She stood with her hands balled into tiny fists, pressing them against her lower lip. She wriggled almost imperceptibly—as though nervous the couple would do something inappropriate, yet fervently hoping they would.

I nudged her. "I bet I know what those holes are for."

The young man and woman simultaneously shucked off their nightshirts. They were now completely nude. Stepping toward the plexiglass, they slipped their arms through the holes and caressed each other.

"*Told 'ya*," I whispered in Sally's ear. "Wanna join me in there later, when everyone's gone?"

She flashed me her big teeth and playfully shoved me. Inwardly, I groaned.

Well, Dakota…you're becoming a first-class cad. Seducing a vulnerable and psychologically troubled girl? Nice job. Your grandparents would be very proud.

The door opened and Dr. Malone came in. "Sally, did you explain to Dr. Stevens and Miss Krüsh how the study works?"

"There's no need, Doctor," I said. "It looks pretty self-explanatory. But the couple on the HDTV"—I pointed at the back of the white room—"I take it they're in a room behind those two doors?"

"Precisely, Dr. Stevens." Malone gestured at the computer monitors. "As you can see, we have electrodes measuring all aspects of the subjects' levels of sexual attraction—respiration, pulse, pupil dilation, and erogenous zone response. And, in what we call the 'private' room, there are infrared cameras monitoring skin temperature."

"How romantic," Svetlana said.

"My field of expertise is human sexuality, Miss Krüsh," Malone said. "If it's romance you seek, I suggest you visit the English department."

Svetlana glared at Malone. "And what if the subjects in the *private* room are overcome by their desires?" She waved dismissively at the HDTV. "Are we also to be treated to X-rated *cinema-vérité*?"

I chuckled at her comment, but Malone frowned.

"No, Miss Krüsh," he said. "If the subjects in the private room start getting out of hand, doors will open and they will be forced to leave. There were a couple of incidents—years ago, before I refined the experiment—but none recently."

"I could use something to drink," I said.

"Sally," Malone said, "get Dr. Stevens a bottled water."

"Actually," I said, "is there a soda machine in the building?"

"Yes, on the second floor," Malone said. "Sally, please show him."

"Yes, Dr. Malone."

I followed Sally out to the hallway. We passed an office with a queue of students out the door. They and the students inside were filling out forms on clipboards.

"New subjects?" I asked Sally.

"*Potential* new subjects," she said. "They complete a questionnaire and have their picture taken, then we contact the top ten percent to serve as test subjects."

"How does one make it into the top ten percent?" I asked.

"There are several factors." She pushed her eyeglasses up her nose. "Physical attractiveness and open-mindedness are certainly important, but Geoff says there's also an X-factor."

"Interesting," I said. "Have *you* been a test subject?"

"I applied," she said, starting up a staircase. "But when Geoff saw that I'm majoring in psychology, he asked me to be his assistant instead."

"Congratulations. You also became his girlfriend. How did that happen?"

"I don't know." She shrugged holding on to the handrail and kept going up the stairs. "We just hit it off, I guess."

The second floor hallway was empty and dim. The only light came from a Coke machine in a nook, and the front windows at the end of the hall. Pointing, Sally led the way toward the soda machine.

"There it is," she said.

"I'm not really thirsty," I said.

"What do you mean?"

"For soda anyway."

Upon reaching the Coke machine, she stopped and looked up at me. The red glow from the machine made her pale skin look like she was blushing all over. In the blouse and short skirt, she looked like my first girlfriend, with legs equally trim and smooth.

When Sally stared at me and creased her lips, I realized that mere flirting wasn't going to get the job done. Mere flirting wasn't going to steal her away from Dr. Malone. Any young woman willing to have rough sex in public won't be seduced by words alone. Bold action was required. Stepping toward her, I backed her against the soda machine until the red plastic "COKE" shell buckled against her butt.

"Dakota!" she hissed. Her eyes darted around the hallway in a panic. "What are you doing?"

Pressing her palms flat against the plastic, she blinked up at me innocently a few times, like she was imitating the ingénue from a teen movie. I removed her eyeglasses and tucked them in my pocket. With her glasses out of the way, I could better appreciate her soft brown eyes and high cheekbones. The girl was eminently kissable.

"You look beautiful today, Sally," I said. "Did you open my present yet?"

"The earrings? Yes, thank you, I love them. I wanted to wear them today, but I knew Geoff would ask me about them, so—"

Gently, I took hold of her head. With one hand on her jaw and the other clutching her hair at the nape of her neck, I tilted her head back and to the side. Her eyes fluttered shut. I started by kissing her tenderly—once.

The second I planted my lips on hers, she wrapped her arms around me and smothered her body against mine.

Sally was only an average kisser, but her nubile body and her eagerness more than compensated for any failings of technique. Her breathing accelerated, grew wheezy and shallow. She murmured something out of the side of her mouth. Spurred on by her murmurs of arousal, I ran a hand down her back, over her skirt, and up the back of her leg to her panties, where I clutched her bijou butt. "Mm!" she yelped into my mouth. She stiffened, then relaxed. We kissed for another minute. Finally, she uncoupled her lips from mine and rasped against my shoulder.

"Dakota…we…we have to stop."

"Why?" I kissed across her cheek. "There's no one here."

"Because I'm hot for you. I *want* you." Her eyes flicked to a doorway across the hall. "See that room? It's a lounge with a couch."

Pretending I hadn't heard her, I unbuttoned the top button of her blouse, pushed the leaves apart, and pinched her BDSM collar in my fingertips.

"Sally?"

"Yes?"

"What kind of man makes his girlfriend wear a collar and call him 'master'?" I asked. "I'll tell you—an insecure one."

"I don't think Geoff is insecure," she muttered.

"Of course he is." Still holding her butt, I squeezed it for emphasis as I talked. "And what are you doing wearing a *collar*, Sally? How long have you known this guy?

Maybe two months? You're a brilliant, beautiful *Harvard* girl, for God's sake. You shouldn't be a slave to *any* man." I kissed her neck, then used my fingers to thread some loose tresses behind her ear. "If you were *my* woman, you wouldn't be wearing a collar. You wouldn't be subservient to me. You'd be—"

She gazed at me with eyes starving for praise. "You really think I'm beautiful, Dakota?"

"Absolutely. I love this skirt on you, by the way."

"Geoff got it for me," she said.

"Yeah? Did he get you those saddle shoes, too?"

She gave a start. "How'd you know that?"

"The saddle shoes go well with that skirt," I said. "It's a very sexy outfit—in a Catholic schoolgirl kind of way."

Sally pouted, stared at the floor.

"What's wrong?" I said.

"Geoff says I'm cute, not sexy," she said.

"*Geoff* is an idiot, Sally."

She giggled. "I can't believe I met you. Where did you *come* from?"

Wrapping my arms around her, I picked her up off the ground and kissed her again. When she spoke next, it was in a breathy, little girl voice—another ingénue affectation, but, because it was straight into my ear canal, an effective one.

"Dakota?" she said. "Could we go somewhere together? Maybe tomorrow? I'm so sick of classes and working, and Geoff never takes me anywhere."

"Sure thing," I said. "But I don't want you staying with him tonight."

"Okay, I won't."

"I'll pick you up at your dorm in the morning. We'll make an entire day of it. We can do anything you want."

"*Anything* I want?"

With a twitch of her eyebrows, she wriggled her breasts against me. Instantly I was filled with an overwhelming urge to scoop her up, carry her to the lounge across the hall, and savagely dent the couch cushions with her. Taking a second to catch my breath, I put her down, yanked up her skirt, and spanked her once on her backside—hard. The spank resonated in the empty hallway.

"Ow!" She rubbed her bottom. "Dakota!"

"Enough with the babe in the woods routine." I put her glasses back on her. "I'm as attracted to your mind as I am your body, Sally."

She nodded. "All right."

"Now, I want you to take the rest of the day off and do something nice for yourself." I opened my wallet and handed her a hundred dollars. "Go get your hair or nails done, or buy yourself a pretty outfit."

"Okay, but…what do I tell Geoff?"

"I'll take care of it. Just leave. I'll tell him you're sick."

She hugged me. I held her head against my chest and stroked her hair.

"If he calls you later, just play sick," I said. "Think about what you want to do tomorrow. I'll pick you up in morning—eight o'clock. All right?"

She nodded against my chest. Then she mumbled something.

"What's that?" I asked.

"I said, 'Kiss me again, Dakota?' "

I kissed her for a good thirty seconds, until we heard a door bang shut downstairs. When we pulled apart, I said, "Now I really *am* thirsty."

"Me too."

I bought us a couple of sodas and walked Sally downstairs to the back exit. She drank some of her soda and daintily wiped her lips with her fingertips.

"Hey, Dakota?" she said.

"Yeah?"

"That guy that was here earlier—do you think he was crazy, or was he telling the truth?"

I wanted Sally to reach her own conclusions about Dr. Malone, so I played dumb.

"The truth about what?"

"You know—about his daughter being abducted and Geoff having something to do with it."

I shrugged. "What I think isn't important. I don't have to be around the guy. What do *you* think?"

She pinched up her lips like a kewpie doll's.

"I'm not sure yet. But I *am* sure about one thing."

"What's that?" I said.

"How much I like you."

She bounced up on her tiptoes, kissed me, and skipped down the steps to the sidewalk gate. Opening the gate, she blew me a kiss. I "caught" the kiss and pressed it to my heart.

The second she disappeared down the sidewalk, I closed my eyes and bowed my head in shame. I had no doubt that I would soon be successful in extricating Sally from Malone's clutches.

But how was Sally going to react when she inevitably learned my wooing her was a sham? A sham fabricated for ulterior motives. Ulterior motives that involved her father.

This was going to be a problem.

21

Watching the Stars
Carousel Around Him

Back in the observation booth, Svetlana was seated in front of a computer screen while Malone hovered over her shoulder explaining the data to her. The other technicians were gone, so the two of them were alone in the room.

When I shut the door, Svetlana whipped around with an irritated look that seemed to say, "Where have you been?"

"Sorry it took me so long," I said. "Sally got sick. I had to see her out."

"Sick?" Malone slowly stood.

"Yeah, I put her in a cab and sent her to the infirmary."

Malone frowned. "Hmm...perhaps I should go see her."

"Better not," I said. "She was really burning up. I think it's the flu."

"Well, there's not much use in my sticking around," he said. "I can't interview all of those applicants by myself."

"Where are you parked?" I asked.

"A garage, a few blocks away, why?" Malone said.

"I think we're in that same garage. We'll walk with you."

"Fine," he said. "Give me a few minutes, and I'll meet you outside. I need to lock up and dismiss the applicants down the hall. Be right out."

Outside, Svetlana was visibly agitated—a far cry from the calm and collected woman I'd met in the Au Bon Pain courtyard the other day. A car whisked by on the street, and then it was dead silent again.

"Svetlana, what's wrong?" I asked.

"There is something about that man that disturbs me," she said. "Just having him look at me, I feel violated."

"Well, finding those photos and blood in his apartment didn't help," I said.

"No, it did not."

"Did you get a chance to ask him who funds his research grant?"

She stared at the bus stop shelter across the street and shook her head.

"I find my ability to think escapes me in his presence," she said. "I fear if I were to play him in chess now, I would lose."

On our way to the parking garage, Svetlana and I walked behind Dr. Malone as he dissertated on sexual attraction, including his discovery of what he had humbly termed the "Malone Magnification Effect."

"When a subject realizes that another subject finds him or her sexually attractive," Malone explained, "it causes his or her interest in the other subject to increase, which magnifies *that* subject's interest in the other, and so on in an endless loop, culminating in some kind of sexual expression, like intercourse."

As we entered the garage and started up the ramp between the parked cars, I attempted to translate Dr. Malone's principle into layperson's terms.

"I get it," I said. "Basically what you're saying is, we get turned on because the other person is turned on by us."

"Not quite," Malone said. "What happens is each subject's interest in the other is *magnified*. I'm sure Miss Krüsh understands the principle." He smiled at Svetlana over his shoulder. "And has no doubt experienced it herself. Numerous times."

"Miss Krüsh has no interest whatsoever in your *principle*," she said.

When Malone turned around again, she stared daggers into his back. After a long uncomfortable silence, during which the only sound was the echo of our footsteps in the garage, I finally posed the question I'd been waiting to ask him.

"Dr. Malone," I said, "I understand your research isn't funded by the university—that you have an independent research grant. Who, may I ask, is your benefactor? I'm curious because I'm having trouble getting a grant for my sabbatical project. Maybe your benefactor would be willing to sponsor me?"

"I sincerely doubt it," he said. "My sponsor insists on remaining anonymous. All I can say is, he's a very wealthy man who wishes me to be successful in my research."

"Come on," I said. "Surely you can tell me more than that. Just give me a hint about his identity."

We reached the top of the garage ramp, turned and continued up to the next level.

"This much I will tell you," Malone said. "I've found foreign philanthropists to be the most sympathetic to my work. Now, I'd appreciate it if you—"

Ahead, Stinky was sitting on the trunk of a red BMW. He was bookended by two wiry young men, maybe 25, wearing hip-length black leather jackets and sunglasses. With their arms crossed, the young men looked like a couple of extras from a low-budget Mob movie—the lean and cocky bodyguards to a pudgy boss. The three of them stood as we approached the car. Malone stopped in his tracks.

"I told you, sir," Malone said to Stinky, "I don't know anything about your daughter."

"Shut up. I *know* you took her," Stinky said. "Ursula Teller—sound familiar?"

Svetlana blinked at me. I knew we were thinking the same thing: one of the sets of photos, and one of the test tubes of blood, had been labeled with the initials "U.T."

Easing around Svetlana, I carefully removed my collapsible striking baton, looped my wrist through the strap and concealed it, still collapsed, in my hand behind my hip. When Stinky and the two bookends started toward us, I positioned myself in front of Svetlana and Dr. Malone. Stinky and the bookends stopped.

"This here's the guy I told you about," Stinky said.

"Tough guy, huh?" said the left one.

"No, not really," I said. "I prefer sex to fighting. Ask your girlfriend."

"Smartass, too," said the other one.

"Actually, I consider myself a *wit*," I said. "You know—in the tradition of Voltaire? Listen to me—of course you don't know, you're a moron. So, how about it, Stinky…take that shower yet?" I sniffed the air. "No? Tell me you at least put on deodorant."

"Like I said before, buddy," Stinky said, "this doesn't involve you. Dr. Malone knows where my daughter is, and he's going to tell me."

"Listen," I said, "there's no need for anybody to get hurt here. I'm sure Dr. Malone will be happy to sit down and discuss this with you. So, why don't you take these two clowns"—I waved my free hand—"back to Rent-a-Schmuck, and the four of us will—"

"That's it!" The guy on the left dropped into a karate stance. "You're *done*, buddy!"

He let out a loud shout and pumped a series of karate punches in front of his chest, alternating his punches left-right-left, and advancing until his fists were only a foot from my torso. It was an impressive display, and against a novice fighter it might have been intimidating. I, however, am not a novice fighter. Since he was off balance during his little demonstration, and since *balance* is the cornerstone of all martial arts, I concluded he didn't know what the hell he was doing.

Bending my knees slightly, I anchored my feet in a solid stance. The moment Karate Guy shouted and started to pump his fists again, I put an end to it. Deftly pivoting on the balls of my feet and swiveling my hips, I pasted him in the jaw with a gorgeous left hook.

In the annals of punches, mine had to be one of the best ever thrown. It was such a beautiful punch, connecting so sublimely with his jaw from out of his blind spot, and delivered so efficiently with all my weight and shoulder strength behind it, that I wanted to ask the garage attendant later if I could view the security tape, maybe get a copy for my archives. Karate Guy's legs crumpled beneath him. He plopped on his butt on the cement, dumbly watching the stars carousel around him.

Then the other guy pulled something from his jacket pocket. He paused for dramatic effect and pressed a button. A knife blade flicked out and glinted in the light.

"A switchblade?" I grimaced. "Bit of a cliché, don't you think? Now, *this*, on the other hand…" I raised my hand holding the baton and, with a snap of the wrist, instantly telescoped it to its full two feet of striking steel. "*This* is more original." I couldn't see his eyes behind his sunglasses, but his hesitation said he concurred. "Walk away, kid," I said. "Whatever Stinky's paying, it's not worth getting your wrist broken."

"We'll see about that."

He stepped forward brandishing the knife. He was more cautious than his buddy had been.

"That's it," Stinky said, easing away from the car. "You keep him busy while I deal with Dr. Malone."

Knife Guy came toward me in a low crouch, holding his knife arm back and jabbing it toward me every so often. As a rule, tough guys for hire aren't well-trained, and their hand-to-hand skills tend to follow deeply grooved patterns based on what's worked for them in the past. I kept my eyes on the knife, but in my periphery I was observing Knife Guy's footsteps, trying to figure out his footwork pattern.

Before jabbing with the knife, he two took sidesteps, followed by two stutter-steps forward. I waited for him to repeat the pattern twice, and when he started to repeat it a third time, I brought the baton crashing down on the back of his hand. The knife clattered under the BMW. By the way he screamed, I knew I'd shattered all of those thin and sensitive bones.

He regained his composure quickly though, and while my stance was still open he kicked me in the thigh, precariously close to my groin. I replied by lashing out with the baton again—a solid strike across his collarbone. He fell to the ground, writhing in pain.

"Dakota," Svetlana said, "behind you!"

I spun around. Stinky was straddling Dr. Malone on the pavement, throttling him. "Tell me where she is! Tell me or you're dead! Tell me!"

Dr. Malone's face was red. He tried to talk, but only croaking sounds came out.

"Stop!" I struck Stinky on the shoulder with the baton, but he kept throttling Malone. I struck him again, this time across the arm, but he still wouldn't let go. Finally I pulled my gun and shoved it in his face.

"Enough!" I shouted. "Now back off!"

When he let go, Dr. Malone got to his feet coughing and holding his throat. He staggered to the BMW and opened the door.

"Dr. Malone," I said, "wait for the police."

He either didn't hear me or acted like he didn't, because he jumped in the car and started it. He squealed out of the parking spot, nearly running over Karate Guy and Knife Guy in the process, and sped out of the garage. I hurried over to Svetlana. Her pupils were dilated.

"Are you okay?" I asked.

"I am physically unharmed, if that is what you mean."

"Good." I gave her my car keys. "Go get my car. It's up there. Walk slowly and take deep breaths. I'm going to talk to Stinky here."

She nodded and walked away. I pointed my gun at Karate Guy and Knife Guy.

"You two...beat it," I said.

They rose unsteadily to their feet and stumbled down the garage ramp. I holstered my gun and pocketed the baton.

"All right, Stinky," I said, nodding to him, "it's just you and me now."

"Go to hell."

"Look, you *want* to be nice to me," I said. "I'm an ex-FBI Special Agent investigating Dr. Malone's involvement with the girl you saw earlier. I've investigated a number of kidnappings, and something occurred to me."

"Oh yeah? What?"

"Your level of anger and desperation is exactly like what I've seen in the parents of kidnap victims," I said. "I think your daughter really was abducted and that you, correctly or incorrectly, believe that Dr. Malone is behind it. The bottom line is, I want to talk to you."

He looked at me in disbelief, then his head sunk and he began to sob.

Ugh...another person crying. First Mrs. O'Toole, and now this guy. *Should I put a hand on his shoulder, say an encouraging word?* This was the part of the job nobody trained you for. I hadn't liked it when I was a Special Agent, and I liked it even less now that I was independent. I was walking over to him when Svetlana pulled up with the Mercedes.

"Listen," I said to him, "come back to my hotel with us. I'll buy you lunch and we can talk. What do you say?"

Nodding, he continued to sob. I held out a hand and helped him to his feet.

"I'm Dakota Stevens, and the woman driving is Svetlana Krüsh," I said. "What's your name?"

"Kevin," he said. "Kevin Teller."

"Nice to meet you, Kevin." I opened the back door of the Mercedes for him. "I have just one request."

"What's that?"

I pinched my nose. "My hotel has an excellent shower."

He nodded and slid inside. As soon as I got in the front, Svetlana drove down the ramp toward the exit.

"Can we stop by my van first?" Kevin asked.

"Sure," I said. "Where's it parked?"

"The IHOP. Know where that is?"

"Yes. But what's there?"

"Change of clothes," he said. "But mostly something else."

"What?"

"Evidence," he said.

22

THE ALL-OVER, FULL-BODY KIND

Back at the hotel, after Kevin got cleaned up, the three of us went downstairs to the hotel restaurant for a late lunch. Svetlana had skirt steak; I had a Caesar salad with wood-grilled shrimp; and Kevin, clearly comfortable as our guest, had page five of the menu. It was obvious the man hadn't eaten much in days, so I didn't bother him with questions while he was eating. But when the waitress came around with the dessert menu, I waved her off and started putting the screws to Kevin.

"Listen, Kevin," I said, "I didn't invite you here so you could break the restaurant's eating record. I want to hear your story. You said your daughter was abducted in May. Start with that, telling us everything that's happened since then." I glanced at my watch. "And please be brief. Svetlana has another appointment soon."

He wiped his mouth with a napkin and dropped it in his plate.

"Sure, Dakota," he said. "Since May, when Ursula disappeared, I've been on the road. I took a leave of absence from the force—that's back in Des Moines—borrowed

239

a van from a friend, and followed Malone across the country."

"Where did you start?" I asked.

"Chicago," he said. "Ursula was a junior at the University of Chicago. Straight-A student. Here."

He showed us a shopworn photograph, in which a curvy blonde girl wearing a St. Patrick's Day hat stood on a bridge with a green river in the background.

"Chicago River on St. Patrick's Day?" I asked.

"Yeah." He gulped and hurriedly put the photo away. "So, just the facts, right? Here goes. In January, Ursula participated in Malone's study. But afterwards, when Malone pursued her for a date, she told him she wasn't interested. Two months after that, Ursula disappeared.

"The FBI investigated—for about a week—and then the lead agent tells me, 'With kidnappings,' he says, 'after the first forty-eight hours, the chances of finding the missing person decline rapidly.' And then he says, 'Chances are, Ursula's dead.' Says it cold just like that. I wanted to kill the sonovabitch. Then he says they'll keep the case open, but they have to scale back their resources. That's when I got the van and started my own investigation.

"Ursula kept a journal—she was an English major— and she wrote how Malone kept pursuing her. He was calling her as late as April, a month after he left. She reported it to the Dean, but the Dean said that since Malone had never worked directly for the university, there was nothing they could do."

His eyes started to tear up. He sipped some ice water.

"You're doing great, Kevin," I said. "Keep it together. After Chicago, where did you go?"

CHRIS ORCUTT

"Oberlin College, in Ohio," he said. "That was the next place Malone was supposed to do his study. But there wasn't enough interest, and he left a couple days before I got there. So I decided to look into the schools he was at *before* Chicago. I backtracked my way west— Colorado College, University of Arizona, University of Las Vegas, UCLA, and Stanford University. And guess what I found?"

"Other girls had disappeared?"

"Bingo." He opened a thick manila envelope and handed over a sheaf of papers and photographs. "All told, fourteen girls have gone missing from schools where Malone performed his sex study."

Sifting through the papers and photos, I quickly recognized the girls' initials and faces from the evidence we'd discovered in Malone's apartment. Finally I learned the names behind the mysterious initials:

Tabitha Andersen
Vicki Crane
Anya French
Tamara Goldwyn
Amber Holt
Jennifer Leigh
Heather O'Neill
Stacy Prentiss
Nora Reese
Veronica Snow
Isla Suarez
Ursula Teller
Mercedes Vonn
Mallory Waters

241

While I jotted the girls' names into my pocket notebook, Svetlana laced her hands together on the tablecloth and leaned across the table.

"And what pattern, if any, did the disappearances follow?" she asked.

"Good question," I said. "Svetlana is a chess grandmaster"—I jutted my head in her direction—"so she's really good at patterns."

"All of the girls disappeared after Malone left," Kevin said. "Usually within two months of his departure. All of them either applied for, or participated in, his 'study.' They were all attractive and unique-looking in some way. In other words, they didn't all have blonde hair like my Ursula, or—"

"Kevin," I said, "what is Ursula's blood type?"

"Excuse me?"

"Her blood type."

"Why do you want to know?"

"It might be important," I said. "Just humor me, okay?"

"A-B negative."

"You're sure?" I asked.

"Yes, of *course* I'm sure," he said. "She got in a car accident last year and lost a lot of blood. It was touch and go because her blood type's so rare. The blood bank had trouble coming up with enough A-B negative for her."

I wagged the sheaf of papers and photos.

"What about the other girls in here? Do you know their blood types?"

"No." He crossed his arms.

"What's this photo of?" I showed him the photo. It was a picture of a dilapidated brick building taken from a hilltop.

"I was getting to that," he said. "It's an abandoned warehouse outside of Montreal."

The back of the photo had GPS coordinates on it.

"And these coordinates," I said. "The location?"

"Yeah," Kevin said.

"Is this where you think the girls are being held?" I asked.

"No." He frowned down at the table. "I wish. I think it's like a distribution center…for the girls."

"How did you find it?" I asked.

"I got lucky."

Kevin described how, while he was at Stanford University, he spoke to a woman in Payroll. When he told the woman about Ursula's kidnapping, she gave him the only permanent address the university had for Malone—an apartment in Montreal. Kevin then drove east to Montreal and staked out Malone's apartment for a week. When Malone showed up, it was late at night, and the next morning he drove to the warehouse. Other vehicles showed up, including two windowless vans, and they all left an hour later.

"I tried to follow Malone from there, but he lost me," Kevin said. "I didn't want to tip him off that I knew about the warehouse, so I took that photo and went to the Mounties. You know, the Royal Canadian Mounted Police."

"Yes, I know who the Mounties are, Kevin," I said. "Go on."

He shrugged. "That's it. That's all I've got. I spoke to the chief superintendent, but he said they didn't have any probable cause to investigate."

I held up the photo of the warehouse. "May I keep this? There's someone at the Bureau I want to share it with."

"Go ahead," he said. "I contacted the lead agent on my daughter's case and told him everything I'm telling you, and *he* gave me the blow-off."

"Well, I'm *not* giving you the blow-off." I flipped to a fresh page in my notebook. "What's Malone's address in Montreal?"

He told me, and I wrote it down. Svetlana leafed through the photos and documents, and then handed them back to me.

"How about these files on each of the girls?" I said. "Can we keep them? It would make our work a lot easier."

"Sure, I've got copies," he said, handing me the envelope. "In fact, back in my van, I've got *boxes* of stuff. Believe me, Dakota...Svetlana...Malone's behind this. I just hope I can find my daughter before the bastard permanently shuts down his *study* and disappears."

"I can't guarantee anything," I said, "but I'm pretty confident the Bureau will get involved now."

"That would be great," he said. "I've been doing this all alone for months. I'm exhausted, and I'm broke."

"I wish I could help you out," I said, "but I'm not in a position—"

"Thanks, but I'm fine. I've been getting by with carpentry gigs."

"Look, do you have a phone number? A place where agents can contact you, so they can look over all the other evidence you've gathered?"

"My cell phone broke, and I haven't had the money to replace it," he said. "Just have them go to the IHOP parking lot. My van's the red Dodge in the back corner, Iowa plates of course."

I took out $50 and handed it to him.

"No, I don't want—"

"To get yourself a cab," I said. "I can't drive you back. I'm sorry."

He nodded meekly and pocketed the money. "Thanks. Both of you. You've taken a huge weight off me."

We shook hands with him, and he left. When the waitress came with the check, I charged it to my room and gave her a generous tip. She poured us coffee, and Svetlana and I sat in silence. While gazing out the window at the Charles River, I put down my coffee cup and spoke.

"I hope I did the right thing," I said.

"By…?"

"By not sharing the photos we found, or mentioning the blood samples."

"I believe you were wise to omit them," Svetlana said. "You should not get his hopes up prematurely. Better to share when you have more data. What will your next move be?"

"As soon as we're finished here, I'm going over to the Bureau office in Government Center and discuss this with an agent I know there."

Svetlana gave me a wry smile. "Is this the agent who was *helping* you at eight o'clock yesterday morning?"

"Yes," I said. "I'm hoping I can convince her to look into Malone a little bit—maybe find out who his mysterious benefactor is."

"May I be of assistance?"

I sipped my coffee. "You mean with talking to her, or something else?"

"Research," she said.

"Yes, that would be great—thanks. What'd you have in mind?"

"Looking into the disappearances at the various schools, perhaps contacting the parents of the missing girls. Inquiring about their blood types, for one thing."

"All right." I slid the sheaf of papers and photos back into the envelope, and handed it to Svetlana. "Just be careful. Make up a cover story for why you're contacting these people. I don't want Malone to get wind of this and blow town."

" '*Blow town*'?" A puzzled look came over her face as she stirred cream into her coffee.

"An American colloquialism from old gangster movies," I said. "It means 'to leave a place rapidly and without warning.' 'Fly the coop' and 'skedaddle' mean the same thing."

"I will be discreet," she said.

"I really appreciate your help, Svetlana," I said. "I'm not crazy about the drudge work—like calling people or researching stuff on the internet. I *can* do it, mind you. I just don't *like* doing it."

"Understood," she said. "And what will you be doing tomorrow?"

"Continuing to persuade Sally to dump Dr. Malone."

"So...*seducing* her?" Svetlana said.

"*No*—taking her on the town." I sighed. Who was I kidding? "Yeah, seducing her basically."

Svetlana shook her head and clucked her tongue.

"Listen, Svetlana," I said, "do you think I *like* this so-called 'case'? I don't. The more I get to know Sally, the more I see she's a sweet girl who's starved for attention and affection. She has serious daddy issues—so serious that, at the drop of a hat, she'll get involved with any older alpha male who shows her a speck of attention. I don't *want* to toy with her like this, but what I'm learning about Malone tells me she's better off getting her feelings hurt with me than she is staying with Malone and having who-knows-what happen to her."

Svetlana nodded. "You are right. I am sorry if I seemed judgmental."

"Forget it." I looked at my watch and stood. "How about I drive you where you have to go, and then I'll head over to Government Center?"

"That would be most helpful."

Taking a final sip of her coffee, she dabbed her mouth with her napkin and stood. We both stared at the battle royal of plates where Kevin had been sitting—the culinary carnage—and looked at each other.

I shrugged. "I guess the man was hungry."

"Hungry?" Svetlana said. "Dakota...I have seen *wolves* less ravenous."

When I got to the Boston FBI office in Government Center, I was told that Special Agent Suzuki was in a meeting and I'd have to wait. Initially I waited in the FBI reception area, but the receptionist, a supercilious young man, kept eyeing me. Then, knowing how many cameras were watching me, I became self-conscious. I told him to tell Agent Suzuki that I would be in the lobby, and rode the elevator downstairs.

Since it was a Saturday, the newsstand and coffee vendor were closed, so I couldn't get anything to drink, but one of the shoeshine guys was working. When his chair became available, I climbed up, requested a "deluxe" shine, and read my copy of Chandler's *The Little Sister*. I must have really gotten into the story. The next thing I knew, the shoeshine guy, an African American man who looked like he'd been doing this for a living since Truman was President, was shaking my leg—hard.

"*Come* on, son!" he said. "Time to go!"

My shoes had never looked better. I put my book away and paid him, adding a nice tip. As I climbed down from the chair, Agent Suzuki emerged from an elevator and scanned the lobby. Spotting me, she walked over.

"Why don't you have a cell phone like the rest of the world?" she asked.

"Haven't needed one. My pager works fine. Why—have you missed my voice?"

She sighed and hitched up her purse. "It's been a long day, Dakota."

"Buy you a drink?" I said.

She hissed through her teeth considering it. I grinned and rubbed her shoulder.

"Too soon?" I said.

She smiled. "No, a drink would be nice."

"How about that Mexican place over by Faneuil Hall?" I said. "Is it still around?"

"Which one?" she said. "There are like four."

"Let's walk over and see," I said. "You can tell me about your day."

"Okay."

We exited the building through the revolving door and set out across the stark concrete courtyard of Government Center. It was a pleasant evening, still light out, and when I put my arm around Jen, she responded by leaning on my shoulder. As we walked, she described a Charlestown bank robbery case she was working. They knew who the perps were (a local crew), but they couldn't get any corroborating witnesses. She mentioned a number of other agents by first name and complained about how slowly the wheels of justice turned, and so forth.

I didn't listen very closely because I didn't have to; I'd lived it, so I knew her frustrations. I also knew she just needed to talk, to purge herself of all the negativity she'd absorbed during the day so she didn't take it home. Finally she achieved catharsis, and when we stepped on the outdoor escalator that led down to Faneuil Hall and Haymarket Square, she held on to me quietly.

"This is totally unexpected," she said. "And, according to the girls in D.C., it's a far cry from your usual M-O."

"What do you mean?" I asked.

"This," she said. "Picking me up after work, letting me talk about my day, taking me out for a drink. Boyfriend stuff. Maybe they're wrong about you. Maybe you *are* good for more than a casual hookup."

"I like to think I am."

As we crossed the street, I was reminded of a bitter fact: Ashley had left me only a few days ago. This snapped me out of the fantasy that I was living in Boston and dating Agent Suzuki. The fact was, I was here on a case, and I'd come to see her this evening not to be a loving boyfriend, but to solicit her help. Plain and simple, I was *using* her, and I didn't like it.

Miraculously, the Mexican restaurant I remembered from my college days still existed. Inside, we were seated in the bar at a window table with a view of the passing tourists. I ordered drinks and *tapas*, but in the meantime another server brought us a basket of homemade tortilla chips and salsa.

"Look, Jen," I said when the server left, "I *did* want to see you tonight, but…"

"But what?"

"I have to be honest…I didn't come just to see you. The case with Sally Standish and Dr. Malone has taken a turn, and I need your help." While Jen ate chips and salsa, I gave her the condensed version of everything Kevin Teller had said earlier. "My instincts tell me there's a very real case. All I ask is, go interview him and look at the evidence he has. Apparently he's got a ton of material in his van."

"Jesus, Dakota—his *van*?"

"Hey, don't judge the guy," I said. "He's been following Malone around the country for months. Yes, he's living in his van, in the IHOP parking lot. But look at it this way—at least it's the *Cambridge* IHOP. It could be 'Ruh-veeuh.'"

She chuckled, then said, "It's just…I'm swamped as it is, Dakota, and tomorrow's Sunday—my only day off, and—"

"Go over there in the morning. You and agent whatshisname—you can meet Kevin for breakfast. Talk to him for half an hour. Please?"

"All right. Breakfast." She dipped a chip in salsa and ate it. "But he'd better not be a kook, Dakota."

"He's not, I promise," I said. "And one other thing."

"What?"

"Dr. Malone doesn't work for Harvard. He's funded by an independent research grant. I need you to find out who finances his Sexual Attraction Study."

"I can try," she said.

"Thanks. But that's tomorrow morning." I reached across the table, took her hand and started massaging it. "As a little thank-you, after drinks and *tapas* how about I take you home and give you a massage? You know—the all-over, *full-body* kind?"

23

THE SUITCASE CONNECTED

When I arrived at her dorm the next morning, Sally was already waiting at the curb with a compact hard-shell suitcase at her feet. She was wearing a bateau-necked, blue-and-white striped French sailor's shirt with holes that exposed her smooth shoulders. That, and another short skirt. I let out a quavering deep breath and prayed for strength.

Nineteen-and-a-half years old or not, my client's daughter or not, the girl had irrepressibly gorgeous gams. Making matters worse—as I parked the Mercedes with the engine running and she approached the door—Sally's new sophisticated shoulder-length hairdo with the smooth part and wavy styling, her saucy cat-eye glasses, and her winsome smile all bespoke seductive intentions. She seemed to be under the impression that we were going on a sexy getaway together. I got out and went around the car.

"What's with the suitcase?" I said as I put it in the back seat. "I wasn't planning on doing an overnight."

"Plans can change," she said. "But never mind that— aren't you forgetting something?"

Standing on her tiptoes with her hands clasped behind her back, she thrust her chest in my direction and swiveled her hips. I couldn't tell if she was showing off her sailor's shirt, or her breasts—a pertly tempting eyeful that I'd first admired in the pool the other day.

"That's a lovely top, Sally," I said. "Is it new?"

"Yes, I got it with the money you gave me," she said. "But not the *top*, silly. Me! Aren't you going to give me a kiss?"

"Of course," I said.

I heaved her off the ground and kissed her. A clique of girls leaving the dorm gawked at us and whispered to each other on their way by. I put Sally down and opened the car door for her, but she enveloped me in a hug before I could put her in the car.

"We're going to have so much fun today," she said.

"Absolutely," I said, patting the car roof. "Jump in, so we can get started."

When she was inside, I walked around the car and got behind the wheel.

"Nice ride," Sally said. She blew through her lips, imitating the muffler's flatulence. "Where'd you get it, a junkyard?"

"No, it was my grandfather's," I said. "And be nice. She's a good old girl."

"Sorry."

Her skirt had ridden way up her legs.

"Sally," I said, averting my eyes, "fix your skirt, please."

"Oops." She giggled and smoothed it down. "Better?"

"Yes," I said. "Now, where are we going?"

"Well, I've given it a lot of thought *and*"—she squeezed my arm—"I want to go to the beach."

"The beach?" I said. "It's late September, Sally. It'll probably be too cold to swim."

"I don't care," she said. "You said we could go anywhere I want. I haven't been to the beach in years, and that's where I want to go."

"You mean you used to go to the beach, and you never learned to swim?"

She frowned and slapped me in the arm. "Are you taking me or not?"

"Okay, okay, the beach it is." I played with a lock of her hair. "But no whining. Now, which beach?"

"How about the Cape?" she said. "Yeah, Provincetown! I've never been."

"That's a really long drive, Sally."

"Please?"

"I guess we could take the ferry," I said. "All right… Provincetown it is."

The instant I pulled away, Sally lunged across the gap between our seats and snuggled up against me. I put an arm over her shoulders and steered one-handed. As I turned on to Memorial Drive, I habitually checked the rear-view mirror. A parked white van did a U-turn and slipped into traffic one car behind us—textbook position for tailing someone. There were two men in the van. I crossed the Harvard Bridge and turned on to Soldiers Field Road, heading toward Boston.

"Dakota," Sally said, "what's that smell?"

"The exhaust," I said. "Sometimes a little bit leaks into the vents."

"We're not going to die from carbon monoxide, are we?"

"No. Just crack a window if you're concerned."

I glanced in the rear-view again. The van was still back there.

"Why don't you get a real car?" she said.

"Because I'm a humble academic, sweetheart."

"I'm only teasing." She ran a finger down my cheek. "You're so handsome, I wouldn't care if all you had was a bicycle."

"Oh...you're sweet," I said.

"I'm bored." She rapped a knuckle on the stereo. "Can this thing play tunes or what?"

"Sure. It has a cassette deck."

"Cassettes? God, Dakota, *nobody* listens to those anymore." She rested her head on my shoulder. *"Geoff* has a CD player."

"Maybe," I said, "but *Geoff* is also an insecure twerp who makes his girlfriends wear BDSM collars."

Sally hitched away from me and sulked against her door.

"What's wrong?" I asked.

"You said *girlfriends."* She picked at a hole in the seat upholstery. "You think he has other girlfriends besides me?"

"I'm sure of it," I said. "Think about it, Sally—the guy's gone from college to college all across the country. Do you really think you're the first young woman he's had a *master-slave* relationship with?"

Sally clenched her jaw and huffed. She pounded on the door.

"Take it easy," I said. "Look in the glove compartment. I think I have some cassette tapes in there."

She opened it and rifled through the contents. "Just two," she said, pulling them out.

"What are they?"

" 'Tchaikovsky's Greatest Hits.' "

"And…?"

" 'The Best of Steve Lawrence,' " she said.

"Yeah, that one."

She popped it into the cassette player and turned up the volume. "Who the heck is Steve Lawrence?"

"Why, he's only the coolest, swingin'-est lounge singer from the sixties Vegas scene. Come over here and listen."

Lawrence's up-tempo, Latin-lounge arrangement of Cole Porter's "Night and Day" came over the speakers. It was one of my favorites. Hugging Sally with one arm, I steered the wheel with the other and snapped my fingers to the beat. I started swaying and singing along. Soon, Sally began to laugh and sway with me as I slalomed the Mercedes through the thin Sunday morning traffic.

The van was still behind us in the far left lane, so when the traffic on Storrow Drive slowed for a merge, I swerved to the right and exited at Charlesgate. Skirting the Fenway, I ran a red light and sped the wrong way down a one-way street.

"Whoa, why'd you do that?" Sally said.

"There was a slowdown back there. We need to get to the ferry."

Despite my swift, evasive driving, somehow the white van had managed to stick with me. There they were—two cars back. Glad for the reassuring heft of the gun under my arm, I resigned myself to their presence and wove through traffic down Boylston Street toward the waterfront. Sitting up on her knees on her seat, Sally sucked my earlobe and acquainted my shoulder with her breasts.

"Stop it, Sally," I said. "I'm trying to drive."

"I can't help it, Dakota. You get me so…mmm!"

One of her hands serpentined down my stomach. Just then, my pager started beeping.

"Now look what you've done!" I said. "You made my beeper go off!"

She laughed.

"Slide over and fasten your seat belt, honey," I said.

"That's the first time you've called me 'honey.' "

"Buckle up, Sally."

"Okay." With one last lingering suck on my earlobe, she complied.

I checked my pager. It looked like Agent Suzuki's office number. I'd call her back from a pay phone at the ferry terminal.

I was still on Boylston Street. Glancing in the rearview mirror again, gauging the van's distance and speed, I tried to think of a stretch of road where I could lose it. There wasn't one. I was better off parking somewhere near the waterfront and losing them on foot through the narrow streets. Then I'd buy Sally and myself ferry tickets, and we'd board at the last moment. I had a plan.

When we reached Long Wharf, where the terminal was, a thick fog was rolling in from the harbor. Through the fog drifting across Atlantic Avenue, I glimpsed a parking garage a couple blocks down. While the white van was stuck behind a bus, I sped past the parking garage, turned and circled the building to the rear entrance. There was an empty spot on the second level. I parked and jumped out of the car.

"Come on, Sally," I said, "we have to move."

"What's wrong?"

"Nothing. But we don't want to miss the next ferry, do we?"

"I need my suitcase," she said.

I grabbed it out of the back seat and hustled us toward the stairwell.

"When we get in the terminal, I need to make a phone call," I said.

She smirked. "Oh…your *beeper*?"

"Right."

On Sunday mornings in late September, ferry terminals are ghost towns. This is particularly true of foggy Sunday mornings. My and Sally's footsteps echoed in the empty terminal as we crossed to the ticket booth.

The clerk was a sullen young man in his twenties with a tiny tuft of black facial hair beneath his lower lip. He was sullen until Sally hugged me, and then he became outright hostile. I bought us tickets for the next ferry, which left in twenty minutes, and asked the clerk where the phone booths were.

"*Phone booths?*" He rolled his eyes at Sally. "Seriously, girl? What are you doing with this fossil?"

"You know what a phone booth is, right?" I said. "A little box you go into to make a phone call."

"Man," the clerk moaned, "we ain't had one of those in *years*."

"Great customer service skills, sonny," I said. "By the way, you've got some dirt under your lower lip."

He rubbed at the tuft of hair, causing Sally to burst out laughing.

"That's my soul patch, you dick," the clerk said.

As we walked away from the ticket booth, Sally poked me in the arm with something.

"Here's my cell," she said. "I need to use the bathroom."

Consulting my pager, I started dialing the number.

"Go ahead," I said, "but the ferry leaves in ten minutes."

"I'll be out in two." She pointed at the ladies' room. "Time me." She put her suitcase handle in my free hand. "Hold this, please?"

I nodded and watched her enter the ladies' room. On the phone, the line picked up.

"Suzuki," she said.

"It's Dakota," I said. "What's up?"

"I have some bad news."

She described how she and her partner had arrived at Kevin Teller's van at eight o'clock this morning, and that he was dead by an apparent self-inflicted gunshot wound to the head. Aside from his body, a Glock 9-millimeter, and a duffel bag of clothing, the van was empty. The only prints in the van and on the gun were Kevin's. Finally, the boxes of files and other evidence Kevin had alluded to were gone.

"But Jen," I said, "there's no way he killed himself."

"We interviewed some of the IHOP staff. They said Teller was depressed and unstable."

"Of course he was depressed," I rejoined. "The guy was living out of a *van*. Look, Jen…this was a *hit*. Did you see the file about my predecessor on the Standish case? A PI named Tommy O'Toole was killed in his car while staking out Malone's apartment."

"I'm sorry, Dakota," she said, "but there's nothing else I can do."

"You could at least inform the Director," I said. "Sally and some of her classmates might be in a lot of danger."

"I'll email him about it," she said. "But there was one other thing. I found out where Malone's funding comes from. It's a nonprofit called International Psychology Research Foundation, based in Dubai. There's no company website, but I called a guy I know at Treasury, and he said a prince in the Saudi royal family bankrolls it."

I was gazing out the terminal window. The fog was drifting across the brick-paved wharf.

Then, behind me, a man's voice said, "Hang up the phone." Something hard jabbed into my lower back.

"Look," Jen said over the line, "I wish I could do more, but I have to go."

"Yeah, me too. Bye."

I hung up. The voice behind me said, "Where is the girl?"

Whoever this guy was, he had a faint accent—French, maybe. My palm gripping the suitcase handle felt clammy, and I became aware of the strength in my arm. In a flash I recalled a story my paternal grandfather used to tell me. Once, while waiting for a train in Boston's South Station, he was standing with his suitcase exactly like I was now, when a man came up behind him, jabbed something into his back, and demanded his wallet. I hoped grandpa's story was true, because I was about to do likewise. I jerked my head toward some vending machines.

"There she is now," I said.

The second I felt him turn, I wheeled around with the suitcase, putting all of my shoulder strength into whipping it up and behind me. It was like I was executing a powerful tennis backhand with the world's heaviest racquet. I braced myself for a gunshot, but the next thing I knew, the suitcase connected with the man's head, cold-conking him where he stood. Carried along by the momentum of the suitcase, I was still spinning around when he crumpled to the floor.

It turned out he *was* holding a gun on me: a Colt .45 ACP. I took it, along with the ID from his wallet. He had a Quebec driver's license, with an address in Quebec City. His name was Jean-Luc, he was 42 years old, and he was balding with a dark goatee. I stripped the gun and threw the pieces in separate garbage bins. Jean-Luc was beginning to stir when Sally emerged from the ladies' room and gaped at him on the floor.

"Is he okay?"

"Sally, take the suitcase and come with me," I said.

"What happened?"

"No questions. Let's go." I grabbed her arm and ushered her toward the exit.

"Did you hit him?" she asked.

"I'll explain on the ferry," I said.

As we stepped outside, I put an arm around her and kept the other inside my jacket, on my gun. In the dense fog, I couldn't distinguish anything more than fifty feet away, which made me nervous. I scanned the wharf. Aside from a flock of seagulls, spectral in the fog, fighting raucously over a scrap of bread, and a couple of ferry deckhands sharing a cigarette by the loading ramp, the wharf was empty. A shrill blast from the ferry horn echoed across the lot.

"That's the warning signal, Sally," I said. "We have to move."

As we approached the ramp, the deckhands put out their cigarette. Handing them our tickets, I noticed their bloodshot eyes and the musky smell in the air. It wasn't tobacco they were smoking. I hustled Sally onboard and upstairs to the outdoor balcony seating area, where I peered around the bridge at the stern. I wanted to see who boarded after us.

"This sucks," Sally said. "Just great—we'll get all the way to Provincetown and the beach will be socked in by fog."

"Actually," I said, "I think once we're out on the water, the fog will disappear."

"Hmmph," Sally said. "Well, what are we standing out *here* for, Dakota? Let's go inside and snuggle."

"In a minute, Sally. Be patient."

The deckhands were attaching the stern chain when, far away out of the fog, two voices shouted for them to wait. As the voices drew nearer, two men materialized out of the fog, jogging toward the ferry. One of them was Jean-Luc, holding the side of his head; the other was a very tall, broad-shouldered redheaded man. His hair was so glaringly bright that it acted like a beacon through the fog. On women I found this particular shade of fiery red positively mesmerizing; but on men it made me cringe. When the deckhands stopped hooking up the chain and waited for the men to board, I knew we had a problem.

"Sally, honey"—I tugged her by the wrist—"come with me. Quickly, and no arguments."

"What's happening?"

I dragged her downstairs, through the passenger cabin, to a bathroom, where I stepped inside with her and shut the door. She pawed my chest and stood on her tiptoes to kiss me.

"A smelly bathroom on a boat, Dakota? I've heard of the mile-high club, but never the *sea-level* club. Well... if you insist..." Grinning, she fumbled with my shirt buttons.

"Stop it, Sally." I pushed her off me. "We don't have much time. I'll explain everything in detail later, but right now I need you to be quiet and *listen*. My name is Dakota Stevens, but I'm not an academic. I'm a private detective. I used to work for the FBI. Your father and the FBI Director hired me to get you away from Malone. That man you saw on the floor inside the ferry terminal? He's a hit man, and I'm pretty sure he's working for Malone. He and another man are boarding the ferry as we speak, and I think they're after you. I can keep you safe, Sally, but only if you do exactly as I say. Do you understand?"

"*Hit men*? Why do they—"

"Hush, Sally. I have to step out now. As soon as I leave, lock the door, and don't open it for *anybody* except me—no matter what."

She stared dumbly at me. Her face was pale. I slapped her cheek.

"Ow! Dakota!"

"Sally," I said, "what are you going to do?"

"Lock the door when you leave and…don't let anybody in."

"Except me. And don't talk or make any noise."

The ferry horn blasted, and the hull shuddered with a loud, low vibration. We were underway. Sally clawed at my jacket.

"Dakota, don't leave. Please. I'm scared."

"Hey, it'll be okay." I kissed her and jounced one of her curls in my fingers. "By the way…I really do love your hair."

She gave me a brief, tight-lipped smile.

"That's my brave girl," I said. "I'll be right back, I promise."

I opened the door and peeked up the passageway. The door to the bow was open. A salty cool breeze, tinged with the tang of marijuana, wafted in. I craned my neck for a better view. The two deckhands who'd been at the stern were sitting Indian-style on the ferry deck between the gunwale and a pickup truck, smoking their joint again. I looked the other way, into the passenger cabin. A pair of elderly women sat near the window, chatting. At the far end of the cabin, the door to the stern was open, but I saw nothing outside.

I slipped out of the bathroom. As soon as I heard the door lock behind me, I pulled my gun. Concealing it against my hip so I didn't frighten the old ladies, I hustled through the passenger cabin to the stern door. I crouched and peeked outside.

Across the stern, Jean-Luc and the big redhead were leaning back against the port-side gunwale, surveying the cars on the deck. Fog drifted past them like smoke. Big Red muttered something to Jean-Luc and marched toward the bow between the cars.

Jean-Luc was smoking a cigarette. When he turned around and peered down at the water, I tiptoed out the door. Directly outside against the bulkhead was a life jacket locker. Holstering my gun, I carefully opened the locker, slid out a life jacket, and crept up behind Jean-Luc. I got within six feet of him before his shoulders tensed up.

As he started to turn around, I rushed in, bear-hugged him around the thighs, and heaved him over the gunwale. He landed hard on his side in the water, making a loud splash, but the roar of the engine and the churning of the propellers muffled the sound. He surfaced, shook a fist at me. I tossed the life jacket down to him. No sooner had he clutched it to his chest than the fog consumed him.

One down, one to go.

Drawing my gun and concealing it in my jacket pocket, I set out between the cars, toward the bow. I needed to find Big Red before he found Sally. Now that we were some distance into the harbor, the ferry picked up speed, causing the fog to swirl around the bulkhead and the cars up near the bow. One second I'd see a car, and the next it would vanish in the fog.

When I rounded the bulkhead corner, the deckhands were still sitting on the deck, smoking their joint. I peeked into the starboard passenger cabin. Sally's bathroom door was still closed. I didn't hear any noise in there or see Big Red, and he wasn't up on the balcony level, so I deduced he must be in the port-side passenger cabin.

I crossed the deck to the door. It was closed, but there was a glass porthole. Big Red was in there all right, yanking doors open and scanning the seating area. I waited until he reached the stern door. As soon as he grabbed the doorknob, I ran on tiptoe to the bulkhead corner just outside the stern door. Hanging on the superstructure above me was a large lifesaver. I took it down carefully and held it in my left hand while steadying my gun hand.

Around the corner, the door banged shut. Big Red lumbered toward the stern looking around. The fog swirling between us was so dense that, even less than ten feet away, all of him except his flaming hair became a dark shape in the soupy gray-white mist. Briefly I considered heaving him overboard like his buddy, but Red outweighed me by a good fifty pounds, and any kind of grappling with this big boy could go horribly wrong for me. Instead I waited until he was looking sternward, and then I snuck up behind him in the fog. When I was six feet away, I leveled my gun at his back.

"Hands up, Red. I have a gun aimed at your spine."

He complied.

"Now turn around. Slowly."

He did. His face was heavily freckled, and he wasn't smiling. Obviously I couldn't shoot him, but somehow I had to convince him that I *would* shoot him, so he'd jump off the boat instead.

"You've got two choices," I said. "Either you *jump* off the boat with this"—I held up the lifesaver—"or I *shoot* you off the boat with this." I aimed the gun at his head. "If I were you, I'd choose the lifesaver."

He frowned. Clearly he wasn't happy with his choices, but after a few seconds' deliberation, he nodded at the lifesaver.

"Good choice," I said. "By the way, I don't like male redheads. There's something creepy about you guys, like you were bred in a government experiment that took a turn. No offense." I jabbed the gun at him. "Now go, and I'll throw the lifesaver over the side to you."

Scowling, he slung his heavy legs over the gunwale, lowered himself down and let go. When I heard the splash, I ran over to the gunwale and winged the lifesaver down. The lifesaver was heading straight for his head when the fog swallowed him up. Hopefully I hit him, the big schmuck. I holstered the gun and ran back to Sally's bathroom. Vomiting sounds emanated from inside. I knocked on the door and announced myself. Sally's voice faltered.

"Duh…kota?"

"Yes, it's me, Sally," I said. "You can open up now. The bad men are gone."

The door squeaked open. I slipped inside.

"I've been puking the whole time," she said.

"Seasick?" I said.

"I guess." She ran the faucet and washed out her mouth. "What happened to the men? Did you kill them?"

"No, I didn't *kill* them. They're fine. Swimming back to Boston as we speak."

"What?!"

"Get yourself together, come out in the passenger cabin, and I'll tell you about it. See you in a few minutes."

Grabbing her suitcase, I went out and commandeered a bench against the bulkhead with a view out the window. I put the suitcase on the floor. Just as I'd predicted, now that we were out in Massachusetts Bay, the fog was lifting, giving way to azure skies. P-Town would be beautiful.

Sally emerged from the bathroom looking slightly less green but still nauseous. She staggered down the corridor, steadying herself with her hands against the walls. When she reached me, I laid her on her side and rested her head on my lap. I removed her glasses and stroked her hair.

"We've got about an hour until we reach Provincetown, Sally," I said. "Close your eyes, stay quiet and I'll tell you everything. This whole thing started when the FBI Director summoned me to Washington, D.C. to meet your father…"

24

A Postcard New England Indian Summer Day

To her credit, Sally was remarkably resilient. Within minutes of stepping onto solid ground—the pier in Provincetown—her stomach settled and she was her usual perky, flirtatious self. Surprisingly, however, she didn't broach the subject of the men on the ferry, nor did she want to discuss what I'd told her during the trip. It was as though all that happened a lifetime ago and was now forgotten.

Sally might have forgotten about the two attackers, but I hadn't. Strolling away from the pier, I kept her close as I formed a plan of where to go and what to do for the next few hours.

I bought us a picnic lunch of lobster rolls, coleslaw, potato salad and bottles of iced tea, then rented us a couple of bicycles, the larger of which had a big basket on the back. I put her suitcase in the basket, hung the bag with the picnic lunch from my handlebars, and led Sally on a brief tour of Provincetown.

I began with the seemingly endless gauntlet of shops, galleries and restaurants along Commercial Street—the main drag in P-Town. Several shops were closed for the season; these were obvious from the dry leaves and litter banked up in front of their entrances.

We coasted down the length of Commercial Street to a small, bayside cove and a complex of seaside bungalows formerly known as Mayflower Cottages. The summer before my junior year in college, I had worked here as a handyman for a German immigrant named Klara, whose father had been the chauffeur for German Field Marshal Rommel. I was confident her story was true because she'd shown me a picture of herself as a toddler standing with her father and Rommel in front of a convertible Mercedes-Benz sedan.

From Klara's place, I led Sally across Route 6 to the entrance for Race Point Beach. We pedaled down the beach road through the scrub pines and sand dunes to the Atlantic side of the Cape. Parking the bikes, we walked out on the beach together, bringing the suitcase and lunch. To the north, the beach was deserted; to the south, about half a mile away, a couple of kids and their parents were flying a kite. There were no footprints on the sand. In fact, aside from some seaweed and driftwood left at the high tide line, this stretch of beach was pristine.

Sally proved well-prepared for our outing, having packed two big beach towels, sunscreen, swim towels and a digital camera. Without warning, she quickly shed her skirt and top, nearly giving me a heart attack until I saw she was wearing her maraschino cherry swimsuit underneath.

Once we spread out the towels, she asked me to put sunscreen on her. I did, but in brisk, fatherly fashion so she wouldn't get ideas. We sat and ate our picnic lunch while breakers crashed lazily down at the shoreline. Seals surfaced in the cresting waves, eyed us curiously, and dove back underwater. Delighted with this serendipitous encounter, Sally snapped photos of them.

It was a postcard New England Indian summer day—clear skies, temperature in the low sixties, and a gentle and steady offshore breeze. The lobster rolls, mostly tail meat, were delectable. When we got to the coleslaw and potato salad, because they'd given us only one fork Sally kneeled beside me and fed me from the containers. After lunch, I made a pillow of my leather jacket and lay on my back. Sally lay on her side and cuddled against me. As she took hold of my hand, her BDSM collar glinted in the bright sun. I reached out and gently lifted it off her collarbone.

"Doesn't this thing bother you, resting on your collarbone like that?"

"Sometimes," she said. "Like if I run, and it bounces up and down, it can hurt. I get bruises once in a while." She touched my gun in its shoulder holster. "What about *this* thing? Isn't it uncomfortable having it under your arm all the time?"

"Sometimes."

I looked out to sea. Miles offshore, an oil tanker crawled along the horizon. Oil made me think of Saudi Arabia, and then I thought about what Jen had said—a member of the Saudi royal family backed the company that funded Malone's study. Sally tapped my shoulder.

"Dakota?"

"Yeah?" I said.

Sitting up on her elbow, she rested her head on her palm and stared at me.

"All that stuff about Geoff, those other girls, the man that was killed—was that true?"

"Yes."

"I just can't believe Geoff would be involved in stuff like that. Abducting girls? Human trafficking? He doesn't seem—"

"The evidence is pretty strong," I said. "I've told you the truth about everything, Sally."

"That's a *lie*." She jabbed me in the chest.

"What are you talking about?"

"Me...how you feel about me," she said. "Pretending you like me. You've been lying about *that* the whole time, haven't you?"

"Hold on a second." I turned on my side and mirrored her pose: my arm bent at the elbow, resting my head on my palm. "Yes, I'll admit, at first I was pretending I liked you. I was hired to lure you away from Dr. Malone, and I needed to make you interested in me. But..."

"But"—her eyes sparkled—"you've fallen in love with me?"

"Not quite," I said. "Just like it'd be absurd for you to say you've fallen in love with *me*. Not after a few days, right?"

She shrugged. "Mm, I guess."

"Let's put it this way...you've *grown* on me, Sally. A lot. I'm attracted to you and...your youthful exuberance."

She glanced at the towel, swallowed, and locked eyes with me again.

"Attracted to me...like, physically?"

"Absolutely," I said. "You're a beautiful young lady."

"Really?" She fidgeted on her towel. "Like *what* about me? Most guys think I look geeky."

"All right, I'm only going to say this *once*. Ready?"

She nodded enthusiastically.

"First of all"—I ran my hand down her hip and thigh—"your legs are stunning."

"Stunning?"

"Shush," I said. "I love how your ears stick out a little bit, your wonderful high cheekbones, and that prominent forehead of yours. It's like you've got an alien brain in there."

Smiling, she wriggled off her towel onto mine. "Yeah? You know what I like about you?"

"I'm not finished," I said. "Finally there's that lower lip of yours—how it's always pouty and shimmering, begging to be kissed. That lip should have a poem written about it."

She laughed. "It *is* begging to be kissed, Dakota."

Before I could resist, Sally threw her leg over me, shoved me on my back, and straddled me. Dipping her head, she dragged her lower lip up across my chin stubble and kissed me.

"I like how you're like classically handsome," she said. "Like...the star of an old-timey movie. And *strong*—a real man's man."

"Actually...I like to think of myself as the man that man's men look up to. A man's man's man."

"Stop fooling around." She caressed my cheek. "You're strong. I feel safe with you. You're smart, too. Even if you *aren't* a Ph.D."

Still straddling me, she kissed my neck and rubbed her chest against my shirt.

"So," she said, kissing me, "since we find each other so attractive…once this case is over…maybe we could—"

"No way."

"Why not?" She sat up and thumped her fist on my chest. "Do you have a girlfriend?"

"Nope. Broke up a few days ago," I said.

"So, what's the problem?"

"Well, for starters," I said, "your father is friends with the FBI Director, and I'm just starting my private detective business."

"So what?" She rolled off me and back onto her towel. "Why's that matter?"

"It just does," I said. "There's also the difference in our ages."

"Oh—you're too *old* for me, is that it? Because you don't look old, Dakota. At *all*. Seriously, you're better-built than *any* of the guys in my dorm."

"Thank you, honey." I smiled and touched her cheek. "No, the issue isn't my being too old for you. The issue is, you're too *young* for me."

Her face scrunched up. She stomped a heel against her blanket.

"That's a stupid double-standard," she said. "For you to—"

"Sally, you're a bright girl with a lot of potential, but you don't know what you want yet. You're definitely not ready to have a committed relationship with a grown man. If you and I got involved right now, I'd give us about a week. Some other guy would catch your eye, and you'd leave me in the dust."

"No, I wouldn't!" She scooped up a fistful of sand and slung it behind her.

"Listen," I said, "I don't think you'd do it intentionally. You just can't help yourself. In every way—academically, socially, sexually, emotionally—you're figuring out what you want, what you like and don't like. I also think you'd wear me out. I bet you're an insatiable little minx in bed."

Looking coyly at me, she spoke with that breathy, ingénue voice again.

"No...but with the right man...I could be."

"See?" I said. "*That's* what I'm talking about."

"What?"

"The coy, come-hither looks, the breathy, baby-girl talk. I'm a grown man, Sally. I want a strong, smart, independent, beautiful *woman*, not some Lolita-esque flibbertigibbet. Do you understand what I'm saying?"

She stared at her blanket. After a tense couple of seconds, she finally nodded.

"Do you?" I said.

"I've never read *Lolita*, but I understand the reference," she said.

"Listen, Sally...you're young. Trust me...you don't want to be tied down to a guy—any guy. In fact, I suggest you take a break from boys for a while. Enjoy your girlfriends, maybe make up with your roommate Megan. And when you *do* decide to date again, date some boys your own age."

"Boys my own age don't like me," she said.

"I seriously doubt that. I bet you only *think* they don't like you because they're standoffish. They're probably intimidated by you."

"Maybe." She shivered and put on her skirt and top again.

"You're not going for a swim?" I said. "After two hours and two bad guys to get here?"

She looked at the water and shook her head.

"Sally," I said, "the most important thing for you right now is to stay away from Malone. Those men were bad news. Did Malone ever say anything about Montreal?"

"Yeah, he invited me to go up there with him," Sally said. "In a few days. I wasn't sure I could do it because I have classes. He asked if Megan might want to join us."

"Interesting," I said. "Sally, I need you to do me a favor."

"What could I possibly do for *you*?"

"Two things," I said. "First, we need to talk to Megan. I think the two of you are in danger. Here, look at this." I handed her the photo of the list of girls. "That's a photo of a page from Malone's day planner. Look at numbers five and eight. Sound familiar?"

As she studied the photo, her face morphed from confusion into shock.

"These sound like me and Megan," she said. "But why are they crossed out?"

"I'm not sure," I said. "I *think* it's because that's a wish list of girls he's looking for, and when he found you and Megan, he crossed them out. By the way, do you know any Asian girls who fit the description of number two on the list?"

"Mm...nobody really. Oh, wait...maybe Jade. You know, from tennis intramurals?"

I thought back to the other day, when I was coaching the girls and Malone was watching them from the stands with binoculars.

"Sure, I remember her," I said.

"What about the 'buxom blonde' mentioned here?" Sally asked.

"I think that was Teller's daughter. I've seen her picture, and she looks like the girl described on the list."

"Teller was the man found killed this morning?" she asked.

"Yes."

She handed the photo back to me. "This doesn't prove anything. Certainly not that Geoff is involved in human trafficking."

"Maybe not," I said, "but two things I discovered the other day are very suspicious."

I told her about the test tubes of blood and the encrypted flash drive of photos—photos of girls who had disappeared.

"I need to ask you something, Sally," I said. "What's your blood type?"

"A-B negative. Why?"

"Ah-hah," I said. "What if I told you that all of those test tubes of blood were A-B negative, and that the young women in those pictures—the ones who've disappeared—they might be A-B negative as well?"

Sally shivered and drew her knees into her chest. Her eyes gaped.

"I...I can't believe this is happening."

I put my arm around her. "Sally, I need you to stay away from him. No more working at the lab, no more Malone period. Which brings me to the second part of the favor. You need to let me take you home to Connecticut."

"*Home?* No way."

"You're not safe in Cambridge, Sally—even after Malone leaves. Most of the young women at the other colleges disappeared a month or so *after* Malone folded up the tents on his study."

She continued to clutch her knees to her chest and stare out at the ocean.

"You've given me a lot to think about," she said. "Honestly, I'm kind of overwhelmed by all this, Dakota."

"That's understandable." I stood, offered her a hand and helped her up. "Come on, we'll walk on the beach for a while, and talk about this some more. Then we'll go back to Cambridge."

She put an arm around me and we strolled down the beach on the wet sand, just above the hissing foam.

———◆·◈·◆———

When we returned the bicycles to Provincetown, I hired a cab to take us to the garage in Boston. The Mercedes didn't appear to have been disturbed. The engine was slow to start, but after a few tries it turned over and I drove us back to the Charles.

There, I installed Sally in the room next to mine, leaving the connecting door open so I could keep tabs on her. When she put on a movie, I called Svetlana. Muzak played in the background on the other end of the line.

"Where are you?" I asked.

"Saks, in Boston," she said. "Shopping."

"Did you have a chance to—"

"So far, everything Mr. Teller told us appears to be accurate," she said.

She explained how she had spent her day calling the parents of the missing girls.

"All of them corroborated his story, Dakota," she said.

"I was afraid of that."

"Perhaps when you speak with the FBI next, you could share this with them."

"Actually, I already heard from them."

I told her about the call from Special Agent Suzuki. I gave her the name of the Saudi-bankrolled organization that funded Malone's research, and how Agent Suzuki had found Kevin Teller dead in his van this morning.

"That is very distressing," she said. "But perhaps now the FBI will get involved, yes?"

"Maybe," I said. "I'll discuss all of this with the Director the next time I talk with him, but I'm not sure it'll make a difference."

"Dakota?" she said.

"Yeah?"

"I am standing at a register with an armload of clothing. Is there anything else?"

"What about the girls' blood types?" I asked. "Did you—"

"A-B negative," she said. "All of them."

"Wow," I said. "That can't be a coincidence. This has really turned into a case now. Mind if I call you tomorrow? In the afternoon, maybe?"

"Certainly," she said.

"Have a good night."

"You as well."

After I hung up, I checked on Sally. She was asleep on her bed with the TV playing. I shut it off. I draped a blanket over her, sat in an armchair and watched her breathe for a while.

25

A GENTLE, AVUNCULAR SQUEEZE

At five o'clock the next morning, I rolled out of bed, worked out in the fitness center, and swam thirty laps in the hotel pool. Once showered and dressed, I woke Sally, waited for her to get ready, and ate a quiet breakfast with her in the restaurant downstairs.

Afterwards I escorted her to her first class—Professor Cantor's "psychos" class, as Sally termed it. She had her arm around my waist during the entire walk. Passing faculty gave me the stink-eye, but I ignored them. Sally's sense of safety was more important than what other people thought about me.

"Hey," she said. "Maybe going home isn't such a bad idea. When were you thinking?"

"Tomorrow morning?" I said.

"So soon?"

"I'll feel better when you're home with your parents, Sally. Tell you what—we'll take our time driving. We can stop for lunch someplace, maybe go to a movie or something. What do you say?"

"I'd love that!" She hugged me with both arms. "Okay, tomorrow morning then."

I glanced at my watch. "Let's get you to class."

In the amphitheater, Sally sat next to a strapping young man who shook my hand with an adamantine grip.

"Dakota," Sally said, "this is my friend, Darryl. He's on the hockey team. I'll be fine for an hour."

"Darryl," I said, "you'll watch out for Sally?"

"You bet," he said. "Anybody messes with her, I'll knock their teeth down their throat."

Sally smiled crookedly.

"Okay then," I said.

Confident Sally would be safe for a while, I slipped out and went hunting for a pay phone. I needed to talk to Director Reeves.

Pay phones, and especially phone *booths*, were becoming scarcer by the day. I sensed the time was fast approaching when I'd have to bite the bullet and get a cell phone. Miraculously, I found a wall-mounted pay phone in the lobby of the building next door. As I dialed Director Reeves's number, the lobby doors kept opening and banging shut behind me.

Once he got on the line, I explained that I'd successfully taken Sally out of Dr. Malone's clutches, that I'd installed her in the room adjoining mine at the Charles, and that I would drive her home to Connecticut tomorrow morning.

"Fine, Stevens," the Director said. "Put it all in your report. Tomorrow, then, we'll consider the case officially closed."

"But actually, sir, it isn't," I said. "I believe Special Agent Suzuki emailed you about this. At least fourteen young women have been abducted by Malone's people and—"

"I'm going to stop you right there, Stevens," he said. "I'm extremely busy this morning, but I want to be very clear about what's going to happen. Are you listening?"

A door banged shut behind me. "Yes, sir."

"You will deliver Miss Standish to her parents in Connecticut," he said. "You will return to New York and hang out your PI shingle—I might even be able to throw you a few cold cases to get you started—and you will forget about this business with Doctor Ma—" Another door banged shut behind me. "What is that racket? It's very annoying."

"Doors, sir," I said. "I'm in a lobby, on a pay phone. But what about all the evidence I've uncovered?"

"What evidence?"

"The list of girls? The photos of girls and the test tubes of A-B negative blood I found in Malone's apartment? Mr. Teller's testimony, the photos he showed me, and the fact that he was murdered? The fact that a Saudi prince backs the nonprofit that bankrolls Malone's research? Sir, there's way too much evidence to ignore."

"Stevens, I'm not arguing with you about this," he said. "The reality is, all of your so-called *evidence* is circumstantial at best, and none of it has been legally obtained—there's no chain of custody. You know it, I know it. As for the photos and Mr. Teller's testimony, well…the man is dead and there wasn't a speck of evidence in his van. I have my best agents working the missing persons cases you're referring to and—"

"Your 'best agents'?" I said. "Like who?"

"That's none of your business, Stevens," he said. "It seems I need to remind you—you are no longer a Bureau employee. Listen carefully. Unless you want to be charged with obstruction of justice, I expect you to immediately drop this matter regarding Teller, get Miss Standish home safely, and refocus on your PI career. Are you hearing me, Stevens? Is this getting through?"

"Yes, sir."

"Good. I'll inform Mr. Standish of your success with Sally and tell him you'll have her home tomorrow."

"Fine."

"Before I go," the Director said, "there's one thing I'm curious about."

"What's that, sir?"

"What did you say to Sally to convince her to leave Malone?"

I knew that saying what I was about to say was a bad idea, but the Director's condescension had gotten my blood up, so I decided to let it fly. When the lobby door opened and banged shut again, I turned and winked at a couple of coeds walking in.

"I didn't *say* anything to her, sir," I said loudly into the phone. "I seduced her."

The girls gaped at me and hurried past.

"What!" the Director shouted. "You…you couldn't have! To have *sex* with Harold's daughter—an innocent and vulnerable young lady! Stevens, I'll—"

"Relax, Director…I didn't have *sex* with her. I just charmed her. Have a nice day, sir. Goodbye."

I hung up.

When I met Sally after class, her hockey friend Darryl tried to crush my hand again shaking me goodbye. I was tempted to retaliate, but I let it go. I was pleased that at least one young man Sally's age was concerned about her welfare. Sally and I said goodbye to him and crossed Harvard Yard together.

"Darryl's nice, isn't he?" Sally said.

"Seems like a good kid," I said. "Why? You like him?"

"Mm…*maybe*."

"God, you're fickle, you know that?"

She giggled.

"Hey, I've been doing some more thinking," she said. "I'm done with Geoff. You're right—he's treated me really badly. Besides, if he's actually behind the abductions of those girls…"

"I was hoping you'd say that."

I led us past the newsstand in Harvard Square and headed down J.F.K. Street toward my hotel.

"Where are we going now, Dakota?"

"Back to the hotel," I said. "I have a surprise for you."

"Mm, I *like* surprises."

A matronly woman at the front desk gave me a scornful look when I walked by with Sally literally hanging all over me. I replied with a boyish exaggerated shrug and led Sally to the elevator.

As soon as the doors closed, she jumped into my arms, wrapping her arms and legs around me, kissing me like I was a soldier just returned from war. The rational, adult part of me knew I should put the kibosh on this mischief before it got out of hand, but the impulsive teenager in me was enjoying it.

Sally made little "mming" noises as she kissed me, like a starving person sampling items at a buffet and being overcome because everything is delicious. Her behavior reminded me vaguely of a girl in college, a reputed nymphomaniac, who'd been interested in me, but whom I'd regrettably ignored. When the feelings of guilt started bubbling up again, I reminded myself that Sally was almost 20 years old; she was of legal age. Besides, it was only kissing.

When the bell dinged for my floor, Sally was still bear-hugging me with all four limbs. Staggering off the elevator with her on me, I passed a pair of businessmen. One of them gave me a discreet thumbs-up and a guy nod (jaw set, eyebrows clenched). I walked like Franken-stein's monster down to the hall to my room, swiped my room key and entered.

At the foot of my bed, I took hold of Sally by the waist and pushed her off me. There was so much suction in her lips that, when I uncoupled her, they made a loud pop in the room, like a plunger being pulled off a tile floor. I held her at arm's length. Her soft brown eyes were dilated, her breathing rapid and shallow. I sat her on the bed. Unfortunately Sally mistook my action as her cue to throw off her jacket and start unbuckling my pants.

"No, Sally." I grabbed her wrists. "That's not the surprise. Look…I want you to take off your blouse—*only* your blouse—and lie face-down on the bed with your eyes closed. Okay?"

She nodded and complied. Grabbing one of my neckties, I sat on the bed and tied it over her eyeglasses. Except for a pink satin bra, her shoulders, back and neck were bare. Her skin was remarkably smooth and creamy. She wagged her feet and murmured into the covers.

"What's my surprise?" she said.

"Hush," I said, removing my coat. "And no peeking."

Quickly, I went into the bathroom and got a hand towel, then pulled the bolt cutters out from under the bed. Threading the hand towel through Sally's collar so the towel protected her neck. I carefully clamped the bolt cutter jaws down on the metal collar.

"What are you doing?"

"Never mind. Just *don't* move, Sally."

In the end, I was disappointed by how easily the bolt cutters severed the collar; they sliced through it like it was electrical solder. When the teeth clamped together, I put the bolt cutters aside and prised the collar apart.

"Okay," I said, "sit up slowly."

As she did, I pulled the collar off her neck and tossed it on the rug. With the blindfold still covering her eyes, Sally patted her throat. I led her to the edge of the bed so she faced the mirror, and removed the blindfold.

"Wow...I have my neck back." She stroked it with her fingertips, craned her head side to side and smiled at herself in the mirror. Then her gaze shifted to me. Her eyes were wet. "Thank you, Dakota."

"You're welcome, Sally."

I pecked her on the nape of her neck and gave her shoulders what I thought was a gentle, avuncular squeeze, but Sally interpreted my gesture differently. Spinning around, her big teeth bared in a lustful snarl, she shoved me onto my back. In the cat-eye glasses, the brimming pink bra, and that perpetually pouting lower lip, she was terribly sexy, so when she clambered on top of me and kissed me, grinding her slippery mouth and chest into me, I couldn't blame myself for surrendering, at least initially, to her advances. However, when she reached behind herself to unlatch her bra, I stopped her.

"Enough, Sally. There's no need for that. Come here."

I pulled her down to me and cradled her in my arms. She began to cry. The crying turned into weeping, which rapidly turned into sobbing—loud, wracking, convulsing sobbing. For the third time on this case, I found myself faced with a person in misery.

I can't describe how uncomfortable and helpless her sobbing made me feel. Although I wanted to tell her to stop, I knew this was the best way for her to get the poison out, so I let her sob into my shirt. Stroking her hair and kissing her cheek from time to time, I reassured her that everything was going to be okay.

In Sally's case her misery was so pronounced, it was as if she were releasing a lifetime of sadness and confusion: about her sexuality, her relationship with her father, her academic life, everything.

From the moment I'd met her, I sensed she was a troubled young lady; however until now I hadn't realized just *how* troubled she was—damaged, possibly. Given the amount of psychological and possibly sexual abuse Malone had likely inflicted on her, Sally, in my opinion, needed to be checked into a good psychiatric hospital for a while. At the very least, the girl was extremely fragile and needed counseling. My job now was to keep her intact and bring her home safely to her parents.

Once Sally had pulled herself together, I drove her over to Malone's apartment. Malone never went home during the day, Sally said, so it was safe. She'd left some clothes there that she wanted back, and I wanted to secure those test tubes and any other evidence I could find.

When we got inside, the apartment was empty. Nothing but bare floors and walls, and dust outlines where the furniture had been. On the way out of the building, while Sally kept lookout I used my ASP baton to jimmy his mailbox, but that, too, was empty.

From the North End, we drove over to Volvap Hall in Cambridge to get some paperwork Sally had left there, only to discover that the observation booth and Malone's office had been cleaned out as well. There was nothing to even hint that Malone had been there.

"This is really weird," Sally said. "Why would he just *leave* like this? Without telling me or anybody?"

"Because his 'research' is just a front, Sally," I said. "And when Malone and his thugs figured out I was on to them, they hightailed it out of town."

"I guess you're right."

As we walked back to the car, I noticed it had turned very cold. After days of mild Indian summer, autumn was settling in. The cold air had a tangy crispness to it that portended possible snow tonight. When we got in the car, I started the engine and ran the heater.

"Sally," I said, "I want you to call Megan and Jade and have them meet us at the hotel right away. I need to talk to them."

"About what?"

"About Malone and the fact that they're in danger," I said. "But don't tell them anything on the phone. Just act like it's a social visit."

"Okay." She took out her cell phone. "I'll call them now."

Because the girls weren't of legal drinking age, we couldn't talk in the hotel bar, so when they showed up at the Charles, the four of us went into the restaurant and ordered nachos, mozzarella sticks, French fries and milkshakes. Megan and Jade had never met each other before, but in minutes they were getting on famously. I called the "meeting" to order by dinging my water glass with my fork.

"Listen, girls," I said, "the reason I wanted you here is because I believe you're all in serious danger. Please listen carefully to me, and hold any questions until *after* I'm finished."

I gave Megan and Jade an abridged, five-minute version of the explanation I'd given Sally the day before, mentioning that I was a former FBI agent, that I'd been hired by Sally's father and the FBI Director, that Malone was the prime suspect in the abductions of fourteen college girls from other campuses, and that he had recently disappeared.

When I finished, Megan and Jade looked at each other and rolled their eyes. Then I showed them the photo of the "shopping list" of girls. When they read crossed-out item numbers two and eight ("Asian girl with long hair [very black hair]" and "female athlete, hardbody type; blonde or Latina") quizzical expressions came over their faces.

"Why are they crossed out?" Jade asked.

"I think it's because he found girls who fit the bill— *you*, Jade; and *you*, Megan." I drank some of my vanilla milkshake. "I have another question. Do you girls know what your blood type is?"

"Of course," Megan said. "Mine's A-B negative."

"So's mine," Jade said, looking at Megan. "What a coincidence."

"You should find this really interesting then," I said. "The fourteen other girls who have been abducted? Guess what their blood type is?" I nodded grimly. "A-B negative."

She and Megan stared at each other. After a moment, Megan slowly turned to Sally and glared at her.

"Damn you, Sally—I always knew he was a creep." She shook her head, sighed, and stuffed a giant clump of nachos in her mouth. She swallowed and dusted her hands. "How do we know we can trust *you*, Dakota? Let's see some ID."

"Of course." I pulled out my Massachusetts State PI license, and my SOCXFBI (Society of Ex-FBI Agents) membership card.

"All right." Megan nodded at my credentials. "What do we do?"

"The most important thing right now is getting you girls safe," I said. "I think you and Jade should stay with Sally tonight here in the hotel. Think of it as a sleepover.

Then, when I take Sally home tomorrow, I'll ask her father to contact the Harvard police. I want people watching the three of you for the next couple months."

"Why so long?" Jade dipped a mozzarella stick in tomato sauce. "You said Malone took off."

"Because," Sally said, "apparently the girls were all abducted like a month or two *after* he left."

"Correct," I said. "Megan, where do you live?"

"Concord. Why?"

"Concord, Mass?" I said.

"No, Concord, Alabama," Megan said, waving another clump of nachos. "Of course Massachusetts. Duh."

"What about you, Jade?"

"San Francisco," she said.

"How about this?" I said. "What if Sally and I drove you both to Megan's house tomorrow morning to stay for a few days? Would you be able to go?"

"That depends," Megan said. "I have Crew practice at six. Could we leave, like, at nine?"

"Sure."

"I don't know if I can," Jade said. "My parents won't want me missing so many classes."

"Listen, girls…this isn't a game. We're talking about your lives and your freedom. Take the days off from school. If you're concerned about your courses, contact your professors, tell them you have a family emergency and ask someone to take notes for you."

When all three girls looked at each other at the same time, I realized how Pollyannaish my suggestion was.

"Sorry," I said, "I forgot this is Harvard, where if you come to class without a pencil, no one will loan you one."

"Dakota went to MIT," Sally said.

"But dated several Harvard girls, so I know the deal," I said. "Anyway, do whatever you have to do to skip your classes for a few days. We'll meet here in the lobby at nine o'clock tomorrow morning, okay?"

They all nodded.

"Great," I said. "Sally, let's you and I take Megan and Jade back to their dorms so they can pack their bags, and then I'll bring the three of you back here. You girls can order room service, anything you want."

"Maybe you'd buy us some *booze*, Dakota?" Megan wagged her eyebrows at me. "Hm?"

"No." I patted her hand where it rested on the table, then winked broadly at all three of them. "And don't even *think* that because there's a minibar in your room with a variety of alcoholic beverages, that the three of you can imbibe and have a pillow fight in your underwear. Understood?"

The three of them squealed and bounced in their chairs. A waiter across the room spun around at the commotion. Shaking his head, he withdrew into the kitchen.

"One last thing." I picked up a French fry and pointed with it. "If you girls *do* decide to have that pillow fight...*I'm* the referee."

26

FATE OR DESTINY DECIDES

One hectic hour later, after rounding up the girls' things and installing the three of them in Sally's room, I called Svetlana at Cabot House and asked her to come over and join me downstairs at the hotel bar. As far as I was concerned, the case was over and I needed a drink. Or five.

I was sitting at a lounge table, watching one of my (and my grandfather's) favorite *Rockford Files* episodes— the one with sassy, brassy-haired Shelley Fabares, who hires Jim Rockford to find buried loot from an old bank robbery—when Svetlana walked in.

Two listless businessmen perked up in their barstools and not so discreetly craned their necks for a better look at her. If she noticed them leering, she didn't show it; instead she glanced at my beer and said to the bartender, "A Pinot Grigio, please." Sitting down at my table, she crossed her legs and skeptically regarded the ceiling-mounted TV.

"What is this?"

"*The Rockford Files*," I said. "He's a TV PI."

"Ah. And what is it you enjoy about the show?"

"Rockford's wit. The con games he uses to get information. The beautiful women that hire him." I jutted my chin. "Like Shelley Fabares here."

The waiter brought over an absurdly full wineglass. He smiled at her as he set it down.

"Thank you." Turning to me, Svetlana said, " 'Beautiful women'—I can see why you would like such a program."

"But it's stuff like this, too." I pointed at the TV. "Watch."

On the program, Jim and the woman were in his Pontiac Firebird, evading another car that was chasing them. Turning a corner next to an auto lot, Jim spies a tractor-trailer car-carrier with its loading ramp down. He drives the Firebird onto the upper deck of the car-carrier, and the pursuing car races past them, none the wiser.

"Is that slick or what?" I said. "I want to do that someday when I'm being followed."

"The presence of the tractor-trailer seems a convenient coincidence, but"—she sipped some of the wine—"it is mildly amusing." She pointed at my beer glass. "I thought you vowed never again to drink while on a case."

"The case is over," I said. "Sally, Megan and Jade are safe in Sally's room upstairs."

"Who are Megan and Jade?" she asked.

I explained that I believed they were two of the girls crossed-off on Malone's list.

"Tomorrow," I said, "I'll drive them to Megan's house in Concord, take Sally home to her parents in Connecticut, and that's that."

Out of nowhere, Svetlana clapped her wineglass down on the table so hard, I thought it would shatter.

"But *what* about all those abducted young women, Dakota? Who is looking out for them?"

"Hey, calm down, Svetlana," I said. "The FBI. At least that's what the Director told me this morning. I explained everything that's happened, but all I got for my trouble was an epic chewing-out."

Putting down my beer, I looked her level in the eyes and told her about the Director's humiliating lecture.

"Svetlana," I said, finishing my monologue, "I did what Mr. Standish and the Director hired me to do, which was to get Sally away from Malone. We're just going to have to trust that the Bureau will continue to investigate the girls' abductions."

Faintly shaking her head, Svetlana stared at me with her wineglass poised halfway to her mouth. Her hand holding the glass trembled slightly. For a moment she looked like she was going to throw the wine in my face.

"There is something I do not understand," she finally said. "You no longer work for the FBI, correct?"

"Correct," I said.

"And why did you leave the FBI?"

"Many reasons," I said. "The reports, the bureaucracy, the politics. Having to do everything 'by the book.' "

" 'By the book,' " she said. "Interesting. However… if you abandon this case, will you not be doing exactly that—going 'by the book'?"

Svetlana was beginning to get on my nerves with her Socratic questioning. I literally had to bite my tongue to prevent myself from lashing out at her. Once I'd calmed down with a few deep breaths, I was able to respond in a more measured tone.

"Svetlana, everything you're saying is right," I said, "but here's the thing. The Director said if I pursue Malone further, he'll have me charged with obstruction of justice. I can't afford to be indicted for a crime while I'm trying to get a private investigations firm off the ground. As far as I'm concerned, that's checkmate."

Svetlana sipped her wine and swirled the glass.

"I find it interesting that you would use a chess analogy," she said, "because I too am seeing your situation in terms of chess. Many of my greatest victories on the chessboard came because I snatched them from the jaws of defeat. The positions were entirely unfavorable for me—I was outmatched in material, tempi, or space—but what I did have was a willingness to make bold moves, to sacrifice material, and to *commit* to a line of play."

She tossed her hair over her jacket collar, put down her wineglass and leaned across the table toward me.

"Dakota, we have only known each other for a few days, but I sense you have it in you to become a great detective. However, in order to do that, you are going to have to overcome your training, the 'official' way of doing things. You will have to step out of the shadow of the FBI and take risks. Not all of your future cases will be as simple as seducing a confused, insecure college girl away from a psychopath. You will surely face much more formidable opponents in the future.

"I know you run a risk going against the FBI Director," she continued, "but...'no risk, no reward.' And if you solve this case—a case that seems to involve international human trafficking—think of it. In one fell swoop, you would be rescuing who knows how many young women from something worse than death, and you would solidly establish your investigations firm. And if you solve the case, if you break such a ring, the FBI will not be arresting or indicting you; they will be rushing to claim you as one of their own and to take the credit."

I nodded to myself considering what she'd said. I drained my beer and waved to the barman for a refill.

"I appreciate your faith in me, Svetlana. Especially considering, like you said, that we've only known each other for a few days. And while I appreciate your point about 'no risk, no reward,' and your accomplishments in chess, there's a big difference between what you do and what I do. Chess is a game that takes place on a board, in a controlled environment. But my work takes place in the real world—a harsh, unforgiving and often violent world. If *you* take a risk in chess, what's the worst that can happen? You lose the game. But if *I* take a risk, I can lose my livelihood and people can die. I'm sorry, but I'm letting the Bureau handle the Malone case from now on. Besides, I'm not ready for a case involving an international conspiracy yet."

"I have learned that we do not get to decide when we are ready," Svetlana said. "Fate or Destiny decides." She laid a hand on my forearm. "Dakota, I think it is your destiny to solve this case. You *must* do it."

"I'm not pursuing the case, Svetlana, and that's final."

She gazed at the tabletop for a few seconds. When she looked up at me again, her eyes were steely and her jaw was clenched.

"I wish you well with your firm," she said, "but do not bother to contact me when you return to New York. I have decided not to rent out the first floor of my building. Perhaps I turn it into exercise room and practice studio for my chess. I will decide when I go home tomorrow night."

"That's fine." I shook her hand. "Nice meeting you. Thanks for your help."

She stood and shouldered her purse. Turning to leave, she stopped in her tracks and glared at me.

"There is one other detail you might find interesting," she said. "That nonprofit, the International Psychology—"

"Yeah, the one backed by the Saudi prince?" I said. "What about it?"

"The Saudi prince in question is a hemophiliac," she said. "Blood type A-B negative."

"That *is* interesting," I said. "Hopefully the Bureau will take note of it."

"Goodbye then," she said.

"Bye."

She walked out. The woman had a lovely walk. I'd miss it.

On the TV, Jim, the girl, and her dead husband's partner were in a barn, digging holes to find the stolen loot. It was the end of the episode. Damn it. I'd missed the entire second half while being lectured at by Svetlana.

When the bartender came over with my beer, I chugged half of it and asked him to bring me another one right away. Then, beer in hand, I went out to the phone booth in the lobby, closed the door and called Special Agent Suzuki.

"Hey, Jen," I said when she answered, "I was thinking. How about you pack a swimsuit and a change of clothes and come over here and join me for dinner? The Bureau's treat. What do you say?"

"Dakota," she said, "I think it'd be best if we...said goodbye."

"Why? We had a good time the other night, didn't we?"

"Yes, but your case is over. The Director called me personally this morning and was very firm—I am not to provide you with any more assistance. Oh, which reminds me...my partner will drop by first thing in the morning to pick up the gun we lent you."

"Fine, but this isn't about the case *or* assistance," I said. "It's about you. I like you, Jen. I need you tonight."

"But that's *tonight*. You go home tomorrow."

"So?"

"So...I'm not some woman you can just hook up with because you're lonely and we happen to be in the same city. I'm not a damn *flight attendant*, Dakota."

"I never said you were. And I don't think I've treated you like one."

She groaned. "Look, I have to go. We had fun. Let's not spoil the memory of it, okay?"

"Yeah, I understand," I said. "Take care of yourself, Jen."

"You too, Dakota. Bye."

27

WHEN I CAME TO DIE

The next morning, I checked the girls and myself out of the Charles Hotel and drove us out to Concord. It was rush hour on a weekday, but since most of the traffic was on its way *in* to Boston, we made good time. Fittingly for the first day of October, a dusting of snow had fallen overnight, making for a pretty ride.

I took the girls to the historic Concord Inn for a late breakfast. The three of them gossiped in rapid girl-speak and joked and laughed the entire time. I was glad to see that Sally and Megan were getting along again, and Jade and Megan both seemed much less uptight together than when I'd dealt with them individually. A few times during breakfast, however, I poignantly felt my age. Like when Megan took a cranberry scone out of the bread basket, declared herself "The Scone-y Monster," and crumbled it against her mouth while making comical munching sounds. Sally and Jade, apoplectic with laughter, thrashed in their chairs.

The girls' hijinks drew unwanted attention from other diners, including a long table of twenty wom-en—from yoga-fit young moms to pearl-adorned elderly matrons—who turned in unison and stared at me, as if to say, "Why aren't you with *one* woman your own age?"

I was relieved when we finally left. Sadly, by now the temperature was up, and the snow dusting was gone. From the car back seat, Megan gave me directions to her house and continued to joke around with Jade. Once we were outside the village, Megan directed me down a road that passed the entrance for Walden Pond. When Sally saw the sign, she grabbed my arm.

"Dakota, can we stop?" she said. "I've never seen Thoreau's cabin. I've always wanted to see it."

"Well, it's not his original cabin," I said. "It's just a replica they built for tourists."

"You've been here before?" she said.

"Of course," I said. "When I was in college, I used to come out here to clear my head. It's very peaceful."

"Well, *I* want to see it," she said. "Who knows when I'll be over here again."

"We can go if you want." I glanced in the rear-view mirror. "Megan, Jade—how about it? Want to see Thoreau's place?"

Megan shoved her head between the front seats and rested her chin on my shoulder

"Lame!" she said. "My house borders the south side of the park, Dakota. My family's hiked in there so many times, we made our own path. That's a hard pass."

"Me, too," Jade said, looking at Megan. "Sounds *super*-lame."

"Hard pass?" I said. "What, Megan? Speak English, Miss 'Perfect SAT Verbal.' "

Sally giggled. " 'Hard pass' means she'll pass on it. But will you still take me? On the way back? Please?"

"Sure," I said.

Past Walden Pond, there was a lot of road construction. Several times we were stopped by a flagger and forced to wait while the traffic crept one-way through a construction site. When we finally turned in to Megan's driveway, she groaned.

"Oh...my...*God* do I hate the construction around here," she said. "That took like, what—half an hour? That *should* be like a five-minute drive. Ugh!"

Her house was at the end of a long driveway. Typical for Concord, it was a big and boring white Colonial with black shutters and a red door. Nearby were a detached garage and a shed. There were no cars in the driveway.

"Are either of your parents home, Megan?" I asked.

"No, my dad works in Boston, and my mom does volunteer stuff. Why?"

"I wanted to talk to them about this situation with Malone."

"Chill, Dakota," Megan said. "I'll be fine. I'll tell them all about it tonight, I swear."

"All right." I gave her and Jade each a business card. "The number on there is for my beeper. Tell your parents they can call—"

"Your *beeper?*" Megan and Jade looked at each other and sniggered.

"Seriously?" Jade said

"I know, right?" Sally said.

"I'll tell them, Dakota," Megan said. "Thanks for breakfast."

"Yeah," Jade said, "thanks, Dakota."

"You're welcome, girls. Goodbye."

They each grabbed a suitcase and a knapsack of books and got out of the car. Outside, Megan rapped on Sally's window.

"Bye, bitch," she said.

"Bye, bitch," Sally said.

Waving goodbye to Megan and Jade, I waited until they entered the house, then pulled away. It took us another twenty minutes to get back to Walden Pond, but when we turned in to the parking lot, there was only one other car. There were no buses either, which I was grateful for because that meant no school kids. Outside, I took my survival pack out of the trunk and slipped it on.

"What's that for?" Sally asked.

"It's a survival pack." I closed the trunk.

"Like we're really going to need it out here," she said, waving a hand. "This isn't exactly the wilderness, Dakota."

"No, but we're going into the woods," I said, "and anytime you go into the woods, the rule is…*Never underestimate Nature.*"

She covered her mouth to muffle a yawn. "Whatever."

"Hey, don't make fun," I said. "You're with a former Eagle Scout, my dear."

"Oooh, I feel so honored." She rolled her eyes.

"Do you know what the Scout motto is, Sally?" I led us down the gravel path toward Thoreau's cabin. " 'Be Prepared.' *Anytime* you go into the woods, you need to have a few basic items on you."

"All right, I'll play along," she said. "Basic items… like…?"

"A compass. Fire-starter and dry tinder. First-aid kit. Bottled water. Emergency food. A knife. Cordage. A tin cup for drinking and cooking. Emergency blankets and—"

"Oh, like those aluminum thingies?" She put her arm around my waist and rested her head against me.

"Actually, they're Mylar, but they're shiny so they look like aluminum." I stopped, took my pack off one shoulder, unzipped a pouch and pulled out an orienteering compass. "Do you know how to use one of these?"

"What's that—a compass?" she asked.

"Yes."

"No, I don't." She stared up at me with her hands clasped behind her back.

"Would you like to learn?" I asked.

With her lips pursing in amusement, she slowly shook her head.

"You little city wench." I put the compass away. "I ought to lose you out here. Then we'd see how smart you are."

"Yeah," she said, "it'd probably take me a whole *hour* to find Megan's house and have a pizza delivered."

I chuckled and pulled her against me. I walked with my arm over her shoulders telling her about Thoreau. When we got to the replica cabin, the door was open, revealing the contents inside: a table, a writing desk and three chairs, a fireplace with a woodstove, a firewood box, and a bed.

"That's *it*?" Sally said. "That's all he had? Seriously, how did the guy not die from boredom?"

"Well, the village is only a couple miles from here," I said. "As I understand it, he would go into town a lot and eat dinner with the Emersons."

After a look at the outside of the cabin, we started down the path toward the pond. Sally gesticulated over her shoulder.

"I thought it would be…you know…bigger," Sally said. "He lived in *that* thing for two years?"

"Well, again, I don't think he was out here the entire time," I said. "Do you know how much the cabin cost him to build?"

"No." She punched me gently in the arm. "But I bet *you* do."

"Twenty-eight dollars, twelve and a half cents."

"They had half-cents back then?"

"Yup."

"Crazy," she said.

Ahead, a wooden sign stood at the trailhead. It was a quote from *Walden*. We stopped, and Sally read it aloud:

> I went to the woods because I wished to live de-liberately, to front only the essential facts of life, and see if I could not learn what it had to teach and not, when I came to die, discover that I had not lived. — Thoreau

"So"—Sally poked me in the ribs—"what's it mean?"

I led us down the trail. "Didn't you read *Walden* in high school?"

"Yeah, sure, but…that was like three years ago. Besides, what's with all of the *not's* in there? It's confusing."

"It means," I said, pulling her close to me, "that he built a cabin in the woods and lived there for two years because he wanted to live elementally, without technology and modern conveniences. He wanted to see if he could live in Nature, on Nature's terms, and he was curious what he'd learn from the experience. The book *Walden* is his report on what happened and what he learned."

"Damn you're smart!" She grinned up at me. "How many times have you read it?"

I shrugged. "Ten or twelve."

"*Twelve times!* What?"

"Sure. It's a great book. Hold on a second."

Fifty feet or so down the trail, directly next to a conspicuous "NO BICYCLES" sign, was a man in his mid 20s on a mountain bike. He was snapping on his helmet.

"Excuse me," I said. "You can't ride that in here."

He threw his shoulders back and jutted his chin at me. "You work here or something?"

"No, but there's a sign." I pointed at it.

"Screw you," he said and pushed off.

"What a jerk," Sally said to me.

"Yeah, but the world is full of them, my dear." I breathed deeply of the fresh air. "You know…I've always wanted to live in a cabin like Thoreau. Or at least I like the *idea* of doing it."

Sally looked up at me, biting her lip. Her eyes flashed.

"If you do it, I'll do it, too! We could do it together!"

"That would kind of defeat the purpose," I said. "Thoreau's experiment was about a person living *alone* in the woods, having to face himself and Nature. I'm pretty sure he didn't have a twenty-year-old minx shacking up with him."

Sally laughed.

"If he had," I continued, "he wouldn't have written his book. And if somehow he *had* managed to write it, that quote back at the trailhead would have gone, 'I went to the woods because I wished to live deliberately, to front only the essential facts of life…well, that is until *Little Sally Sexpot* came knocking on my door, after which the two of us spent all our time holed up in the cabin copulating furiously, like rabbits.' "

" '*Sally Sexpot!*' " She slapped me in the stomach and laughed harder.

As I walked with my arm around her, a gentle autumn breeze came up, fluttering her hair against my fingers. For a blissful moment I forgot all about the thirteen-year chasm between our ages. I felt like I was back in college and the two of us were dating. A week ago, when Director Reeves had forced me to take this case, a case whose sole mandate was to entice a privileged college girl away from an unsavory professor, I never would have imagined I'd actually come to *care for* the girl in question. But I liked Sally. Not only did she make me feel ten years younger, she also made me more optimistic about my future; I wasn't a guy in his early thirties at a dead-end in his career and his relationships; I was a still-young man embarking on a new adventure.

Gnawing at the back of my mind, however, was the awareness that these past few days with Sally had been a pipe dream. When I got her home to Connecticut,

I would be rudely reawakened into reality. Right now, though, it was just the two of us in the colorful woods around Walden Pond, strolling the foliage-flanked and acorn-strewn paths. I resolved to enjoy the remaining few hours we had together. We strolled in silence for a while, following the trail up a gradual rise until we were on the far side of the pond. At a bend in the trail, we stopped and stared down at the placid water. Stepping in front of me and draping her arms around my neck, Sally stood on tiptoe, craned her head up, and kissed me. We kissed for a couple minutes. In the distance, a woodpecker drummed on a tree, and I thought I heard the crunch of acorns underfoot somewhere down the trail. When we opened our eyes, Sally was beaming at me. She hugged me tightly, resting her head against my heart.

"I don't want to go home, Dakota." Biting her lower lip, she looked up at me with a rebellious flash in her eyes. "Let's do it—let's pull a Thoreau! Just leave everything and move to Alaska together! Let's do it!"

I chuckled. "What about Harvard?"

"I'll...take a leave of absence. They let students do it all the time."

When I chuckled again, she frowned and jabbed me in the ribs. "Oh, I forgot. I'm too *young* for you."

About ten feet behind Sally's shoulder, where the trail cornered and descended the other side of the ridge, was a sugar maple with long branches that jutted into the trail. The flame-orange leaves rustled, and then I noticed another flame-orange object coming up and around the corner of the trail. It was a head of red hair.

It was Big Red from the ferry.

28

THE RACE OF YOUR LIFE

I yanked Sally behind me and reached into my jacket for my gun. My stomach sank when I realized I no longer had a gun; Jen's partner had collected it from me this morning. What could I use for a weapon? I had a Swiss Army Knife in the survival pack. *No...my ASP baton.* When Big Red started toward me, I pulled the baton out of my pocket, flicked my wrist, and telescoped it. He stopped.

"Dakota," Sally said behind me, "what's going on?"

"Sally," I said, "I need you to run."

"Run? Where?"

"Back to the car and get help. Don't argue with me. Go! *Run!*"

Sally turned and took off, her footfalls fading into the woods behind me. Feeling the adrenaline start to course through my body, I slowed my breathing and deliberately focused on curbing the onset of tunnel vision. By staying calm, I was able to slow everything down, so that the events of the next minute felt like five.

Big Red started after Sally, but I jumped in front of him and shuffled side to side in a loose fighting stance, cutting him off. He betrayed his frustration by throwing a wild haymaker at my head—which, luckily, I ducked.

Dakota, this guy might be slow, but he's a good four inches taller than you, fifty pounds heavier, and he's as brawny as a lumberjack. This is life or death. You have to strike to <u>kill</u>.

His arm was still across his body from his punch follow-through, exposing his entire side and elongating his neck. I sprang forward, planted my feet, and, with every fiber of strength I possessed, smashed the heel of my fist and the butt of the baton handle into his larynx. It lurched in his throat.

But the human body can be remarkably tough and resilient, and certain men, like Big Red, are a lot tougher than the average person. Although he grunted and coughed, after a moment he shook off the blow. When he looked at me again, his lip was quivering and his eyes gleamed with rage.

Squatting slightly in a wrestler's stance, tucking in his chin to protect his throat, he crept toward me. I shuffled to the side, set my feet, and delivered a combination of two stiff jabs to his nose, followed rapidly by a slash with the baton that glanced off his skull. But before I could withdraw my baton arm, he grabbed me by the wrist, spun and hammer-threw me into some brush off the trail.

Somewhere behind me, a woman shrieked and went quiet. *Sally!* Scrabbling to my feet, I sprinted down the trail with Big Red galumphing in pursuit. In a clearing ahead, Malone and Jean-Luc held a squirming Sally by the arm. I moved toward them, but when I entered the clearing, Jean-Luc, smiling wolfishly with nicotine-stained teeth, pointed a snub-nosed revolver at me.

I stopped. He dragged the barrel across Sally's temple and drilled it into her cheek. She whimpered and gazed pleadingly at me. She flicked her eyes to Malone, who was calmly smoking a cigarette.

"Geoff, make him stop!" she said. "He's hurting me!"

Malone flicked his cigarette at her, hitting her in the face. It bounced off onto the trail, where it smoldered in the dirt.

"Ow!" Sally said. "You bastard—you almost hit my eye!"

"Shut up, Sally. You are not to speak unless you are answering my questions." Malone removed his sunglasses and dangled them from his fingers. He stepped closer to her and examined her neck. "Where is your collar, Sally?"

She stared at the dirt and didn't say anything.

"I asked you a question," he said.

"Leave her alone," I said. "I cut it off her. She's not going to be a sex slave to an insecure psychopath anymore."

With a faint smile on his lips, Malone nodded over my shoulder. I heard footsteps behind me, and as I turned around, Big Red punched me in the ribs. I felt like I'd been broadsided by a steel girder.

The pain in my side was instantaneous and severe; he'd broken at least one, probably a few, of my ribs. With the wind knocked out of me, I dropped to my knees in the dirt, painfully coughing.

Malone placed his fingers on Sally's cheek and glided them down the contours of her neck, breast, ribs and backside. Sally's legs quaked and her eyes dilated enormously; she was experiencing an adrenaline dump.

"I'm afraid our time together is over anyway, Sally," he said. "Soon you'll have a new master. But in the meantime, you *will* continue to serve me."

Slowly, I got to my feet. To say it *hurt* to breathe was the understatement of my life. As Malone whispered something to Sally, I stayed hunched over with my hands on my knees. I wanted Malone to think I was incapacitated so he'd feel safe approaching me.

It worked. He strolled over.

"As for you, Mr. Stevens," he said, "I have—"

As soon as he stooped over me, I sprang to my feet and unleashed a blistering uppercut—a punch so fast and devastating, Bruce Lee would have been proud. When my fist connected with his nose, I felt a soft crunch, like a chicken bone breaking, then the warmth of blood. Malone screamed, staggered backwards and fell on his ass. He sat there, bleeding. Then, smiling gruesomely, he snapped a handkerchief out of his pocket and held it on his nose. Standing up, he brushed himself off and shook his head.

"Mr. Stevens," he said, "you might think such antics make you seem tough, but they only make you look weak."

"Maybe," I said. "But I'm not the one with a badly broken nose. Good luck looking like yourself again."

"Jean-Luc," Malone said, "I want you to walk this man into the woods, shoot him in the head, and cover his body with leaves. Be sure to do it some distance off the trail so he won't be found until spring."

"Gladly," Jean-Luc said.

Jean-Luc grinned at me again. The beauty of the fall woods made his teeth even more unsightly.

"Dakota!" Sally whimpered.

Jean-Luc clamped a hand over her mouth.

"It'll be okay, Sally," I said.

Big Red put his hands on his hips and stared at me. "*I* will deal with him."

"No, I need you to carry the girl," Malone said. "Jean-Luc will dispose of him while we go back to Megan's house and get her and Jade."

"Why are we bothering with them?" Big Red said. "Let's kill him now and be on our way."

"Malone," I said, "listen to me. Be smart—let Sally go and leave. Sally's father is best friends with the Director of the FBI. Stop for a second and *think*. If you kidnap her, in about ten minutes the FBI and every Podunk police force in the Northeast will be combing the countryside for you. They'll have helicopters, roadblocks, dogs, SWAT—"

"I highly doubt it," Malone said, giving me a pitiful look. "We will be safely across the border before that happens."

Jean-Luc smiled at me and wagged his eyebrows. Still digging the gun barrel into Sally's cheek, he removed his other hand from her mouth and groped her breasts. Squealing, Sally tried to slap his hand away, and when she couldn't, she leaned over and bit his hand. Jean-Luc yelped and let go of her. Sally staggered away from him. While everyone's eyes were on Sally, I pressed the baton against the ground, compacting it, and slid it up my jacket sleeve.

"The little cunt bit me!" Jean-Luc said. He sneered and jabbed the gun at her.

"Put the gun down," Malone said.

Reaching into his jacket pocket, Malone produced a small case, opened it, and removed a hypodermic needle. While Sally was looking in my direction and hyperventilating, Malone lifted her skirt and jabbed the needle into her butt. Sally's eyes went glassy, her knees buckled, and Big Red scooped her up and slung her over his shoulder.

"Excellent," Malone said. "Now walk off the trail with her and wait in the woods near the road. I'll get the car and meet you. Understood?"

Big Red nodded and walked off into the woods with Sally.

"What did you inject her with, Malone?" I said.

"Merely a tranquilizer," Malone said, "to calm her down. Jean-Luc, you know what to do. And remember— take him well off the trail, and cover his body with leaves. Goodbye, *Mister* Stevens."

I glared at him. "You're making a big mistake."

Putting on his sunglasses, Malone chuckled, spun on his heels and strolled away. I could hear him laughing to himself as he disappeared down the trail. Holding the gun on me, Jean-Luc lit a cigarette, then motioned toward the woods with the gun. I walked very slowly into the trees off the trail, letting the compacted ASP baton slide down my jacket sleeve until its handle was concealed in my fist.

My only play here was to either stay very close to Jean-Luc—within two feet so I could use the baton—or get as far away from him as I could. The gun he was holding on me, a .38 snub nose, tended to be inaccurate beyond 50 feet, so if I could put fifty feet between myself and that gun, I had a chance. First, though, I'd try to get him close to me.

As we shuffled through the leaves, down the back side of the ridge toward a swamp below, I pretended to trip. This triggered a jolt of pain in my ribs so intense that it felt like I'd fallen on a subway third rail. Hunched over on my knees, feigning catching my breath, I waited for Jean-Luc to get closer so I could take him down with the baton. When he was a safe ten feet away from me, he stopped and grinned.

"Get moving," he said.

I reluctantly got to my feet and started walking again, faster this time to increase the distance between us. The swamp was getting closer.

"Slow down," he said.

"You said, 'Get moving,' " I said. "Which is it? Make up your mind."

Slaloming between the trees, fifty or so yards away, was the mountain biker who'd been rude to me earlier. Ahead, on the edge of the swamp, was a massive syca-more tree, a good four feet in diameter, with a couple of long branches fallen around its base. This was as good a situation as I could hope for; with that mountain biker so close, Jean-Luc would be reluctant to fire his gun. I pointed at the mountain biker.

"Look at that punk, would you?" I said. "No respect for the rules."

The second Jean-Luc turned to look, I sprinted for the sycamore.

"Hey, get back here!" Jean-Luc said.

I grabbed a sturdy six-foot branch and ducked behind the tree trunk. As he ran toward the tree, I listened to his footsteps. As soon as I knew which way he was coming, holding the branch like a giant baseball bat I swung blindly around that side of the tree. The branch struck something, there was a grunt, and when I emerged cautiously from behind the tree, Jean-Luc was stumbling around holding the side of his head.

Between the suitcase the other day and now the tree branch, I was batting a thousand with this guy.

Blood trickled down his temple, cheek and chin. With a snap of my wrist that held the baton, I telescoped it to its full length and rushed him. He was still stumbling in a circle, wildly brandishing the pistol, when I reared back and swung the baton at his wrist with everything I had, like I was hitting a tennis forehand winner. The way he screamed—even worse than Knife Guy had the other day—I knew I'd shattered every bone in his wrist. The gun fell, cartwheeled across the leaves and plopped into the swamp.

His scream stirred the bloodlust in me, and I could feel my jaw quivering with the desire to hurt him. Continuing to stagger in circles, he gingerly cradled his wrist with his other hand.

A few feet away, some leaves smoldered where his cigarette had fallen. As Jean-Luc stumbled toward the swamp, I followed calmly behind him, squashed the cigarette out, and cracked him behind the knee with the baton. He yelled again and toppled over into the muck. When he got his head out of the water, he scrabbled around in the muck, tried to stand, and started to sink.

Panic-stricken, he clawed desperately for the solid ground where I stood—a torturously close six feet away.

"Please," he said. "Please!"

"Where are the girls?" I asked.

Sinking steadily, he looked around with darting eyes. "What?" he said.

"The fourteen girls you already abducted. Where are they?"

His eyes bulged. "Quebec City. The docks. I tell you everything, just help me!"

"When are they being smuggled out?" I said.

He had sunk down to his chest now. "Four days, container ship!"

"What's the name of the ship?" I asked.

"*Al Barr*! Arab name. Please!"

"Where are they going?"

"Dubai!"

The muck was now up to his chin.

"I can only imagine what sick things you did to those girls," I said.

"Please! I beg you!"

I turned and walked away. Behind me, I heard him shout, but it quickly became a watery yelp and then was muffled completely. I didn't look back. Running up the ridge, I glanced at my watch: eighteen minutes past.

At the top of the ridge, I pulled the bottled water out of my pack and guzzled all of it. Then I sat down on a fallen tree to compose myself.

All right, Dakota…think. Calm down and think.

From here, the parking lot is about three-quarters of a mile away. Malone and Big Red are probably just getting back to their car. Option A: you could sprint back to your car and drive after them.

No, scrap that. It'll take too long.

Okay then...Megan said her backyard abutted the south side of Walden, and that her family had blazed a trail in here from her house. Hopefully, she wasn't exaggerating. With the road construction, it'll take Malone and Big Red a good twenty minutes to reach Megan's house. Which brings up Option B. Find that trail and cover the mile or so of woods before Malone and Big Red reach Megan's by road.

Remember, though—uneven, wooded terrain is twice as tiring as flat ground, so it's going to feel like two or three miles.

Dakota...this is the race of your life.

I put away the empty water bottle, got out the orienteering compass and took a bearing. Due south was the hill in the woods where I'd seen the mountain biker earlier. Once I reached that spot, I would run east, where I hoped to find the path that would lead me to Megan's. I put the water and compass away, re-shouldered my pack, and started running.

Here was the payoff for keeping myself in such great shape. With my breathing and stride perfectly synced, I gracefully hurdled logs and old stone walls, dodged stumps, leapt across ditches. Aside from the lightning bolts of pain in my ribs, I felt like a perfectly tuned machine. I felt like I was seventeen years old again, running cross-country through the woods at the Millbrook School. The difference was, I was stronger, better trained and had more endurance now than I had as a teenager.

As long as I stayed focused, nothing was going to prevent me from making it to Megan's and rescuing Sally.

Nothing.

Hang in there, Sally. I'm coming for you.

When I reached the top of the hill, I took another reading with the compass. Then, off to my right, I heard the mountain bike. He was about 50 yards away diagonally and pedaling fast along a trajectory that intersected with mine at the bottom of a short hill. I needed that bike. I sprinted straight ahead.

He and the mountain bike dipped into a gully and were temporarily out of sight, but I could hear his chain rattling and knew we were on a collision course. Then the mountain bike launched off a rise, and as soon as the tires hit the ground, I broadsided him with a body check that knocked him off the bike. While he groaned and struggled to his feet, I hopped on the bike and turned south.

"You asshole!" he yelled. "Who the hell do you think you are? Get back here! I'm calling the cops!"

"Harvard Fellow!" I shouted back, and rode away.

Pumping the pedals, I was able to cover the rugged, hilly terrain through the woods twice as fast as I had by running. Turning east, I rode for a few hundred yards, constantly checking south for some kind of trail. I was about to turn around when I spotted a narrow stripe of dirt through the trees. At first I thought it might only be a game trail, but as I turned down it, I noticed the remnants of shoe prints in the dirt—shoe prints of various sizes and soles, going in both directions, as if people had entered the Walden woods and returned along the same route. I kept following the path south.

When the path reached a stream, I forded it by walking rock-to-rock and carrying the bike on my shoulder. On the other side, the path became very faint as it traversed a meadow, but after riding in circles for a minute, I picked it up again and kept going. Finally I reached a stand of birches. Through breaks in the trees I glimpsed the backyard of a white Colonial—with black shutters. Sighing with relief, I raced the bike down the rest of the path, dumped it on the lawn and, heaving to catch my breath, staggered to a sliding glass door.

The door, and the entire house for that matter, vibrated with the sound of dance music with a bass-heavy beat. I rapped on the glass. Nobody came. I rapped again, harder this time, and peered inside. A perfect Martha Stewart kitchen sneered back at me. I ran around the house to the front door, opened it and went inside.

The music was coming from a doorway to my right. Stepping into the room, I glimpsed floor-to-ceiling bookcases crammed with books, framed photos and knickknacks. In my periphery, a light-colored blob squirmed around on a brown object. The brown object was a leather sofa, and the squirming blob was Megan and Jade. Stripped to their underwear, they were making out on said sofa. Averting my eyes, I located the stereo and shut it off.

"A-hem!" I said.

"Dakota!" Megan said. They sat up and covered themselves. "What the hell! Get *out* of here!"

"Be quiet and listen," I said. "Malone kidnapped Sally, and they're headed here."

At first they gave me looks of disbelief, but then their eyes flicked across me—the mud on my shoes, the twigs in my hair, and my generally sweaty, disheveled appearance.

"What?" Jade said. "How do—"

"Listen to me," I said. "Megan, what's the most secure room in the house?"

"I don't know…my dad's office maybe."

"Good. Go barricade yourselves in, and call the police."

"All right."

"Wait," I said. "Is there a gun in the house?"

Megan slipped on a T-shirt. "My parents are Massachusetts liberals, Dakota."

"So, no gun? Not even a twenty-two?"

"Nope."

Across the room was a fireplace with a set of brass fire tools. I grabbed the poker. It felt solidly constructed. Emblazoned on the handle, however, was "MADE IN CHINA," which hardly inspired confidence.

"What are you going to do, Dakota?" Jade asked.

"Get Sally back." Outside I heard the distant crunch of tires on the stone driveway. "All right, you two—go lock yourselves in, call the police and be quiet until help comes. Go!"

Megan and Jade scooped up their clothes and ran upstairs, leaving me with a loudly ticking grandfather clock across the room.

The priority here was to get Sally back. If I needed to kill or severely injure Malone and Big Red to accomplish that, so be it, but revenge wasn't the priority. Rescuing Sally was. And for that reason, I needed to be covert.

Outside, the car stopped and the engine shut off. Glancing out the front window, I saw an oversized black SUV with tinted windows. I ran to the kitchen, slipped out through the sliding glass door, closed it, and ran around the house to a spruce tree on the corner, where I ducked down and waited. The SUV doors opened and shut, and Malone and Big Red started up the walkway. Malone was talking.

"We have to be quick about this," he said. "Find them, sedate them, grab them and leave."

"Why hasn't Jean-Luc called?" Big Red said.

"No reception, I'm sure," Malone said. "Never mind him. Just find the girls. Now quiet."

They opened the front door, crept into the house, and shut the door. Bent double, I ran to the SUV, memorized the license plate, and walked alongside it peering in the windows. It was too dark to see inside.

I darted around the SUV trying the doors, but they were all locked. I was holding the fire poker. If it came to it, I could smash a window to get Sally out, but the noise would alert Malone and Big Red.

Ducking down on the side of the SUV opposite the house, I rapped on the window and spoke into the door crack.

"Sally? Sally, listen to me. It's Dakota. You've been drugged. Honey, I need you to wake up and open the door. Hurry, Sally." I rapped on the window some more. "Sally? Please, honey."

Inside the SUV, something bumped against the door. There was a moan. I heard fumbling against the latch, and then the door unlocked. I yanked it open and Sally spilled out, her hands bound behind her back. Her eyes flickered open.

"Dakota," she said.

"I've got you, sweetheart."

I picked her up in my arms, shut the car door with my hip, and ran as fast as I could with her for the shed. Fortunately it was unlocked. When I got Sally inside, I laid her gently on a chaise lounge cushion, took out my knife and cut the zip-tie around her wrists.

"Be very quiet. Okay, honey?" I stroked her hair. "I'll be back as soon as I can."

I covered her from head to toe with a rumpled tarp, so if anyone peered in the window from outside, she would just look like a covered-over pile of junk. Before leaving the shed, I scanned the yard out the window. All clear around the house. I slipped out. Closing the shed door behind me, I sprinted across the lawn to the shrubbery by the front door.

Lining both sides of the front walkway was a thick evergreen hedge, about three feet high. Given that I only had a fire poker for a weapon, my best play was to disable Big Red with it, retreat, and then ambush Malone in close quarters when he was alone. Holding the brass poker at the ready like a baseball bat, I crouched down behind the hedge and waited.

I just hoped the girls had called the police like I'd told them to. I wasn't sure how long I could hold out with just my wits and a Chinese-made fireplace tool.

The wait was interminable.

After who knows how many minutes, there was shouting from upstairs in the house, and then I heard footsteps banging loudly down the stairs.

My limbs were shaking. Sweat pooled on my lower back. I breathed slowly through my nose to keep myself steady. I'd only get one shot at this.

The door squeaked open, and Malone walked out. For an instant I debated whether I should club him first, but I stopped myself: Big Red was the real physical threat.

"Come on!" Malone said, passing just above me. "They called the police!"

A foot stepped over the threshold and the door squeaked closed. I jumped out of a squat into a batter's stance and swung the poker at Big Red's skull.

But at the last second, he lurched backwards.

Instead of connecting squarely with his skull, the poker hook ripped through his cheek and shattered several of his teeth. Blood sprayed across the white siding. Big Red let out a long, pathetic whimper that sounded more like a wounded animal than a human being. Cradling his mangled jaw in place, he stumbled down the walkway toward the car, where Malone stood aiming a gun at me.

Malone stared at me for a good ten seconds, unconsciously flexing his hand on the gun handle, as if debating whether or not to shoot me.

Finally, as though he'd reached a decision, he gave me a smug look and slipped on his sunglasses. He was less than twenty feet away, so there was little doubt that he'd hit me. I braced myself for the gunshot.

Then he got into the SUV and slammed the door. As soon as Big Red got in, Malone started the engine and roared away.

I studied the bloody poker, still clutched in my shaking hands. Tossing it on the lawn, I ran back to the shed and yanked the tarp off Sally. She stirred.

Her eyes flickered open. She smiled at me.

As I caressed her cheeks, tears rolled down mine.

29

MY WILLPOWER WAS DOWN TO FUMES

From the moment the Concord Town Police showed up, I tried to explain the situation but gave up when the pair of young cops ignored me and flirted with Megan and Jade instead. Recalling how I'd found the girls earlier—making out in their underwear—I knew the cops' efforts were in vain. The girls and I smirked at each other while the cops played macho hero.

As soon as the cops left, I called Director Reeves, but Mrs. Greer said he was unavailable. I left a message explaining that Dr. Malone had attempted to kidnap Sally Standish and two other girls, and I pleaded with Mrs. Greer to have the Director call me back immediately. Next I called Jen Suzuki's office number, got her voicemail, and left her the same message I'd given Mrs. Greer. Then Megan's mother, the patrician and horse-faced Mrs. Archambault, arrived. I told her the entire story, too, only for her to behave even more skeptically toward me than the cops had. Although Megan corroborated everything I said, I was too overwrought and exhausted to project my usual self-confidence. Leaving my business card with Mrs. Archambault, I asked her to call me sometime the next day. Finally, when the paramedics finished patching up Sally and me, I had them drop us at my car in the Walden Pond parking lot.

From there, operating on autopilot I started to drive Sally home to Connecticut. When I reached I-495, however, I noticed she was dead asleep in the passenger seat. Then I caught a glimpse of myself in the rear-view mirror and actually shuddered at the sight: matted hair, blood, dirt, bruises, and a torn shirt. Even though the paramedics had taped my ribs, the pain of sitting up in a car, folded in half, was overwhelming.

I pulled off the highway at the next exit, washed my face and hands in a gas station rest room, and went into the first decent motel I saw: Country Slumbers. The motel was across the road from a small shopping plaza with a couple of restaurants, so we wouldn't have to drive anywhere else today.

I checked us into a room with two double beds in the rear of the motel, where my easily recognized Mercedes wouldn't be visible from the road. I carried Sally into the room, laid her on one of the beds, turned on the A/C, and closed the heavy drapes on the windows. Then, steeling myself with a deep breath, and while staring at the Currier and Ives print wallpaper, I removed all her clothes but her underwear and tucked her under the covers. Sally murmured something and fell back asleep.

I brought in our luggage, including a case that contained a Remington 870 12-gauge pump shotgun. I kept the shotgun in the car trunk for emergency situations like this. Once it was loaded with double-ought buckshot, I laid it on the floor under my bed. In the bathroom, I gazed at myself in the mirror, and, thinking I might have missed messages earlier, checked my beeper.

Neither Director Reeves nor Jen Suzuki had called.

In fact, nobody had called.

I couldn't believe it.

When he'd summoned me to D.C., the Director had assured me if I discovered evidence that suggested a federal crime, then the Bureau would get involved. Well, I'd found fourteen test tubes of blood and photos of fourteen abducted girls; I'd seen evidence gathered by Kevin Teller (since deceased); and I'd just foiled the attempted kidnapping of three more girls, one of whom was the client's daughter.

What more did Director Reeves need?

Standing there in the harsh, flickering fluorescent lighting, I could feel my blood getting hotter, my pulse increasing, my breath growing shallower and more rapid. I was incensed. The Director probably thought if he ignored me, I'd go away.

Well, was he in for a surprise.

Locking the door and exiting quietly, I walked around the motel and across the road to a liquor store in the shopping plaza. I bought a bottle of Maker's Mark Kentucky Straight Bourbon, and went into a phone booth outside with a clear view across the road of the motel entrance. This way, I'd be able to see if anybody pulled in there.

Tearing off the bottle's red wax seal, I unscrewed the cap and had a long chug of the bourbon. Ah...I could feel the stresses melting away. With the liquor still pleasantly warm in my throat, I dialed the operator and called the Director's office again—*collect* this time. Mrs. Greer accepted the charges, telling me this time that the Director had left for the day.

"Put him on the phone, Mrs. Greer," I said sharply. "Now!"

"Very well," she said, and placed me on hold.

During the uncomfortable silence—a silence during which it occurred to me that this might very well be the end of my career—I had another swig of the bourbon. When he clicked on the line, he took a couple breaths before speaking.

"Stevens," he said, "I've had enough of this. This case is *over*. Have you returned Sally to Mr. and Mrs. Standish yet?"

"No, sir, I haven't."

"And why not?"

"Didn't you get my message?" I said. "Because Malone and his men almost kidnapped her. Actually, they almost kidnapped Sally *and* two of her friends from school. Sir, the Bureau needs to put out an APB for all of the border crossings in the Northeast. It's a black Ford Expedition with tinted windows." I gave him the SUV's license plate information. "This all happened a couple of hours ago, so if you hurry—"

"Stevens!"

"Yes, sir."

"Sally—is she safe now?" he asked.

"Yes."

"And the other girls?"

"Yes, sir."

"Very good," he said. "There was an attempted kidnapping, but you thwarted it. Seems your experience and training with the Bureau saved the day, Stevens. Good work. There's no immediate danger *now*, correct?"

"Well...yes, but—"

"But nothing," he said. "As of this moment, I'm *ordering* you to drop this case. Return Sally to her parents A-sap and—"

I had another slug of the bourbon and said, "Pardon me, Director, but you told me if I discovered evidence of a federal crime, then you could get involved. Sir, in addition to the evidence I mentioned to you the other day, I now know where the fourteen abducted girls are being held in Canada, and where they're being smuggled to—Dubai, sir. Malone has been working as the roper for a human trafficking, forced prostitution ring for a member of the Saudi royal family."

There was a long inhale and exhale on the other end of the line.

"Even if what you're saying is accurate," the Director said, "because it's taking place in other countries, it's out of our jurisdiction. Put it in a report and I'll forward it to the appropriate people at Interpol."

"A report?!" I said. "Sir, in a few days the girls are being smuggled to Dubai in a container ship!"

"That's the best I can do, Stevens. Now I'm ordering you to drop this. Take Sally back to her parents, send me a report about today's events, and do *not* call me anymore. Goodbye."

He hung up. I was about to pound the phone handset against the switch hook when I stopped myself and gently replaced the receiver. Hooking my bottle of bourbon, I returned to the motel. There, I dug Sally's cell phone out of her purse, went outside and called her parents. I got an answering machine. Not wanting to worry them, I simply left a message that my plans had changed, that I would have Sally home midday tomorrow, and hung up.

Back inside, Sally was sleeping soundly. I quietly closed the door and wedged the desk chair under the doorknob. Once I'd put her phone back in her purse, I rummaged through my suitcase in the dim room, located my toiletry kit and carried the kit and the bottle of bourbon into the bathroom. I shaved between swigs of bourbon, and then I got in the shower.

I probably spent forty minutes under the hot water, trying to wash away the stresses of the case and my worries about those abducted girls. What was going to become of them? If I sent a report to the Director, would it reach the Interpol authorities in time, or would it just end up in bureaucratic limbo, passed around between agencies forever while the girls suffered alone and without hope?

As I was rinsing the shampoo out of my hair, the shower door rolled open. Startled, I squinted my eyes open before all the shampoo was gone. It stung like hell. Someone stepped inside the shower stall, and the door slid shut. I now was able to see clearly.

Before me was Sally Standish, smiling and swiveling her hips. Every inch of her was lusciously nude. I gasped in some water at the sight of her, and when I finished coughing I pretended to be outraged.

"Sally, you can't be in here!"

"Gimme a second. Please? I need a shower."

Squinting without her glasses, covering her chest with her forearms, she maneuvered into the spray beside me. Then she noticed the open bottle of bourbon on the tub shelf. She picked it up in both hands and sniffed from the opening. Her nose crinkled up.

"What's this?"

"Maker's Mark Kentucky Straight Bourbon," I said. "Not for underage girls."

She took a sip. "Yuck."

She handed me the bottle, wrapped her arms around my ribs and squeezed. I winced. She let go and stepped back from me.

"Oh, did I hurt you? Why all the tape?"

"It's my ribs. The redhead broke some of them."

"In the woods?" she said. "When you were rescuing me?"

"Yeah."

"I'm really sorry, Dakota," she said. "About everything."

"It's not your fault."

I had a swill of bourbon and put the bottle on the tub shelf, away from the shower spray. When I turned around again, I got a long, unimpeded look at Sally's sublime body—the tiny frame and smooth legs, the compact backside and flat stomach, and the one part of her anatomy slightly incongruous with her otherwise dainty physique, the part of her anatomy only truly appreciable now that it was laid gloriously bare—her breasts. Full yet gravity-defying, they were like ripe fruit on a sturdy sapling. With a thickness in my throat that made breathing difficult in the steamy air, I felt my lust for her rising in my body like flood water behind a dam. In seconds, the struggle between my amygdala and my frontal lobe was so intense, my entire body trembled.

"Sally...you shouldn't be in here, honey."

"Please, Dakota?" She gazed up at me with puppy-dog eyes and that succulent lower lips of hers beading water from the shower spray. "I was scared out there all alone."

"Sally, we—"

She rested her head against my chest and tenderly placed her hands on my waist. Tracing the ridges of my abdominal muscles with her thumbs, she shivered a little.

"Whoa. Seriously, Dakota...you're, like, *crazy* built."

"Thanks. I work out a lot."

"It shows," she said. "Would you...wash my hair?"

"I think I should get out of here and let you do it," I said.

She caressed my arms. "Stay with me. Please?"

"All right."

I angled her head backward into the spray, and she closed her eyes while I worked shampoo into her hair. Her eyes were still closed when she squeezed my waist.

"You saved me today," she said. "Geoff almost abducted me."

"But you're safe now," I said.

"Yes, thanks to you."

As I rinsed the shampoo out of her hair, I had to make a conscious effort not to watch it ooze and dribble over her breasts. I stared over her shoulder at a crack in the shower tile. I felt her breasts compress against my stomach. She kissed my chest.

"I...I want you to know...how grateful I am," she said, "and how much you mean to me. I want—"

"You don't have to do anything," I said. "Sally, please...get out of here before we do something we regret."

"I know I don't *have* to do anything," she said. "I want to. And believe me, Dakota, I won't regret it. Actually, I'll regret it if I *don't* do this."

Smiling up at me, she took hold of my wrists and guided my hands to her breasts. Reflexively, my hands began to massage them. I gritted my teeth. My groin throbbed against her stomach. Kissing my chest, Sally looked into my eyes and said, "I want you, Dakota. I *need* you."

With that, my prefrontal lobe shut down. Abruptly cranking off the faucet and yanking the door open, I grabbed the bottle of bourbon and picked up Sally by the waist. She let out a kittenish squeal and waggled her feet. I planted her outside the shower and climbed out next to her on the bathmat. Sally wriggled in place and nibbled her lower lip as I dried her off. Water droplets misted her face, giving her a dewy look; I left them.

Then she dried me off, staring into my eyes the entire time, and when she was finished, she blindly flung the wet towel over her shoulder into the bedroom. Still nude, she picked up her eyeglasses from the sink counter. Slipping them on, she struck a cheesecake pose by bending her knees and sticking out her chest and butt.

"Ta-dah!" Sucking her cheeks together so her lips puckered, she spread her fingers and motioned from her head to her toes. "My 'sexy nerd' look. You like?"

My chest pounded. I had to gulp to create an airway. "Very much."

She kissed me, minced into the bedroom, and—glancing at me over her shoulder—reached into a pouch on her Rollaboard. With titillating slowness, she removed a comically long accordion strip of condom packets. Humming, wagging the strip from her fingertips, she minced over to my bed making bedroom eyes at me, peeled the covers off, tossed the strip of condoms on a pillow, and lay down on her side facing me. Stretching out her legs and rubbing her feet together almost imperceptibly, she bent her elbow and propped up her head with her hand. Some of her hair dangled over her breasts; clenching her eyebrows in annoyance, she tossed the hair over her shoulder.

The sight of her nude body, as smooth and creamy as a pearl, was dizzying. Between the days of flirting with her, kissing her, seeing her lovely figure in that maraschino cherry swimsuit and her legs in those obscenely short skirts; between making out with her next to the soda machine and on the hotel elevator; between her hanging all over me in my car and her relentless barrage of coquettish looks and breathy, high-pitched come-ons—my willpower was down to fumes. Quaffing the bourbon and feasting my eyes on her from the bathroom doorway, I knew that any further resistance was futile: the two of us sleeping together had been fated since the beginning of this case, and I was powerless to stop it.

"You're sure about this, Sally?" I shut out the bathroom light, went over to the nightstand, put down the bottle. "You swear you don't feel coerced or anything?"

"Please." She rolled her eyes. "Dakota, I've never wanted to do this with *anyone* like I want to with you." Grinning, she adjusted her eyeglasses and traced her fingertips over her curves. "Besides, if anybody's being coerced here, it's you." She patted the mattress. "Come, lie down. Let me reward my hero."

Slowly, I lay down on my back beside her. "My ribs are on fire."

"I'll be super-gentle," she said. "I promise."

"I don't know if I can do this, Sally," I said. "These broken ribs have pretty much knocked me out of commission."

"Shh."

She pressed a finger to my lips and started kissing down my chest and stomach. Skating her breasts tantalizingly against my skin, she lowered her petite body down mine by straddling me and hooking her feet over my legs. Every few kisses, she paused to push up her glasses sliding down her nose.

"*You* might be…out of commission," she said sweetly, "but *I'm* not. And anyway, who said…*you* had to do anything? I'll do *all* the work." She moved her hair out of her face, kept kissing downward. "Besides…your most important body part…seems fine." Upon reaching my groin, she moistened her lips and raised a jaunty eyebrow. "*Perfectly* fine."

❖◆❖

Afterwards we took a nap, and Sally slept with her head on my shoulder into the early evening, when I made us get up. We got dressed, walked over to a pizza parlor across the road, ordered a pepperoni and mushroom and soft drinks, and brought the food back to the motel. As we ate on the bed, we watched a movie about a ditzy blonde who follows her boyfriend to Harvard Law School. When the movie was over, I switched off the TV.

"Hey!" Sally said.

"We need to talk," I said.

"About what?"

"About what happened, and what's going to happen—starting tomorrow."

Sitting cross-legged with her back against the headboard, she reached for another slice and gave me a bite.

"I'll tell you what happened," she said, grinning. "We had mind-blowing sex—that's what happened." She gazed pensively across the room. "Kind of makes me wish someone would try to kidnap me every day."

"Don't say that, Sally," I said. "Remember—there are still fourteen girls missing. You, Megan and Jade were almost three more."

"You're right. Sorry." She took a bite of pizza. "As for tomorrow, I go home—so what?"

"So...you've been through a lot of trauma over the past couple of months," I said.

"*Trauma?*" She scoffed. "Like what?"

"Oh, I don't know," I said. "How about almost being abducted by your boyfriend? A boyfriend who made you wear a collar and left you chained up in his apartment like a dog."

She froze in the middle of chewing and gaped at me. "How'd you know about that?"

"I searched his apartment and saw the cable," I said. "The point is, Sally, you need therapy."

"Therapy? *Please.*" She resumed eating.

"May I be blunt?" I said.

She shrugged.

"First, I think you've got daddy issues," I said. "You also show signs of bipolar disorder—wild mood swings between elation and depression, as well as some pretty impulsive behavior."

"Are you calling me *crazy*, Dakota?" she said. "Thanks a lot."

"No, I'm not saying you're *crazy*, Sally, but I do think you need treatment. Although the daddy issues and the bipolar stuff don't concern me as much as something else."

"What?"

"The sex stuff," I said. "Like earlier—how you could only express your gratitude toward me through sex."

"Are you saying you didn't *enjoy* it?" she said. "Because it was the best sex I've ever had! Do you regret it?"

"No," I said. "But I do feel a little guilty, like I took advantage of you."

"You didn't take advantage of *me*, Dakota," she said. "When I got in the shower, I knew what was going to happen, and I wanted it to happen. But forget about us. You said, 'the sex stuff.' What other *stuff* are you talking about?"

"How about the months you were with Malone? The BDSM collar? The 'master-submissive' role-playing? How about the fact that your boyfriend was operating a human trafficking ring right under your nose?"

"I think you're exaggerating how *traumatic* these things have been on me," she said. "Get real."

"Okay," I said, "how's *this* for real? What about Malone forcing you to have sex with him in public, where you could have been caught anytime? Huh?"

She looked at me blank-faced.

"I followed you one night last week," I said, "and yes, I saw the two of you going at it on Acorn Street."

She dropped her pizza slice back in the box and held her face in her hands.

"Did he make you do that a lot?" I asked.

She nodded without saying anything.

"Wouldn't it help to talk to somebody about it?"

She nodded again and began to cry.

Wonderful, Dakota. Here we go again.

Propping myself up on the pillows, I fortified myself with a long chug of bourbon and a bite of pizza, laid her head on my chest and let her cry. After a good fifteen-minute cry, I got her some tissues and held her hand while she blew her nose.

"So will you agree to get counseling?" I asked.

She nodded and turned on her side to face the wall.

"Okay," I said, "it's been a long day. Let's get some sleep."

I double-checked that the motel room door was locked and chained, and for extra security, I re-wedged the desk chair under the doorknob. After I brushed my teeth, I made Sally brush hers, and then I tucked her in and kissed her goodnight. Retrieving the shotgun from under my bed, I leaned it against the wall between the headboard and the nightstand where I could grab it in the night if necessary.

I slid under the covers and shut out the light. A few minutes later in the darkness, above the plangent hum of the A/C unit, I heard Sally in her bed softly weeping.

"Sally?" I said.

"Yeah?"

"If I let you come over here and I held you, would it make you feel better?"

"Yes."

"Do you promise you won't turn it into something sexual?"

"No," she said. "But I'll try."

"All right, come on over."

I heard her covers flap open, and within two seconds she was in my bed, spooning her bijou backside into me. I kissed her neck and stroked her hair.

"We have to be up early, Sally," I said. "It's time for sleep."

"Okay," she said over her shoulder. "But I should warn you, Dakota…in the wee hours, like three o'clock…"

"Yeah?" I said.

"I tend to wake up from extremely erotic dreams," she said. "Goodnight."

30

THE STANDISH HOUSEHOLD MILIEU

Late the next morning, after sleeping in and enjoying a leisurely breakfast at Waffle House, Sally and I set out in a cold drizzle for Greenwich, Connecticut. Since it was after rush hour, the highways—I-495, I-290, the Mass Pike, I-84 and now, I-91—were virtually empty. As I drove, Sally cuddled against me, curling her legs beneath her in that enchanting feline way that only svelte, petite women can. The two of us had been quiet for many miles when she finally broke the silence.

"I'm going to miss you, Dakota." She kissed my cheek and rested her head on my shoulder.

"I'll miss you, too, Sally."

"Remember what you said on the beach the other day—about me being too young for you?"

"I do," I said.

"Well, I've been thinking about it a lot." She retreated back to her seat and crossed her legs. "I think you're wrong. I think I'm the perfect age for you." She turned to me. "But…I'm willing to wait. You realize, in five years I'll be twenty-five."

"So?"

"*So*, let's say this…in five years, if our paths cross again and we're still attracted to each other, we'll get together. By then, I'll be a grown woman, like you want."

I chuckled, patted her leg.

"Don't laugh," she said. "I'm very serious."

"A lot can change in five years, Sally."

"Yeah—we might feel even more strongly for each other. Did you consider that?"

"You're right," I said. "Okay. In five years, *if* our paths cross again, and *if* we still have feelings for each other, it's a deal—we'll get together."

"You swear?" She held out her hand.

"I swear." We shook on it.

When we reached the I-95 exit for Greenwich, home of the Standishes and legions of other WASP families, Sally gave me turn-by-turn directions to a row of mansions overlooking Long Island Sound. Hers was a rambling brick affair. Perched high on a bluff, it was visible from the lower main road, as was the hedge-lined serpentine drive that led to it. As we neared the driveway gate, Sally visibly stiffened in her seat.

"Stop the car for a second?" she said. "Please, Dakota?"

I pulled over and rolled down the windows. A salty cool breeze wafted into the car.

"Are you okay?" I asked.

"My parents are going to be on my case the second I walk in the door."

"Relax and take a breath," I said.

"I just *know* they're going to be all judge-y about Geoff," she said.

"Maybe, but you'll survive it."

"Will you come in with me?" she asked.

"Of course. I'm sure your father will want to talk to me as well."

She took a few deep breaths.

"Ready?" I said.

She nodded. I turned into the driveway and pressed the call button on the intercom. A few seconds later, the gate whirred open and we started up a seemingly endless series of hedge-lined switchbacks.

"Look, Sally," I said, "whatever you do, don't tell your parents about your BDSM collar, or about you and me fooling around, and *definitely* not what happened between us last night, okay? We went through a life-and-death ordeal yesterday, and that often causes men and women to—"

"Relax, Dakota." She squeezed my hand. "It'll be our secret. Always."

"Thank you." I squeezed her hand back. "While we're on the subject, you probably shouldn't discuss your sex life at all with your parents. Your father looked on the verge of a heart attack when he hired me. If he learns the truth about your sexual exploits, it might kill him. Besides, I was hired by the Director of the FBI, who's friends with your dad, and—"

"I promise I won't say a word, Dakota," she said. "About any of it. But there's something I want you to do for me before you go."

"What?" I said.

"I'll tell you later."

I parked the car in a cul-de-sac in front of the house and shut off the engine. When we got out, I was struck by how much the house, a sprawling brick monstrosity in the neo-Georgian style, looked like one of the buildings in Harvard Yard. There was even red ivy growing up trellises on either side of the front door. The rest of the Standish household milieu became apparent the moment the front door opened and we were greeted by a Hispanic woman wearing a gray maid's uniform. I didn't think they even made those uniforms anymore.

"Miss Sally," the woman said, "it is wonderful to see you. Your parents, they are very happy you come home."

"Thank you, Rosa." Sally kissed her on the cheek and handed her her suitcase. We followed her inside.

She led Sally and me down a hallway lined with landscape paintings into a great room. Across the room, with a fireplace blazing behind him, Mr. Standish sat in a maroon leather club chair reading the *Hartford Courant.* A trim and petite brunette woman in her mid-forties sat in a matching chair licking her forefinger and turning pages in *Travel & Leisure* magazine.

"Mr. and Mrs. Standish?" Rosa said. "Sally is here."

Tossing the magazine aside, Mrs. Standish leapt from her chair, minced across the room to her daughter, and hugged her. Mr. Standish carefully folded his newspaper and set it on an end table before rising slowly to his feet. With a slight limp in his right leg, he walked over to Sally and his wife and stood awkwardly beside them, wearing a forced smile and patting his daughter's arm. Rosa took Sally's suitcase and disappeared.

"Oh, my darling, darling baby girl!" her mother chirruped. "You're home, safe and sound!" She let go of Sally and grabbed my hands. "And all because of you, Mr. Stevens! I cannot express...oh, Mr. Stevens, you simply must stay for lunch!"

"Thank you, Mrs. Standish, but I'm afraid I can't. I have a new case."

"Oh, that is most disappointing. Are you sure you won't stay?"

"I really can't. Sorry."

"Another time perhaps?"

"Perhaps."

Mr. Standish frowned. "Mr. Stevens, I thought you were bringing Sally home *yesterday*."

"I was, Mr. Standish." Thinking of something James Bond says in *Goldfinger*, I surreptitiously tapped Sally's ankle with my shoe. "But something big came up."

Sally clenched her jaw to keep from laughing.

"Something big?" Mr. Standish said. "What was it?"

"May we speak in private, sir?" I said.

"Yes, well...let me congratulate you in front of Sally and Mrs. Standish." He shook my hand. "Fine work, Mr. Stevens. Fine work."

"Thank you, sir."

"Come into my study with me and we'll settle up."

I started to follow him down the hallway. Behind us, Sally called out, "Dakota, be sure to see me before you leave, okay?"

"Of course, Miss Standish."

Mr. Standish led me into a study. The walls, like the ones in Sally's dorm library, were dark wood and lined with books. The room felt like one you'd encounter in an English Lord's manor house; the only thing missing was one of those giant antique globes for recounting your worldwide adventures. He gestured at a brass bar trolley with crystal liquor decanters on it.

"A drink, Mr. Stevens? You've certainly earned it."

"No thank you, sir."

He hobbled behind a desk, sat down with a grunt, and bade me sit in the armchair on the side of the desk. Taking my seat, I had a rush of *déjà vu* remembering a scolding 16 years earlier in the Millbrook School headmaster's office. I took a breath and let it pass. Mr. Standish folded his hands across his stomach and stared at me unflinchingly.

"Before I compensate you for your work on this case," he said, "there is one question I need an answer to."

"What's that, sir?"

"Mr. Stevens…in the course of your investigation—that is, while you were wooing my daughter away from Dr. Malone—did you discover any evidence to suggest that Sally is…*sexually active?*"

"Sir, forgive me, but I don't think it's appropriate for me to discuss your daughter's—"

"Come now, man—did you or did you not find evidence to suggest that my daughter is no longer a virgin?"

A wave of pity for Sally swept over me. Soon, the poor girl would undergo this exact interrogation.

"No, sir," I said. "Nothing. In fact, her relationship with Dr. Malone seems to have been entirely platonic."

"But…what about all of the nights she spent in his apartment?" Mr. Standish said. "Your predecessor, Mr. O'Toole seemed quite convinced that—"

"He was wrong. I believe Dr. Malone and Sally were simply working late, Mr. Standish. Sally *was* his assistant, after all."

"Ah, I guess that explains it. Excellent news, Mr. Stevens."

"That being said, sir," I continued, "I believe this entire incident has scarred your daughter significantly. I'm no psychiatrist, but I strongly suggest she receive counseling."

"*Counseling*? Don't be ridiculous. For what?"

"Well…trauma, for starters."

He sighed. "Yes, I can see how this has all been quite traumatic for her." A sympathetic look came over his face. "I suppose I could make a few calls."

"Good," I said. "Sir, while I have you here, there are a few other things you need to know. Including something that happened yesterday."

"Ah, the *big thing* that came up, preventing you from coming yesterday, correct?"

"Um…yes, sir."

"Well?"

I told him about Kevin Teller's death, the disappearances of the girls on the other campuses, the photos and test tubes of blood I found in Malone's apartment, and, finally, about the attempted kidnapping of Sally, Megan and Jade.

"When the girls return to school next week," I said, "they'll all need increased security for the next couple of months. All of the fourteen girls I mentioned were abducted a month or two *after* Malone left."

He shrugged. "Fine, fine. I'll call the president and arrange the security."

"For all three girls, sir? Please?"

"Yes, Mr. Stevens—for all three girls." He opened the desk center drawer, pulled out a check and thrust it at me. "Your room at the Charles is already paid for. However, *this*, I trust, will cover any expenses you incurred."

It was a cashier's check for twenty-five thousand dollars. Guilt—thick and palpable guilt—rose up in me. Guilt for succumbing to his daughter's charms. But as I sat there and breathed, the feeling passed. With trembling fingers, I folded the check and tucked it in my wallet.

"And then some," I said. "Thank you, sir."

"I'm very grateful to you, Mr. Stevens, for getting my sweet Sally away from that horrible man," he said. "Is there anything else I should know?"

"No, sir. Except to say that your daughter is a wonderful girl, and you're very fortunate to have her. Despite this lapse in judgment, she—"

"Mr. Stevens, I don't need you to tell me how great my daughter is." With effort, he got to his feet. "If there's nothing further."

"What about the fourteen abducted girls, sir?" I said. "I spoke to Director Reeves about them, asking him to get the Bureau involved, but he was intractable. Perhaps if *you* talked to him, he might—"

"I *won't* be doing that," he said. "I'm not telling the Director how to run his shop. It's probably time you got on your way." Opening the door, he led me out to the foyer. His voice, louder than it had been in the study, suddenly took on a much more chipper tone. "So, Mr. Stevens…back to Manhattan now?"

"Yes."

"Hopefully that check will help get your practice off the ground." He shook my hand and opened the front door. "Goodbye, Mr. Stevens."

"Actually, sir…Sally wanted to see me before I left."

"I don't think that's appropriate, Mr. Stevens."

"Wait, Daddy!" Sally yelled.

Her voice came from the second floor somewhere, followed immediately by the pounding of footsteps. A streak flashed across the landing and onto the stair banister. It was Sally, sliding down the banister on her butt like she was riding a horse sidesaddle. At the bottom, she vaulted off, landed with a flourish like a gymnast, and stood demurely next to her father, who frowned at her.

"Daddy wishes Muffin wouldn't do that," Mr. Standish said.

"Sorry, Daddy," she said. "Muffin wants to show Mr. Stevens something before he leaves, okay?"

"Well…all right, but don't take too long. We need to have a talk, you and I."

"Yes, Daddy."

Kissing her father on the cheek, she walked me outside and around the side of the house. We crossed a broad, sloping lawn until it stopped at a fence on the edge of the bluff. A long set of stairs led down to a beach. Out on the Sound, a cabin cruiser drifted by.

"Nice view"—I turned to her and grinned—"*Muffin*."

Sally rolled her eyes. "Yeah, yeah."

"What kind of muffin?" I asked.

"Blueberry."

"Mmm…toasted." I ribbed her. "My favorite."

"Mine too." She ribbed me back. "That's how I got the nickname."

"So," I said, "what did you want me to do for you?"

She pointed at the driveway. "Drive down to the gate. I'll ask you down there."

She started walking diagonally up the lawn, toward an arbor built into a tall hedge.

I returned to the car in front of the house. After a few tries, I got the engine started, and when I reached the gate at the end of the driveway, I parked and shut it off. A second later, the passenger door opened and a beaming Sally lunged inside.

"What did you want to ask me?"

"I want you to kiss me," she said. "One super-long, hot kiss before you go."

"I don't know if that's such a—"

She pounced against me and started kissing me in a frenzy.

"Easy, Sally," I said, "my ribs."

"Oooh, sorry. How about…?" She jutted her head at the back seat and wagged her eyebrows.

"Okay, but *just* kissing," I said.

She was out of the car in a hummingbird's heartbeat. Five seconds later she was on top of me in the back seat, crushing her breasts into me, cupping my neck with her hands, grinding her pelvis against mine, and making little sighs of pleasure. It took all the self-control I possessed to keep from fondling her in reply.

The rain, which had been drizzling on and off all day long, increased in intensity until it was drumming on the car roof. The water gushed down the windows like we were in a car wash. We kissed like this for a good ten minutes—until I became aware of the passing time. Gently but forcefully I pushed Sally off me and sat up. Sally was still clinging to me.

"Please don't leave," she said. "Not yet."

"I have to go, honey."

"It's pouring out there," she said. "Kiss me some more."

"Sally, with the two of us," I said, "it won't stay 'just kissing' for long."

"But…I love you, Dakota."

I winced. "Oh, honey…you only *think* you love me."

"Shut up…I know how I feel!" Her eyes were tearing up. "Don't you love me?"

"I think you're a wonderful young lady, Sally. Wonderful." I snapped a Kleenex out of the box on the floor and dabbed her eyes with it. "But we don't know each other well enough to *love* each other."

"Well, I don't care what you say," she said. "I love you, Dakota. And in five years, when I'm a woman, you and I are going to be together."

"You know that in five years I'll be close to forty, right?"

"I don't care," she said. "You'll be the coolest, sexiest forty-year-old guy alive."

"Not forty, Sally." I tapped her nose. "*Close to* forty."

"Whatever," she said. "You'll still be the hottest man I've ever known."

"All right." With a glance at the rain streaming down the windows, I smiled and removed her glasses. "*That* deserves one more kiss."

"*Oh no.*" She hastily unbuttoned her blouse. "It deserves a lot more than that."

By the time we finished with each other, my car had been blocking her driveway for half an hour. We'd run a hell of a risk. The car windows had fogged over, the rain had slowed to a mist. Lightheaded, I got out of the car with her to say goodbye.

"Sally," I said, hugging her, "promise me you'll get counseling? Impulsive stuff like that"—I tapped the back window—"isn't healthy. Do you understand what I mean?"

"I do." She ran her hands over my chest and shoulders. "I will. I'll talk to somebody, I promise."

She looked up at me, visibly struggling to keep herself together. After a few seconds, she planted her head against my chest and started to cry.

"Hey, easy," I said. "You're going to be fine. Now, I want you to go back to Harvard and focus on your studies. There will be plenty of time for boys later. You have oodles of potential, Sally. Don't waste it on a profligate lifestyle, okay?"

" '*Oodles*' of potential? You really think so?"

"Yes."

I gave her a final kiss, squeezed her hands, and got back in the car. The starter gave me trouble again, but when the engine finally turned over, I rolled down my window and smiled at Sally one last time. She leaned her elbows on the window frame.

"I love you, Dakota."

She waited for me to reply in kind. I didn't say anything.

"Could I write to you sometime?" she said.

"Sure. My home address is on here." I gave her my business card. "I want you to stay out of trouble, okay? But if you ever have a major emergency, you can call—"

"Yeah, your *beeper*." She forced a smile and kissed me on the cheek. "Goodbye, Dakota. Be careful. I love you."

"Goodbye, Sally. Be good, sweetheart."

As I drove away, she followed me out to the road. I watched her in the rear-view mirror blowing kisses and waving to me.

And then I went around a hedge-lined bend, and she was gone.

31

NOT BY A LONG SHOT

I'd only driven a few miles from Sally's house when paranoia set in. What if, after I left, Sally had returned to her house sobbing? And what if, when her parents asked her what was wrong, what if Sally blurted out that she was in love with me, adding, "And, oh, by the way, mommy and daddy, it was the best sex I've ever had!"

Given Sally's proven instability and the fact that in my pocket I had an un-cashed cashier's check from her father for twenty-five thousand dollars, I was justifiably concerned. So, when I glanced off the highway and spied a branch of Mr. Standish's bank (the same New York bank with whom I had my own meager accounts), I exited immediately, went inside and cashed the check.

Back in the car, I tossed the brick-sized envelope of cash on the passenger seat and stared at it. Was that *it*? Could a chunk of money make up for everything I'd put myself through for this case?

Let's see...over the course of a week I'd...wooed a 19½-year-old girl at her blue-blooded father's behest... seduced a Bureau colleague...uncovered a human trafficking ring...beat up a pair of rent-a-punks...tormented a grieving father who was later murdered...alienated a potential business partner...extricated the girl from her bad situation...gotten some ribs broken and nearly been killed...walked away while a man drowned in a swamp... disfigured another man with a fire poker...saved the girl and two others from kidnapping and forced prostitution...pissed off the Director of the FBI...and last but not least, for good measure...shtupped into a breathless stupor (several times) the girl I was hired to rescue.

Nice job, Dakota. With all of it.

As I continued to stare at the envelope of cash, the emotion I felt was disgust. I was disgusted with my behavior of the past week. More to the point, I was disgusted with myself because I knew what needed to be done, but I was too chicken to disobey Director Reeves. Instead of boldly going after Malone, smashing his human trafficking ring, and rescuing those girls, I was letting myself be intimidated by the Director—all so I could walk away from the situation hassle-free with some hush money, and launch my PI firm.

Looking at the car key in my hand, I thought about whose car this used to be: my grandfather's. A no-nonsense, highly principled Mainer, he would not approve of my quitting this job until it was finished. And that's exactly what it was: unfinished. Come to think of it, my paternal grandfather Al, another Mainer—although a charming scoundrel and sometime bootlegger during his life—would say the same thing. They'd both tell me that, succeed or fail, I had to see it through.

So would PI Jim Rockford. Rockford would be getting bonked on the head every ten minutes, and coming to in alleyways and on beaches, but he'd keep going. He'd keep yanking on the string until the whole thing came unraveled.

This case wasn't over, not by a long shot. Sure, I'd rescued Sally from Dr. Malone, but what about those fourteen other young women? Director Reeves said he had his "best agents" investigating their disappearances, and that he would forward my report to Interpol. But if I really believed him, why did I feel guilty?

I felt guilty because, deep down, I knew it wasn't true. The man was just placating me.

Considering the picture that had come to light, it would be downright criminal of me not to see this case through. A Saudi prince had hired Malone to acquire a variety of attractive American college girls to be used for his sexual purposes, and, because the prince was a hemophiliac with the rarest blood type of AB negative, the girls would also serve as living blood banks for him. I'd encountered a lot of scumbags in my time, but they all paled next to this prince and Malone.

I knew where the girls were being held, as well as when and how they were being shipped to Dubai. And, most infuriating of all, I knew from the smug look he'd given me at Megan's house yesterday that Malone was a remorseless psychopath, and that if I didn't intervene, he'd get away with not only these fourteen abductions, but countless others to follow.

When I critically examined my behavior during this case, I had more than lived up to Jen Suzuki's epithet about me as "the hot mess." Especially deplorable were my seducing Agent Suzuki and succumbing to Sally's charms.

But here was a chance for me to redeem myself. Here was a chance to bury the "hot mess" label once and for all. Here was a chance, like the Classics scholar Helen had encouraged me, to be heroic—a modern-day Odysseus. I recalled her chestnut hair and her pensive, grey-green eyes when she'd said I was now on Joseph Campbell's Road of Trials:

> *"This will be a dark time for you, a time of struggling in the wilderness, alone without the support of a big government agency. But…I believe if you fight your way through this period, and overcome the challenges you'll face, on the other side of it will be success and satisfaction beyond anything you've ever known."*

And then I remembered another beautiful, brilliant woman giving me similar advice in the past week—Svetlana. I had gotten angry with her the other day because she'd confronted me with the truth. Recalling our conversation in the Charles hotel bar, I now recognized she was right—about all of it. Snatches of what she'd said to me replayed in my mind:

> *"I sense you have it in you to become a great detective."*
>
> *"You will have to step out of the shadow of the FBI and take risks."*
>
> *"In one fell swoop, you would be rescuing who knows how many young women from something worse than death, and you would solidly establish your investigations firm."*

Svetlana. She was the missing link. She was the gal Friday, maybe the partner, I'd been looking for.

I had to talk to her. No—more than that—I needed her. If I wanted to solve this case, I needed her help.

I had to talk her immediately. In person.

Right now.

I checked my watch. It was three o'clock. Svetlana had mentioned she was returning to Manhattan tonight, but I didn't know if that meant rush hour or late evening. From here it would take me three hours to get back to Cambridge, or two-and-a-half if I lead-footed it. I crammed the envelope of cash in the inside pocket of my jacket and slipped the car key into the ignition.

After a few tries, I got the Mercedes started and tore out of the bank parking lot like I'd just robbed the place. Squealing off the highway at the next exit, I zoomed down back roads and eventually merged onto the Merritt Parkway eastbound.

I accelerated the car up to 85 mph and raced back to Cambridge.

32

MUCH EASIER ON THE EYES

My beloved Mercedes 280SE, a car that that had served me faithfully from when I first got my driver's license, died at a stoplight on Mass Ave near Harvard Square.

I was about a mile from Cabot House, where Svetlana was staying. It was pouring rain, but rather than wait around for a tow truck, I simply pushed the car into an illegal parking space and ran across Cambridge to the Radcliffe Quad.

At Cabot House, a student monitor buzzed me in. I was soaked, so naturally she eyed me with suspicion.

"How can I help you, sir?"

"I'm a friend of Svetlana Krüsh, the chess champion. She's—"

"Oh…I'm sorry, sir. You just missed her."

I stared blankly at the girl.

"She went home," she said. "To New York."

"How was she traveling, do you know?" I asked.

"I'm sorry," she said. "How…?"

"By plane, car—"

"Right…the train. If you hurry, you might be able to catch her. South Station."

"Thanks."

I ran out of the residence hall and down the street, glancing over my shoulder every so often for a cab. Back at the Mercedes, I tried starting it again, but the car was having none of it. I locked it up and kept running down Mass Ave, toward Boston.

I almost reached Central Station before a taxi deigned to stop for me. Not that I could blame the ones that had passed me. Some guy running in the dark in a rainstorm? They probably thought I was fleeing the scene of a homicide.

Motivated by the $50 bill I shoved through the plexi-glass porthole, the cabbie raced me to South Station. I bolted inside and scanned the departures monitor. The next train to New York was leaving in ten minutes. I was zigzagging through the crowd in the kiosk area when a woman's voice called to me from a flower stand.

"Dakota?" The woman had dishwater blonde hair and nicotine-stained teeth. "It's me, Laura. Remember? Freshman dorm?"

Now I remembered her: Laura Sargent, the snobby Music major who'd turned me down for a date—one of only two girls to do so during college. I remembered seeing her here ten years ago, at this very kiosk.

"Hi, Laura. Listen, I have to—"

"What're you doin' in town? Do you *live* here now? Last I heard, you were in D.C. Are you still with the FBI?"

"Laura, I'd love to talk, but I have to catch somebody. Sorry."

"Wait…how about a drink later? We could—"

"Another time maybe." I spied the pre-wrapped bouquets of flowers on her kiosk. "How much for these? Oh, whatever. Here." I tossed down two twenties, grabbed the flowers and took off.

"Bye, Dakota!"

I ran up the stairs and through the station searching for Svetlana's gate. At the very end of the cavernous terminal, I saw a group of men leering at someone and ribbing each other. As I got closer, I saw who they were leering at: Svetlana in a short belted trench coat that showed off her legs. Even the Amtrak employee checking tickets, a dowdy middle-aged woman, was sneaking an envious peek. Svetlana was third in line to go out to the platform. I had to act fast.

My hair was dripping, so I took a detour through the food court, grabbed a fistful of napkins and dried myself off the best I could. When I emerged next to her platform entrance, she was already gone.

Through the open doorway I glimpsed her wheeling a Louis Vuitton suitcase down the platform. Unsure what to do, I considered the Amtrak woman and something occurred to me: Deep down, most middle-aged women are hopeless romantics. I went to the front of the line and showed her the flowers.

"That's my girlfriend, the one that just went out," I said. "I need to ask her to marry me, but I don't have a ticket."

She nodded and smiled. "Sure, honey...go ahead. Good luck!"

I ran outside. The rain was streaming off the platform roof. Three train cars down, Svetlana was about to board.

"Svetlana Krüsh!" I shouted. "Wait!"

Initially she looked annoyed to hear someone shouting her name, but as she turned and peered down the platform, she recognized me. For a nanosecond, her face brightened, before returning to its default intensity. I caught up to her at the train door.

"Please don't leave," I said. "I'm sorry about the other day. Here, these are for you."

"Thank you, Dakota," she said, "but there is no need to apologize. You were right—I am not a detective. I am a chess player. That is what I know, and I need to focus on what I know."

"No, Svetlana," I said. "You have an untapped talent for detective work and you need to pursue it."

"Perhaps," she said, "but..."

Other passengers rubbernecked at us as they boarded the train. Down the platform, the locomotive engines idled loudly. Svetlana compressed her lips and eyed the car door.

"Don't leave, Svetlana," I said.

"We will see each other again, Dakota. We both live in Manhattan and we know how to reach each other. And I will still rent you the basement of my building if you want."

"I don't care about that," I said. "Look...can we talk about this? It's really important."

"Dakota, my train is leaving any minute."

"Take the next one."

"This is the last train tonight. I have a blitz tournament at the Marshall tomorrow."

"The Marshall?"

"The Marshall Chess Club," she said. "My base of operations. Now I really must go. Thank you for the flowers. Call me sometime soon and we will make arrangements regarding the office space. Goodnight."

She turned and was about to step into the train when I blurted out, "Svetlana, you were right! About all of it! Don't go!"

She turned around and stepped under the platform eaves beside me. "You have my attention."

"I was wrong to say we should drop the case," I said. "I only said it because my old boss, the Director of the FBI, was pressuring me. I care, Svetlana. I care about those girls. I do. Hear me out, please."

In a rapid monologue I told her about everything case-related that had happened since the two of us argued in the Charles hotel bar: returning to Malone's, only to find the place cleaned out; foiling the kidnapping at Walden Pond; and learning that the fourteen abducted girls were being held at the waterfront in Quebec City, and that they were being shipped to Dubai by container ship in three days. I decided not to mention Sally and me ravishing each other, and I capped my speech by saying I'd given Svetlana's advice a lot of thought.

"The bottom line is," I said, "I need you, Svetlana."

"Oh?" She squinted at me. "How?"

"Well, for starters, I have to go to Quebec City and I don't speak French," I said. "Stanley said you speak two or three languages."

"Six."

"Languages?" I said.

She nodded.

"Wow. And French is one of them?"

"*Oui*," she said. "That means 'yes.'"

I gave her a waggish smirk. "Look, can we talk about this...inside maybe? There's a bar in the station. Even if you—"

She shook her head. "There is no time for socializing. You said the ship with the girls leaves in three days?"

"Yeah."

"There is much planning to do," she said. "We must drive up tonight and—"

"We can't," I said. "My car's dead."

"Then we must fly to Montreal and rent a vehicle," she said. "First I will call the Marshall to cancel."

Handing me her suitcase, she took out her cell phone, dialed a number and walked down the platform beside me.

In that moment it seemed like the reason the universe had brought me this case was so Svetlana and I could meet and join forces. We were a born team, each instinctively complementing the other's strengths and weaknesses. But what exactly should her role be in my burgeoning agency?

She was far too intelligent and talented to be a mere *assistant*, a glorified receptionist. However, she didn't have any detecting experience, so I couldn't justify making her my partner.

Chuckling to myself, I thought about the two mugs that work for PI Jake Gittes in *Chinatown*. Svetlana would be like them—an associate—except much easier on the eyes.

She hung up and put her cell phone away.

"Before I forget," I said, "we should probably get me one of those."

"A cell phone?"

"Yeah." I lifted my jacket and showed her the beeper on my belt. "I think it's time."

"There is a store at the airport," she said. "Dakota… just to be clear…are you hiring me? That is to say, will I be receiving a paycheck for my services?"

"You'll get a percentage of my fee."

"And what is your fee for this case?"

"After expenses?" I said.

"Yes."

"Let me see…nine, carry the one…and…*nothing*."

"Nothing?" She looked at me in disgust. "You are quite the negotiator."

I shrugged. "I'm not very good with money."

"From now on then," she said, "*I* will handle the money."

"Deal. You can start by handling this."

Reaching into my jacket, I pulled out the envelope of cash, pocketed a half-inch of it, and slapped the envelope with the rest into her hand.

"What is this?" she said.

"Expense money from Sally's father. Handle it."

Her eyes dilated at the sight of the bulging envelope, then narrowed as she tucked it into her purse. This was my first sighting of Svetlana's mercenary nature.

As we walked inside together, the Amtrak woman pressed my arm and grinned.

"I take it she said yes."

I looked at Svetlana, who eyed me skeptically.

"Yes," I said. "Yes, she did."

"Congratulations," the woman said. "You know…I have a good feeling about you two. I think you're going to be very happy together."

"Thank you," I said. "So do I."

I held out my arm, Svetlana looped hers through it, and we walked through the station. We must have cut quite a figure together because men and women alike, including scowling Laura at the flower stand, turned their heads as we passed.

"Oh," Svetlana said, "while we are on the subject of money—"

"I didn't know we were still on that subject," I said.

"We are," she said. "You should know that each of the abducted girls has a reward for her return. Together, the fourteen rewards are considerable."

"Really?" I said. "How much?"

"I think it best if you do not know," she said.

Outside, I hailed a cab by whistling sharply. Svetlana patted my shoulder.

"Dakota?" she said.

"Yes?"

"The next time you do the fake proposal gambit with me…"

"Yes?"

"You should give me a *ring*, not flowers," she said. "No self-respecting woman would say 'yes' to a proposal made without a ring."

"Svetlana, you're the U.S. chess champion, correct?"

"That is correct," she said.

"All right, *Champ*." I smiled and opened the cab door for her as it pulled up. "Let's go solve this case."

Taking hold of my hand, she muttered something in a foreign language and eased into the car.

ABOUT THE AUTHOR

Chris Orcutt has written professionally for over 25 years as a novelist, short story writer, speechwriter, journalist and playwright. *A Study in Crimson* is his eleventh book.

Orcutt is the author of the critically acclaimed Dakota Stevens Mystery Series, including the Amazon bestseller *A Real Piece of Work*. Orcutt's short story collection, *The Man, The Myth, The Legend*, was voted by IndieReader as one of the best books of 2013. His modern pastoral novel *One Hundred Miles from Manhattan* (an IndieReader Best Book for 2014) prompted *Kirkus Reviews* to favorably compare Orcutt to Pulitzer Prize-winning author John Cheever. In 2017, Orcutt released *The Ronald And Other Plays* and a humorous memoir about the writing life entitled *Perpetuating Trouble*.

As a newspaper reporter Orcutt received a New York Press Association award, and while an adjunct lecturer in writing for the City University of New York, he received the Distinguished Teaching Award.

If you would like to contact Chris, you can email him at corcutt007@yahoo.com or tweet him: @chrisorcutt. For more about Orcutt and his writing, or to follow his blog, visit his website: www.orcutt.net.

EXCERPT FROM *A REAL PIECE OF WORK*

Book 1 in Chris Orcutt's Dakota Stevens Mystery Series is also available. *A Real Piece of Work*, the 1st novel in the series, delves into a world of art forgery, secret identities and murder. Following is the opening of *A Real Piece of Work*.

Back in my FBI days, during soporific stakeouts when I dreamed about the life I might lead as a private detective, I never imagined the job would one day require me to scuba-dive across a half-mile of ocean brimming with sharks.

Basically, anything capable of eating me was absent from my business plan.

Right now, despite the Caribbean sun on my face and the piquant salt air in my nose, I wished I were back in snowy Manhattan, safe behind my desk, listening like Sam Spade to some elegant dame tell me her troubles. Instead I had a 20-year-old scuba bum and my bikini-clad associate, Svetlana Krüsh, all but shoving me into the water. They stood silently beside me as wave after wave spanked the hull. Under my wetsuit, the heat began to rise.

"You're positive they're both on there," I said, nodding at the 80-foot motor yacht in the distance.

"According to the chambermaid," Svetlana said, "they left together this morning."

"And we're sure they're, ah, busy?"

"I am told they never leave the room."

She adjusted her bikini strap. After three days down here, Svetlana had only a whisper of a tan, but the way the leopard print hugged her aristocratic curves, you didn't care. Kyle, our alleged guide, leered at her. I grabbed him by the mouth and pinched his cheeks together.

"How about it, *dude*?"

"Wha?"

"Our friend on the yacht."

"Already told you—guy runs their slip says they put out every morning, come back around one."

"What time we got?"

With a flourish, Svetlana held out her watch. High noon.

"How long to get over there?" I asked.

"Half an hour, tops." Kyle scratched in his ear. "Quit stalling, man. I've gotta meet somebody at Sloppy Joe's soon."

I looked over our stern. Key West was a purple mist on the horizon. I turned back to the yacht.

"Let me see, one more time."

Svetlana passed the binoculars. While the captain and his mate read newspapers on the bridge, three bodyguards sunned themselves on the bow. Conover and his mistress had to be inside, doing what mistresses and CEOs of financial services companies did.

"*Moneta*?" Kyle said. "What the hell kind of name for a boat is that?"

"Goddess of money," I said. "Greek, I think."

"Roman," Svetlana said.

"There you go—Roman. We know what he worships anyway."

To the south dark clouds were creeping in, and the mounting wind flapped Svetlana's hair across my cheek. Between their boat and ours was a gulf of iridescent blue-green water that looked like it would take a week to cross. I wanted to call it off, but if I chickened-out now, in two weeks my business would shrivel up. Besides, Mrs. Conover was counting on us. I handed the binoculars back.

"Ready, Mr. Stevens?" Kyle said.

"Stop with the 'Mister' already. It's Dakota." I strapped on the flippers. "Why am I doing this again?"

Why? Because Mrs. Conover had made it sound so simple—snap a few photos, collect a big check. "I'll cover any expenses," she said. "Consider it a vacation…take a week, a month—I don't care. Just catch the bastard."

Svetlana nudged me. "Because you are sucker for jilted women. Especially when they are rich." She handed me a mask. "And don't forget, a blizzard is starting in New York, so we must catch six o'clock out of Miami."

I spit in the mask, rubbed it around and put it on.

"Sharks?" I said to Kyle.

"Sure. Blacktips, a few bulls maybe. No big deal."

I squatted down and slipped into the vest with the scuba tank. Kyle showed me the buttons for the buoyancy compensator.

"So, Miss Krüsh," I said, "while I'm risking life and *limb*, what will you be doing?"

She donned a pair of Dolce & Gabbana sunglasses and tied a mocha sarong around her waist so it hung fetchingly off one hip.

"Wave when you finish, and I swoop in like cavalry." She plopped down behind the wheel, crossed her runway legs and rubbed sunblock on her shoulders. Kyle jammed the regulator in my mouth.

"Remember what Nietzsche said, man—the shit that doesn't kill you makes you stronger. Trust me, you're gonna love it." He tipped backward into the deep.

I patted the vest's waterproof pouch to check for the camera and plunged in…

www.ingramcontent.com/pod-product-compliance
Lightning Source LLC
Chambersburg PA
CBHW060349260626
47160CB00006B/2251